IN LONDON,

What would make you rethink your entire life?

BE IJOS MIL

E BOA CEITMA !

22/10/21

In London, Still

H.S. Fernandes
Translated by A.I. Birosel

IN LONDON, STILL

H.S. Fernandes

Translated by A.I. Birosel

London – United Kingdom

2020

In London, Still

Original Title
Ainda em Londres

English Title
In London, Still

Copyright © 2020 H. S. Fernandes

Cover/Illustration:
Fellipe Ladeira

Cover Photo:
Helder Sidney Fernandes

ISBN: 979-86-640817-4-9

Social Media, Sales and Contact:

Instagram: @hsfernandesescritor
Instagram: @hsfernandesauthor
Facebook: @inlondonstill
E-mail: hfernandes.hsf@gmail.com

To my friends, family, readers and especially to my husband, Sergio, my mother, Dolores, and my dear friend, A.I. Birosel who made this version a reality. This is a dream come true.

Thank you all for being by my side.

H.S. Fernandes

Table of Contents

Chapter One – In London, Still

Just another grey day of too much rain in *London*, nonetheless for Eduardo the sun shone as never before since his arrival in that city. That day was more than perfect; his reward for too much sacrifice, too much pain, too much eating crow. 'After almost 10 years of so much coming and going, so much effort and new beginnings, I've finally reached the place where I want to be. Yes, I'm in *London* still, even though I can't celebrate this conquest with you. In *London* still, without any reason to be here,' he thought, taking a deep breath while he left by an *Uber* for another day of work.

It was true life hadn't been just fun and games for Eduardo since he had migrated from *Brazil* to *London* years ago. After all, being a *Latino* immigrant in this country, even as a resident wasn't nearly as easy as having been born here or even having come as an expat. He learned soon after arrival: the lives of expats and immigrants are singularly different, for the latter is someone who decides to leave his country and everything in it behind to start a new life in a foreign land.

Yes, on that March morning, still with its wintery winds and temperature, it was a 'sunny day' for him regardless of the heavy rain that pelted the region of *Hyde Park* where he lived. After all, his much dreamt of and deserved promotion to director of operations for Latin American markets would finally become official.

Early that same morning he had laid out his favorite suit, shirt, and tie on his bed. He thought back to the woman he still loved: 'Oh, how I wish you were here my love. I loved it when you would help me choose what to wear on special occasions.'

Eduardo decided he wouldn't have breakfast at home so as not be late or heighten his anxiety. On the way to work, he stopped at his best friend's place to give him a ride. He also worked at the same asset management company.

"Good morning Martin! Isn't today a beautiful day in *London*?" He quipped as his friend got into the car.

"You must be going crazy Eduardo!" It is 7° Celsius and pouring rain," he responded. "Ah! Today's the big day, isn't it? Yes, it's a beautiful day my friend, and I'm very happy about your promotion. You deserve it more than anyone and have waited too long for this recognition." Martin went on, remembering that this day had indeed a sweet flavor for his friend.

Martin and Eduardo had become great friends since the time both were hired by the company to work in the renewable energy market as specialists in asset management. The year they started the market had begun to warm up after the 2008 financial crisis and the company was hiring specialists for the European market and the Americas. Eduardo's knowledge of the Brazilian market and his ability to speak both Portuguese and Spanish landed him a position for investments in Brazil's Northeastern region. They were three for the Brazilian market alone. The country was booming, not having been affected by the crisis; many projects were ongoing or in operation, even though the country was already facing generalized saturation with the Worker's Party as it reached the end of its third government trifecta. The fact is, there were various wind energy projects and a few for solar energy that had been or were being installed in order to meet the Brazilian energy demand. Good for the region and excellent for Eduardo, who was the right person at the right time when he was called for his interview.

After three years of working in an area unrelated to his profession in *Brazil* and restarting from zero—not to mention that his degree was invalid in the *United Kingdom*—he was finally able to resume his career in what he knew and enjoyed doing. He and Martin were hired in the same batch of new specialists at *Tottenham Equity*.

When he left his native land, he also left a position as director in a multinational. But he had done it for love.

On the day he was hired, a new phase began for Eduardo and he was radiant. Reestablishing his career, although as a specialist; compared to his previous jobs, the position was a breakthrough in his *London* life.

Eduardo and Martin got out of the car and walked up to the reception of *The Shard*, the tallest building in London. Standing right next to the famous *London Bridge* in *The City*, a region of *London* where the most important banks and financial service companies in the country and the world are concentrated.

They went through *The Shards'* turnstile and walked through to the bay of elevators. Head offices of the corporation were located on the twenty-third floor. They passed through the small reception area of *Tottenham* with a "good morning" to everyone there and went on separately; Eduardo went to the right, to the office of his boss who was expecting him.

"Good morning Eduardo! Excited?"–his new boss, Anton Muller, VP Operations of the corporation boomed, as he received him with the director of Human Resources at his side. Anton had been with the company since the headquarters were moved from *Frankfurt* to *London*, about thirty years ago. He was a typical German.

"I'm anxious to assume the division Anton, and would like to thank you and the company for your confidence in me and for the opportunity that I've been given," Eduardo replied. He was a little nervous, aware of the fame for being a demanding boss that the Vice President had—"I hope I can exceed your expectations"—he tried on a smile, in an attempt to relax more.

Eduardo didn't know what to expect from Anton at that moment. Before his promotion, he hadn't exchanged more than a dozen words with the man. Eduardo's previous boss had always dealt with him directly in the past; and when he left the firm he indicated Eduardo as his substitute. Anton together with HR had invited him to participate in the selection process with outside candidates, and it was during this selection process that Eduardo had actually started interacting with Anton. But up to now, their relationship had been very formal.

"You are here by merit, my esteemed friend, and I am certain that you will contribute even more when you take over the entire region! Aside from understanding the technical intricacies, I believe that a good manager should understand well the cultural issues too—among the candidates, none better than you with the ability to perform such a role."—Anton acknowledged, pleased with his own perceptions during the selection process. "Amy here will take you to a meeting room to discuss with you all of the details of your new position. If you can perform as a director as well as you have as a specialist for these past years at the firm; I am certain that we will all turn out winners"—he went on—"not to mention that your command of the languages of *Latin America* will be especially advantageous in communications with the region"—he added with a wink.

"I'll do my best." Eduardo concluded.

Eduardo and Amy moved on to a meeting room and spent the rest of the morning dealing with all the intricacies of the new position: attributes, goals, training, travel and everything else relative to the duties of a company director.

From that day on, Eduardo managed three analysts for the Brazilian market, as well as the analysts for the other Latin American countries, running an eight-member team. Additionally, he started earning a significantly higher yearly salary, not to mention the result-based bonuses offered by the firm. "This achievement isn't mine. It's ours," he thought, as he said his good-byes to Amy, while leaving the meeting room.

That was one of the best Mondays in the last ten years for Eduardo, and the occasion demanded some serious partying. Crossing the *London Bridge*, not far from *Monument Station* was one of Eduardo's favorite pubs, *The Walrus and the Carpenter*—one of those places with a name so peculiar to the UK—an eponymous pub, after Lewis Carroll in this particular case. So, at the end of the day, Eduardo and Martin walked over for a pint (or more, in truth) of beer to celebrate.

They arrived at the pub around eight in the evening. It was very cold, but at least the rain had stopped. As no tables were available—this place was always filled with people who worked in the region and liked to meet up with friends to drink after work—they decided to drink standing at the bar. In the summer, your best bet would be outside, taking advantage of the last rare rays of sunshine. They stayed talking, drinking and having fun until eleven that evening when most pubs in *London* close and afterwards, moved on to *Soho* where a few bars are open until late at night.

"How was your meeting this morning with Anton?" Martin asked.

"Man, I was a little tense at the beginning, but afterwards I calmed down. I think he was very satisfied choosing me, at least that was what he led me to believe"—Eduardo responded—"I'll also have to visit the operations in the region so that I can accompany them up close. He said he doesn't want management based only on analysis of reports. He said that he would make use of my knowledge of Portuguese and Spanish and make some changes in our remote control policy of operations in the more distant places like *Latin America.* And that he would start those changes with me."

"That's excellent news, Eduardo. You'll also be able to see your friends in *Brazil* more often, making use of your business trips. That's great man!"

"My thoughts exactly," Eduardo smiled in response.

Conversation and drinking went on all night and when they couldn't drink another drop of alcohol, the two finally decided to leave. It was almost five in the morning and they hadn't even stopped to eat anything that night.

Martin lived in nearby *Southwark*, while Eduardo was north of *Hyde Park* near the *Marble Arch* in the *Saint George's Fields* area. In the state they were in, neither had the most remote possibility of using the *Underground* which certainly awaited passengers on their way to another days' work. So, each called for his ride with *Uber App*. Martin's car arrived first, so he said goodbye with a bear hug and, "Congratulations once again, my friend".

"Thank you so much, Martin. I know that you've always wished me well at the firm and thanks for your sincere friendship. You may be English, but you're a good guy," Eduardo said as the two said their good-byes roaring with laughter at their private joke.

From the pub, Martin's place wasn't far. He lived in a great little flat on *Union Street*, right down the road from the *Southwark Station* of the *Jubilee Line*.

Eduardo entered his address at *Burwood Place* into the *App*. His was a small flat, only one bedroom and elegantly, though spartanly decorated; and only four blocks from the northeast tip of *Hyde Park*. There was an ample sitting room with a sofa and small coffee table, an armchair, a floor lamp, a mirror one of the walls, a large abstract painting on the one opposite, and a TV on the wall next to a door opening onto the balcony. In the dining area there were simply four chairs surrounding a table. The kitchen was fully equipped with everything imaginable for that space; Eduardo enjoyed cooking in his free time. It had a nicely sized bathroom, and the room where he slept contained a king-sized bed and a walk-in closet. The entire flat, with the exception of the kitchen had wood tile flooring throughout—a rare privilege in a city where carpeting was the norm in small residences.

Eduardo was the kind of guy who believed that less was more. He also didn't care for knick-knacks or a lot of paintings on the walls. Not to mention that it was a lot less to bother with on cleaning days.

His ride arrived five minutes after Martin had left. Eduardo was driven off in the direction of home. Only a few blocks away, Eduardo felt queasy and asked the driver to stop before he lost everything he drank the night before. The car had already reached the east side of *Hyde Park* in the direction of his flat. He apologized to the driver and said that it might be better if he walked the rest of the way, rather than have something disagreeable happen in the guy's car. The driver got the message and pulled over.

"Will you be alright?" his driver asked, mildly concerned.

"Yes, I'll be fine. I just need to walk a little to clear my head. In ten minutes I'll be home. Thank you!" Eduardo replied as he turned and walked into the park.

Eduardo walked along the bike path and in all honesty, he was stumbling more than walking when suddenly, a passing bicycle hit him in the arm, propelling him to the ground.

"*Mon Dieu!*" the cyclist exclaimed in French. "Are you all right?" She asked, now in English. "Here, let me help you up."

"I'm fine," Eduardo replied, "it was my fault. I shouldn't have been walking on the bike path; my apologies for that."

While she helped Eduardo up, the cyclist, a very pretty woman nearing her forties, waved to her cycling companion who had stopped a little beyond them when she realized what had happened.

"Everything is fine, dear,"—the woman shouted in French to the adolescent who turned to wait for her—"it's nothing serious. I think the guy just had a little too much to drink."

"True." Eduardo said in French.

Surprised, the woman's face became suffused as she realized that he had understood her comment. The blush on her face was made even more evident, contrasting with her very pale complexion.

"Yesterday was a big day for me, and I think I exaggerated my celebrating"—he continued in French—"once again, I apologize for the inconvenience. Have a good day miss."

"It is I who must apologize for that last comment"—she continued as she remounted her bike—"good day to you too. I hope you are alright."

In contemplation, Eduardo stood watching the two cyclists until they disappeared from view as they turned in the direction of the *Hyde Park Bandstand.*

Eduardo moved off in the direction of his home, but unknowingly (perhaps due to his being drunk) arrived instead at his old flat in *Mayfair*. He still owned the flat, but had rented it out to a couple with a son over a year ago. He always thought it was way too big anyway. The building was on *Davies Street* near *Grosvenor Square*, a ten minute walk from *Marble Arch Station*. 'After everything that happened, it made no sense my staying there,' he had thought when he decided to move.

Plodding up to the floor of his old flat, he turned his key in the lock, but the door wouldn't budge. Fumbling with his keys— too drunk to find what he wanted—his alcohol-dazed mind refused to cooperate. Leaning against the door to steady himself; he tried again to find the right key as he slid to the floor, motionless. "Gabrielle…Brie, my love, open the door, please. I can't find my key," he whispered into the crack between the door and its casing as he twisted from where he sat sprawled, lips nearly touching the painted wood.

In Eduardo's mind, he was back in another time in life. All at once realizing where he was, he leaned back against the wall and began to sob helplessly, "why did you do this to me? How could you leave me that way Gabrielle?" Eduardo raved drifting off to sleep where he sat, slumped beside the door in the cold corridor, dreaming of home.

In London, Still

Chapter Two – *Beauté Cosmetics* and the Restaurant at *Rue Lamennais*

A little more than ten years ago Eduardo lived in *Rio de Janeiro* and at only twenty-eight years of age had reached the apex of his career. He was the Chief Financial Officer (CFO) of a French cosmetics company. The plant was located in the metropolitan region of *Rio* which he visited on at least a weekly basis to meet with the operations management, but headquarters were at the *Centro Empresarial Mourisco* in *Botafogo*. Aside from the CFO and his department, this was also the offices of the Chief Executive Officer (CEO), the director of marketing, the administrative/HR director, and the people from internal auditing, legal, and compliance who were also there. The main office of the *Beauté Cosmetics' Rio de Janeiro* branch was made up of around seventy employees distributed over some two hundred square meters of modern office space and meeting rooms, but the plant in *Duque de Caxias* had a head count of over two thousand employees spread out in a single-story complex surrounded by two acres of lush greenery. It was a billion-dollar operation that the French company had in *Brazil*. After all, the beauty industry in *Brazil* has always been very strong and lucrative.

Eduardo had always been competent and courageous, arriving at the height of his career very young, entirely through his own merit. Whenever he didn't know how to do something, he would often say he knew a little something on the subject and immediately rushed off to hit the books and the internet to study up on the matter. When reading wasn't helping, he would go after traditional learning. What was important was to not lose the opportunity, including learning opportunities: he was an excellent student. He liked numbers and he liked to read. His mother once had hopes that he might choose engineering as his profession, but what he most identified with was accounting. Soon after graduating college he went on to specialize in economics and finances, two areas that had fascinated him during his college years.

His contact with the English language began early and in his teens he decided to learn Spanish too. However, it was only after he began at *Beauté* did he decide to learn French.

Still in college, he participated in a selection process for one of the highly sought-after *trainee* positions offered yearly by *Beauté Cosmetics*. Due to his excellent work and business acumen, before even finishing his internship his boss offered him a job opportunity as a financial planning analyst. It wasn't too long before the company realized that he also had a talent for management. He was an opinion former, motivated, and an excellent salesman for his own ideas. By twenty-five he was already manager of Financial Planning and Analysis (FP&A) and by twenty-seven he had been promoted to CFO when his own boss became the new Director of Operations in *Brazil*.

Aside from a competitive salary and benefits, as a director, Eduardo also travelled frequently to the corporate office in Paris. He was a business class frequent flier and when he could, he would catch a Friday flight preceding his work commitments to enjoy *Paris* a little—one of his favorite places—or visit other cities in *France* or around *Europe*.

Every time he stayed in *Paris*, whether for work or on his weekends off, Eduardo explored somewhere new. He would delineate a small area of the town to walk and take in every square meter. Of course, he had his favorite places where he would occasionally make a repeat visit and explored new perspectives. He appreciated good wine (though not a *connoisseur*) and good food.

"France is a great place to explore new gastronomic experiences, but cuisines other than French should be tried too. For example, there are good Greek and Middle Eastern restaurants," he commented at one time to a colleague.

The main office of *Beauté Cosmetics* in *Paris* was located near the *Avenue Champs-Élysées*. So when he could, Eduardo would try to find hotels nearby and savored walking to work. For him, being in *Paris* meant not losing too much time on the subway or in taxis—one of the best things to do in that city was to walk.

When he stayed on weekends before or after a week's work, he would go to the region he wanted to explore and there he would do everything on foot. He would visit the neighborhoods or sections of town he had passed by earlier and thought might be interesting—without anyone else's suggestion—and loved losing himself on those walks. When it was time to eat, his approach was no different: normally, stopping in front of any restaurant, well known or not, he would look at the menu in the entry and decide there and then whether he would go in, sit down to eat, or try somewhere else. If the place didn't please him, he would move on to the next, until he found what he wanted.

Eduardo also wasn't very in to frequenting expensive restaurants or those with *Michelin* stars, but during one of his visits his boss invited him to dinner at a star-rated restaurant along with the other directors who were also in *Paris* for the convention. The secretary had made the reservation for the closing of the event.

The restaurant was on *Rue Lamennais*—behind the *Champs-Élysées Monument*—with it's classic architecture, exceptional *décor* and lit by beautiful chandeliers—a refined environment—marvelous service and menu, with impeccable presentation of each dish.

"I'm certain that you will all enjoy this experience," his boss said as they entered the restaurant.

Frédéric Capitaine, a man of sixty some-odd years had been in the vice presidency of the company for the past fifteen. *Beauté* was only his second job when he was thirty, beginning his career at the company in the commercial area. He climbed steadily to higher positions within the group until he reached the position of Vice President of Finances, controlling all of the financial directors for all the regions the company operated in around the world.

At the table were all the heads of the finance: Frédéric, Eduardo, Chris Peterson —for *Europe*, Jorge Ramirez—for the *Americas*, excluding *Brazil*, Angelique Mordu—in charge of the *Middle East* and the African countries, and Jim Sun Cho— for *Japan*, *China* and *South Korea*.

It was a pleasant evening for everyone. Frédéric started the night off by ordering a bottle of *Dom Perignon* to toast the successful week they had had. That year had been one of great expansion; the market for cosmetics was booming, notably in the developing countries.

The group remained almost until closing, discussing a wide array of subjects: world economy, politics, company guidelines, pleasantries about the personal life of each of those present, as well as the marvelous meal they had shared.

"My, I can say without hesitation that this was the best meal I have ever had," Angelique commented at one moment.

"It's good that you are enjoying it," Frédéric replied.

"I enjoy eating well, but this was indescribable. My *Magret de Canard* was simply heavenly, and the dessert!" Eduardo added,

"I would like to compliment the *chef* for the marvelous dinner he prepared."

"That can be arranged," Frédéric replied as he signaled to the floor manager and whispered into his ear, after which he went off in the direction of the kitchen.

Despite her youth and considering the demanding standards of the profession, Gabrielle found herself well placed among her peers; she was thirty years old and already one of the most fashionable *chefs* in *Paris*. Everyone wanted to know who this woman in a man's world was who had consolidated a position as one of the greats of French cuisine. And so young! The restaurant was always full; with reservations booked months in advance. And open only one year under her command before it achieved a *Michelin* star. Gabrielle was a *phénomène*!

Gabrielle's great motivator to enter this world of *haute cuisine* had been her grandmother. Rare was the year that went by in her childhood that she hadn't spent part of her summer in the home of her grandparents in the *Languedoc* region, in the south of *France*. This custom continued up until her seventeenth year. After that, her visits became rarer until they ended with the deaths of both grandparents.

The *vila* was in the proximities of *Lac Vailhan*, a lushly green and beautiful region. Her grandparents were the owners of one of the several small vineyards in the region, planting almost everything else they consumed from vegetables and fruits to the herbs they used to flavor their family meals. Nothing industrialized. Everything they produced they either consumed or sold in the farmers' markets found throughout the region on the different market days.

Gabrielle had loved helping her grandmother making cheeses and preparing the meals served *al fresco* on those long summer days. When the time came to start college, she chose gastronomy.

Her grandmother, who endearingly called her 'Brie', left her the property after her death, but Gabrielle asked her mother to take care of everything until she could decide what to do with it. Her mother opted to lease the *vila* to a neighbor and with that income Gabrielle paid for her college education.

She graduated *Cordon Bleu* at the age of twenty-four, suffered through some bad experiences as *sous chef* to a few famous *chefs* with more ego than talent and by twenty-eight, was invited by an investor to head his restaurant on the *Rue Lamennais*.

Pierre San-Michel had of course, done his homework. After all, he was a millionaire and didn't get where he was by acting on a whim, not even a beautiful one. One day he went to the restaurant where Gabrielle worked and was impressed with the food. He asked the waiter who the *chef* was, as he wanted to congratulate him. The young man replied softly in Pierre's ear, that the merit, in truth was all Gabrielle's and not the restaurants' *chef*. Pierre didn't lose any time complimenting the *chef* on that day, and as he was interested in investing in *haute cuisine* restaurants, he began to investigate the girl.

At that time the world economy grew exponentially and the *nouveaux riche* from all over the globe loved going to *Paris* to splurge in the shops of the *Galeries Lafayette* and eat in the *City of Lights*' finest restaurants. This smelled of a great opportunity for Pierre. And getting the right *chef* for his restaurant was as important as the marketing needed to attract the clientele.

After tasting Gabrielle's food, he wanted her to be the newest star in the Parisian *cuisine* scene. The next day, he asked a trusted employee to dig up everything he could find on Gabrielle's professional trajectory and personality.

After reading everything about the girl, he decided that she was the one to command the restaurant he was investing in. Before discovering Gabrielle, Pierre had approached several promising *chefs* and *sous chefs* and many others had approached him too. Whispers of the new restaurant at the level Pierre was creating spread like wildfire among the elite of the industry. He had almost resolved to hire an experienced—and expensive— seasoned professional for his restaurant when he discovered Gabrielle's talent and had read sufficiently about her for her to believe he had win-win situation; he would give her the chance to head her own kitchen and at the same time negotiate a salary lower than what he would have paid a renowned someone. Of course, there was enormous risk in this deal, and he would have to increase investment in the restaurant's promotion. But as an *entrepreneur*, Pierre also knew that the bigger the risk, the greater the return on the investment, if all went as planned. And it did.

Pierre met with Gabrielle in his office in *La Defense*, a major business district just 3 km west, outside *Paris* city limits in the *Île-de-France* region of the *department des Hauts-de-Seine*. She was responding to a telephone call from Pierre's assistant who spoke of an opportunity to be the *chef* for a new *haute cuisine* restaurant in the *8th Arrondissement* of *Paris*, near the *Champs-Élysées*.

"Pierre"—his assistant spoke softly into the interphone — "Gabrielle has arrived for her interview."

"She's a little early," Pierre responded on the other side, glancing at his watch, "but ask her to come in."

Gabrielle didn't like to be late for any engagement and usually arrived earlier than the scheduled time.

Gabrielle was a beautiful and elegant woman: a slender body with accentuated curves along her 1.72 meter body, straight dark brown—almost black hair, green eyes and full lips. She looked more like a movie star—especially when she wasn't wearing her *chef's* uniform. She was also a very formal woman and liked her privacy. Nonetheless, she was not straight-laced. She had her *affairs* but kept them to herself. In truth, no one ever knew when she was dating and when she wasn't.

On the day of her interview with Pierre she was wearing a navy blue *tailleur* with a cream blouse, a small *écharpe* at her throat covering her neck and *décolleté,* and heels. Her beautiful hair was knotted in a *chignon*, giving her the more serious air, she believed appropriate for a business meeting.

"Pierre, this is Gabrielle." Linda, his assistant announced softly, as they entered his office.

As he stood and they shook hands—he admired her—impressed with her beauty. He had already seen her in the photos contained in the *dossier* he had on her, but nothing prepared him for her in person.

"It's a pleasure, *Monsieur* San-Michel," Gabrielle said, "and thank you for the opportunity to be here," she went on in her modulated voice.

"Please, call me Pierre," he replied, motioning to one of the groupings of designer armchairs under a bank of windows. "And please, sit."

Pierre was at least ten years her senior, but at that moment he reconsidered his life as a lady's man and confirmed bachelor, imagining himself married to this beautiful woman. "You are aware that it is a job that I'm offering you?" Pierre went on.

"Your secretary informed me that it was a position for executive *chef* but didn't mention any details."

Pierre then went on to describe the project and how he had become aware of her work when dining by chance at the restaurant where she was *sous chef.* He was adamant in mentioning that it was thanks to the waiter who served his table that he heard about her work. If it hadn't been for him, he certainly would have spoken to the *chef* of the restaurant where she worked, certain that the marvelous food he had savored had been his work and not that of Gabrielle.

Gabrielle listened attentively to all that he said without interruption and at the end asked that Pierre clarify a few points.

"Look, the project seems very interesting and has a lot of potential"—Gabrielle began—"however, what worries me is that I am not known. I know my capabilities and the quality of what I do, but I'm not the one who takes credit for it, as you have already concluded."

"I don't think you need to concern yourself with that—Pierre said, trying to tranquilize her—I have an excellent marketing team and they know a great public relations agency here in *Paris*. While we are finishing the work on the restaurant, they can start working on your name. We'll see to it that you start to be mentioned in specialized publications as quickly as possible. Something like: 'the woman behind the great *chef'*—it might sound a little sexist, but you know you're in a male-dominated profession."

"That's true," Gabrielle agreed, nodding.

"And that's only one idea on how to launch your name on the market—Pierre went on—what's important is that you continue to work where you are for the time being, so that we can start working on this. Do you have any restriction in your contract—a non-compete or prior notice clause to leave the company?"

"No, just the usual," she replied.

"That makes our work that much easier," he smiled. The restaurant will be ready in a few months, in the meantime, let's start working on building your name. As soon as the specialized press starts to take interest in you, we will announce that you're leaving your present job to take over our project. You'll have to work just a few more hours a day while you are still there, since you're going to have to sit down with our marketing team to discuss strategy. And we also have to tie-up your contract with me. We can't run the risk of promoting you and then losing you to the competition, can we?"—his smile only reached his lips. "What do you think?"

"I think that's fair, and an excellent strategy," Gabrielle responded, "however, what will my participation be in this enterprise?"

"Gabrielle, you know that today you are unknown, so I will have to invest heavily in your name for this to work. So, I thought that I would offer you something intermediary to start off. A salary better than you are earning now, but less than what your better-known peers earn—for let's say—at least a three-year non-compete. Of course, we will have to think about the terms for all of this. I believe that in that time my company would recuperate what it invests to put your name at the top."

"Look, what you are offering me in terms of professional advancement is something I've dreamed of since I decided to go into gastronomy. I also realize that you are a businessman and that you are thinking of compensation for your risks, in case my name doesn't please the market and you end up with an empty restaurant. It's only fair that you think about your side. For your company I'm an investment, an opportunity; for me, it's a lifetime dream. So, I have a counter-offer. Would you like to hear it?"

"Of course, as you say, I am a man of business. So please, tell me more about your idea."

"Ok, I can accept the salary you offer for the first three years. I could even continue earning what I am getting now, even though my responsibilities increase exponentially. Now, I know exactly how far I can take your investment, and if you are telling me that you will run risks, I would also like to participate in those risks, really get on board with you. So, my proposal is that I hold twenty percent in the restaurant."

"Twenty percent?" Pierre exhaled, surprised. "I come in with all of the capital and you want twenty percent? You don't think that's a little too much?" He smiled at her daring.

"If you guarantee a good market, I can guarantee the quality. And what's more, wouldn't it be better for you to keep eighty percent of a lucrative business than one hundred percent of something that you take a loss in?" she concluded with the corners of her mouth rising into a slight smile.

"You are a very bold woman, aren't you? I admire that," he responded.

"Thank you. And so, do you accept my proposal?" She replied, tilting her head slightly to the side, eyebrows raised.

"Agreed, but what I can offer you is ten percent. However, we can make it so that if we open other restaurants together, your participation can reach up to forty percent of the business, while

I continue to subsidize your original ten; but you *will* have to invest any percentage over that yourself. I am certain that if our enterprise does well, you will be able to pay for your own investment," Pierre countered.

"Then I accept your proposal"—Gabrielle smiling—this time with her eyes too—as she replied extending her right hand: "partners?"

"Partners!" Pierre responded, grinning, he shook her hand.

From that morning on, Pierre and Gabrielle worked hard to bring about what they had discussed, and after a year had passed since the inauguration of the restaurant, Gabrielle had become one of the most consecrated *chefs* in all of *France* and her restaurant had already earned a star in the *Michelin Guide*.

Only days prior to the dinner that Frédéric offered his team at the restaurant on *Rue Lamennais*, Pierre proposed to Gabrielle: "I think we're ready for our second restaurant. The house is always full and we have reservations three months in advance. What do you think? Are you ready for a bigger part in the business?"

"Pierre, I think that's a fabulous idea. But we haven't completed two years yet with our first restaurant. Ok, we do have our first star, but don't you think we should wait a bit more? Or at least until we have a second star? We would be consolidated as a brand and then open another restaurant, perhaps outside of *Paris*?"

"I can't say that I agree, but I will respect your decision. We'll come back to this matter very soon though, Gabrielle," he replied reluctantly.

"Fine Pierre, let's have this talk again in a few months," Gabrielle conceded.

Pierre left rather frustrated. Nonetheless, he always tried to respect his partner's opinions.

Pierre and Gabrielle had a relationship of collaboration and trust. He had noted Gabrielle's strength of spirit and intelligence in their first contact years ago and that led him to trust very much in her character and professionalism.

In the beginning, it had been very difficult for him to resist Gabrielle's beauty, charm and intelligence. Whenever he could, he demonstrated his personal interest in her: inviting her to dinners, on trips, and to events, all of which she declined politely and with class. When he saw that subtlety was getting him nowhere, he decided to go directly to the point. And that was shortly after she had won them their first star.

"A toast to the best *chef* in *Paris*, if not the world"—Pierre exclaimed to the entire team, raising a champagne flute in her direction, "we wouldn't have gotten this far if it weren't for your work—to Gabrielle!"

"To Gabrielle," the team chanted in unison, as they raised their glasses to her.

Gabrielle thanked everyone and without false modesty, told them with a broad grin, that alone she would have achieved nothing and gotten nowhere, proposing a new toast to the team and the confidence that Pierre had put in her since the beginning.

At the end of the celebration, after the others had gone, Gabrielle was alone in the closed restaurant with Pierre. She called out to him that they should leave. She needed to close the restaurant and come back in only a few hours when a new business day would begin. It was already three in the morning.

"No, why don't we stay a little longer or take this celebration to my apartment?" Pierre was drunk and allowing himself to be carried away by his feelings for Gabrielle.

"Pierre, I think you have gone a little beyond your limit. We have to go. I'll call you a taxi," She replied.

"All this time you still don't understand that I want to be with you, do you? I'm in love with you Gabrielle," Pierre murmured.

Gabrielle was aware of Pierre's platonic love for her, but was caught off guard by this declaration.

"Pierre, I hope you remember tomorrow what I am going to say to you now," Gabrielle replied with a slight frown wrinkling her forehead. "I like you very much, but I like even more the confidence, respect, and friendship that we have developed during this short time we have known each other. So I would like to make it very clear to you that it is only that. We will never be together and I would like very much for you to understand that. For me, we are partners and great friends, nothing more."

That was a punch in the stomach to Pierre, even more so since he was used to getting his way with every woman he had ever wanted. But from that moment on, he accepted that there was no chance of them ever being together and understood that they would be just friends; at least, on the outside. And after that, Pierre returned to the womanizing he enjoyed so much before he met Gabrielle.

Chapter Three – At First Sight

Tristan arrived in the kitchen of the restaurant on *Rue Lamennais* and recalled the night before when he had spoken to Pierre about Gabrielle, the real talent in the restaurant where they worked. The two of them had become great friends since they first started working together. But Tristan hadn't told Pierre about Gabrielle because they were friends, rather because she really deserved the recognition.

Just slightly shorter than Gabrielle, Tristan is almost too thin, with sharp features; his dark eyes always flashing his feelings to the world. He has dark, straight, fashionably-cut hair. He's the stereotypical Frenchman; without the beret. Vain to a fault, he adores velvet and detests anything plaid. At home or around town he sports a velvet blazer with jeans and dress shoes, sockless. And no tennis shoes for our Tristan, thank you very much! A dress shirt of pure white or a soft pastel—sleeves folded twice—completed his look. No piercings at all, but there might be a discrete, though highly detailed tattoo somewhere that doesn't show when he is working.

Tristan's never has a shadow on his jaw—always impeccably shaved—even on his days off. He does like a fine thin line of a sideburn delineating his jaw and stretching almost to his mouth. He doesn't have much money, yet his flat glows chic, and of course, it's impeccably clean. An embroidered hand towel in the bathroom with his initials in ivory is always laid out for guests.

For her part, Gabrielle was aware of Tristan's competency and potential and invited him to be her Floor Manager in the restaurant she opened with Pierre. He accepted on the spot.

"Gabrielle!" Tristan exclaimed, as he stuck his head through the kitchen's swinging door: "Is everything ready so we can close the restaurant for the day?"

"Sure, just a few more details, and the kitchen will be ready to close for the day," she responded from the prep table where the kitchen crew was in a meeting. "Are there any more clients in the dining room?"

"Just one last table—*M. Capitaine* with a group of executives. Oh, and by the way, he would like you to make an appearance—I think your dishes made quite an impression on the group he's with."

"Of course!" Gabrielle replied, "Frédéric is one of our most frequent clients, not to mention that he is a true gentleman. Please, tell him that I will be with him in only a few moments, I need to finish up with a few things with the team so I can let them go home. I'll try to be quick."

As Tristan left the kitchen, Gabrielle turned back to the group to conclude the last activities of the night.

Everyone had already finished their last drinks at Frédéric's table. He was motioning again to Tristan when Gabrielle entered the dining room and moved toward their table.

"Good evening Frédéric. Good evening everyone!" Gabrielle exclaimed.

"Good evening Gabrielle," Frédéric responded, "my team of directors for our international operations was impressed by your dishes and would like to compliment you on your marvelous food; especially Eduardo,"—as he gestured in Eduardo's direction—"he is our Financial Director for our operations in *Brazil*."

Eduardo couldn't mask his look of enchantment and surprise when he saw that beautiful woman standing before him. The sensation in the pit of his stomach and his accelerating heart took him by surprise. And everyone at the table noticed his expression as he looked at the girl, but they pretended otherwise, focusing on the conversation.

The executives intoned their satisfaction with the food, the service, and everything else. Eduardo however, remained frozen and couldn't say a word. It was Gabrielle who broke his silence: "I hope you enjoyed our restaurant too, Eduardo."

"Oh, uh, yes, of course"—he managed to get out,—"everything was p-perfect, and all the wines in p-p-perfect harmony with the dishes," he continued.

It was the custom of the restaurant to serve the wine and champagne the client requested before they started serving the food, but the *sommelier* often counseled their clients, suggesting wines that paired well with each chosen dish. If it wasn't possible for a single wine to pair well with all of the orders at a table, he would suggest that the clients request their wines by the glass.

"I hope you enjoyed your stay in Paris?" Gabrielle added, trying to put the guy at ease.

Even she had noticed his reaction and his staring at her. And to tell the truth, she enjoyed being desired, especially since she didn't feel all that presentable after more than twelve hours work and wearing her *toque blanche* and chef's jacket.

"Yes, yes,"—he responded, though still not quite his normal self—"*Paris* is one of my favorite cities; after *Rio de Janeiro*, of course."

To which Gabrielle responded, "ah, I have heard a lot about *Rio*, an enchanting city. I would very much like to see it."

"And have you any plans to open a new restaurant, my dear?" Frédéric interjected.

"We need to consolidate more before thinking about new projects," Gabrielle responded. "A new restaurant would demand my absence here, and I won't be able to do that until I have at least two *chefs* to cover for me in each place."

"Of course, very sensible," Frédéric replied.

The group continued chatting with Gabrielle for a few more moments. Tristan brought the check which was commandeered immediately by Frédéric.

Eduardo and the others left the restaurant and asked the valet for two taxis to take them to their hotel. Frédéric's driver was already waiting to take him home. Eduardo however, decided that he would rather walk, and so, each went his own way.

The restaurant was about ten minutes by car from the hotel where they were staying; perhaps forty minutes at a leisurely pace. This time the company hadn't been able to find an available hotel closer to *Beauté*.

Eduardo walked in the direction of the hotel unable to get the image of Gabrielle out of his head. His pulse was still rapid— inexplicable so. Eduardo knew that he wouldn't be able to sleep that night. He even tried to mentally plan what he would do this last weekend in *Paris* before he went back to *Rio* while he wandered in the direction of his hotel, but he couldn't stop thinking of Gabrielle. He thought: "those eyes, that mouth…and so talented!"

Eduardo wasn't too hard on the eyes either: he was tanned, whenever he could he would take advantage of what *Leblon* beach had to offer, play footvolley with his friends; light brown eyes that appeared green contrasted with his tanned skin; a full head of short dark brown curls, an athletic build with well defined muscles along his 1,85m body—a little over average height for a Brazilian. Eduardo however didn't consider himself really *carioca*. Although born in *Rio de Janeiro*, he wasn't the stereotypical *carioca*—expansive, a loud talker and hitting on all the girls, whether or not they showed any interest in him. In truth, whenever he was with anyone, it was always through the girl's initiative; and he never let his relationships evolve into any kind of serious relationship. His focus was always on work and his career, and that was really where he could be expansive and assertive, very different from the rather shy and reserved *persona* of his private life.

A few guys at the office had even made bets on his sexuality. "It's not possible that anyone as good looking and successful as he is doesn't have a girlfriend. The guy has got to be gay!" they would joke. The truth is, everyone has their own story, and the majority finds it easier to judge just by looking at the book's cover.

Finally arriving at his hotel, that restaurant *chef*—where he had just had dinner—still in his head. He went up to his room, took off his suit, brushed his teeth, took a shower and put on his pajamas before lying down on the king-sized bed.

The hotel was very comfortable and near *Rue des Écoles,* in a typically Parisian building, with slated wooden doors opening onto tiny balconies edged with black wrought iron railings. His room was decorated elegantly, with old works of art and a fireplace in front of the bed. Eduardo felt almost as if he were transported to another era were it not for the modern infrastructure and ample *en suite* bathroom. The continental breakfast was really good too.

Eduardo couldn't sleep thinking about Gabrielle, so he turned on his laptop and tried to concentrate on something else. He decided to research something to do in *Paris* the next day, since he hadn't planned anything before coming, as was his habit. In the end, nothing caught his interest.

Honestly, the only thing that interested Eduardo that night was to think about that woman who had left him speechless—mouth dry—frozen in front of everyone. He felt something in his chest and stomach he had never felt before. He even thought he might be coming down with something. The fact of the matter was he really didn't know how to deal with that sensation. That sentiment was totally unknown to him.

Eduardo tossed and turned in bed that night, got up and went to the balcony several times, and only fell asleep when exhaustion overcame him.

Chapter Four – Urca, Tijuca, Urca

Eduardo had reached a comfortable financial situation at a young age through his own merit and hard work. He was the son of a production manager, who had worked at a big company in the metropolitan area of *Rio*, his mother was a teacher at a municipal school.

When Eduardo was born, his father suggested to his wife *Dona* Julia that no one could take better care of their son than she; and with his manager's salary, they could live comfortably if they were willing to make some minor adjustments to the family budget. She had been a little reluctant, but in the end agreed that at least during Eduardo's first few years she would make the sacrifice of being away from her beloved profession.

Eduardo and his family lived in a nice house in the *Urca* neighborhood and he mainly stayed at home with his mother until he became old enough to start school. Oh, and how he enjoyed that short time, taking advantage of everything the neighborhood had to offer: beach, parks and safety—there was a lot of policing in the area. As his mother had been a teacher, she used her knowledge and abilities to prepare him for school life before he had even started his first year in pre-school. He was a quick learner.

When Eduardo finally grew old enough to go to school, *Dona* Julia decided that the best option would be to try for a place at the selective *Colégio Pedro II*, a traditional federal educational institution with a selection process by drawing lots once all applications were entered. *Dona* Julia was one of the first in line when the time came to apply for a number in the drawing for the upcoming school year. The results would only be made public in fifteen days, which left her very apprehensive for the next two weeks. If Eduardo was not selected, they would have to wait two more years before he could try again for a place in the first year. That would mean two years in a private school which wouldn't be at the same high standard as *Pedro II*.

The day of the results arrived; Eduardo had been selected! The family celebrated their good fortune that night quietly.

Eduardo's childhood couldn't have been better; he was one of the best students in his class and lived comfortably in a loving middle class family. *Dona* Julia tried to occupy her mornings with the routines of the house and in the afternoon helped Eduardo with his homework. Whenever she could, she would take her son for a walk on the *Urca* waterfront or go to the *Rio Sul Shopping Center* or even the *Botafogo* beach. She was already used to not working as a teacher.

Seu Giovani, Eduardo's father always had the same routine during the week: he woke up at six in the morning, spent the day at the factory and arrived home around seven in the evening. He took over an hour to get home at the end of the day as the factory was on the outskirts of Rio. The weekends however, he made certain to spend with his wife and son.

One day, the factory needed to prepare and dispatch an exceptionally large shipment, so *Seu* Giovani called his wife to tell her that he would be home very late. He told her not to worry about dinner since he would be fine eating something at the factory. That was a Wednesday night.

Dona Julia explained to little Eduardo that they would have dinner by themselves that night, since his father would only come home at dawn because of work.

It was four in the morning when the telephone rang in the living room. *Dona* Julia awoke startled by the sound and as she turned to ask *Seu* Giovani to answer it, realized that he hadn't arrived yet. Her heart beat fast. "Nonsense," she told herself out loud, "it's probably him calling to say that he hasn't left the factory yet."

"*Dona* Julia?" A voice asked tentatively as she answered the telephone.

She felt her mouth go dry and her heart beat even faster.

"Yes," she responded, her voice husky with fear.

"*Dona* Julia this is Daniel, the Health and Safety Manager of the company where *Seu* Giovane works," the man continued on the other end of the line.

It was as if her spirit faded away. *Dona* Julia couldn't feel her body anymore.

"Has something happened, Daniel?" she asked, a tremble in her voice.

"*Dona* Julia, unfortunately there has been an accident with one of the forklifts. One of the crates fell from high up and hit *Seu* Giovani. He received help immediately and was taken to the local hospital," Daniel explained.

"*Ai, meu Deus*! But is he ok?" she whispered through her tears.

"*Dona* Julia, we still don't have news. I must ask you to stay calm. We are sending a driver to your house to take you to the hospital. I am on my way there now too. By the time I arrive, we will have more information."

Eduardo became fatherless at the age of eight.

The lives of both *Dona* Julia and Eduardo changed radically that year. Although *Seu* Giovani had an excellent salary, aside from benefits and bonus—that wasn't the case in his absence—

significantly affecting the family budget and consequently, their style of living. *Dona* Julia had only the house and his pension to support herself and her son. What the family received from his life insurance was barely enough to pay up the mortgage. As for the pension, it was less than half of what *Seu* Giovani brought home when he was alive.

Even without the house payments, *Dona* Julia saw that his pension would not cover the rest of their expenses. She had to make decisions so that she and her son could continue living with some dignity and not accumulate debts. She wouldn't wait for the worst.

So, not only did he have to swallow the bitter pill of the loss of his father, Eduardo and *Dona* Julia had to leave their home where they had been so happy. She decided to rent out the house in *Urca* which was worth a good amount, being an expensive neighborhood on the south side of *Rio*. She could pay the rent for a less expensive place and with the difference, complement their income.

Eduardo and his mother moved to an apartment in *Tijuca*—a neighborhood in the north zone of *Rio*—close to *Maracanã* Stadium and *Dona* Julia decided to supplement their income with reinforcement tutoring for neighborhood children and Eduardo's schoolmates.

It was a radical change in both their lives, but as time passed, Eduardo barely remembered the good life he had had in *Urca*—since he hadn't changed schools or friends—he didn't feel the change as badly. He got used to his new life, but still missed his father who had been so loving and present in his life.

Eduardo kept the same small group of friends and was always very studious, nor as an adolescent did he go out very often. Many times, it was his mother who insisted that he go out.

Normally, he was reluctant, but once in a while he would concede and go out with his friends. By fifteen he had become a good-looking boy and the girls wouldn't stop following him with their eyes at parties and at school.

Because of the premature loss of his father, and because he was so close to his mother, Eduardo applied himself more than ever to his studies. He swore to himself that he would give back to his mother the comfortable life they had once enjoyed. Not because he missed it, but because he knew that it would make his mother happy. And so he did: Eduardo grew, and after his studies were over, he made a name for himself early on at work.

As soon as he was promoted to FP&A Manager at *Beauté Cosmetic*, he had a talk with *Dona* Julia, seated in their modest living room:

"Mom," he said; his voice excited, "we need to talk."

"Of course son, what's happened?" She replied as she sat on the sofa beside him.

"As you know," he said seriously, "I was promoted at the firm and of course, my salary is much better. Not to mention all the rest."

"I understand. I suppose that now you will want more privacy. It is quite natural, my son." She replied, patting his hand. She was eating herself up inside, but as an intelligent woman, she knew that one day this would happen.

"Never mother! I can have my privacy in my room, and what are hotels for anyway? And another thing, you never stopped me from bringing my friends or girlfriends home. So most certainly, that is *not* what I'm saying. What I'm proposing to you is that we go back to our home in *Urca*. We can update it and have our old life back. After all, it has been some time now that I am no longer an expense for you and if we go home, I could take over the larger part of the expenses. Of course, Dad won't be there with us... so, what do you think?"

Dona Julia couldn't hold back her tears. "Son that is the best news you could have given your old mother, but what would I do with my private students?"

"You could finish the semester with them while we remodel the house and then you tell them that you won't be doing private tutoring next year. And if you still want to tutor, you can get new students in *Urca*, but I don't think that will be necessary. Anyway, we can make Dad's old office into a study room and I can also use it when I bring work home. What do you think?" Eduardo replied, eager to please.

"Could I decide when we move? But you should decorate the new office however you please. And if I decide to go on tutoring, then I can share it with you."

"Of course Mother!" He answered, delighted.

The two couldn't have been happier.

Six months passed quickly and the two were back in their old house in *Urca*. *Dona* Julia had decided finally that she wouldn't go back to tutoring after all.

Eduardo drove to and from *Beauté* every day, but when he would go to *Leblon* beach or out with his friends at night he preferred using taxis or the subway. It's what he had been doing before moving back to the old neighborhood where he had been born and anyway, parking was impossible anywhere in the southern zone of the city.

One day, not long after their move, Eduardo was in a meeting with his team explaining a few projections to the group, when they were suddenly interrupted.

"Eduardo," his assistant—a twenty-four year-old brunette—blurted breathlessly from the doorway,   "sorry to interrupt your meeting, but your mother is on the phone and it sounds important."

That was at five on a Friday afternoon.

"No problem," Eduardo replied, "I'll take the call in my office. Guys, let's take this up again on Monday?"

Everyone was still agreeing as Eduardo ran to his office.

"Mom, what happened?" Eduardo tensely said into the phone.

"Take it easy son, it's nothing much," *Dona* Julia responded. "I felt a pain in my stomach while I was walking on the beach and fainted."

"What?" Eduardo exclaimed, almost shouting into the telephone. "I'm on my way home now!"

"Son, I'm not home. A couple helped me and brought me to the Emergency at *Copa D'Or Hospital*, but I'm alright now. I'm still under observation waiting for someone to authorize my release. Could you come pick me up?"

"Of course Mom, I'm leaving now. *Tchau!*" He exclaimed as he grabbed his things and headed out the door, full speed.

In just a few short weeks *Dona* Julia was diagnosed with stomach cancer. They were months of treatment and suffering for the family. And to think, that they were so happy having moved back home.

Dona Julia didn't make it.

With the loss of his mother and in her, his best friend, Eduardo closed himself off even more within himself than before, focusing exclusively on his work. He rarely went out, was rarely with anyone, and he never dated anyone for very long— he had promised himself that he would never get involved with anyone. He just didn't want to ever have to deal with loss again. It was too painful.

With his promotion to CFO, his responsibilities also increased and from then on, it was just work, the beach, his gym, and whenever possible, his trips for work or vacation. Whenever he met anyone—which was a rarity since he hardly ever went out—he tried to leave between the lines that he wasn't looking for a serious relationship, which only made the women he briefly got involved with feeling a mixture of frustration and regret.

But life pulls odd tricks on even those most determined not to want something, and Eduardo was no exception. On the night he met Gabrielle, his intent to never fall in love went down the drain.

Chapter Five – Paris, France

Not having planned anything the night before that final week in Paris, Eduardo decided to go out without a plan, something unthinkable for him.

After getting out of bed, washing his face and rinsing his mouth, he dressed in light clothing, put on running shoes, and went out for a run. It was a sunny day. To warm up, he sped down the four flights of stairs from his room grabbing a piece of fruit from the reception on his way out, as he headed toward the nearby *Luxemburg Gardens*. After three laps or so that took only about forty-five minutes, he returned to his hotel. Starving, Eduardo showered and was back in the hotel lobby and on his way to the dining room in short order. He served himself a nice cup of coffee and a few *croissants*, scrambled eggs, cheese, and a slice of cake from the buffet. He topped that off with a second cup and a small bowl of fresh strawberries and blueberries.

Before leaving the hotel he went up to his room for a second time to brush his teeth and grab his backpack, wallet, and passport. He never left his passport in hotel rooms.

By the time he left the hotel for the second time that day it was already nearing ten that morning. Wandering off in the direction of the *Luxemburg Gardens* again, but this time he decided to go to *Montparnasse* and explore on the way. The only thing he was certain of was that he would stop at one of the *créperies* on *Rue du Montparnasse* to have a savory *crêpe* with cider served in a porcelain jar and glass—he loved that.

Taking advantage of the moment, he stopped in at the *Luxemburg Palace and Museum*. Although he had visited the park numerous times to enjoy the gardens or run laps around them, he had never been inside the palace or the museum.

Eduardo thoroughly enjoyed the palace, a beautiful example of XVII century construction with luxurious *salons* and bedrooms; there he could also see the seat of the French Senate inside the palace. He spent the next two hours wandering in its halls. From there, he went to the *Luxemburg Museum*, a small contemporary art museum just next door to the palace, all within the *Gardens* grounds.

It was nearly one in the afternoon when Eduardo left the palace. He crossed the center of the *Garden* admiring the views and people-watching those strolling. Reaching the *Rue Vavin* exit, he went off in the direction of *Montparnasse* where he saw a small *adega* called *Nicolas* and decided to stop. He spent over half an hour browsing in the shop, leaving with two bottles of *Bordeaux*. Since he always brought a backpack on his walks, he put the bottles inside, leaving his hands free. He continued on *Vavin* until he reached the end of the street, turned right on *Boulevard du Montparnasse* to reach the block on *Rue du Montparnasse* where the majority of *crêperies* were located. By that time, it was just past two in the afternoon and he was hungry—time to interrupt his tour for a meal.

Even after having a pleasant morning sightseeing, he still couldn't get Gabrielle out of his head for a moment. Each time thoughts of her overpowered the sights, Eduardo felt a chill in the pit of his stomach.

Arriving at his destiny he saw several *crêperies* and examined their *façades* choosing one with the most pleasing appearance for his meal. He decided on *Le Petit Josselin*. Although it was a little crowded, he liked one of the *crêpes* he saw on the menu posted in chalk on a blackboard sitting on a small easel on the sidewalk by the door. When he was finally seated, he asked for a glass of red wine while he examined the menu. He finally decided on the *crêpe Normande*, one filled with *camembert*, an apple jam and cured ham. He was intrigued with that combination of savory and sweet. A pitcher of cider would accompany his meal.

As the food and cider arrived, Eduardo was finishing his second glass of red wine and probably because of his empty stomach and the delay he was feeling slightly lightheaded. He thought that after he ate he would feel better, except that he forgot that cider also contains alcohol and the pitcher held almost a liter. Eduardo not only did not feel better from the effects of the alcohol in the wine, but was feeling rather drunk after all that cider.

He paid his bill and left the *crêperie* instilled with a courage that only the inebriated possess; he decided to go to Gabrielle's restaurant and ask her out.

The walk to the restaurant would take nearly an hour from *Montparnasse* and he knew that not only was he not up to walking the distance in his state, but if he did arrive there on foot, by that time he would be too sober to still have the courage to ask her out. Eduardo decided to take a taxi. On a Saturday, the car took less than fifteen minutes to arrive at *Rue Lamennais*.

Getting out of the car, Eduardo stood on the sidewalk staring up at the front of the restaurant for almost ten minutes trying to build up the courage to go in. It was already after four in the afternoon. By that time, the effects of the alcohol had begun to dissipate along with his courage which was turning into panic at having to face that incredible woman and invite her out, risking hearing "no" as an answer.

"Hello, good afternoon sir," a low feminine voice said nearing Eduardo who was still contemplating the *façade*. "I couldn't help but notice you as I was coming up the street." Eduardo turned his head toward the sound of the voice he heard addressing him from behind. It was Gabrielle returning to the restaurant after her lunch break. The blood drained from Eduardo's face as he froze in a mixture of embarrassment and enchantment—"you've been staring at our *façade* for quite a while," she continued. "May I help you with something? I work here," she went on as she drew up to his side and stopped.

Eduardo continued speechless for a few more moments which felt like an eternity until he managed: "Oh, yes. No! I mean…" he stuttered to a stop.

"Sorry, but do you need help?" Gabrielle insisted, still not recognizing him from the night before. Most likely because the clothing he was wearing was so very different from the well cut and expensive suit he had worn the night before.

By this time, the effects of the alcohol had dissipated completely and he was finally able to gather his thoughts; breathing deeply: "Your name is Gabrielle, isn't it?" Eduardo asked, already feeling calmer.

"Yes, but from where do you know me?" she began, stopping midsentence as she remembered him. "Ah, you are one of the directors that works for Frédéric, are you not Eduardo?

"That's right." Eduardo replied with a sensation of relief that she had recognized him. "Yesterday I had one of the best gastronomic experiences of my life!"

"Oh, thank you very much for the compliment. I am pleased that you enjoyed our restaurant, but it is still a little early for dinner, no? Besides, the house requires more formal dress than what you are using," she completed, a smile in her voice and eyes.

"No, no. In truth, I was standing here gathering up courage to knock on the door and ask you out."

Gabrielle was surprised at his directness. "What do you mean? You barely know me and you think you can come to my restaurant and expect that I accept an invitation from you?" That self awareness of an independent woman spoke to Gabrielle much louder at that moment than any desire to accept Eduardo's invitation.

"I apologize for being so direct, but I confess that I am not used to asking women out. I really don't know how. I thought being direct and honest with you would demonstrate my respect."

Irritated with his reply, Gabrielle shot off: "Oh, so you mean that women chase after you? That is so conceited of you!"

"Please, excuse me. I don't mean to sound boastful, but that is exactly what happens. I'm extremely timi…"

Gabrielle interrupted him mid-phrase, "I think you should leave, if you don't have a reservation, sir. And the last time I checked, the house was full…all night. Goodbye *Monsieur* Eduardo." She whipped around and went into the restaurant, slamming the door before he could say anything else.

Eduardo walked slowly away not understanding what had happened. He had gone there to invite Gabrielle to do something before his flight the next day and instead, saw someone absolutely indignant with his sincerity. True, Eduardo didn't know how to approach a woman, and it's also true that he never had to: he attracted them like flies to honey.

He even considered going back and knocking on the door to try to retract any misunderstanding, but thought that might just worsen the situation. "What a crazy woman!" he thought finally, entering *George V Station* on *Avenue Champs-Elysées*.

Eduardo returned to his hotel and didn't go out again until his flight on Sunday, so disappointed, he had lost all interest.

Arriving in his room, he lay down for a while to cool down and ended up falling asleep. Waking at around ten in the evening, feeling hungry, and with a slight headache; he swallowed some Aspirin he found in his suitcase, took a shower, dressed, and went down for dinner. Since he didn't feel like going out, he walked into the hotel restaurant and asked for a table. Eduardo ordered a simple meal of onion soup followed by fish and ate alone with his thoughts.

Back in his room again, he decided to work a little until he felt sleepy. Opening his laptop he began analyzing a report he had received that week from Accounting but hadn't had time to review it because of the intense week of meetings and presentations in *Paris*. Less than five minutes later, his mind wandered back to what had happened between him and Gabrielle. He just couldn't understand what he had done to offend her. That might even seem like a lack of empathy on Eduardo's part, but taking into context his limited experience, he just really couldn't find his error.

Unhappy with the whole misunderstanding, he decided to search for answers on the internet. He searched for articles about the restaurant opening, hoping to find something about Gabrielle. When he finished reading he understood her personality a little better, realizing how much she had fought to get where she was, her force of character, and exceptional negotiating capabilities.

It was then that he realized what a fool he had been giving Gabrielle the impression that he thought himself irresistible, and that any woman would want to be with him. Even without meaning to, he had been bragging. Blood rushed to Eduardo's face as he blushed, ashamed of what he had said. But it was too late, not only did he have to catch his flight back to Brazil the next day, but he hadn't the slightest idea how to find her at that time of night.

The next day Eduardo went to the *Charles de Gaulle Airport* and caught his flight back to *Rio de Janeiro*.

In London, Still

Chapter Six – The Misunderstanding

Gabrielle was furious as the door slammed in Eduardo's face when she rushed into the restaurant that Saturday afternoon. Never had she imagined that she would hear from a man— apparently so interesting—something that was so outrageously unforgivable.

"Imbecile! Sexist! Conceited idiot!" She shouted as the kitchen door banged on her way through.

"What's happened Gabrielle?" Tristan exclaimed, startled by her behavior. "Did you and Pierre have a fight?"

"Pierre? Pierre and I are fine!" Gabrielle responded with her voice still burred with anger. "It was that idiot of a Brazilian who was here yesterday with Frédéric," she replied.

"What Brazilian? I couldn't identify the nationality of anyone in *Monsieur* Capitaine's party yesterday," Tristan replied. But before she could interrupt him, he went on, "Ah, the good-looking young *mec*."

"Good-looking!" Gabrielle harrumphed. "He is as good looking as he is a pretentious, sexist idiot. And to think that I thought he was interesting yesterday during that brief conversation we had when I went to meet the entire table."

"But what happened for you to come into the restaurant in such an irate state? I know you aren't the type to take anything lying down, but from where I stood yesterday I couldn't see anything that looked like a misunderstanding between the two of you." Tristan went on, now intrigued, "did you two talk alone after the group left the restaurant?"

"No! I mean yes!" Gabrielle responded, exasperated. "But it didn't happen yesterday. Can you believe that he was just here, in front of the restaurant looking for me?"

"Really?" Tristan drawled, lifting an eyebrow and one side of his mouth in the beginning of a smile.

"Yes, and by chance, I was arriving when I saw him staring at the door like someone trying to drum up the courage to knock."

"*Mon Dieu*! This is getting interesting…" Tristan exclaimed, the other corner of his mouth turning up to join the first in a slight smile.

"Far from it," Gabrielle denied when she saw that smile. "When I saw that handsome man looking at the restaurant, I didn't recognize him at first. But when I did remember him, I became intrigued. Because of course, I had thought he was interesting and very polite yesterday. I only saw what he was really like after I approached him to see if he needed help, since he was staring this way," she indicated with her hand pointing to herself.

"Ok, and then what did he say when you came up to him?" Tristan queried, curiosity piqued.

"He realized that I didn't recognize him and became rather anxious. I even thought it was kind of cute, because the moment he said my name," Gabrielle continued, "I recognized him."

"*Alors*—so, what else did he say?" Tristan blurted out, not able to contain his curiosity any longer.

"At the beginning of the conversation he came off well, complimenting the food, he was very polite, until…" Gabrielle took a deep breath.

"What, what?! You're killing me here!" Tristan demanded, so excited, he almost squealed.

"He invited me out," she said in a rush as she exhaled.

"Whaaaaaaat?" Tristan exclaimed, eyes flashing with glee. "And you said yes, right?"

"Of course not!" Gabrielle replied indignantly, "what does he think I am? That I would accept an invitation from a complete stranger just because I thought he was polite and interesting? Ha!"

"Uh, YES!" Tristan responded so loudly that everyone in the *salon* preparing for the evening turned toward them, alert. "Sorry everyone, go back to work, please," he intoned, lowering his voice back to its normal volume.

"Are you mad, you fool? What hysteria is this?" Gabrielle hissed indignantly.

"Ah Gabrielle, how could you reject an invitation from such a gorgeous man? You're the one who's mad!" Tristan whispered theatrically.

"Look Tristan, when I acted offended to see what he would say, he simply said, 'he wasn't used to asking women to go out with him'. And he even said that it was exactly the opposite!" she whispered, exasperated.

"First of all, I don't doubt that he was telling you the truth," Tristan replied, "and second, I would like to know: just what was the context of his comments?"

"Honestly, I wasn't too interested in any *context*," Gabrielle glared at her friend. "I was just so outraged with his smugness that I lost it. Or does he just happen to think that the same thing happens to me? That I don't flirt with any men, and they just fall all over themselves for me on the street?"

"Well my dear, isn't that exactly what happens? The difference is that the man who 'harassed' you was gorgeous, polite and YOU were interested in him! You women—independent feminists—put everything to lose in the name of foolish truths that exist only in your own heads most of the time." Tristan assessed unimpressed.

Gabrielle wanted to interrupt him, but Tristan put up a hand, "Don't interrupt me, please!" he went on, "Didn't you let your anger get the better of you, overriding your desire to get to know him better by going out with him? So now you are going to listen to me. I am your friend! And if it weren't for me to tell you a few truths, who would? Anyway, whoever isn't excited by you--is terrified of you."

"You like to push the limits, don't you? I am still your boss!" Gabrielle said, jutting out her chin stubbornly.

"So, the same thing that happens with you, a beautiful and interesting woman always approached by men—and I have seen it here in the restaurant, at least a hundred times—could happen to a gorgeous man like him. The difference is that he was being honest with you and you couldn't take it: not the honesty or the competition coming from the opposite sex. You women should stop being so competitive, otherwise you'll never be happy. It's not enough to compete among yourselves; you have to compete with men as well?" Tristan finalized, thoroughly indignant.

"But..." Gabrielle tried to argue.

"No BUTS!" Tristan pushed on, "honestly Gabrielle! We could be talking about the man of your dreams. I don't know, the man who could make your 'happily ever after'. But no, no, no, you just had to be right, didn't you? You just had to assert your point of view, not even letting the poor boy defend himself. Gabrielle, you know how much I love you, but honestly, if you don't soften your tone, you are going to end up all alone, or worse, having to spend your days off putting up with me."

Gabrielle couldn't hold back her laughter after that. "As if you gays were any different," she tried lamely in her defense.

"Yes, with us it is *very* different," Tristan continued, "because we compete when we smell the competition from another gay guy, but we don't compete *with* the men we're interested in! Frankly, you really need to reconsider your basic concepts Gabrielle, so you don't end your days alone. I'm sorry, but someone had to say that to you. *Mon Dieu*! You already dropped that delightfully charming man Pierre. Ok, I do understand your position when you say you don't want to mix business with pleasure. But to brush off a man like the Brazilian, just because you were offended by his honesty? If he is honest to such a degree, you should have grabbed him then and there. Believe me, he is a breed in extinction, girl!"

"But sermons are useless now, aren't they Tristan?" Gabrielle replied, pensive.

"Honestly, you and your obsession with always being right puts everything at risk. I hope the lesson is learnt, don't you Gabrielle? Now please, let me see what's going on in the *salon* because we have to open in little over an hour," Tristan concluded, turned and was off before she could say anything more.

Tristan abandoned Gabrielle to her own thoughts in the hallway between the kitchen and the restaurant *salon* and went to help his team finish setting up for dinner.

Gabrielle returned to the kitchen, but stood thinking about what Tristan had just lectured her on. She stood quietly in contemplation for some time. Could he be right? Did Eduardo really not mean to be cocky? Had she been too hard on him, especially since she hadn't even let him finish at the end? But now, it's too late, she thought.

"Gabrielle?" a voice interrupted her reverie. It was Antoine, one of the *sous chefs*.

"Yes Antoine," Gabrielle responded, waking from her trance, "how can I help you?"

Medium build, with muscles that would turn to fat with age—Antoine, a creature of habit, worked out every day at a gym before going to the restaurant—his muscles were solidly obvious beneath his uniform. He never bothers much with his appearance. To facilitate his life, he just dresses in black—jeans and tee shirts were fine by him—more time to study and experiment.

He loved the simple perfection of Gabrielle's dishes and dreamt of making dishes of his own, so he studied each of Gabrielle's meticulously. Everything was penned into his tiny pocket journal, between its beaten-up leather covers. It contained his impressions, ideas, dreams—his someday perfect dishes.

"The team needs your orientation for tonight's activities." Antoine responded simply and succinctly.

Gabrielle nodded, moving past him toward the center of the kitchen (a tiny wrinkle creased her forehead) and she began talking to the team about Sunday evening. She always liked to have these meetings before opening the restaurant, with the objective of aligning the activities of each *sous chef* and the kitchen assistants and by doing so, improved the logistics during the service. From the moment she began speaking until after the shift was over, Gabrielle had no more time to ponder on that matter again.

The restaurant opened at six in the evening and closed at midnight when the last table paid and the clients left.

The kitchen staff was already on their way out, the last dish having been prepared at 11 o'clock. Gabrielle asked Tristan to close up.

"Certainly Gabrielle, we can take over from here. Have a good evening and try to get some rest," Tristan responded, "I'll see you on Tuesday."

Since the restaurant didn't open Mondays for dinner, Gabrielle didn't work Sundays or Mondays. On these days, Antoine took over the command.

As *sous chef*, Antoine usually skipped the 'meet and greet' with the restaurant customers, so frequently was seen in a day-old beard, slightly disheveled curly brown hair under his *toque*; not because he was a slob or lazy, but because all of his free time went into studying and dreaming of new dishes. His nose, either in a fine cuisine book, or following some delectable smell in the market—barely quivering, like some *Grand Bleu de Gascogne* catching a whiff of his prey, he would doggedly chased his elusive dream dish.

A favorite haunt of his to hunt was the *Marche des Enfants Rouge*, a covered market—the oldest of Paris—less than twenty minutes from the restaurant on Rue Lamennais. Antoine could spend time before work or even between lunch and dinner services at this lovely little market created in 1610, which had become all the rage with tourists. Between the beautifully arranged displays of fruits and vegetables, sat the fresh seafood and fish counters where he was always welcomed warmly. Having worked behind his father's counter there as a kid, he developed a keen interest in food, and from there—who knows—one day, his seafood dishes might be the talk of the town.

Gabrielle was exhausted as she left work. The house was full and almost all of the tables had turned over three times that night. Nonetheless, not even exhaustion stopped her from rehashing what had happened between her and Eduardo that afternoon. Had she been so very rude to him? Had he really not meant to be offensive? The scene kept repeating over and over in her mind.

She got into a taxi to take her to her flat and before she realized it, she was home, having seen nothing on the way except for the reruns of that lamentable encounter in her head.

"*Mademoiselle*," the driver said softly, but there was no reaction from Gabrielle. "Miss," he repeated a little louder, recalling her from her reverie, "we've arrived at your destiny."

"Oh, yes." Gabrielle replied, coming back to reality. "I'm sorry, how much?"

"Fifteen Euros," he replied.

"Here it is, and please, keep the change," she motioned from the back seat as she handed him a twenty and got out of the car. "Thank you very much."

"Thank you, *Mademoiselle*, and if I may, please don't worry about whatever it is that's upsetting you. Everything will resolve itself in the end." The taxi driver put the car in gear and drove off.

Although she didn't know the man, his words gave Gabrielle hope. In that instant, she realized what a fool she had been.

Gabrielle walked up the flights to her flat, took a bath and lay down. She fell asleep immediately. Her weariness wasn't only physical, but emotional too. She couldn't help but feel guilty after all for having treated Eduardo so rudely.

The next day she woke late and had only a cup of coffee, black. She didn't feel like eating anything.

She spent the day reading and by the end of the afternoon, decided to call Pierre.

In London, Still

Chapter Seven – There Will Always Be Another Sunset

Months had passed before Eduardo would return to *Paris*. Although he loved the city, for some time he just didn't feel like going back. After a few weeks had passed since his return to *Rio*, both Eduardo and Gabrielle tried to bury the matter of their disagreement. It was clear to Eduardo that he wasn't Gabrielle's type, and that she had a terrible impression of him. There was nothing that he could do. While for Gabrielle, she realized that she had treated the matter with such complete impulsively that in the end, it was certain that there wasn't even the remotest possibility of they're ever getting together. The two suffered that lost opportunity for some time after the unfortunate event, but as the months passed, neither one thought much about the other anymore.

It was only in the spring of the next year that Eduardo was called to *Paris* by Frédéric so that they could talk about the impact of the US sub-primes crisis. "Eduardo, I am very concerned about this crisis that afflicts the entire world. Here in *Europe* we all suffer because of this situation," Frédéric said in a meeting with Eduardo to discuss how the greatest financial crisis since 1929 was affecting the Brazilian market. "I see little effect yet on Brazil. This five percent drop in gross income in the first quarter isn't something to concern ourselves with yet; however, I am worried it might escape our control. You know very well that the first things people cut in their budgets are the nonessentials. And we sell inessentials. And it will be particularly concerning if the newly ascended lower middle class in Brazil feel the need to cut down on expenses."

"Frédéric, I understand your concerns and I am very empathetic, however you should understand that *Brazil* is going through a peak in consumer buying and this is making money circulate within the country. Even the US Dollar that went up significantly since October is starting to signal a consistent drop in value. Of course this festival of consumption has its limits and yes, I am worried; but not now, or for the upcoming two or three years, perhaps only after 2012. For now, what we need is to evaluate whether the commodities produced in *Brazil* will still have the same relevance in the Chinese, Russian and American markets. Those prices have started to fall and if it continues, then yes, we will have a problem with the Brazilian market—job positions will be lost and consequently, consumer buying will decrease—especially for our products."

Frédéric nodded, "I understand. So, you think we're guaranteed for at least the next three years?"

"Yes, I do." Eduardo went on, "What we can do is evaluate the possibility of opening new markets so that we can export from *Brazil*. Or even develop a mix of different products from those of the rest of *Latin America* so that we can buy from the other regional subsidiaries what we don't have and sell what we produce to them. What do you think?"

"That might be the way to balance things out," Frédéric agreed.

Eduardo had flown to *Paris* for this meeting with Frédéric on a Wednesday afternoon, so they only had two days of discussions. Aside from Frédéric, Eduardo also met with the Consumer Products and HR directors. On Friday afternoon Frédéric invited Eduardo to dinner.

"Of course, it would be a pleasure, Frédéric," Eduardo replied. "What do you suggestion this time?"

Frédéric replied after a moment's thought, "I was thinking of our going to Gabrielle's restaurant again. What do you say?"

Eduardo's heart skipped a beat, which surprised him, to say the least. He thought that he had gotten over what he felt for Gabrielle since his last trip to *Paris*. "Oh, I don't know, Frédéric. How about introducing me to another one of your excellent selections?"

"But I thought you loved the food at that restaurant." Frédéric replied, slightly surprised.

"Sure, it was the best meal I've ever had," Eduardo admitted, "but I know that you like to eat well, and I'm sure that there are other places just as good as, or even better than that one that you could introduce me to last time," he ended nonchalantly.

"Of course; ok, I'm convinced," Frédéric smiled, raising both hands in surrender. "There is this *chef* who is the talk of all of *Paris*, the new darling of the gastronomic world. He's Indian, but his *cuisine* is very much based on French traditions. From what I have read, he came to *France* as an adolescent and fell in love with French *cuisine*. He's already earned his first Michelin star, and the word around town is that it won't be long before he earns his second."

"Wow! So that's where I want to go," Eduardo enthused. If he had done a modicum of soul-searching, he would know that what he really wanted was to go to the restaurant on *Rue Lamennais*.

"Then I'll see with my secretary if we can still get a table. It's two now and I think we're finished here. If you want to go for a walk in the neighborhood while I finish a few things around here, we can meet at seven this evening downstairs, at the entrance. What do you say, Eduardo?"

"If that won't be a problem for you, I would like to stretch my legs a bit."

"Of course, my dear fellow; I will see you at seven sharp and let's hope that we can get a table. Until then," Frédéric responded.

"I'll see you in a while, Frédéric," Eduardo replied as he packed up his laptop and left the meeting room.

Eduardo took the elevator down from *Beauté's* headquarters and walked down the *Champs-Élisées* toward the *Arch of Triumph*. In a short while he reached a small side street he knew that had an open-air market with regional produce. It was a place he really enjoyed going to whenever he was in *Paris*. He never failed to buy cheeses, sausages, jams, and wines from the small producers. There were organic goods too. Everything was of exceptional quality and well worth the annoyance of bringing a larger suitcase.

He walked slowly through the entire market sampling seasonal fruit, the cheeses and hams, tasting the organic wines and sipping an exceptional artisanal cognac. The market was set up in a single corridor of opposing stalls and stands of beautifully, yet simply presented products in a street with pedestrian access only. Ambling around the farmer's market for a second time, he began buying what he wanted. It was then that he heard a woman's voice coming from a cheese and sausage stall where he had stopped just moments before to buy his choices of this trip. He recognized that voice. A tall thin woman was beside him, bending over the cheeses, examining them—her head turned slightly away—while choosing several she chatted with the man standing on Eduardo's other side.

Eduardo's heart soared. "How was this possible? I did everything to avoid seeing her and yet here she is now?" Garbled thoughts tumbled through his mind, "what now?"

Life is full of surprises—for better or for worse—but rarely does it give you a second chance.

Eduardo tried to turn away from the stall before she could see him; but the stall owner who already knew him from his many previous visits, interrupted his get-away. "*Monsieur* Eduardo?" The stall owner's gravelly voice rising above the din of the market, "aren't you going to take anything to *Brazil* this time?"

"Um, uhh," Eduardo cleared his throat, "No thank you, Marcel," he finally responded nervously. "I didn't bring a suitcase that could carry very much this time," he concluded weakly.

That was a lie.

At precisely that moment the woman beside him turned to look at him. Her eyes widened, "Eduardo!" she exclaimed in surprise, "it's me, Gabrielle Debois. You were at my restaurant, remember? And of course, we also…"

Eduardo interrupted her, "Yes, how could I not remember you, *n'est-ce pas*?" Eduardo replied rather dryly. "Forgive me for not recognizing you. Well, I have to get back to *Beauté*. Frédéric is waiting for me."

But Gabrielle simply had to apologize for the discourtesy that had weighed so heavily on her. "No! Wait, please," Gabrielle rushed on, "Let me introduce you to my friend and colleague from the restaurant, Tristan Emérson."

"My pleasure Tristan," Eduardo replied automatically, turning to shake Tristan's hand. "I believe that we have already met at your restaurant."

"The pleasure is mine Eduardo," Tristan responded smiling, thrilled that Eduardo remembered him. "*Pardon*, but I must hurry to get these cheeses back to the restaurant. Antoine needs them immediately." With a shrug and a grin, Tristan grabbed the package from the stand and turned to rush off.

"Tristan, wait!" Gabrielle called out, raising her voice, trying to grasp his arm before he moved through the crowd.

"Don't worry Gabrielle, I've got this!" Tristan answered over his shoulder as he strode away, insisting emphatically, "Take as long as you like. As long as you like, understand?"

Gabrielle shrugged as she watched Tristan disappear into the crowd then turned back to Eduardo.

"I would like to apologize for that day. I didn't have the right to just…" Eduardo began.

"No, no! Please, listen," Gabrielle interrupted him for a second time that day, "I am the one who should be apologizing. I was offended by your honesty and directness with me when I should have felt flattered. Not to mention that I didn't even let you finish what you had to say. I was very rude, and for that I apologize. I am very sorry for not giving us the opportunity to get to know each other better."

"*Nossa*! What a relief I feel now," Eduardo replied, exhaling; feeling as if a knot of tension untangled itself between his shoulders. "All this time I was feeling guilty for not knowing how to talk to you. I realize that I was too direct, but please, be assured; I never intended to offend. I thought you were such an interesting woman that I would really have liked to get to know better. I blamed myself for a long time for the way I spoke to you."

"Not in the least. I was very rude to you and took the defensive. I tend to do that when men try to get close to me. It is I who must apologize," Gabrielle insisted. "Listen, I know you have a previous engagement with Frédéric, but if you're in Paris until tomorrow, perhaps you would like to do something," she asked with a smile as charming as her words.

"Of course," Eduardo replied, eyes shining at this unexpected turn of events, "this might seem insane, but if I can cancel with Frédéric, would you like to do something right now?"

"No, wait! What do you mean?" Gabrielle, taken aback responded, "I'm still in my uniform!"

"What does that matter? We've wasted almost a whole year. Couldn't you get free for one night?"

Eduardo was overwhelmed by an impulse that instant that for him was unimaginable—to break from old habits and do something irresponsible or adventurous for someone so self-restrained as he—unbelievable! In fact, something had changed in him during that reencounter; as if his life depended on this chance that was before him. He had tried hard to avoid seeing Gabrielle again, but there she was in front of him, even more beautiful than he remembered. And so open; this had to mean something!

"*Mon Dieu!*" Gabrielle exclaimed, excited about what they were about to do, "what are we doing?" She hesitated for just an instant, then said decisively, "Ok, then let's do it, now! You call Frédéric and I'll call Tristan."

And at once it hit him, Eduardo's eyes shone even more brightly. He felt something surge from his very core; something he had never felt before. Was this the love he had never felt for any woman? It was as if his personality had magically changed from what it had been since adolescence—but love transformed into a totally different man—had he just been reborn? Life had taught him to never, ever, ever be impulsive; yet, what was so amazing was that *he* had been the catalyst of it all!

Eduardo called Frédéric at the same time Gabrielle was speaking to Tristan. He told Frédéric that something important had happened to him, but he couldn't speak at the moment; that it was something personal. He regretted having to break off their dinner engagement, but he would call Frédéric on Monday, when he got back to *Rio de Janeiro*.

Gabrielle had Tristan's approval before she had even finished telling him why she wouldn't be coming in that night. She asked that he speak with Antoine to take over the kitchen for the night without giving any further details. She also had him recall one of the *sous chefs*–off for the day—to come in to work that evening. Tristan told her not to worry, that everything would be fine in her absence. "And for the love of God, don't say anything foolish or let your twisted feminist attitude screw things up! Oh, and tell me everything tomorrow!" Tristan admonished.

"Leave it to me. I will try to behave. We'll talk tomorrow. *Bisus!*" Gabrielle broke the connection on her mobile with a tap and looked up to speak to Eduardo, "And now?"

"And now we get out of here and do whatever we want!" Eduardo grinned broadly, "and I've got an idea!"

Eduardo took Gabrielle's hand and asked her to accompany him. They entered the subway at the *École Militaire* station and got on the train heading to the north of *Paris*.

During the ride they spoke of many things, mostly just small talk. When they finally arrived at the *Abbesses Station* they got off and moved rapidly toward the *Rue la Vieuville* exit, walking northeast.

"Where are we going?" Gabrielle asked, curious.

"We are going to the best view of Paris. Trust me," he responded, excited.

They finally passed in front of the *Basilique du Sacré-Coeur* and continued walking arm in arm toward the *Montmartre Funicular* kiosk.

"Ah, I haven't been here since I was a teenager, drinking cheap wine and smoking marijuana with my friends," Gabrielle laughed at the memory.

Eduardo tried not to look shocked about the marijuana part. He had never in his life even dreamed of smoking it. Embarrassed, he changed the subject quickly, "anyway, here's a place I always like to visit whenever I'm in *Paris* and it's warm and the days are long. I come to admire the church and enjoy the view. At the end of the day I would usually watch the sunset too. And today is a perfect day for that."

When they arrived at the top, they entered the church, automatically lowering their voices, heads close. It seemed as if they had known each other for years.

As they were leaving, the sun was beginning to set. Eduardo asked Gabrielle to wait a few moments. He went off at a run to the nearest restaurant, ordering a bottle of fine wine and two wine glasses. When he explained to the waiter that he wanted to take everything with him outside of the restaurant, the guy refused to sell him the wine.

"Please, you can sell me the glasses then. Today is a very important day for me and I need not only the wine, but the glasses too."

The waiter hesitated a little more, but finally convinced, he went to ask his manager who quickly approved the odd request of the foreigner. Eduardo paid the asking price willingly. The waiter opened the bottle for him and as soon as Eduardo had everything gathered, off he went at a run again, back to the front of the basilica.

"Hello, would the young lady like to accompany me in a glass of wine while we sit there on the grass and enjoy the sight of this beautiful city? He asked, gesturing solemnly with the hand not holding the wine and glasses, grinning at Gabrielle all the while.

"But of course!" Gabrielle responded. "This is the first time I've done this after so many years, and certainly it is the first time that I've sat on the grass of the *Louise Michel* park drinking such fine wine from a crystal goblet," she said chuckling.

As they walked toward the basilica's stairway looking for a nice place on the grass to sit, Eduardo risked trying to hold Gabrielle's hand. She complied easily, giving his hand a squeeze, and leaving no doubt of what she wanted.

Finally finding the perfect place to sit, Eduardo pulled the cork from the bottle and served their wine. "A toast! To reencounters and the chance meeting that brought us together today," Eduardo proclaimed brightly.

"*Santé!*" Gabrielle smiled happily.

The two continued to chat for some time. They spoke of their lives, their childhoods and how they had arrived at this point in life. Finally, a somewhat disconcerting silence overtook the two.

"Sorry, you were going to say something?" Gabrielle asked.

"Uh, no, I thought you wanted to say something. Wow, the sun is already going down…"

Gabrielle silenced Eduardo with her lips. The two kissed as if no one else existed around them. And while they kissed with such passion, the sun slowly made his exit from the Parisian horizon. Eduardo had never felt an emotion so strong, so alive. At that moment he realized for the first time what it was to be in love.

Gabrielle had felt this emotion a few times before, but this time it was different; this time it felt special.

"I think we missed the sunset," Eduardo murmured.

"There will always be another sunset to be seen from *Sacré-Coeur*," she replied softly, her lips still touching his.

The two started to laugh and went back to kissing.

"I'm hungry. Would you like to get something to eat?" Eduardo suddenly proposed.

"Yes, I am too. I hadn't realized until you mentioned it," Gabrielle replied, "how about if we go to my flat? I can prepare something there for us to eat."

"Are you sure?" Eduardo queried, "I don't want you to think that I am imposing. We can go down and look for something to eat around here."

"But I need to change from these clothes too. I must look like a crazy person wearing a chef's uniform," she insisted.

"Not at all, to me, you are beautiful. I would take you to the opera this instant," Eduardo insisted boyishly.

"Oh right! One point for you," she chortled.

"Well, I didn't realize that I was being evaluated," he grinned mischievously.

The two laughed.

"Let's go! We can find a cab and get back faster," Gabrielle asserted, getting up and moving towards the stairs to get back down to the street below, leaving Eduardo to follow. He caught up, took her hand, and after that, they never let go of each other. The two found a cab and went back to Gabrielle's flat. They rode all the way back holding hands, Gabrielle leaning on Eduardo.

Entering the apartment, Gabrielle took off her chef's jacket revealing her perfect silhouette in a sleeveless blouse underneath and the fitted pants she wore clung to her body.

"Would you like something to drink," she offered.

"We could continue with wine, no?" Eduardo replied, as the two walked toward the kitchen.

"Yes, of course. Follow me," Gabrielle responded as she went to the small electric wine cooler and got a bottle of *Bordeaux;* reaching up, she opened the cabinet above and got two glasses; then opening a drawer with her free hand, she reached for the corkscrew.

"Could you, please?" She asked, displaying the bottle and corkscrew.

"With pleasure!" Eduardo exclaimed.

"What would you like to eat?"

"Anything—I would even eat scrambled eggs!" he said, laughing.

"Oh, I know, I'll make an omelet and salad for us," she decided. While Gabrielle got the ingredients and prepared the omelet, the two continued chatting while Eduardo leaned a hip against the counter next to her, watching. And while they talked, they exchanged loving glances and several kisses.

"I realize that we are only just getting to know each other, but I have something I must tell you," Gabrielle said, mysteriously.

Eduardo, a little apprehensively replied, "yes, of course."

"On that terrible day that we saw each other last, in front of the restaurant, I talked for a long time with Tristan. He's my best friend. And it was he who made me see how rude and unfair I had been with you. To tell the truth, I can't even believe that after all this time we are here together now, talking while I prepare our food."

Eduardo held up a hand to interrupt, but Gabrielle went on, "No, wait. Let me finish. I felt really badly that night after everything Tristan said, thinking about that moment of ours. I was terribly unfair and acted impulsively. And I apologize truly for my behavior."

"But, you don't need…"

"Wait, there's more."

Eduardo was afraid to hear the rest, wanting to escape, but there was no way out. Gabrielle continued, "when I arrived at home it was already late at night, so I decided to call Pierre the next day."

"Who's Pierre?!" Eduardo demanded, unable to hide a wave of jealousy—like nausea—that swept over him. Not even he recognized himself.

"*Calme-toi!* It's not what you're thinking. Pierre and I are partners in the restaurant," she hurried on, noting his expression. "As I was saying, I decided to call him because I felt that something in my life had to change. Get out of my comfort zone. See new sights, learn new things. Not just because of what happened between us that day, but for various other reasons, and especially because I need to be more open to things. I don't know, but I thought that getting out of Paris might help me mature as a person, as a woman."

"What are you talking about?" Now, Eduardo was really confused.

"It's nothing really. At least, I don't think it is. But that night Pierre and I talked about the possibility of opening a new restaurant. A new project, understand?"

"Of course I do, it's a great idea," Eduardo replied, relieved.

"Our present restaurant was conceived and set-up entirely by him. I practically fell into it and only really got involved with the kitchen. Now, I'll participate in the entire project, from choosing the location to the wallpaper. Plus, I'll have a greater share in the new restaurant—financially speaking."

"*Nossa!*" Eduardo exhaled, at once relieved and excited, "that's marvelous! But why do you think that you have to tell me this?"

"Honestly?" Gabrielle replied, "I don't know. After all, we don't know where tonight might lead. I mean, since we met at the market this afternoon, every second has been marvelous, as if we've lived an entire lifetime in a single day. But we mustn't beguile ourselves, *n'est ce pas?*"

"Truthfully, at this exact moment, all I want is to be enchanted by you," Eduardo quipped. They both laughed and he went on more seriously, "and have you and your partner decided on the location of the new restaurant yet?"

Warming to her subject, Gabrielle responded without pause, "well, we've done a lot of research, and finally decided that we wouldn't open another in Paris."

"Then where will it be?" Eduardo queried, curious.

"We'll open our next house in *London*. It's close by and it's a metropolis with over 10 million inhabitants," Gabrielle replied excitedly.

"Wow, that's a great idea!" Eduardo responded. "And how do you command two restaurants at the same time?"

By that time, both were eating. They didn't even bother to sit at the dining table, they ate seated right there at the tiny kitchen peninsula that modestly exposed the upper half of kitchen to the living room.

"At the beginning, it will be rather hectic for me, but I can come and go by *Eurostar*. It's only a two and a half hours trip, and the stations are centrally located in both cities. I'll slowly pass the control of the *Paris* kitchen to Antoine; he's my number two." She detailed between bites.

Eduardo chewed thoughtfully, "excellent idea," he managed after swallowing.

Gabrielle went on, her fork in the air designing her thoughts as she spoke, "as time goes by, I will be doing only quality control—perhaps twice a month. Antoine is an excellent chef. I have great faith in his work." The two continued chatting a little more until Eduardo offered to wash the dishes.

"Ok, while you clean up, I'll take a quick shower and get out of these work clothes," Gabrielle replied going off to the bathroom. After her shower she passed by the living room before she got dressed, to see if all was well with Eduardo; and to give him a kiss. He was sitting on the sofa drinking his wine. The kissing had turned into embraces when Gabrielle's towel fell to the floor, leaving her completely in the buff.

"*Oh, meu Deus, meu Deus!*" Eduardo stuttered pulling back, "I'm so sorry, I didn't mean..." Gabrielle sealed his lips with yet another kiss before she turned and led him to her bedroom. The towel lay forgotten on the floor.

They had an incredible night. Gabrielle was especially enchanted with Eduardo's way of treating a woman in bed, cherishing every centimeter of her body: his kisses, the way his lips travelled lightly over her body; his subliminal concern with her satisfaction; and the explosion of pleasure they both shared at exactly the same moment. How was this even possible on a first date?

They stayed awake almost the entire night. It was four in the morning when they finally fell asleep in each other's arms. Later that morning they awoke without either one feeling uneasy or embarrassed. It was as if they had known each other for years. Gabrielle got up and prepared their breakfast. Seated at the table, they ate and there they remained seated next to each other, talking easily about so many things.

"Would you be able to stay away from the restaurant for one more day?" Eduardo asked with the look of someone who wants to hear a "yes."

Being such a responsible person, Gabrielle wasn't sure that she would feel at ease leaving her team alone with a full house for two nights in a row. When she was about to tell Eduardo that she would have to work that Saturday evening; what actually came out of her mouth was: "Do you want to know something? I am very happy, and I don't know when we will have time together for us again." Inside, she was frightened by her daring, but what she said was, "I'm going to talk to Antoine and Tristan," in a firm tone of certainty.

She ran to the telephone on the side table in the living room and punched in the number of the restaurant. It was already lunchtime and the receptionist answered. *"Restaurant Romarin,* Clarice, good afternoon!"

"Good afternoon Clarice, this is Gabrielle, is everything going well?"

"*Mlle* Gabrielle! Are you well?" Clarice asked sounding slightly worried. "We were all so concerned for you. Tristan spent the morning trying to call; we were just so worried—you are always the first to arrive at the restaurant—yet we heard nothing."

"Everything is fine, calm yourself. There was an unexpected development, but there is nothing to worry about. May I speak to Tristan?" Gabrielle concluded.

"Certainly *Mlle* Gabrielle, I'll find him now." Claire jumped to her feet and sped off in search of Tristan.

A few minutes passed before Tristan came to the phone. With the house already full, it was difficult for Tristan to break away from the *salon.* "Gabrielle!" Tristan sounded like he might have had a heart attack, "what happened?" He blurted, "Why aren't you here? Are you…"

Gabrielle interrupted him, "Calm down Tristan. Everything is fine, actually it's fantastic, but I can't talk much now. I know this sounds insane, but do you think that you and Antoine can manage to cover for me again tonight? I promise to explain everything to you tomorrow."

"Gabrielle, have you completely lost your mind? The restaurant is full and we have a full house tonight too!" Tristan whispered dramatically into the mouthpiece.

"Yes, I think I have, my friend. But please, hold things together for me. Please! I swear, you'll know everything tomorrow. I can't talk now," Gabrielle begged, her voice so soft, it was almost a whisper.

"I must ask Antoine and see if he can cover your absence again, but hold on; I'll get back to you. *A bientôt!*" Tristan whispered. Returning the phone to its cradle, he moved decisively through the packed dining room toward the kitchen.

Tristan called back after several minutes, his voice now normal, he told Gabrielle that everything was taken care of. "But if you don't show up tomorrow, you know that I will hunt you down, don't you? I'll go to your house!" he hissed, pretending anger.

Gabrielle laughed and promised to be at the restaurant on Sunday afternoon.

"Have you thought about what we should do on this fine spring Saturday with that marvelous sun shining outside?" Gabrielle asked walking back from the telephone to the table where Eduardo was still lounging to give him another kiss.

"As tempting as the heat outside may be, what I really want is to take the opportunity to make up for all the time we've lost. Although I don't believe that that can be done by tomorrow," he responded drolly.

Gabrielle grinned widely and agreed.

The two didn't separate until it was time for Eduardo to catch his flight back to *Rio de Janeiro*. It had been truly an unforgettable weekend.

On Sunday morning, Eduardo woke up and could hear the sound of the shower running. When Gabrielle returned to the bedroom wrapped in a towel, he asked, "could you go with me to the hotel? Unfortunately, I have to go back to *Brazil* in a few hours, and haven't even packed my bag".

"Certainly, we can eat something along the way!" she replied, already starting to dress.

The two went to a charming *café* near Eduardo's hotel and ate before he packed his bag and checked out. They stayed together for the few remaining hours before Eduardo's flight and said their good-byes in front of his hotel near the *Champs-Élysées*. They embraced while they talked; the doorman on the look-out for a taxi for Eduardo.

His breath soft on her cheek, Eduardo confessed, "This has been by far, the best weekend of my life. I hope we can be together and repeat moments like these for a long, long time."

"I loved every moment we had together too. I hope you will come back to Paris soon," Gabrielle replied, as she pressed her cheek to his.

"I'll do my best, and if I can't, you could go to *Rio*—how about that?" Eduardo replied, perking up at the prospect.

"Wow, but with this *London* project, I don't know. At any rate, I can talk with my team and Pierre," she said thoughtfully.

A taxi pulled up and the doorman put Eduardo's bag in the trunk.

"I'm sorry, but I really have to go now." Eduardo sighed before their last lingering kiss. He tipped the doorman, got into the back seat of the cab and was off to the airport. Gabrielle remained on the sidewalk. The two held eye contact until the cab and Eduardo disappeared turning the corner. Gabrielle stood there a few moments longer, lost in thought. She called a taxi to take her to the restaurant to see how things had gone in her absence, and to talk with Tristan. After all, they had a lot to talk about now.

Chapter Eight – Restaurant *Romarin*, Good Night!

When Gabrielle arrived at the restaurant, it was already past Sunday lunch time and the *salon* team had already arranged the tables for dinner.

"Good afternoon, Gabrielle!" one of the waiters greeted her, smiling.

"Good afternoon, Philippe!" Gabrielle replied. "Is Tristan back yet?"

"I think he went out for his break, but he should be back soon for dinner." Philippe responded with his good-natured smile.

"Fine, I'll try him on his cell phone," Gabrielle concluded as she made her way to the tiny glass-enclosed office in the back of the restaurant to take care of a few matters, and there she remained for the rest of the afternoon, so caught up in her tasks she forgot to call her friend.

Tristan returned to the restaurant at six and rushed directly to the office, bursting in slightly out of breath, more from excitement than the running. "How could you leave me without any news for almost three days in a row!" he proclaimed indignantly, hands on hips.

"Good afternoon to you too, sir," Gabrielle answered sardonically as she slowly lifted her head from the papers in front of her, focusing far-away eyes and thoughts on her best friend.

"Sorry Gabrielle, but my curiosity is just eating me up inside," Tristan responded; only slightly deflated at her tone.

"Believe me, these past few days I have been busy with much more interesting things than worrying about talking to just anyone." Gabrielle tried, but couldn't hide the light of happiness in her eyes and the lilt in her voice that so clearly contradicted her words.

"Ah, mon Dieu! Tell me everything! Everything! Even the most sordid details," Tristan burst out, unable to contain his curiosity, practically dancing as he gesticulated in tandem with his words.

"Calmez-vous, I'll tell you everything. Here," she pointed to a chair, "sit down and breathe," she giggled, giving up trying to keep her face straight.

The two remained in the *Romarin* office for over an hour, their heads close together, talking quietly. Tristan barely breathed, so closely did he follow the amazing tale flowing from Gabrielle's mouth.

His open-mouthed attention to what Gabrielle was saying broke when they were interrupted by Antoine knocking at the door. Startled, Tristan looked up, his mouth snapping shut.

"Good evening you two. Forgive my interrupting this *tête-à-tête*—which must be truly fascinating—but it's already half past seven and the house is beginning to fill. Since *Mlle.* Gabrielle has not been with us for the past two days and I'd called in the guys who were supposed to be off, today I had to let them rest. So, your help would be more than welcome," Antoine intoned that truth in a mockingly stern voice and went on, "Ah, and Tristan, I do believe our hostess has been searching everywhere for you to help her with organization and logistics in the salon," he deadpanned.

"Of course! You are absolutely right and thank you for taking care of everything during my absence," Gabrielle responded with the same gravitas. "As a matter of fact, we need to talk, because it is probable that I will soon be in need of a new head *chef*. Give us ten minutes more and then I'll see you in the kitchen."

Antoine's heart flip-flopped. He left the back office, closing the door quietly behind him as Gabrielle and Tristan continued to talk. "So," Gabrielle said before the door even closed, going back to her story, "I don't know what will come of this, but I think it will be serious. He has even invited me to stay a few days in *Rio de Janeiro!*"

"*Ç'est très* cool! I've heard that *Rio de Janeiro* is a beautiful city and that the men there are *mar-ve-lous!*" Tristan gushed, his eyes sparkling with mischievousness. They both laughed out loud.

"But seriously," she went on, "I'm worried about all of this because I still haven't spoken to any of the team, and Pierre and I are thinking about opening a second restaurant."

"What! How could you hide something like that from me!" Tristan's eyes grew even rounder with surprise. "This is way too much to happen in just one day, *mec!*"

"I'm telling you now. And please, don't comment with anyone. Not even Jordan," Gabrielle replied more seriously.

"*Bien sûr*, but now you must tell me all about this new restaurant. Please!" Tristan implored dramatically; uniting his hands as if in prayer.

"We don't have time to talk now, Tristan, but let's get together for coffee tomorrow morning and I'll tell you everything. Now, I must go help Antoine in the kitchen, and you have to get out to the *salon. Allez-y, allez-y!*" Gabrielle concluded, clapping her hands together as she rose from her chair. They both went off to their respective stations and the evening's work.

Gabrielle stopped at her locker on the way, to put on her chef's jacket and *toque blanche*. "Good evening everyone," Gabrielle greeted her staff as she entered the kitchen. "I would like to thank everyone here and those that aren't for your efforts these past few days while I was out; especially Antoine, for his excellent work and for his sublime substitution." The team's response was a round of applause. "Ok, everyone back to work—to your stations!" Turning to Antoine, she finalized, "what have we got today?" Antoine quickly updated Gabrielle on the routines for the evening and the two commanded their kitchen together.

For the first time Gabrielle asked Antoine not to go back to his position as *sous chef* in her presence. The evening progressed in the kitchen perfectly without a hitch or snag between the two *chefs*. They worked in perfect symbiosis that night which only confirmed Gabrielle's suspicion that her decision to promote Antoine—after she went on to administrate the two restaurants—was perfect.

At the end of the night, when the kitchen team had already sent out the last dishes and begun final clean-up for the day, Antoine asked Gabrielle for a word. "Do you have a minute for me?" he asked softly.

"Of course, Antoine," she responded, leading the way to the back office with Antoine trailing behind.

"What did you mean when you said you were hiring a new *chef* for the restaurant?" Antoine asked in a worried tone before he had even sat down.

"Antoine, you misunderstood. I can't say very much at this time, but what I can say at the moment is that if there is any hiring in the kitchen here at *Romarin*, it will be for a new *sous chef.* That is, if you accept to be the new head *chef*," she said watching his face carefully.

Antoine felt as if his heart would burst. "What do you mean Gabrielle? What's happening? You're not thinking of..." his voice trailed off with a nearly indiscernible tremble.

"Don't concern yourself with this now. Very soon you will know everything that is happening. I still need to discuss a few things with Pierre, but if you were going to ask if I am leaving my restaurant, then the answer is no," Gabrielle said with a gentle smile, "and if you will permit, I would like to go home now."

"Of course, as you wish," Antoine replied, standing, he bowed slightly and left; clearly with a lot on his mind.

Facing her open locker, Gabrielle removed her *toque blanche* and uniform, dressing quickly. She ran her fingers through her hair, deftly twisting it into a loose bun as she left through the back of the restaurant. She walked to *Avenue Champs-Élysées* and caught a taxi home. She had barely enough strength to remove her shoes, but it was a good tiredness, the kind that comes from happiness. She was in love.

On the other side of the *Atlantic*, Eduardo's flight arrived a little after seven in the evening, Brazilian time. It was an easy flight and having flown executive class, he had slept comfortably most of the time, even managing to watch a movie. Passing quickly through immigration; while he waited for his bag Eduardo went into the duty free shop to buy wine and perfume. He also got chocolates for his team at the office. Three hours had passed since touch-down, including the taxi ride from the international airport on *Ilha do Governador* to his house in *Urca*. He arrived home around ten and during his waking hours that day—from the time he left his *Paris* hotel until he reached his front door—he had only one thought, Gabrielle.

He felt radiant! He had never felt so alive. It was as if he had finally left his protective bubble, as if the personal tragedies that mostly defined him as a person had dissipated. That reserved man--who tried so consistently to avoid serious relationships so he wouldn't have to deal with any more personal loss—had finally lowered his guard. And it was about time—he deserved to be happy.

Eduardo couldn't get to sleep when he arrived home having already slept on the flight. He finally fell asleep around two in the morning. The next day he got up just before ten, took a shower, got dressed and went out. He decided to have coffee at the office so that he wouldn't be any later getting in.

Since that first weekend they spent together, Eduardo and Gabrielle never failed to talk—by phone or *Skype*—every day, however briefly.

Chapter Nine – Project London

On Monday, Gabrielle and Tristan had scheduled breakfast together, but before leaving the flat to meet her friend, Gabrielle called Pierre.

"*San-Michel* Holding, good morning!" The voice on the other end of the line greeted her.

"Good morning Linda, how are you?" Gabrielle responded.

Linda replied, "hello *Mlle*. Gabrielle. I'm fine, thank you."

"Might I have a quick word with Pierre?" Gabrielle inquired.

"Of course, I'll see if he can take your call." The line remained silent while Gabrielle waited. After a few minutes a masculine voice said, "*bonjour* Gabrielle! To what do I owe this honor on a Monday morning?"

"Good morning, Pierre. We need to talk," Gabrielle replied rather abruptly.

"Has something happened?" Pierre replied quickly, sounding worried.

"Nothing to worry about; but I would like to schedule a meeting with you to talk about the project for the new restaurant in *London*. We have the entire project pieced together: budget, location, logistics. And I have almost sold the property my grandmother left me, so I'll have the money to buy in on forty percent of the venture. We need to think about the next steps, don't you agree? I don't think it will be feasible to open the restaurant by this summer. So, we need to think about the opening at least by February or little before the beginning of spring next year," Gabrielle proposed.

"Of course," Pierre replied, "I've been waiting for your position on financing the difference of your participation to reach the forty-percentile agreed. If you're sure that it is well underway; let's talk, but why all this rush Gabrielle?"

"There is no rush," she replied. "Truthfully, I need a vacation and would like to be back before this project takes off. I want to be involved in every step."

"I see," Pierre replied, mulling over her reason. "Hmmm, how is your day today?

"I'm on my way to an appointment now, but am free after midday," she answered without pause.

"Perfect." Pierre proposed, "Shall we have lunch together? We can eat here at the restaurant in the building."

"*D'accord*," Gabrielle replied, "what time?"

"One o'clock in my office, is that ok?" Pierre proposed.

"That's fine. Until then Pierre," Gabrielle concluded, "and thank you for receiving me on such short notice."

"You know I have all the time in the world for you," Pierre responded suavely. Gabrielle laughed and said goodbye to Pierre before disconnecting. As soon as she concluded the call, she grabbed her bag and went out to meet up with Tristan.

The two met at 25 *Rue du Château* around half past nine in *Neuilly-sur-Seine*—the wealthiest suburb of Paris—in front of the *Boulangerie-Pâtissier Maison Lepareur*. They queued briefly as they entered the beautiful shop to order *croissants* and coffee. Gabrielle was also particularly interested in the marvelous *baba au rhum* sold there. She paid for the orders, received the croissants and little cakes, and waited a little more for their coffee. Gabrielle asked for a *latte* while Tristan ordered a double *espresso*.

From the moment they met, there was no lack of subject matter. "Have you spoken to Eduardo since he travelled?" Tristan asked as they left in search of a place to sit.

"Not yet, I was too tired when I got home yesterday and fell asleep. Now it's still too early to call. It's four hours earlier in *Brazil* now. We'll talk later," Gabrielle replied wistfully as they walked on.

"I see. And how are you feeling today after the first day of separation since your weekend together?" Tristan asked, thrilled to analyze even the tiniest details of this new romance.

"Wow, can you believe that I already miss him? It's all been just so very intense, you know? I hope we aren't precipitating things," Gabrielle said with a sigh, a minute frown creasing her forehead. Tristan looked up from his espresso, directly into Gabrielle's eyes and with a serious demeanor, he prophesized: "Gabrielle, I think the chemistry between you two is very clear and it will develop into something serious."

"Do you really," she asked, a little flustered at his seriousness, looking down, she picked at her croissant.

Gesticulating so wildly that he nearly spilled his coffee, Tristan insisted emphatically, "Of course! You two had everything going to NEVER see each other again in this lifetime. He even told you he avoided going to the restaurant on Friday so that there was zero risk of a chance encounter. And just look what happened! You saw each other in a totally improbable place. That couldn't have happened by chance!"

"Well, putting it that way..." Gabrielle seemed to want to foresee the future. She stopped and glanced up as if to search for an answer in the stars, instead she saw only clear blue sky.

Stopping beside her, Tristan shrugged and concluded, "don't be anxious; give it some time to put things in their proper places. Now," Tristan changed the subject before Gabrielle could get a word in, "tell me all about this new project with Pierre."

By that time, the two had arrived at a tiny plaza and sat on one of the benches surrounded by trees. After settling themselves, Gabrielle went on to explain the project to Tristan who listened avidly to every detail on the edge of his seat, not taking his eyes off her. "So that means you're leaving us?" he queried abruptly, too shocked to say anything else as she finished. "Not exactly," Gabrielle replied. "I'll indicate two head *chefs*, one for each restaurant, but I will continue to sign the dishes and manage both *maisons*. In the beginning, I will be more in London than in Paris, but I will be here at least one weekend per month. This will be a great opportunity for Antoine. And yesterday I saw that I can really trust his ability to command the restaurant in my absence. It was so good to see him co-ordinate the team in my presence. He has precisely the qualifications we need. As for the management of the main establishment in Paris, I can do that remotely; and of course, Pierre has already said he would help me with this in whatever I may need. So I can focus more on the new *maison* in London and I'll perform monthly quality audits on the food and service," she concluded looking hopefully for affirmation from her best friend.

"But," Tristan responded despondently, shoulders slumped, "what will happen to me without you?" He was devastated by the possibility of not having his best friend nearby.

"Well my friend," she responded with a sly smile, "I stole you from our last job to stay by my side. I trust your work, and I think this could be an opportunity for you too…" she trailed off. Tristan felt as if his heart had leaped to his mouth. "And just as I will need someone commanding the kitchens with me at both *Romarin* restaurants, I'll also need administrative command. Not to mention that that includes not just administrative issues, but all the internal logistics too. So, I will need a manager for Paris and for London," Gabrielle concluded with a wide grin.

"*Ah, mon Dieu!*" Tristan whispered. "*Ah, mon DIEU!*" Tristan squealed even louder, he grabbed Gabrielle's hand and placed it over his heart for her feel how hard it was beating. "Calm down!" Gabrielle insisted, looking around; relieved to see that only a few passersby even looked their way. "Let me finish. I realize that you have your life here in *Paris* with Jordan, so I don't know how you will bring this subject up with him, but I would like it very much if you were to come to *London* with me. You would not only help me manage the new restaurant, but also set up the *maison* as soon as we begin the pre-operational phase. Of course, if you don't want to, or can't accept my proposal, the position of manager in *Paris* is yours. I will just need to align everything with Pierre."

Tristan couldn't hold back his happiness and let out a shout in the middle of the plaza while he hugged Gabrielle, lifting her off her feet. A few people seated at nearby benches looked up and couldn't help but smile at the contagious elation of the two.

"Gabrielle, now I AM nervous!" Tristan blurted out, thrilled at the news. "It's everything I've ever wanted, going to *London* with you! But I do need to discuss this situation with Jordan first," he continued excitably, "I know he'll like the idea, but we need to see what he can do about a job there. He works with fashion, so I can't imagine it would be too difficult."

"Fantastic! Then talk with him," Gabrielle replied, relieved. "This afternoon I'll have lunch with Pierre to discuss all of this and take the opportunity to talk about the possibility of you coming to work with me in the *Romarin* of *London* too," Gabrielle concluded, pleased with the way things were going.

Calmer, Tristan asked, "ok, so how much time do you think we have before we need to move to *London*? I only ask so that Jordan has time to start looking for a job from here."

Gabrielle thought for a moment and replied, "all will depend on the conversation I have with Pierre today. Let's do this: you talk to Jordan, and tomorrow at the restaurant I'll give you some feedback on the move based on my conversation with Pierre today."

"*D'accord*!" Tristan agreed. They continued to sit and chat a while and they finished eating, after a few minutes they continued to stroll toward the classical botanical garden *Parc de Bagatelle* stopping at the *Louis Vuitton Foundation* located within the *Bois de Boulogne*—the former royal hunting grounds that encompassed these and several other gardens and buildings, including two race courses the impressionist *Musée Marmottan Monet* and the *Théâtre de Verdure du Jardin Shakespeare*— where they wandered through the iconic displays chatting. The museum and cultural center had been recently inaugurated and there was even a venue for concerts.

Concluding their visit at the foundation, they quickly moved into the gardens to take better advantage of the springtime sun of that morning. Tristan and Gabrielle chatted non-stop as they meandered down the tree-lined paths arm in arm. At noon Gabrielle said goodbye to Tristan and walked to the offices of *San Michel Holding* where she had lunch with her partner.

 Her journey on foot took about forty minutes to arrive at the *San Miche*l Holding building. Passing through security at the reception she went directly up to the floor where Pierre had his office.

"Good afternoon Linda," she said as she arrived.

"Good afternoon *Mlle.* Gabrielle, how are you today? Were you able to enjoy a little of this beautiful day we're having?" Linda inquired, noting the color in Gabrielle's cheeks.

"I certainly have Linda. I took advantage of every minute of this marvelous morning. I scheduled this meeting with Pierre for one o'clock, but ended up arriving a little early," Gabrielle concluded.

"That isn't a problem," Linda replied, "I told him you were coming up and he's already expecting you."

Gabrielle thanked her and Linda stood as she motioned for her to pass through, "please, go in."

"Gabrielle! How is my favorite *chef*?" Pierre greeted her delightedly as she walked in, before she had even extended her hand in greeting. Linda closed the door quietly behind her, leaving them to themselves.

"Pierre, you old charmer," Gabrielle answered, smiling back as she walked toward him. Pierre who had risen when she came in, kissed each of her cheeks and murmured in her ear after the last kiss, "don't forget it was you who didn't want me, my dear."

"Oh Pierre, stop it! We've already had this conversation, and you know very well why," Gabrielle chided him, releasing herself from his grip.

"Well, if that's how you still feel, so be it. But you can be certain, I will be right here waiting for you whenever you change your mind," he shot back with a sly wink. "Let's sit here by the windows where it's more comfortable," and where he could have her incredible body in full view he thought, carefully hiding his anticipation behind his outwardly suave demeanor.

"Pierre, you are such an incorrigible womanizer. You would never be capable of loving just one woman," Gabrielle quipped.

"If that's the excuse you need…" Pierre's voice trailed off. He raised an eyebrow instead of concluding that line of thought.

"Look Pierre," Gabrielle said, cutting him off firmly, "I came here to talk about business not our personal lives."

To which Pierre simply drawled, "as you wish my dear, but some things can't be repeated often enough. One of these days you might even say yes."

And at that moment Gabrielle decided that she wouldn't share her happiness with Pierre.

Pierre went on, "tell me, what happened that made you decide to take the project off paper and begin execution? I thought we were going to wait until the end of summer." Pierre was silent for a moment while he studied Gabrielle, his eyes narrowed and then continued, "By the way, you look different today—younger—not that you aren't young and beautiful, but you have an air of adolescence, I would even say happiness. Might I know the motive for this semblance which has, by the way, made you even more beautiful than ever?"

Gabrielle blushed, almost giving away her motive for so much happiness. "Oh, stop it, Pierre! You are embarrassing me. Nothing is happening. I've only thought a lot these past few days and am excited to begin execution of our project. Someone has to go to *London* as soon as possible to start viewing locations for our new *maison*, begin interviews, meet local suppliers, and see to the decoration and furniture. We can't risk leaving any of this to the last minute, and you know how all this can take months. Besides, if we can't get all of our supplies in the *London* region, we'll have to sit down with our local suppliers here and see what can be done about logistics." Gabrielle just couldn't seem to stop talking.

"I see." Was all Pierre said before Gabrielle continued, "So, we are now in April of 2009, and I do realize that we are in the middle of an unprecedented financial crisis; nonetheless, we have a lot of clients from emerging countries who don't care that they pay top dollar to experience our excellent food—the Chinese, Indians, Russians, Brazilians, Chileans…and the list goes on."

"I agree." He stated simply, and off went Gabrielle again, as if he hadn't spoken. "Furthermore, despite everything that is going on, our restaurant has only grown," she concluded firmly.

"Yes, of that I have no doubt," Pierre agreed, "As a matter of fact; I already have the budget approved by the *San Michel* board. We were only waiting for your participation to be able to begin the project. Actually, this is an excellent investment opportunity; since property prices have fallen a lot since October, we'll be able to negotiate a good deal on a long-term lease in *London*."

"That's fantastic!" Gabrielle replied and went on earnestly to open up more details to him, "as far as my part is concerned, I have almost all of it. I am just waiting for the closing on a property I inherited from my grandmother to pay in my part and still keep some capital as a reserve. But if I were to inject the resources I have now and sign a deed of undertaking to pay in the remainder by the end of the project," she suggested, "that way, we could use the balance as part of the *maison*'s working capital. What do you think?" Gabrielle concluded looking Pierre in the eye.

"Super!" Pierre replied, pleased at her adroitness, "but tell me something my dear, when are you thinking of going and how would you like to go about it?"

Gabrielle responded thoughtfully, "I've been working for some time without stopping at *Romarin*, and honestly, I need a rest before starting this new project."

"*D'accord*," Pierre agreed amiably. "But do you have someone to substitute you?" he enquired.

"Look Pierre," she replied, "I've trained Antoine for some time now to assume the kitchen in *Paris*. He is an excellent chef, aside from also having studied at *Cordon Bleu*. To be very frank, I kind of signaled to him about the possibility of his assuming with me the kitchen of the *Romarin* this weekend. Of course, I've said nothing about our project. He was very excited."

"And you are satisfied leaving the kitchen in his hands alone in your absence?" Pierre queried further. Gabrielle responded with full conviction, "I want to take this vacation before going to *London* and I believe that will be a great opportunity to let him prove himself as a grand *chef*. And as you know, he already takes over on my days off. Of course, two days a week isn't the same as taking over altogether, but he has proven his value."

"I see," Pierre intoned, pursing his lips together.

Gabrielle still defending her choice said, "this weekend I took some personal time off and he took over the kitchen on Friday evening and Saturday lunch and dinner. We didn't have a single problem reported."

"But what happened? Why didn't you call me?" Pierre asked, leaning forward, immediately concerned.

"It was of no importance," Gabrielle answered, brushing his question away with the wave of a hand. "But I had to be absent for those two days. On Sunday I went to the restaurant to compensate. The fact remains that he took care of everything very professionally. He was able to call in team members who were on their days off and overcame the situation in an exceptional manner."

"That's great then. So now, tell me about how you think you want to go about this. When do you want to take your vacation and when will you start travelling to London?" Relieved, Pierre had moved back to practical matters again.

Gabrielle continued to present her proposed schedule, "I was thinking of taking the next fifteen or twenty days off and then when I get back to work, I'd stay a week in *Paris* to see how things were managed during my absence, and only then leave for *London*. Of course, until the inauguration I will be coming back and forth; after that, I'll start coming less and less until I actually take over the general administration of both restaurants and their quality control, as we discussed when we started discussing the project."

"Of course, that's perfect Gabrielle," he replied, satisfied with her well thought-out planning.

"So, in this case, we will have two head *chefs* and me. Ah, and I would also like to take Tristan to help me in *London*. I've already spoken to him today before coming here," she concluded. This time, there was no request for approval in her tone of voice.

"I imagined that sooner or later you would propose that." Pierre said, mockingly pursing his lips together imitating a kiss, he continued, "and how about his boyfriend situation?

"I spoke to him regarding that possibility," she replied, deliberately ignoring his puerile attempt at humor, "and Tristan said that he would speak with Jordan. Let's see."

"Very good, then shall we eat?" Rising from his chair Pierre concluded their meeting, brushing off her put-down.

"*Mon Dieu*, I had forgotten," Gabrielle replied, smiling and standing up to accompany him.

The two left the office and took the elevator up to the restaurant. It was a rather small open-air terrace with several tables spread out along one side of the rooftop of the building. The menu had only three options for the main course, with a green salad, and a wide variety of *canapés*. Actually, it was more of a rooftop style bar; with the meal options to attract clientele only at lunch. Despite the limited options, they were exceptionally good and the menu changed daily. The menu was boldly hand-written in chalk on a blackboard standing near the rooftop elevator. Two other framed blackboards hung on the side wall listing the *canapés* and *tapas* of the day.

Since it was a gorgeous sunny day, the place was packed, but Linda had already made a reservation for the two. They sat in a part of the terrace with a lovely view of the *Torre Eiffel*. While they waited after ordering, they continued quietly discussing the upcoming plans.

"Where are you planning on going for your two-week vacation," Pierre asked, abruptly changing the subject.

Again Gabrielle hesitated to share her private life with Pierre, given his unsavory history with her. "I haven't decided yet, but certainly somewhere hot," she replied with a wide smile and a sparkle in her eyes.

The two left the restaurant around three in the afternoon and Gabrielle said goodbye to Pierre when the elevator reached his floor. Leaving the building, she walked toward *La Défense* subway station and took out her cell phone to call Eduardo. It would be the first time they talked since they had said goodbye the previous day. Looking at the screen, she saw a missed call from Brazil—it wasn't Eduardo's cell phone—but it was certainly him calling from another number. Gabrielle called back immediately.

"*Alô*," Eduardo answered briskly, not even bothering to look at the caller information displayed, despite the garish color against the black background.

"*Bonjour*! How are you today? Did you have a good flight?" Gabrielle asked happily as soon as he answered.

Immediately recognizing her voice, he replied quickly, "I'm sorry Gabrielle, could I call you back shortly? I am resolving a very serious problem here at the firm."

"Of course! Call me when you can," she replied. She heard an "ok," and the phone went dead. She stopped in her tracks—having understood absolutely nothing of what had just taken place—she worried about his coldness on the phone. Walking on as she put her cell phone away, by the time she reached the platform she had decided that she would remain calm; after all, could she have been so mistaken about Eduardo again?

In London, Still

Chapter Ten – Brazil in Crisis

Frankly, the day hadn't started at all well for Eduardo that Monday. Despite the talks he had had the week before with the chief executives at *Beauté Cosmetics* in *Paris*, the atmosphere of apprehension at the head office caused by the world-devastating financial crisis had not been alleviated. To the contrary, based precisely on those talks with Eduardo, the parent company board made a decision that crushed the Brazilian subsidiary; Eduardo included.

When Gabrielle had called, Eduardo was in a meeting with the entire Brazilian board of directors discussing the issue with the *Paris* board via video conference, the reason for his monosyllabic responses.

"That proposal is unacceptable Frédéric!" Eduardo shouted, raising his voice over the grumbles around the table. He was unimaginably furious: "How can you just halt 50% of Brazilian production in a market that is going exceedingly well—thank you very much—just to benefit the factory workers in Europe?" He demanded, lowering his voice at the sudden silence in the room, "This is simply unacceptable! How could any of you possibly expect any Brazilian market fidelity after it gets out that in order to protect European jobs you fired employees in Brazil?!"

"Calm yourself Eduardo; you have to understand that..." Frédéric tried to argue but was interrupted by Eduardo. "Forgive me Frédéric, but my view is that you are treating us like a second class country—even though our bottom line is nearly equal to that of the whole of Europe—all in the name of protectionism," his voice finally breaking with frustration at the unfairness of it all.

Eduardo opened his mouth to start speaking again when the Brazilian CEO, Flavio de Lucca, jumped in, "Calm down Eduardo," trying to pacify the situation, "we cannot conduct this kind of conversation in that tone. I realize that we are all upset with this news, but we have to find an intermediary solution. Frédéric," he went on, "what is the deadline for implementing this decision and what are the impacts relative to our central office here in *Rio*? Will we be losing management jobs as well?"

"Flávio, we haven't defined that yet, but I would say that the maximum would be ninety days to plan everything and immediately begin implementation," Frédéric replied, also moderating his tone. "I comprehend Eduardo's frustration, especially since he was just here explaining that this situation *de merde* of the rest of the world is not affecting the Brazilian cosmetic market. Either way, either we must divide this cost or we risk losing everything since here we run the risk of strikes if we leave *Europe* to absorb the entire cut. And that might result in irreversible consequences."

"I understand," Flávio nodded, tentatively conceding the point.

Frédéric went on to defend the decision in a more conciliatory tone, "I realize that it may sound like we are treating *Brazil* as if it were nothing, but the fact is, we must divide this burden, at least until the economy recovers."

"Frédéric," Eduardo took advantage of his brief pause and pushed forward his defense, "that's not exactly how I see the situation. At any rate, let's believe that the motive of this sacrifice of the Brazilian employees is noble. How will you manage the costs? It's obvious that the cost of cuts at the plant will be equally high here in *Brazil* as those in *Europe*, and I believe that *France* has slightly higher salaries because of your higher minimum wage. But what's going to happen with logistics and tax costs? And what if the Brazilian government decides to charge a retaliatory import tariff—even increase our IPI—or something of that sort—what then?"

"Look Eduardo," Frédéric replied, talking through clenched teeth, "that's why we have stipulated this three-month period, and we are counting on your support in this study; you are after all, the one who knows these matters best." He looked like a ventriloquist. His lips never moved.

"So, you want me to be party to all of this?" Eduardo asked grimly, making an effort not to lose control again.

"I'm sorry Eduardo, but I don't recognize you; not the way you're acting," Frédéric said without any discernible emotion. "You have always been the most sensible of people I've ever worked with." He continued—as he glanced around the table in *Paris*—never once looking at the camera or screen in front of him, "why this now?"

Standing up, Eduardo faced the camera as he calmly and clearly articulated his sentiments, "Frédéric, I would like to thank you for your compliments, it is an honor: first because I think of you as a friend and second because I have always liked having you as my boss. You are a great leader and mentor. But you must forgive me; if there is one thing that I cannot tolerate, it is injustice. And to punish *Brazil* because *Europe* is going badly..." he opened both hands—palms upward and shrugged (the archetypical Brazilian body-language of disbelief) then shook his head emphasizing his denial and continued, saddened and almost regrettably: "truly, I cannot find this fair and cannot condone it." Eduardo hesitated for an instant and then continued, "Without a doubt, I am part of this team and will do all I can to help. But I want to make very clear that I will also do whatever I can to convince all of you" he said pronouncing each word carefully and clearly, as he looked from face to face around the tables of *Rio* and *Paris*, "to minimize the negative impact on the Brazilian operations as much as possible." And with that he exhaled softly and sat down.

"*D'accord,*" Frédéric agreed explosively, "then we are all agreed!" He slapped both hands on the table as if to seal *Brazil's* acquiescence. "*Alors,* we shall begin the studies here at once! As soon as we have a preliminary outline of the action plan we will meet again. It's also highly probable that Eduardo must come back to *Paris* very soon."

The moment passed and the meeting took on a milder note, lasting another hour. Eduardo finally left the meeting room drained. Never in his life had he gone through a situation of confrontation like that, but his conscience would never allow him to shrink away from any of what was happening or going to happen.

When the meeting ended, Flávio asked Eduardo to stay a few minutes as he dismissed everyone else. "Eduardo," Flávio turned to him as soon as they were alone, "I want to thank you for taking up the fight for our operations," he gazed out the window as if searching for the right words and then continued, "you were very brave. I just hope that this doesn't come back at you!"

"Look Flávio, I realize that at the end of the day people normally worry about their own neck. After all, we all have bills to pay and mouths to feed; but I can't take this lying down! It's just not fair to our people! And as to jeopardizing me, I believe that Frédéric is a professional and won't take my stand personally. Sure, from what I know of the French, they don't like to be contradicted. And they can even be vindictive; but I can't believe that kind of thing coming from Frédéric or any of the directors that were at the meeting, for that matter."

"I hope not," Flávio replied, pausing momentarily to mull over Eduardo's words before he did a one-eighty and said blithely: "So, shall we eat? Where shall we go today? I heard there is an excellent new sushi house that opened near the *Botafogo* Shopping Center." He smiled, his perfect teeth gleaming, while he wondered how long it might take to find Eduardo's replacement—the French board would never live down that embarrassing confrontation without payback even if Frédéric might.

"Thanks Flávio, but I'll just order something by phone and stay in today. Maybe I'll just have a sandwich at my desk," Eduardo replied, declining the invitation. The two went their separate ways; Flávio toward the elevator, Eduardo walking back to his office on the same floor. As soon as he closed his door he tapped in Gabrielle's name on his cell phone and waited as the call completed.

"Bonjour mon amour. Ça va?" he spoke softly—as if to whisper in her ear—wishing desperately that he was at her side.

"Ça va bien, et toi?" Came Gabrielle's disembodied voice through his Bluetooth earbud full of concern which her own apprehensiveness had generated.

"Not too great, but it's only work stuff. Please forgive me for my coldness on the phone earlier, but I was in the middle of a meeting with all the directors here in *Brazil* and the head office in *Paris*."

"No need to apologize," Gabrielle replied quickly, relieved her suspicions were proven totally unfounded.

"Do you mind if we don't talk about my work right now," Eduardo asked, anxious to change the subject.

"Not at all; actually, I want to speak only of good things with you. After all, this is the first time we talk since you left. So, how was your trip back to Brazil?" She replied, promptly changing the topic.

"It went smoothly. I slept almost the entire flight. The only downside was that I couldn't fall asleep after I finally went to bed. And today I got to the office with big problems to resolve," he replied, feeling as if her calming voice were a restorative, he even smiled for the first time since that disaster of a meeting.

"Don't worry, dear. All will be ok in the end, and if it's not ok, then it's not the end," she paraphrased John Lennon, smiling.

"I hope so," he replied, brightening, "I didn't know you were a Beatles fan. But what about you, did you go to the restaurant yesterday? Did you talk with your friend? What's his name again?" Words tumbling suddenly from his mouth as his humor improved.

She laughed, delighted: "isn't everyone a Beatles fan? Oh, Tristan you mean. Yes, we talked a lot," Gabrielle let out a sly laugh, "…about everything!"

"*Santo Deus*! Don't embarrass me!" Eduardo was at once flustered and amused with her silliness.

"Not to worry! Tristan is my best friend and confidant," she giggled, not in the least repentant of her teasing.

"I am happy, truly," he insisted earnestly. "I have very few friends and none so intimate. I think I may have problems getting involved with other people," he ended with a self-depreciative laugh.

"I think you fixed that problem this past weekend," she responded as Eduardo laughed timidly and quipped, "that might very well be. And I think it's entirely your fault, but I don't regret any of it!"

"That's good!" She agreed emphatically. "I don't regret anything between us either. And I hope we can be together soon," she added tenderly.

"Me too," Eduardo replied, nodding as if she could see him. "I don't know what's happening to me, but it's as if we've always been together and being far from you makes me miss you terribly—something I've never felt before," he ended with a sigh.

"Oh, how I love to hear you say that," she murmured. "I was thinking, perhaps we don't have to be apart for so long after all. Were you serious when you said I should visit *Rio*?"

"Was I serious? As far as I'm concerned, you should have come with me on yesterday's flight!" he replied, sitting up straight in his chair.

"*Oh, mon Dieu*! What's happening to us? Have we become teenagers again?" Gabrielle laughed and paused before continuing, "so, I've got two weeks of vacation a fortnight from now. I'm going to need this time to get my head around the new restaurant project. So, I was thinking…"

"When are you arriving?" Eduardo jumped in, ecstatic at the thought of seeing Gabrielle again. "Oh, wait!" he cried, interrupting himself, "I think I have to be in *Paris* sometime in the next few weeks, but Frédéric still hasn't set the date."

"Oh, but I was so excited already about being there with you Eduardo," Gabrielle pouted, disappointed that her plans might fall through.

"But wait!" Eduardo exclaimed. "Do you know what—to hell with that! I want to see you soon too, and I'm not going to sit here waiting for the company to decide when I'm going to *Paris*. Can you get away this Sunday? Right! We are not going to wait for two weeks."

"But…" Gabrielle started to say.

"No, no, no—you come next Sunday," he insisted. "That way we can spend the next two weeks here and soon after that I'll be there with you again. What do you think?" Eduardo declared, triumphant.

"Well, I…" Gabrielle began, but Eduardo interrupted her again, "Gabrielle, let's not over-think this, otherwise we'll rationalize this too much and you will end up not coming, or worse, come here when I'm there!"

Gabrielle laughed, hesitated, gave up, and caved in; all in the blink of an eye. Agreeing with Eduardo she proclaimed, "you know—you're right! I'm going to talk with Tristan and Antoine, and tell Pierre that I bought my ticket for next Sunday!"

"*Maravilha!*" Eduardo whooped, jumping from his chair. "I know it's still early days, but I think I'm in love with you."

Silence. Gabrielle felt a chill grip her heart.

Seconds passed. Slowly, Eduardo sat back down; waiting, unsure. "Gabrielle, are you there?" Eduardo said quietly.

"Ah, ah, yes…" she replied nervously. "I'm sorry; I just…you just took me by surprise, that's all."

"Don't worry, you don't have to say that you are in love too," Eduardo blurt out, as the thought that perhaps the old Eduardo

111

of before last Friday might be his better version after all, flashed through his head.

"*Calme-toi*, let me speak," she said talking quickly without taking a breath, so that he couldn't interrupt this time, "just because I was taken by surprise doesn't mean that I didn't like hearing what you said, or that I don't feel the same way. I am in love with you too. I can't stop thinking about you. I can't stop wanting to be with you. This is all very crazy, *n'est-ce pas?*" She ended, taking a deep breath.

"It really is crazy. I never thought I would feel like this," Eduardo mused aloud. "All that nonsense I've heard about past lives suddenly seems almost sensible now. How is it even possible that I feel like this for someone I've known for only three days?"

"*Voilà!*" Gabrielle cried. "That's what it is—our connection is from lives past!" she quipped, though half-seriously.

Gabrielle and Eduardo continued their lovers' prattle several minutes more, making the most of their new-found *affaire du coeur*.

As soon as they disconnected, Gabrielle called Antoine and then Tristan scheduling a meeting with the two for the next day during the interval between lunch and dinner services.

Gabrielle arrived early that Tuesday at *Romarin*. Taking advantage of the rare quiet, she organized documents and control spreadsheets to leave everything in as much order as possible for her two-week absence. Before any of the kitchen crew arrived at work to do the day's prepping, she called Pierre to communicate her decision to move her vacation forward.

Pierre balked. He tried arguing against this sudden change of plans, insisting that it would cause unnecessary problems with the restaurant's flux if she had only a week to leave everything in order for her trip. Gabrielle however rejected Pierre's arguments and told him that she trusted her team and was positive that all would go well, and even in the worst-case scenario they would always be free to contact her. At that, he conceded defeat and finally agreed.

He also tried again to find out the motive of this precipitous vacation, again asking where Gabrielle was going. She, as usual, didn't want to go into details and sidestepped his attempt. Gabrielle knew very well that he still had a 'thing' for her, and she certainly didn't want her personal life becoming an obstacle to their professional relationship. Pierre seemed incapable of understanding that for her, he was only a partner for whom she had respect and trust, but nothing more.

By the time Gabrielle finished talking with Pierre, the kitchen crew was starting to arrive, and two hours later, by eleven that morning, the *salon* team also came trickling in.

The remainder of the morning and the lunch service were equally uneventful, so by three in the afternoon the house was emptying of its last lunch clients and the kitchen had finished sending out dishes; already concluding their clean-up routine.

Coincidentally, both Tristan and Antoine arrived at *Romarin's* doorstep at three thirty in the afternoon. It was their day off and they had gone to *Romarin* only to meet with Gabrielle. She was already waiting for them in her tiny office at the back of the restaurant squeezed between the walk-in freezer and the changing rooms.

After the two seated themselves in her office, Gabrielle closed the door and leaning against the lintel. She went directly to the point, unfolding the entire project and officially presented her promotion offers to them both. Delighted, Tristan and Antoine accepted their new positions. Standing; they all shook hands and kissed each other on the cheeks—truly happy for one another—before all three sat down again to continue. Tristan excitedly confirmed that he would be coming with her to *London* and announced, "Jordan loved the idea of living in *London* and has already started using his contacts for a job indication in the *City*".

Gabrielle went on to inform them that she would be going on vacation in less than a week and would hand over the administration to the two of them immediately. She would remain exclusively in the back office during that entire week providing support to both and clearing up any doubts that might arise as to how to manage the *maison*. This last detail caught them by surprise, and each expressed his apprehension at the suddenness of so much responsibility. She mollified their concerns and said with conviction, "You guys have nothing to worry about. I'm fully aware of the quality of your work, and another thing, you'll have the entire week to come to me here at the office with any doubts or questions. But otherwise, you should pretend as if I am not here. Antoine, as of today, you are the new head *chef*, and Tristan you are effective immediately, the new house manager. Congratulations!"

"Thank you for your confidence in me Gabrielle," Antoine stood again, this time kissing her hand as he thanked her.

Tristan was dazed by the suddenness of it all, could only ask, "but what of the other two weeks?"

Gabrielle smiled and replied, "if there are any problems, you know that you can call me immediately, but you both should realize that you are both taking over at once. As for you MM. Tristan, this shall be your trial run for London since you will be taking over that *maison* as of its inauguration."

"*Oh, Mon Dieu!*" Tristan burst out. "But can I do it, Gabrielle?" he squawked, fanning himself vigorously with both hands. Antoine rolled his eyes and half grinned at Tristan's outburst. He wanted to jump up and down with excitement himself, but he left that thought in his head, precisely where it belonged.

"That's for you to say," Gabrielle replied honestly, "give it your best and I am sure that all will be well. And don't think for a minute that because we're friends, I'll demand any less of you! Consider this all a test. If I see that you really don't have the aptitude to assume any more than the coordination of a team of waiters, we will sit down and talk and review your position. As a matter of fact, I know you know a lot about wines, but perhaps you can start thinking about courses to take to increase your knowledge?"

Gabrielle's seriousness had the desired effect. Tristan took a deep calming breath, straightened his shoulders, and responded with resolve, "Very well. I will do everything I can to exceed your expectations Gabrielle and thank you so very much for giving me this opportunity."

"Guys, I'm counting on you and I know that you'll do an excellent job." Gabrielle said, then went on to complete, "and both of you should start to think about your substitute. If you think you have someone to promote from your team, let's do it and bring aboard someone new to substitute them. Otherwise, bring someone in from outside. The point is it's you who should start to resolve this tomorrow."

Antoine and Tristan looked at each other than turned to Gabrielle and said almost in unison that their day off had ended as of that moment. They got up and left her office to begin their search for their respective substitutes.

Gabrielle appreciated their attitude. She was also tranquil knowing that they worked very well with each other. Regardless of a certain rivalry, if not outright hostility that tended to exist in some *maisons* between the kitchen and salon teams, Gabrielle was proud of her exceptionally united house team.

In London, Still

Chapter Eleven – *Rio*, The Marvelous City

The week before Gabrielle's trip passed quickly and with the exception of some very minor issues Antoine and Tristan had required Gabrielle's assistance to resolve, everything had gone wonderfully smooth. Eduardo's week, on the other hand, hadn't been all that great. But the expectation of seeing Gabrielle had served as a shield, helping him deflect many of the company's problems.

Sunday finally arrived and Gabrielle took off on a direct flight to *Rio de Janeiro* from *Charles de Gaulle,* landing at the *Galeão* several hours later.

Eduardo could hardly stand the suspense. He wanted so much to see Gabrielle to hug her, to kiss her, to fully enjoy every second she was by his side.

Her flight arrived at nine that evening but Eduardo had been there waiting since seven. He wasn't about to risk missing a single second with her. By the time Gabrielle's flight had finally appeared on the electronic arrival board, Gabrielle was already disembarking, following the signs down the long corridor marked "*Saída* – Exit" overhead. He walked swiftly down the wide open public corridor reaching the international exit doors to wait for her behind the containment tape that made a semi-circle around those swinging doors.

He watched the doors swing open and close several times as the green-lighted passengers quickly single-filed through the customs review area, unlike their red-lighted counterparts whose unlucky baggage would suffer the indignities of physical examination, until he suddenly caught sight of her in the distance. The most beautiful woman he had ever seen. She was the one; he knew deep inside that she was the one he would marry.

The moment she saw him, Gabrielle was off like a shot to reach Eduardo and without any self-consciousness, let go of her suitcase behind her and still behind the divider tape, she hugged and kissed him as if no one else was there, as if there were no tomorrow. That kiss was cinematographic; two beautiful people who had yet to realize that they had met the one great love of their life. While they kissed and hugged ardently, they could feel each other's hearts racing and the heat of their bodies rising—at any moment they both might erupt. Time stopped for them—and there they stood suspended in time—speechless.

People who circulated in the area stopped and stared. Some even searched for hidden cameras, thinking it must be a scene from some steamy Brazilian soap opera. One woman who observed them poked her husband in the ribs with her elbow and muttered, "*Meu Deus*! How long has it been since those two have seen each other?" He glanced up over the rims of his glasses, smiled; he turned and continued walking on in silence.

In fact, Gabrielle and Eduardo had lost a lot of time that they could have been together. Finally, and much to their delight, Life, Destiny, or whatever had made it possible for the two to re-encounter almost a year after the first time. And there had of course, been that little hiccup of a disastrous encounter on the sidewalk in front of the *Romarin* which Destiny also had a hand in fixing. But finally, there they were—the happiest couple in the airport!

After a long while just holding each other, they were finally able to talk:

"Oh my love, how much I have missed you," Eduardo proclaimed. "It seemed like forever!"

"Yes, it was an eternity! I couldn't bear my eagerness to get here! I'm so glad this week passed so quickly for me!" Gabrielle whispered.

"That's wonderful, Brie!" Eduardo went on, "Because for me this past week was awfully long. But I talked with Frédéric and my CEO and told them that I needed ten days before getting involved with those problems that are coming."

"Brie?" Gabrielle repeated, surprised. "*Je suis choqué*, the only person who called me that was my grandmother. Ah, how I loved my grandmother. Everything I am I owe to her!"

"I'm sorry, I didn't know," Eduardo rushed to apologized, "it just came out naturally, but I can…"

Gabrielle interrupted him, putting a finger to his lips, "No Eduardo. Please call me Brie." And she silenced any further argument with another kiss.

After a few moments Eduardo pulled his lips away without releasing his hands from her waist and said, "so, I wanted to make it a surprise, but: I'll be on vacation as of tomorrow for ten days and only go back to work on next Thursday. And since Friday is a holiday here—Labor Day—we'll have another long weekend together before you catch your flight back to *Paris* that Sunday evening."

"*Mon Dieu*! What wonderful news!" Gabrielle cried out. "I was already happy just being with you only during the nights and for the weekends!" she exclaimed, delighted.

"I didn't want to say anything because I wanted to surprise you with everything I've planned for us," Eduardo explained, grinning broadly.

"What are you talking about?" Gabrielle queried expectantly.

"Come on dear, it's getting late. Let's go home and I'll tell you everything along the way," Eduardo replied, enjoying her curiosity. He took hold of the handle of her luggage, put an arm around her waist and started toward the closest exit. The two went to the parking lot of the *Galeão* where Eduardo had left his car and got the most direct route to *Urca*. While they chatted, Gabrielle kept her hand on Eduardo's thigh, and whenever he could, he placed his hand over hers, squeezing gently in a gesture of affection. The two could feel the energy that passed between them—palpable, electrifying.

During the drive, Eduardo detailed everything they would do during the next two weeks. In all honesty, Gabrielle knew very little about *Brazil* and had imagined that they would stay in the city of *Rio de Janeiro*, the most famous of Brazilian cities to the rest of the world. She hadn't concerned herself much with what else she might like to do. She knew little about the city other than its famous tourist attractions. But what she wanted most was just to be with Eduardo, so she was overjoyed with the idea of spending the entire time with him.

Though attentive to Eduardo's every word and movement, Gabrielle eyed the city with curiosity as they passed through it fairly rapidly. From afar she could see the spectacular *Cristo Redentor* atop the *Corcovado*—the 'hunchbacked' mountain—standing dramatically illuminated against the ebony sky, arms outstretched—protective, welcoming—overlooking the city off to the right. Eduardo followed the perimeter of downtown giving her the highlights and pointing out those more interesting—passing the *Teatro Municipal*, through *Cinelândia*, nicknamed for its many movie theaters, with its theaters, bars, nightclubs, and restaurants between towering monumental buildings; they finally reaching the MAM, its lines glaring starkly white against the black night sky, as if to invite viewers to further admire the modern art exhibited within —finally turning off to take the seaside avenues toward the *Zona Sul* of the city. They passed through *Flamengo* and *Botafogo* neighborhoods before finally reaching the entrance to *Urca*.

She could appreciate the city for what it truly is, one of the marvels of the modern world. Gabrielle was enchanted, even at night with the fascinating mixture of modern and old buildings interspersed with lovely little pockets of green plazas, but nothing left her more enthralled than when they entered *Urca*. It was as if she had passed through a magical portal when they reached the neighborhood on *Avenida Pasteur*, its main thoroughfare. Not five minutes had passed, but she couldn't contain her excitement any longer, "*mon Dieu!*" she exclaimed, fascinated. "What is this place?"

"Wha--what?" Eduardo replied, suddenly startled from his concentration on the road.

"Are we still in *Rio de Janeiro*? How is it possible? How can there be such a magical place as this inside the city? Where are we?" she exclaimed, her words tumbling one over the other.

"We are home, my love. This is *Urca*—a piece of paradise in the city of sin," he replied, smiling with the pride of a *Carioca*. "But you haven't seen anything yet, it's too dark."

"*Phénoménale!*" She cried out her voice husky with emotion. "Have you always lived here?" she asked.

"I spent part of my childhood here, but after the death of my father, my mother had to rent out our home and we went to live in a less expensive place far from here. When I got my first big promotion I convinced my mother to return to our home."

"How marvelous, Eduardo," she said, touched by his story.

"Unfortunately," he continued, "she enjoyed very little of our return."

"Yes, I remember you told me what happened to her, but I didn't realize that you had to live somewhere else because of your loss."

"I had wonderful parents. Unfortunately, I lost them very early, earlier than reasonable to expect," he replied as his eyes brimming with tears.

"Forgive me for bringing up these sad memories, my love," she murmured as she reached out and touched his chest with her palm, as if to absorb his pain.

"No," he replied, shaking his head, "you have nothing to apologize for." He went on to explain, "I have always buried these memories deep inside, these feelings that I rarely bring to light, but when I do, they come with the force of a tempest. It's not your fault. In truth, it's God's fault. He took the people I loved most in this life away from me. That's why I find it so hard to open up to others; but with you it's different. We hardly know each other, but I feel as if I can speak freely with you about anything," he concluded earnestly, wiping his eyes with the back of his hand as he took control of himself.

"I am so happy that I can help you feel so at ease with me that you can open up like this. I will always be ready to listen to you. I also have my traumas, but I try hard not to associate them with any god, if only because I don't believe in God," she replied sincerely.

By this time they had parked in front of Eduardo's house but continued to talk in the car.

"I understand," Eduardo replied, "but for me it is very difficult not to believe in God; my parents were very religious. They weren't fanatical or anything, but always taught me the idea of the Creator. I've never stopped believing in Him, but since my mother died, I stopped conducting my life around any communication with God. Since she passed away, I never went to church again or even prayed."

"The death of my father didn't affect me as much as my mother's did. First, because I was very small when he died and with time, I understood that it had been an accident, a fatality. But with my mother...with her death I became very angry, because when we could finally get our lives back, that damned sickness took her. Anyway, I don't want to talk about this anymore. You are here to relax and enjoy these two weeks we have together and that is what we are going to do!"

Gabrielle lightly swiped at the remaining tears from the corners of Eduardo's eyes with each thumb as she looked into his eyes. "You're right, my love. Let's enjoy every single moment, but if by chance you feel the need to share anything with me, just tell me."

Eduardo cleared his throat and thanked her, "we're here, my love. This is the house I was born in. You are most welcome Brie."

They got out of the car and Eduardo retrieved Gabrielle's baggage from the trunk, following her up to the front door then into the house. He showed her the entire house and they ended with the kitchen.

"Wow! It's a beautiful home. Has it always been like this?" she asked.

"Not really, no," Eduardo replied, "it was remodeled right before we moved back in."

"It's very beautiful," Gabrielle replied as she admired the modern details in the kitchen.

"And we are only a few meters from the sea," Eduardo went on, grinning at the thought.

"What? I don't believe it! I love the ocean!" she gushed, excited with the possibilities.

"Me too; *Rio de Janeiro* is my favorite city," Eduardo chuckled with evident pride.

"It may very well become mine too after these next few days," Gabrielle exclaimed with a wide grin. Unable to resist, Eduardo pulled her toward him and kissed her passionately.

Still holding onto her shoulders, Eduardo gently released her from their kiss, grinned rather shame-faced said, "look, I have a confession to make." He paused, took a breath and blurt out: "I don't know how to cook anything!" Then continued quickly, "there's probably something frozen in the freezer and some other stuff that's easy to fix in the fridge, like eggs, cheese and perhaps some sausages and cold cuts. Please don't judge me."

Gabrielle let loose a gale of laughter. "I can't believe that a man with such good taste for restaurants and wine like you can't prepare his own food! And just how were you able to tempt other girls into coming here?"

"Brie" he replied solemnly, "you're the first girl I've brought home in a very long time."

"Seriously?" she asked, looking doubtful.

"Seriously," Eduardo answered earnestly, "I've always tried to keep my relationships away from here because I didn't want to impose my furtive encounters on my mother. Not that she would have minded, but I preferred it that way. And after she died, it became something of a habit. I'm just the solitary type."

"So, how did you do it?" She was too curious to uphold any mundane sense of overrated propriety.

Eduardo let out a bark of a laugh, but explained in his usual serious manner, "here in *Brazil* there is something we call a motel. It's like a hotel, but it's used for just two or three hours or just a single night—some are quite luxurious. Nothing like the motels in other countries that are just for people to sleep on road trips—anyway, you go on a date or to a party and then go there with the sole purpose of…well, you know," he concluded with a shrug and a foolish grin.

Gabrielle couldn't resist any longer and burst out laughing. "But how very interesting; I'm sure!" She managed through her laughter, "I wonder why we don't have those in *France*?"

"You know," Eduardo replied grinning, "I've asked myself why this type of accommodation doesn't exist anywhere else I've travelled too. Is it because we Brazilians are more perverted or more practical than the rest of the world?"

This time they both laughed.

"Anyway, if you wish," she finally managed to say, "I can teach you a few things in the kitchen so that you can survive when you are far from me. Would you accept me as your teacher," she asked invitingly with a sly grin.

"Would I?" Eduardo sidled up to Gabrielle and grabbed her around the waist, "of course I would!" He laughed pretending to leer, pursing his lips and making loud kissing noises as she giggled at his antics.

After rummaging through the refrigerator and pantry, they ended up preparing a board of cheeses and cold cuts and opened a bottle of wine. Actually, it was three bottles throughout that long ardent night of lovemaking. The two were awake almost until dawn.

The next day Eduardo woke up a little before Gabrielle, took a shower and as he was leaving the room trying not to make any noise, she called out, "Where are you going, my love?"

"Good morning, my love," he replied happily. "I'm just going to buy something for our breakfast."

"No, wait! Let me go with you," she replied, jumping out of bed.

"But it'll be quick," Eduardo responded, "I'll do it while you're showering."

"But I want to walk through the streets of *Urrrr...*" She couldn't pronounce it.

"*Urca!*" He laughed.

"That's it, *Ur-ca.* I'll take a quick shower and we can go together," she insisted.

"All right," Eduardo agreed. "I'll be in my study going through my e-mail—to see if there's anything important–I still haven't disconnected from my work yet."

"Fine darling; I'll meet you in the study in a few minutes," she replied stretching luxuriously. Eduardo watched her as he walked over to the bed, bent over and kissed Gabrielle on the lips and left with a smile on his.

The two walked out of Eduardo's house hand in hand with Gabrielle looking curiously around, she didn't tire of saying how charmed she was with *Urca*: so many trees, the tiny beaches, the bucolic atmosphere, the people who passed and said, "*bom dia*" as they passed, and the bars—so many! She couldn't believe that she was in a metropolis the size of *Rio de Janeiro*, and when she saw the *Pão de Açúcar*, Eduardo told her that it was that very *Sugar Loaf* Mountain that shielded the *Urca* from the rest of the world. It was that lone sentinel of a mountain that protected *Urca* from the effects of the outside world.

Eduardo and Gabrielle arrived at one of the innumerous neighborhood *barzinhos* and decided to eat there seated at the counter. The tiny *café*—although called a *"little bar"* in Portuguese—was a curious mixture of old and even older. With little more space than could hold a row of a dozen fixed bar stools and barely enough room to squeeze past, it had a single solid black granite counter running down the center in an "L" formation. For some reason lost in time, the wall behind the stools had its upper half covered in aged bronze mirror, while the bottom half was covered in dulled black and white square tiles set on their ends, a pattern repeated on the floor but worn down the aisle where thousands of feet had tread over the decades. The miniscule modern steel-clad cooking and prep areas as well as the coffee machines behind the bar extended along a narrow counter flush against a black granite covered wall. A huge ugly neon backlit board hung directly across the front top half of the wall; listing dozens of fresh juices, sandwiches and assorted snacks with unlikely glaring garishly colored images above and hand-written prices inked in next to most items. Along that same back wall to the rear of the narrow establishment (not on the breakfast menu) were rows and rows of bottles of *cachaça* also known as *pinga* in other regions. In the only remaining empty spot hung a single framed *Mil-reis* bill—one of the long forgotten Brazilian currencies that suffered death by inflation. And above that a plain bronze plaque screwed to the granite wall read simply: *"Fundação 1936"*.

The cash register was set dead center on top of the bar and encased behind glass on three sides. There was only a miniscule pass-through at counter height flanked by a few ID cards, a bus pass and an odd key taped to the glass—a forgotten lost and found—the tape already curling brown at the edges of the items; they partially obscured boxes of gum and jars of individually wrapped green mints and red-brown cinnamon balls. The guy behind the glass was further camouflaged behind dozens of packs of cigarettes and boxes of candy bars stacked on tiny ledges on the upper half of the glass front and sides.

Facing toward the street there was even more crammed into that narrow space. The short foot of the "L" counter extended almost flush with the sidewalk and had a solitary large covered acrylic box resting on it—half-filled with a single type of bread—*careca*. Underneath that was an old-fashioned glass-fronted warmer with a variety of tepid snacks, including slices of pizza, pigs-in-a-blanket, and assorted savory pastries rested on greasy parchment doilies. The entire front of the establishment opened onto the street, sealed only at closing with black iron grates and a rolling steel door that met the edge of the sidewalk by thick bars sliding into holes in the cement and fitted with enormous *Papaiz* locks.

Strong sweetened black *cafezinho* served in tiny but well-worn thick white ceramic demitasse cups—hot enough to burn the unwary lip—was placed before them almost before they were seated. They ordered the typical slightly sweet *careca* bread with its soft "bald" crust, something between a *brioche* and a hotdog bun, together with salted butter and *frescal* cheese; an absurdly icy blend of *acerola cherries*, *papaia*, and orange juices that arrived in tall gasses filled to overflowing on age-worn saucers; and a bowl of fresh *açaí* and granola with two spoons made up their simple morning meal.

As they were finishing, wanting to take advantage of the clear day, Eduardo asked if she would like to see the city from the top of *Pão de Açúcar*.

"What kind of question is that?" she laughed. "Can we go now?" she asked, taking a sip of her *cafezinho* finally cool enough to finish off without scalding her.

"Yes," he laughed, "but we have to get a taxi. Or, if you prefer, we can go home and get the car."

"Let's go get the car," she replied.

The two finished their breakfast and walked back to Eduardo's place arm in arm, got into the car and started toward the aerial cable car of Sugar Loaf Mountain.

Gabrielle had always believed that she lived in one of the most charming cities in the world, but she required less than thirty seconds to yield to the beauty of the city of *Rio de Janeiro*. Arriving at the top of *Pão de Açúcar* in the glass-enclosed gondola swaying its way slowly up to the top of the mountain, she could see the vistas of sea, mountains, and forest, and nestled into that communion of nature was the beautiful pulsing *Cidade Maravilhosa*. She fell in love with its charms.

"What a marvelous city Eduardo!" she exclaimed. "I want to know every little piece of this paradise."

"Don't worry, my love. We have all the time in the world. This is just the beginning," he replied, leaning against the railing as she gazed at the *Corcovado* and the towering Christ the Redeemer, he kissed her.

They stayed on *Pão de Açúcar* enjoying the magnificent views of the city and distant mountains for almost two hours before returning to their car. And so they began one of the best tours of Gabrielle's life: Eduardo took her to *Leblon* where they ambled along the beach enjoying the sun for a while. Gabrielle couldn't believe there was so much beauty, including the people. And how those men and women lived so well with their own bodies—perfect or not—to the point of walking both on and off the seafront dressed only in their bathing suits. At one point, while Eduardo drove around Lake *Rodrigo Freitas,* she couldn't help but notice a young man who came walking in their direction, five blocks from the beach carrying a bag while wearing only a *sunga,* barely covering his genitals, and *Havaianas*. 'How marvelous; what unabashed absence of modesty,' she thought—"I'm enchanted with the simplicity and liberty from pretensions of the Brazilians, Eduardo," she said.

"Brie, *Brazil* is made up of many '*Brazils*'. You are only seeing one small corner of the whole. Brazilians can be very conservative too," he replied, after glancing at what she was looking at before swiftly returning his eyes to the speeding cars surrounding him that changed lanes without bothering with signals and always close enough to see fine salt crystals on their polished bumpers.

Stopping just beyond the opposite side of the lake, they took another hour to meander the tranquil cobblestone paths of *Catacumbas* ecological park and made swift work of the climb to *Sacopã* Outlook where they could see the entire *Lagoa Rodrigo de Freitas*, and part of the eponymous Jockey Club, the *Leblon* beach they had just left, and the bicentennial Botanical Gardens, established by the then Portuguese prince regent *Dom João*. Reaching the bottom of the cobbled paths after frequent stops under the canopy of Atlantic Forest in order to admire several of the dozens of statues along the way, Gabrielle declared herself hungry, so they returned to the car and continued around the lake to the nearby *Copacabana* Fort, the once premier defense against attack by sea, seated on a promontory that separates the two world famous beaches: *Copacabana* and *Ipanema*.

It was already close to five in the afternoon by the time the two seated themselves outside the packed *Café 18 do Forte* and ordered seafood appetizers and typical Brazilian dishes as their main courses, accompanied by white wine. They enjoyed the relaxed seaside atmosphere, contemplated its privileged view of *Copacabana,* and chatted between bites and sips into the dusk of the *Cidade Maravilhosa.*

It was already long after nightfall when they returned home to rest; the next day they would fly out early to the city of *Recife.* Eduardo wanted to take Gabrielle somewhere neither of the two knew, so he surprised her with a three nights visit to *Fernando de Noronha.* She knew nothing of the twenty-one-island archipelago, 350km off the northeast coast of *Brazil,* other than it had been designation a World Heritage Site by UNESCO for its environmental importance. It was going to be a wonderful adventure for both of them.

The trip to *Fernando de Noronha* was simply incredible! They enjoyed every minute: *Pig Bay*—reached by a beach hike, followed by snorkeling in calm waters that were protected by reefs and rocks, abounding with colorful marine life; the *Two Brothers Rock*—a tiny island with beautiful little coves, the *Conceição* beach and its spectacular sunsets, *Morro do Pico,* and so many other interesting sights to see, not to mention the thrilling scuba diving lessons. Both Gabrielle and Eduardo were spellbound by the islands and their warm transparent waters.

"This is paradise Eduardo!" Gabrielle exclaimed as they returned from a dive, squeezing the water from her hair, "thank you so much, you've given me the best moments of my life!"

"Anything to make you happy, *meu amor*; and we are only halfway through of our vacation! When we get back to *Rio* there is still so much more to do and places that I want to take you to," he replied grinning happily, his teeth shining white against his newly darkening tan.

Those days in *Fernando de Noroha* were idyllic, the sea, the tours, the *cuisine*. The two enjoyed eating fish and seafood of all kinds—everything always so fresh. They stayed in a simple yet delightfully cozy Bed & Breakfast at *Pig Bay*.

The two held hands and hugged each other constantly, rarely straying beyond one another's fingertips. When they were awake in their room, they were making love as if there was no tomorrow. On one late afternoon they walked along a deserted beach they had discovered—after all, it was the middle of the week and there weren't many tourists about—they enjoyed the sea, the sand, and the sun—when between kisses and gentle fondling their excitement grew and they made love there on the lonely beach. It was them and Nature. They were Adam and Eve in all the splendid glory of original sin; before any evil ever came into the world.

On Friday night they flew back, tanned and exhausted but happy, to *Rio de Janeiro*. Arriving in *Urca* a little after eight, they took the time only to drop their bags inside the front door and were off on foot to explore the tiny seafront of the neighborhood, bathed by the waters of the *Guanabara Bay*. Within moments they found an appealing neighborhood pub among many, where they sat outside among the several tiny tables packed tightly together and took full advantage of the balmy evening for beers accompanied by an infinity of traditional Brazilian appetizers and *tapas*—Gabrielle was particularly infatuated with the little fried balls made with fresh manioc *purée*, or *aipim* as Eduardo called it, filled with sundried shredded beef; the decadent slivered and grilled *filet mignon* and onions drowning in *Catupiry* (a molten mild creamy white cheese) eaten with crusty bread; and the delightful *camarão empanado*—*giant prawns dressed in a Choux* made with shrimp broth then enveloped individually— breaded and deep fried—exposing their bright orange head and tail still attached; all so quintessentially Brazilian.

Gabrielle's remaining days in Brazil were equally fascinating. The two spent the weekend exploring *Angra dos Reis,* a playground of the rich and famous and that little jewel of a historic town of *Parati* with its pretty docks overflowing with colorful little boats that mimicked the pastel colors of the small flat-faced houses that lined the narrow cobblestone streets. That next week they drove up one winding road to *Corcovado Mountain* to visit the *Cristo Redentor* through the *Atlantic Forest* and came down an older, darker, narrower road on another face of the mountain where she saw wild orchids and bromeliads clinging high up in the trees and flashes of colorful birds and once, a toucan flash overhead between mountainside and treetops—she was enthralled. They visited the *Teatro Municipal* a lovely example of turn of the twentieth century architecture, the result of the fusion of two competing architectural projects, one by a Brazilian, the other by a Frenchman. And so many other fantastic places all within the city of *Rio de Janeiro*. One of the places Gabrielle liked best was the unforgettable *Vista Chinesa* an observation deck honoring the Asian immigrants in the form of a pagoda, erected high above a part of the *Tijuca Forest* called the *Alto da Boa Vista*. There, from high above, she could see the perfect symbiosis between nature and the jewel-like *Cidade Maravilhosa*.

"What a magical place," she sighed.

As her trip was finally reaching its end, the two decided to spend that final weekend at home together, going out only to enjoy *Urca* and its many beach coves. For Gabrielle, the bucolic air of the neighborhood brought back such great memories of her own infancy and adolescence with her grandmother Millie, as she called *Madam* Emilia.

Gabrielle made a point of cooking for Eduardo during those last days and seized those moments to fulfill her promise to teach him the basics of cooking. The two had a great time, they laughed long and hard at Eduardo's antics and the messes he made in the kitchen trying to learn cooking procedures and the dishes that Gabrielle taught him. Eduardo at one moment even dusted Gabrielle's face with flour as she tried to teach him to make homemade bread. Laughing and chasing her around the kitchen, he caught her around the waist and spun her around kissing her and in the heat of the kitchen they made love against the kitchen counter, both covered in flour, the rising dough forgotten in their equally rising passion.

That last weekend was the moment of greatest intimacy between the two. It was then that each came to realize that they wanted to be together forever. However, they would soon feel the agony of having to say "*adieu*" when it came time for Gabrielle to pass through the reinforced security at the airport for her return flight that Sunday. They were in love.

Waking up that Sunday morning and while Eduardo prepared breakfast for the two, Gabrielle already feeling the bitter sweetness of their oncoming separation, said, "I want to thank you for the best days of my life. You have made me very happy these past two weeks. I wish that time would stop so that I wouldn't have to be away from you."

Feeling a tightening in his throat Eduardo replied, "you don't have to thank me, they were simply the best days of my entire life too! I've never felt this way before. In truth, I never knew what that happiness was that everyone always talked about. I've deprived myself of this my entire life afraid of the pain of loss."

"I love..." Gabrielle tried to stop herself, but the words had already come out of her mouth.

Eduardo's heart skipped a beat.

"I, I, I mean," Gabrielle stuttered, trying to rectify herself.

Eduardo rushed up to where she was standing and touched his palm to the side of her face, brushing her cheek softly, tenderly. "I love you," Eduardo declared softly, "and I don't want to be far from you."

"I love you too!" Gabrielle burst out.

The two hugged each other and kissed deeply.

After some moments had passed as they stood side by side leaning against the kitchen counter, Gabrielle with her head resting on Eduardo's shoulder said, "Eduardo let me say something."

"Yes," he murmured into her hair, memorizing its sweet scent.

"Don't allow deceptions or your personal tragedies define you. I am so very happy that you have opened your heart to me, but if in the future adversities follow you again, especially in matters of the heart; don't close the door to possibilities just because you want to avoid suffering. It is not possible to make the omelet without breaking eggs," she said smiling up at him.

"I try Brie, but it's stronger than I am," Eduardo replied hanging his head, "this fear I have is because of the losses I've had and it makes me want to avoid opening myself up to deeper relationships. But you have broken its hold on me. The moment I saw you at *Romarin*, I knew that it was love. What I didn't know was how to deal with it since I had never felt that way with anyone. It was nothing like the love I had for my parents; it was something that stunned me at the time. It felt as if there were was a multitude of frozen butterflies flying around in my stomach," he said simply and from the heart.

Gabrielle smiled with the glow of love in her eyes, "I am so happy that I'm the one who brought this change about in you. Now, more than ever, at this moment, I want to be with you forever; but we can't foresee the future, you must keep your heart open to the possibilities," she insisted.

"But why are you saying this?" Eduardo replied as a slight crease marked his forehead, his voice growing a little husky.

"I don't know. It was just something that I feel needed to be said; but our moment is of happiness, so let us be happy!" she cried joyously.

"And what shall we do about the distance?" Eduardo queried, oddly more curious than concerned.

"That's simple!" Gabrielle exclaimed. "We will try to be together as much as we can and we will see in what direction we go! Of course, I am frightened about what I am going to feel the moment we have to say *adieu* at the airport. What gives me courage is to know that because of your work, we will always be together. Don't worry. All will be well..." and her voice trailed off as each became lost in their own thoughts.

Eduardo went back to making breakfast as he mulled over what she had said. They ate and then dressed for their final walk around the neighborhood. They went to the beach one last time and enjoyed that Sunday morning sun for a while, then had lunch at a little *boteco*—not unlike the open air pub they had been to when they flew in from *Recife* returning from *Fernando de Noronha*—not far from Eduardo's house. There Gabrielle was introduced to *feijoada*—the Brazilian national dish that in *Rio* is made with black beans; pork offal—from ears to tail; *paio* – a dried pork loin sausage of Portuguese descent; and salted beef in thick cubes, served with coarsely ground and then fried *manioc* flour; sliced oranges to 'cut' the fat; and ultra-finely sliced long slivers of kale sautéed in olive oil and garlic. Gabrielle couldn't help but compare it to *cassoulet*, a typical French dish of the *Languedoc* region and one her grandmother Millie's specialized in.

The two returned home to rest and shower before going to the airport. It was still early so they made love before napping and cuddled quietly together for a long while like spoons fitted one against the other. Since Gabrielle's arrival in *Brazil* they had both enjoyed showering together, but as they were getting out of bed that afternoon, Eduardo turned and asked Gabrielle to let him go first because he wanted to take a look at his email while she showered and dressed. Gabrielle shrugged and thought it was only slightly odd but didn't question it as she laid back against the pillows.

Eduardo showered quickly, dressed and walked over to the bed, bent down and kissed Gabrielle. "I'll be in the study while you get ready, Brie."

"That's fine, my love. I'll meet you there soon."

Eduardo walked out but passed his study door quickly and quietly on the way to the front door, closed it soundlessly, got in his car and drove off. He was back before she noticed he had left. By the time Gabrielle left their room pulling her luggage on its rollers behind her, Eduardo was seated behind his desk reading email.

"I'm ready," she said brightly from just outside the door of the study, "we can go whenever you want."

"Of course, my love," Eduardo responded, glancing behind him as he walked toward her. Reaching her he put an arm around her, pulling her close, kissed her gently on the lips and said, "ah, how I love you Brie. I know it seems too soon to say that, but I love you and am going to miss you very much."

"I love you too Eduardo. It's something inexplicable. But some people say you can fall in love with someone in a second. Incredibly, I think that is our case, my love."

With his free hand Eduardo took her suitcase as they continued arm in arm out the front door and to the car where she got in as Eduardo put her bag in the trunk. As they drove off, Eduardo was a little tense. Quiet.

After they had been driving for a few minutes, Gabrielle broke the silence in the car, "Is everything all right, my love? You seem a little nervous."

"No, it's nothing. Just nerves with your leaving, I guess. I really don't know what I'll do without you," he said pensively.

"I don't know what will become of me either my love, but we will find our way. Of that I am certain," Gabrielle responded after a moment's pause. They continued in a companionable silence through the city, each lost in their own thoughts.

Finally arriving at the Galeão, Eduardo parked the car and retrieved Gabrielle's luggage. Eduardo pulled her bag along with one hand and held tightly onto her hand with his other. They passed slowly through the check-in line and after their turn at the counter, walked slowly, still hand-in-hand, up to the security entrance for the international gates. There they stood silently, shoulder to shoulder behind the tape barrier as others passed through until, "the time has come, my love," Gabrielle said quietly as she turned and faced him, "I will not say '*adieu*', only '*au revoir*'. And once more, thank you again for the most incredible moments of my life. Tomorrow when I get to the restaurant, I will call you on Skype. Shall we do that?" she ended gently.

"Wait! I, I, I…" Eduardo's voice trailed off.

"Is everything alright Eduardo?" she asked concerned.

"It's just that I…" his voice trembled, "while you were in the bath I ran to the *Rio Sul*, that shopping center nearby, and I…" his voice trailed off a second time.

"What's happening, my love?" she asked again.

"Will you marry me?" he finally asked in a rush. Using his thumb and forefinger, Eduardo pulled from the watch pocket in his jeans a white gold engagement ring incrusted with a beautiful white diamond that he had bought just hours earlier from a famous jeweler at the *Rio Sul*, offering it to her as he knelt on one knee. He had acted on impulse in a way he had never imagined possible before meeting her. But he just couldn't let this wonderful woman walk through those gates and go back to *Paris* without him doing what his heart demanded.

That was the day when Eduardo quashed all reason and allowed his emotions to take him where they would. She stood there astonished, her mouth making a small round o, while around her the 'ohhhs' and 'aaahhhs' echoed throughout the crowd close enough to see and hear his request as those further away pressed closer to see what had happened, everyone waiting for her answer.

In London, Still

Chapter Twelve – Yes, Yes, Yes

Gabrielle was inside the jet at cruise speed but couldn't sleep or stop thinking about that minute that had preceded her passing through the security check doorway:

"Will you marry me," Eduardo had asked.

"What?!?" Gabrielle exclaimed, "Have you gone mad Eduardo? My love, I do love you, but it hasn't been two months since we've been together."

"Haven't you ever heard that the best way to prove that two people were made for each other is to put them together on a vacation trip living together twenty-four hours a day," he countered.

"Have you gone completely mad? I never…" she replied still in shock.

"My love, we were together for two weeks and never even had an argument, so we must be made for each other," he continued still on one knee with pleading eyes, "Will you marry me Gabrielle Debois?"

"Well, of course I want to marry you! I want to spend my entire life with you Eduardo!" she replied, her voice resounding her conviction.

All of those circulating or passing that first security check stopped to watch the scene evolve and when she uttered the awaited "yes" they all applauded. Of course no one needed to understand what was being said in French; the scene spoke for itself.

Eduardo rose and slipped the ring on her finger, kissing her ardently. More clapping and cheers from the crowd of strangers while various comments on the romanticism and beauty of the scene pulsed around them.

They finally said their goodbyes.

"My love, I have to go or I'll miss my flight," she murmured.

"Yes, of course Brie. Although I would love for that to happen," he replied smiling wryly.

"Stop Eduardo; let's talk more about this insanity tomorrow, alright?" she replied seriously.

"Whatever you wish my love. So long as we are together forever," he replied, kissing her one last time before she showed her passport and ticket to the guard and passed through the doors entering the security queue with the passport check after that to finally reach her flight gate.

'Forever'—how relative that one little word is.

Eduardo stood behind the tape barrier watching until Gabrielle was lost from sight.

Gabrielle was brought back from her reverie by a voice: "Miss, Miss, would you like chicken or beef for dinner?"

"Chicken or beef, Miss?" the flight attendant queried a second time.

"I'm sorry, what?" Gabrielle asked shaking her head as if to clear her jumbled thoughts, "could you repeat that please?"

"Would you like chicken in wine sauce or beef Miss, for dinner?" The question repeated a third time.

"The *coq au vin*, please," Gabrielle replied.

Gabrielle dined and when the hot drinks were being served she asked for Chamomile tea hoping it would relax her. Even so, she only fell asleep a few hours later.

Eduardo left the airport dazed by everything he had had the courage to do that day: run to the jeweler, ask for her hand in marriage in front of all those strangers in one of the biggest Brazilian airports. "I must be going crazy after all," he muttered to himself as he sped along the *Linha Vermelha* toward home.

The next day Eduardo woke up early and went for a run along the *Guanabara* Bay. He needed to release some endorphins after so much emotion in just one day. While he ran, he never did manage to wipe the wide grin of happiness from his face.

When he arrived at the office around nine that morning, he picked up a note on his desk with a request that he call Frédéric in Paris as soon as he got in.

"Good morning Frédéric, how are things there?" he asked, determined to hold onto his good mood.

"Good morning Eduardo. Nothing is very good. How was your vacation—were you able to rest?" Frédéric enquired more coolly then he intended.

"What I can say is that I am very happy for the days off I had, and I have only you to thank, Frédéric. As a matter of fact, not only for that, but we will speak later on that," Eduardo replied.

"I'm glad you are excited my friend. I was worried about you in our last meeting, and when you asked for a few days, I didn't hesitate. I think I made the right decision, even in the middle of this terrible crisis that I see no way out of," Frédéric said with even less enthusiasm.

"Don't worry Frédéric," Eduardo said sincerely, "I will do my best to find a fair solution for operations here in *Brazil* as well as for *France*!"

"I am well aware of that," Frédéric went on, finally unthawing toward his *protégé*, "you are one of my best executives outside of *Paris*, Eduardo. I am pleased that I may count on your help." He went on in a more serious tone, "What I would like to discuss however, is your coming to *Paris* as soon as possible. We have prepared an outline of what should or can be done and we need you here so that you can assist in finalizing everything and of course, put our decision into motion."

Eduardo could barely contain his excitement but didn't let it transpire to Frédéric. Of course, he had planned to tell him everything since it was he who indirectly had initiated his great happiness by presenting him to Gabrielle. "When would you like me to get there?" he asked, his voice calm.

"Eduardo, see if you can get a flight at least by tomorrow night and get your return flight with an open date, please. We don't know how long it might take to reach a final project once you've arrived."

"Of course, I understand perfectly," Eduardo closed his eyes and with a huge grin threw his free hand to the sky as if his favorite soccer team had just scored a goal. His exaltation was a soundless roar. He had to try hard not to jump with joy.

"Then please, confirm your arrival with me and do come with ideas in your head, Eduardo. And also, be aware that there is no way to avoid cuts in *Brazil*, even if the crisis in the rest of the world isn't affecting the market there."

"Ok," Eduardo replied, "and don't worry, I'll think of some alternatives and keep an open mind, but I ask that you also keep an open mind, alright?"

"Of course; that's it then," Frédéric finalized. And with that they both hung up.

Eduardo was off like a shot to ask his assistant to get him a ticket to *Paris*. After that he requested a meeting with his entire team to get updated on everything that had happened in his absence. When he finally got back to his office at the end of the day, he saw that Gabrielle had *skyped* him:

"*Bonjour* my love, I still haven't been able to stop thinking about yesterday. Call me when you can, ok? I can imagine that you must have a really busy day today. Kisses and I love you."

Eduardo called Gabrielle as soon as he finished reading her message. "Hi Brie, sorry for not calling earlier, I've been incredibly busy today. But you haven't been far from my thoughts for a single second."

"Good evening my love!" Gabrielle answered, so happy to hear his voice. "I thought that you might be having a really busy day. Mine was much more tranquil since it was my day off, so I resolved some things at home. The restaurant is really quiet today, so I asked Antoine to take care of everything. By the way, how are you, my dear?"

"I'm dying of *saudades*, I really miss you so much Brie," he groaned. "But at least the turmoil of the day made time pass faster today so, it was one day less without you by my side."

"How very charming you are. Now tell me, how are we going to carry on our married life with you living there and me here, *hein*?" Gabrielle asked half joking.

"I don't know, but I do know that I want you for the rest of my life!" Eduardo replied, more serious this time.

"I know," she agreed, "but we have to resolve this situation."

146

"How about discussing it over dinner together on Wednesday evening?" Eduardo asked grinning.

"I'm not sure that I am very good for you Eduardo, I think you might have lost your mind completely," she laughed.

"It's not insanity," he insisted more seriously now, "tomorrow night I catch a flight for *Paris* on business. It happened sooner than I expected, my love. Isn't that marvelous?"

"*Ah, mon Dieu*! That is fantastic!" She cried, delighted. "Then this is what we shall do, don't reserve a hotel. Obviously, you will come and stay with me at home. Then early tomorrow morning I'll have a key made for you and you can pick it up at the restaurant any time during the day on Wednesday," she ended excitedly.

"Not to worry, my love," he replied, "I'll arrive in *Paris* late morning on Wednesday, so I won't be going to *Beauté* headquarters until the next day. I'll go directly to *Romarin* from the airport. Would you do me the honor of having lunch with me *Mademoiselle*?"

"But of course, *Monsieur*," Gabrielle laughed, "but you will have to wait until the lunch rush has calmed."

"Of course I'll wait! Actually, after spending two weeks with a certain famous *chef*, I know practically everything there is to know about *haute cuisine*," Eduardo laughed, "so if you need a helper in the restaurant kitchen…"

"You are so very funny, are you not?" she shot back, joining in his laughter.

"No," Eduardo replied, soberly, "but I am very happy and very much in love with the most beautiful woman in the world."

"And who may I ask is this woman that you have not presented to me?" Gabrielle asked, acting the shrew.

The two began laughing uncontrollably at their nonsense. As their mirth died down, Gabrielle wiped a tear of laughter from one eye and said, "My love, I cannot remain on the telephone any longer. I need to finish with some things here before I go to work tomorrow."

"All right Brie, we'll talk more on Wednesday then. Tomorrow will be another hellish day of work here at the office because of my upcoming absence," Eduardo replied.

"Not to worry my love. Take care. I love you," Gabrielle concluded softly.

"I love you too," Eduardo whispered. Ending the call, he went back to work in his office for the next few hours while Gabrielle revised the entire *London* project, pausing from time to time to gaze at her engagement ring.

In fact, the next day Eduardo was in back-to-back meetings with his team, Flavio, HR and Admin, and Legal, aligning thoughts, suggestions and finally, the proposal, planned presentation, and responses that Eduardo would take with him to *Paris*. Everyone agreed by the end of the day that their proposal was the best alternative for a bad situation.

Gabrielle left home Tuesday morning to meet with Tristan before going to the restaurant, since that was his day off. Over coffee, she told Tristan all about the trip and the wonderful places she had visited, the *Marvelous City*, *Fernando de Noronha*, and the enchanted *Urca*, which now rolled easily off her tongue. "The *Fernando de Noronha* archipelago— paradise!" she gushed. She also told of Eduardo having nicknamed her "Brie" and how touched she had been by that, since it was only her now deceased grandmother—her most favorite person in the world—had ever called her that. A good omen surely. And leaving the best for last, she told the wide-eyed Tristan of Eduardo's romantic request for her hand in marriage, providing the now open-mouthed Tristan with all the minute details and how she had said "yes," her eyes shining with tears of joy. Tristan couldn't contain his happiness for his best friend. He picked her up and whirled her around, squeezing her tightly until neither could breathe, so enthusiastic were his congratulations.

"Now you have to think about how you're going to tell 'you know who'," Tristan blurt out after seating himself again his enthusiasm suddenly wilting. "You know how he feels about you even after being rejected at every attempt. And what's more, he doesn't even know about your involvement with anyone else Gabrielle."

"I know Tristan," she replied now serious, "I spent some time yesterday thinking about that. The fact is, during my absence the entire process of opening the new restaurant in London was concluded, including the financial contributions. Today I'm only going there for the signatures of *San Michel Group* and myself, formalizing the 60%-40% partnership in *Romarin* of *London*."

"*Mon Dieu*! What are you going to say?" Tristan asked, a worried expression on his face as he leaned toward her placing a hand on each of her shoulders.

"Well," she replied, with a wane smile, "I was thinking about signing everything and when everything is in my hands, I would just tell him."

"Oh, Gabrielle, don't do that!" Tristan exclaimed horrified, "Close the deal today and since Eduardo will only be here for a few days, maybe even weeks, leave off telling him until after

Eduardo goes back to *Brazil*. Then you tell Pierre that the request was done here. Don't you dare put your lifetime project at risk like that," he continued shaking a finger at her sternly for emphasis. "You don't know what kind of reaction Pierre will have getting that kind of news. The fact is, from this moment on, you're going to find out what kind of man your partner really is. And need I say who is also in love with you," Tristan concluded.

"Do you really think that's what I should do Tristan?" Gabrielle asked, now even more concerned.

"*Ma petit chérie*, believe you me, you are going to find out who the real Pierre is when he finally realizes that he will *never* have you. Do you really want to know before you close the deal on the new restaurant with him? You don't know if he will be vindictive or rancorous. It's one thing you as the woman who rejects him but has no one in her life…" Tristan's voice trailed off and then he concluded direly, his brow wrinkled in worry while he gestured, pretending to threaten her with a pistol made of each hand, "But to know that you are happily married to another man, well…" his voice died away, the worst remaining unsaid as the pistols dissolved into his pale hands quietly at rest in his lap.

She stared silently at Tristan's hands for a moment then suddenly said, "you're right; but I'll have to explain to Eduardo first and get this story straight with him, and only then tell Pierre this version."

"I'm certain that he will understand," Tristan replied relieved, "and then it'll be easier to convince him to alter the date of the engagement. Of course, you won't be able to tell anyone about this, the new date will have to be the official one for everyone," Tristan stated matter-of-factly, "and don't forget to take off that ring!" he concluded glancing at it rather wistfully.

"*Bien sûr*, you're right," Gabrielle concluded, removing her ring, she put it in her bag and then suddenly looked back up at Tristan with a wolfish grin, "you're turning out quite the Machiavellian, *cher ami*!"

They convulsed with laughter, each holding onto the other until finally, Gabrielle reminded him, shaking an index finger at him pretending to scold, "and don't forget, you can't mention any of this to Jordan either!"

"*D'accord*!" he replied. "The fewer that know about this the safer it will be. The revamped official story will be better for everyone."

The simple truth was that Pierre was madly in love with Gabrielle; although he pretended well, he never stopped thinking about her. In all honesty, he only agreed to open the new restaurant in *London* because he thought that the distance might cool that passion down. Only time could confirm his theory.

That day was uneventful for Gabrielle at the restaurant. She had asked Antoine to work that day so that she could be brought up-to-date on everything that had happened during her absence. To start with, she was very pleased that she hadn't received a single call from either him or Tristan asking for help or telling of a problem that they couldn't resolve.

The two shared control of the kitchen at lunch hour and they spent the afternoon together in a closed meeting. Gabrielle complimented his performance and confirmed that her absence had only ratified her original choice. She also appreciated the fact that he had chosen a colleague as his substitute, as Number Two in the *maison*.

Gabrielle informed him that as of that day the *London* project would officially begin and that she would be in the restaurant only to provide support and to resolve administrative matters. Of course the review of all of the kitchen procedures, as well as testing and presentation of new dishes would continue to be her privilege since the signature trademark of *Romarin* was hers. But she promised him the release of a note to the specialized press on the expansion of the restaurant also stating that Antoine would take over as the *chef* of the Paris *maison*. Antoine was more than satisfied with her generosity and thanked her warmly for her trust and faith in him.

It was close to five in the afternoon when Gabrielle finally rushed off to Pierre's office to formalize the new venture with him. They chatted for a while and signed all of the documentation, but something seemed slightly off with Gabrielle. "Are you all right my dear? Is something bothering you?" Pierre asked.

"No, no Pierre," she replied, "I'm just a little anxious with this change. Now that everything has solidified, I'm feeling the weight of responsibility."

"I understand perfectly, but you are a woman of both competence and ambition. I believe that *Romarin* of *London* will be an even greater success than *Paris*," he stated firmly.

"Thank you for your confidence," she responded, "I appreciate it."

The two continued talking for a while about the new project and then Gabrielle excused herself, returning to the restaurant to start the evening service, this time no longer as *chef* responsible for the kitchen, but as a newly-formed partner. And from that moment on, the baton was passed to Antoine.

Wednesday came quickly and with it, Eduardo. The two met at the restaurant but soon Gabrielle asked him to go with her to her apartment. There she explained everything about her business venture with Pierre and described his advances during the past few years. Eduardo was incensed with jealousy as the tale came to light, but Gabrielle quickly soothed his feathers swearing that she had never given her business partner any margin or opportunity and that it would not be at this fabulous time in her personal life that that would change. She went on to explain that she could not control what he felt about her and that her entire career was at stake, so she would just have to play her cards impeccably so as not to jeopardize her life project.

"And anyway my love, I will be in *London* and I believe that this silly fixation of his will cease to exist," she brushed the matter off with the flick of a hand.

"Brie, I don't know if that's true. But I do trust you and that's what counts," he said reaching for her and sealing his faith in her with a kiss. "Let's do this your way. You announce our engagement on the day I return to *Brazil*."

"Thank you, *mon amour*," she replied, planting a kiss in the palm of his hand. "You can trust in me one hundred percent. I would never betray your trust, much less with Pierre. I've always seen him as a friend, someone with much more experience, something of a mentor."

"I do trust you," Eduardo whispered, taking her in his arms and embracing her tightly.

Eduardo did in truth did trust Gabrielle completely, but without even knowing Pierre, he also knew that passion didn't fade just because of distance.

Eduardo stayed in *Paris* for two weeks, working out the best solution possible for the production of *Beauté* in *Brazil*. Those days were intense and stressful, but to know that at the end of the day he would be in the arms of his beloved gave him great comfort. After much discussion and debate, by the end of those two weeks Eduardo realized that that final solution wasn't what he had hoped for. He had lost that battle but received a promise from Frédéric that he would have a position for him in *Paris*. Eduardo had confided in him about his relationship with Gabrielle and from the looks of things Frédéric both supported him and promised to help; since Eduardo had commented that it wouldn't make much sense his remaining at the Brazilian office after the losses the subsidiary was about to sustain.

"I can't promise you a position as director my friend but as a specialist, certainly," Frédéric avowed.

"Thank you Frédéric," Eduardo replied. "I hope I'm not being selfish or unethical for not wanting to remain in *Brazil*. For me a new opportunity in another country would be the best option after everything that is about to happen."

"Do not concern yourself my friend, you would not be the villain for thinking about yourself for a change," Frédéric concluded soothingly; extending his hand to shake Eduardo's as he walked him out of his office.

Gabrielle spent her days during those two weeks preparing everything for her first trip to *London* where she would stay for at least a month. The entire time she was with Eduardo she tried to give him strength to deal with that difficult situation at his work.

Professionally, it was Eduardo's greatest moment of adversity, but he was also happy to know that on the personal side, he was with the most marvelous woman that life could possibly have given him.

The time had come for Eduardo to return to *Brazil* bearing the bad news about the cessation of some operations in his homeland. The possibility of a transfer to *Paris* gave him some small relief from this heavy burden. He felt guilty and worried that people would comment that he had sold them out for personal advantage—a rung up the corporate ladder—even though at best, it was less than a lateral move in the corporation.

Eduardo left Gabrielle's apartment on a Sunday morning. "I'll see you soon, my love. These last weeks have only confirmed my decision not to let you escape, to have asked for your hand there in the middle of all those people in *Brazil*," he said smiling.

"And I too am so happy that you did, but don't forget: officially, that request was made today!" she reminded him.

"All right Brie. Thank you for the wonderful nights we had in your kitchen learning new things. I'm becoming something of an expert. And would you believe it, I really love the whole food thing!" he declared puffing out his chest in pretending pride as he laughed at himself.

"That is wonderful, my love! It also brings us so much closer together," she replied, grinning and leering she went on, "now I do hope our love-making has also been just as worthwhile," she laughed.

"Was it worthwhile?" He shrugged. "Maybe, just look at my sad face," Eduardo replied playfully making a moue of sadness and deflating his puffed-out chest.

They both laughed, silly in love with each other. Eduardo hugged her, and kissed her, then left. So different was this good-bye from the last; their confidence in their mutual love and new-founded complicity left them glowing with the courage of certainty.

Gabrielle already had her *Eurostar* ticket for tomorrow afternoon, but she decided to drop by Pierre's office early to tell him about the engagement and clear up everything before she left. Pierre confirmed his availability for their meeting as soon as Linda transmitted her request.

Tristan would go with her on this first trip in search of an appropriate site for the new *Romarin*, so they agreed to meet on the platform at *Gare du Nord* station thirty minutes before the train would depart. She also mentioned that she was on her way to Pierre's office to tell him about her engagement to Eduardo.

"Good luck with that, Gabrielle," Tristan said as he ended the call, a minute frown turned down the sides of his mouth.

She was going to need it.

In London, Still

Chapter Thirteen – Breakfast in *Hyde Park*

He was already waiting when Gabrielle arrived early at Pierre's office. "Good morning Linda," Gabrielle said as she entered the elegant reception of the presidential suite of *Group San-Michel*, "has Pierre arrived already?"

"*Bon jour Mademoiselle* Gabrielle, yes he is expecting you," Linda replied from behind her sleek glass-topped desk.

Before Linda could get up to escort her to Pierre's office, Gabrielle had already crossed the black granite floor—reflecting the several dove grey leather chairs and small sofas of the reception with its sparkling vases of freshly cut flowers on every glass and polished aluminum table—toward Pierre's doorway. She turned, thanking Linda as she knocked on his door, and went through, without waiting for a reply. The scent of the freshly cut flowers followed her.

"Good morning, my dear!" Pierre boomed from across the room and behind his desk where he was seated. "I thought you were already on your way to *London*." He smiled languidly as he avidly watched her walking toward him.

"Good morning. No, my ticket is scheduled for later this morning," she replied simply, her heels clicking on the stone floor as she crossed the wide expanse. She extended her hand to shake his as she leaned over his desk. He quickly grasped her offered hand with both of his and brushed it with a kiss.

"Please, let's sit more comfortably," Pierre said gallantly as he released her hand, gesturing as he came from around his desk, kissed her on both cheeks and walked her back the way she had come. He perched on a wide arm of one of the large opposing sofas, his backed close to the bank of windows and the light to his back; while Gabrielle sank into one of the down-filled matching club chairs placed facing the other set and perpendicular to the sofas, so that the morning sun wasn't in her eyes. He had deliberately ignored the grouping of pewter grey raw silk covered high-backed wing chairs under the bank of windows that was closer to his desk, and chosen the larger sofa grouping just beyond it in his more than generously proportioned office. It had crossed his mind that she might take a seat on the down filled sofa facing his so that he might later sit beside her.

She brushed one hand lightly over the luxurious graphite mohair of one twin of matching club chairs positioned closest to the large down-filled sofa dressed in black and grey herringbone tweed that Pierre's decorator had chosen, before setting her bag down on the enormous round black marble coffee table, its thick curved aluminum legs reflecting her own. The entire room was a statement of masculine luxury. The only remotely feminine touches were the bright riot of purple-hued flowers in tall crystal Baccarat vases—sitting on each block of polished black marble serving as side tables between each pair of club chairs—and the *aubergine* raw silk pillows set meticulously on edge between the seats of the twin sofas.

Opposite to the two seating groupings were two massive gleaming ebony conference tables. The closest to Pierre's desk was round and seated four while that nearest the entry and opposite the sofas was an elongated oval seating twelve. The recessed ceiling lights made them glow softly. A huge blank TV screen hung on the ebony paneled wall at the entry and below that, a sleek clean-lined cabinet on which stood an exquisite 6-piece late 19th century *Rocaille* sterling silver *Boulenger* coffee and tea set. The tables were surrounded by precisely aligned identical polished aluminum and black leather *Herman Millers Eames 'Group Management'* chairs with pneumatic lifts —the sole exceptions to the entirely French decorated office space. Despite the antique rugs strewn over the *Nero Absolute* black granite floor and excellent examples of early abstracts on the walls, the room seemed curiously cold to Gabrielle.

"So, are you excited about everything?" Pierre queried as soon as she settled in her seat.

"Yes," she replied, "very excited, Pierre. I think *London* might be an even bigger success than *Paris.*"

"My thoughts precisely," Pierre agreed, nodding. "Well my dear, how might I assist you?" He looked at her enquiringly as he crossed one leg neatly over the other.

"Well Pierre, it's something rather personal that has been happening with me these past months; and since aside from partners, our relation is also based on friendship, I wanted you to be one of the first to know. I wouldn't want you to hear from others before I had a chance to tell you personally," she said, trying to lead up to the point gently.

"Has something serious happened Gabrielle?" Pierre asked suddenly concerned, half rising from his perch on the sofa arm.

"No, no, it's nothing like that. Everything is fine with me. In fact, everything is wonderful with me," she replied with a slight smile.

"Oh, good," Pierre let out his sigh with relief, uncrossing his legs. "So tell me then, what is it that is happening that you need to share with me?" His curiosity now thoroughly piqued.

"*Bon* Pierre, some months ago I met a person and we have become intensely involved with one another."

Pierre did try to hide his shock, but was unsuccessful. Even so, Gabrielle ignored his expression of stupefaction and pushed on with her explanation. "Anyway, yesterday he asked for my hand in marriage, and well, I have accepted," she concluded with a wide smile.

Flabbergasted, Pierre's jaw dropped, his heart skipped a beat, and he could no longer contain himself. Red-faced, he suddenly shouted, "What is this tale Gabrielle! I've never even heard of any boyfriend of yours and now you come to me engaged?" He was completely enraged—spittle spraying as he shouted—he rose completely from his seat to tower over her.

Her smile slipping, Gabrielle maintained her calm, "I am very sorry Pierre, but boyfriend or not, if I marry or not is none of your concern! I simply felt the obligation to tell you personally because I respect you and would not like this to reach your ears as mere gossip. After all, we are partners, and I believe friends," she concluded in an even, controlled tone.

Pierre took a deep breath and rasped, "You know very well that it is not just a friendship that I want to have with you!"

Gabrielle responded, staring him down, "Pierre, what you would like to have with me is irrelevant," she snapped. "I am not here to fulfill your desires Pierre and frankly, from the very beginning I have left it very clear to you that I have no interest whatsoever in you as a man." She continued slightly more moderately, "you may be very charming and attractive, that is undeniable; but I do NOT mix business with pleasure, ever. The day we sat down to discuss business the very first time, any attraction at all became absolutely out of the question—either I would be your partner or your lover—both, never!"

Her words seem cruel and biting to Pierre. His voice took on a whining tone as he took a step back from the impact of her brutal honesty, "But you never even gave me a chance to prove that that is possible." He pleaded, "You never..." Tempers were running high and Gabrielle interrupted him before he could finish, saying abruptly, "what I have always left more than clear to you is that there would never be anything between us. Or have I by any chance ever let anything transpire to the contrary?" she demanded.

"No," he paused, just for an instant. "But I never gave up hope," he continued in a rush, "but if it's a question of marriage, we could have arranged that." He cried out in anguish, "I love you, Gabrielle!" Suddenly changing tack, his posture more menacing, "is it possible that you are blind!" he demanded angrily glaring at her.

Gabrielle enraged, stood and responded coldly, looking him straight in the eye, "you are confusing me with some other kind of a woman, Pierre! What are you thinking?" She demanded, "that I should need a man to marry me for some kind of masculine protection, or perhaps for money?" Her words like whips, lashed at him, "I am the mistress of my destiny! I make my own decisions for myself. If I decided to marry, it is because I love him! The End!" Taking a deep breath, she lowered her voice and continued, more conciliatory this time, "And please, I have not come here to fight or to justify my actions, but as a courtesy and to tell you before you heard from others," she concluded with a slight shrug of her shoulders.

"Well I..." Pierre blustered, but he was so unhinged that he could no longer reason and without thinking, he grabbed Gabrielle by the arm and tried to kiss her on the mouth. Gabrielle avoided his lips, turned her head away and slapped him hard with her free hand, jerking her other arm free from his grip. "Don't-you-ever-try-to-do-that-again! Never!" She said through clenched teeth, chest heaving, her eyes brimmed with unshed tears, but she didn't give an inch. "Don't you ever dare try to kiss me against my will Pierre! I have never in my entire life let any man get away with that kind of sexual abuse, and you most certainly are not going to be the first!" She hissed; her voice filled with rage. "You are my partner not my owner, UNDERSTAND!" She finally yelled.

"Oh my God, what have I done?" Pierre taking a step back from her blast of fury fell seated on the sofa, totally ashamed of what he had just done. "Please!" he implored, "please forgive me Gabriele. I don't know what came over me. Forgive me! I hope this doesn't..." his voice died away as suddenly the door burst opened.

Linda had heard the rising voices from the reception but had decided not to interrupt unless Gabrielle really needed help. She stood in the doorway, one hand still on the knob, the other holding her cell phone ready as she stared from one to the other.

Gabrielle took a deep breath and a step back, picking up her bag from the table, "we are putting an end to this conversation now, Pierre. I will be in *London* for the next few weeks and I hope that will be sufficient time for us to calm down and review our relationship going forward," she said with deadly calm.

"Of course, my dear; you are absolutely right. I am so embarrassed by what I did. Please forgive me," he responded. His veneer was no longer quite so polished in the eyes of either woman.

"There is nothing to forgive Pierre, but when I return we will have a conversation about our situation at *Romarin*. I am a practical woman, so we shall not let an entire project fall through because of something personal. And, we shall also review who will take care of the restaurant on the part of *San-Michel Group* from now on."

"No, please, don't say that. I'm sorry..." Pierre insisted.

Gabrielle held her palm up to stop him, "*adieu.*" She took another deep breath, turned with her head held high, back erect, and passed by Linda on her way out.

Linda stepped aside and inquired softly, "is everything all right *Mademoiselle* Gabrielle?" She silently closed the door to Pierre's office without a backward glance.

Gabrielle paused for an instant, turned and placed a hand on Linda's arm, giving it the slightest squeeze, "yes, everything is fine Linda, thank you."

Gabrielle walked out of the reception, took the elevator down to the ground floor lobby of the building and reclaimed her suitcase from the *concierge;* stepping onto the sidewalk, she fell apart. Sobbing uncontrollably, she stumbled once as she walked toward the station, rolling her suitcase beside her—she wept— not because of the sexual attack, but because she had just lost a friend. Of course she had known that he felt something for her, but she had never given him the slightest glimmer of hope. And after all the time that had passed, she thought that it was only the inconsequential banter of a playboy. Nothing could have prepared her for the obsessive reaction that he had demonstrated or his pitiful apologies.

Even with the gravity of the situation, Gabrielle was determined that she would not be the victim. After all, she had taken firm hold of the reins during the situation and had put Pierre in his place—which was why she decided not to tell anyone of what had transpired; not even Eduardo. After a few more tears, she shook her head and thought to herself, 'I have more important things to worry about now!' Wiping her tears with a tissue she found in her pocket, she put on some lipstick using her cell phone as a mirror; digging around a little more in her bag, she found her sunglasses, put them on and walked on purposefully.

Feeling ready to face the world, Gabrielle arrived at *Gare du Nord* not long afterwards, excited to find Tristan and get on their way in search of the perfect location for the new restaurant in *London*. "Halloo! Gabrielle! I'm over here!" She turned her head toward the sound of her name automatically, recognizing Tristan's voice above the rumble of the voices of the crowded station. She caught sight of a hand fluttering wildly over the heads of the crowd as he waved trying to catch her attention as he continued to shout her name; she laughed and waded as quickly as possible through the human maze in his direction.

Finally reaching him, she hugged him, sunglasses in one hand while she held onto her suitcase with the other and asked brightly with a grin, "All ready for our change in life?" Breathless from shouting, Tristan hugged her back, released her and hooked her free arm in his as they walked toward the train, answering with a question, "yes! But tell me quick, how was your little chat with Pierre?"

"Ah," she replied, "it couldn't have gone better. All squared.'" Too excited, he didn't notice the wavering of her smile as he playfully wiggling her arm trapped by his and insisted, "but what did he say?"

"Nothing much Tristan; let's focus on our planning, ok?" She replied, trying to change the subject, "Have you gone over the list of places we're going to visit?" Suddenly noticing her demeanor, he realized that Gabrielle wasn't 'ok'; something had happened between her and Pierre. But since she didn't want to open up about it right then, he glanced at her out of the corner of his eye as they continued slowly toward the train, limiting his conversation to the work at hand as she requested. 'When she's feeling more at ease to talk,' he mused, 'she'll tell me'.

"Yes, I've already called several of the places as close as possible to *Mayfair*, like you asked. And I made reservations at the *Hyde Park Intercontinental,* so we'll be able to do most of our visits on foot. Oh, and I scheduled a few meetings already with some prospective suppliers too. I asked for Antoine's help on that," he concluded.

"Perfect!" she replied, already forgetting about the morning's disaster as she set her mind to the work at hand. "Let's hurry then, and continue our talk on the train," she said as it was their turn to step inside.

The trip took about two and a half hours. Getting off at *Saint Pancras Station,* they went directly to the hotel. Using the *Piccadilly* line of the *Underground* when they disembarked, they were only a few steps from their hotel at *Hyde Park Corner.* Since they were such close friends, and in order to get a better room, they decided to divide a *suite* with two beds. The hotel was marvelous, their *suite* overlooked *Green Park,* and had plenty of space to work and go over the samples. Gabrielle thought their choice was perfect.

Those four weeks flew by quickly while Gabrielle and Tristan visited the possible locations for *Romarin,* met with prospective food suppliers for the kitchen, architects, and visited show rooms and shops for the *décor,* and equipment.

During the third week they found the perfect location in *Mayfair,* one of the most expensive and luxurious neighborhoods of *London,* near *Hyde Park* but rather off the beaten track for most tourists. It was on *Mount Street,* one of *London's* most iconic streets. Charming and nestled deep within the neighborhood this narrow one-way street was filled with restaurants and high end shops on the ground floors of beautiful red brick four and five story buildings built in the late 1800's in ornate Flemish and early French renaissance styles which had so delighted the Victorian sensibilities. Gabrielle fell in love with the location the moment she set foot inside—it was perfect!

She negotiated all of the contractual conditions and sealed the deal; *Romarin* would open its doors at *Mount Street*, number 24. To celebrate, she and Tristan walked a few steps up the street to No. 20 and had a lovely late lunch at *Scott's* where they enjoyed a taste of English seafood at one of *London's* iconic restaurants. Gabrielle was in love with her new location—eye candy everywhere and so much to explore!

At the same time, they were resolving things with the restaurant, both Gabrielle and Tristan were flat hunting. Their budgets and wish lists were vastly different though, so they separated every time one went to visit a prospective flat. Gabrielle decided she would live right there in the neighborhood even though the rent was exorbitant in that region. Nonetheless, that's what she wanted, even if it had to be a small studio to start out.

Her intent was actually to buy a place with the funds remaining from the sale of the property she had inherited from her grandmother part of which had been used to buy into *Romarin* of *London*—she never tired of the feel of that name rolling off her tongue—'*Romarin of London*'! Of course, she realized that the money would only serve as a down payment, but at least she wouldn't be paying rent and it would be hers—anchoring her to her new life. Besides, it was a great buyer's market because of the crisis affecting all of *Europe*.

Unable to find anything really close by, she chose a flat in *Chelsea*, less than twenty minutes by public transport or taxi to the restaurant, and a nice long walk when she wanted to think and stretch her legs. She opted for a one-year contract and would see where she would go from there. Tristan was undecided between two options: one in *Bermondsey* which wasn't quite the expensive or desirable neighborhood yet, and something nice could still be had for a decent price, and *Notting Hill* which was twice the distance, but he would pass by *Kensington Gardens* and *Hyde Park* every day on his way to work. Always the practical minded, Tristan finally opted for the closer with its single bus ride so, *Bermondsey* it was, but only after several long nightly discussions with Jordan on the phone.

Even up to her ears in work on the new restaurant project, Gabrielle never failed to find time to chat with Eduardo every day. They used everything available, *Skype*, land line, mobile, even SMS. They left love notes during the day for each other and whispered from their respective beds late into the night, until Tristan would exclaim, "enough!" from his bed, and the two would laugh and shout in unison, "*bonne nuit Papa Tristan!*"

Finally, the time came for Tristan and Gabrielle to return to *Paris* with the agreement for the ten-year *Mayfair* lease with an even longer option signed by Gabrielle and the owner. The final agreement only required the signature of a representative of *Group San-Michel*, and that was still Pierre's responsibility. Gabrielle also brought back almost the entirety of the renovation phase contractors already chosen: builder, decorator, and architect, not to mention that with assistance of Tristan, several food and drink suppliers were already aligned with too. Naturally, there were items that they didn't find in *London*, so they would search *France* or elsewhere for whomever could offer better cost-benefits for *décor* and specialty items, and of course, among their own suppliers for the wine list which was very specific for the already existing *Romarin* dishes to be served at *Romarin of London*.

That was another thing that had been decided during this trip, Gabrielle would create some new dishes exclusive to *Romarin of London* and others would be exclusive to *Paris*, that way curiosity could pique *London* clients to experience the delightful differences or opt for favorites in *Paris* and vice-versa.

Execution of the remodeling phase of the schedule was to commence in less than two months, by which time both Gabrielle and Tristan must have moved definitively to *London*. Aside from leading the sessions with the architect and decorator, Gabrielle would use this time in *Paris* to create and test new dishes to launch on the new menu for *London* since she wouldn't have her Parisian professional kitchen at her new *London* flat to work in. But as soon as she bought her *London* flat, a professional kitchen would be the first item on her to-do list!

By now, it was already June and works should start by mid-September. Gabrielle thought everything was going just as planned.

Chapter Fourteen – Off With Their Heads, By Order of Napoleon

The month Gabrielle spent in *London* busy with the preparations for her move and starting the renovation project passed quickly for Gabrielle and Tristan, but not for Eduardo. After his return from *Paris* he had to put into effect *Beauté Cosmetics'* appalling plan to reduce the number of employees and deactivate production lines. That hadn't been easy for him. Not professionally, because he suffered massive pressure from the employees and the unions. He was accused of having masterminded the dismissal plan since he was the head of finances at the company, so it seemed evident to many that he was responsible for the cost cutting bloodletting. And not personally—since he hadn't agreed with a single iota of the dismissal plan and line cut-back of the company—his vote had been cast for the loosing argument.

Eduardo suffered grim emotional distress from implementing such unfair job cuts in *Brazil* and also because he had to accept products coming from *Europe* at a higher cost in order to maintain jobs on that continent while those same production lines were closed in *Brazil*. 'It's outrageous!' he fumed.

The first week was markedly difficult. When he met with the union representatives, they immediately suspended negotiations, walking out before even hearing the remainder of the plan and called for an immediate general strike. It was chaos—almost 100% of the production line employees joined the picket lines, and the grumbling and low morale at the main office was almost as bad. By the second week, Eduardo had managed to ease the tension somewhat and convinced the opposition that there was no other way to go about it; either they sacrificed part of the jobs, or *Europe* would close down the entire Brazilian operation, but by that time, the news had already hit the media and spread like wildfire damaging, perhaps irreparably *Beauté's* image in *Brazil*. Luckily, Eduardo thought, the news remained local, never spreading beyond *Brazil's* boarders.

The initial demand in *Paris* had been that the job cuts would total 50%, but Frédéric had left a margin of negotiation open for Eduardo to work with. By the time the damage was inflicted, thirty-five percent of the factory employees had been laid off—from line workers to supervisors—maintenance, gardeners, and kitchen personnel, even plant management and R&D took a hit; one of the plants was deactivated, and a good swath of support personnel in the *Botafogo* office were hit—not a single department remained unscathed.

The Brazilian subsidiary offered outplacement services as part of the exit package for all personnel who had been let go to help them find new jobs as quickly as possible. That was no small relief for Eduardo; since he knew that the Brazilian economy was stable, booming even, regardless of the crisis affecting the *United States* and *Europe*. Chances were about as good as they were going to get for rapid placement in the market.

By almost the end of a month of battle, Eduardo was feeling the pain; he had lost weight and slept badly, and had no appetite for food or even his runs, but not once did he share these troubles with Gabrielle who every day exploded with happiness, excited about her new project and progress. He decided that he couldn't, no; he wouldn't take that away by burdening her with his work problems. Her happiness kept him going, regardless.

Nonetheless, the greatest setback Eduardo suffered was in mid-July when the worst had passed and things were calming down. He called Frédéric to update him on events in *Brazil*.

"Ah, Eduardo it's good that everything is ending well," Frédéric said at one point of the call.

"Good? Good for whom, Frédéric? Certainly not for the people who were so unfairly let go," Eduardo vented; dispirited and too sapped to pretend anymore.

"Look Eduardo, there was no other way out. Unfortunately, the majority of our shareholders are not in or from *Brazil*. They left us with no option except to pressure us into taking this action. Believe me when I tell you my friend, we all lost out," Frédéric sympathized.

"Perhaps," Eduardo replied, trying hard to be positive, he went on, "anyway, let's look to the future and hope that this downward spiral of your market ends soon."

"That's the spirit!" Frédéric exclaimed. "We take a few steps back so that soon we can move forward," was the vapid platitude Frédéric ended on.

"Well, I don't mean to put any pressure on you Frédéric, but have you thought about how I can contribute to the operations in *Paris*? After everything that's happened here, it doesn't make much sense my continuing on in command of financial operations in *Brazil*," Eduardo finally introducing the true point of his call.

"*Bon* Eduardo, unfortunately, and as you well know, things here aren't going very well and heads went to the block here too— not only at our factories throughout *Europe*, but also here at headquarters. I had to let a lot of good people go," Frédéric said, sighing heavily.

"I understand, but we agreed that you would bring me to *Paris* to work with you," Eduardo insisted, his unease rising.

"Yes, but unfortunately if I do that now, I would be taking on a fight with my HR. You understand, don't you? How could I possibly justify letting so many qualified Frenchmen go and then bring a Brazilian onboard with us in *Paris*?" he rationalized disdainfully. Eduardo froze. He couldn't believe what he was hearing. Blood rose to his face and he felt a fury overtake him, almost letting it transpire over the phone. And yet, feet firm on the ground, he inhaled deeply and let the air out slowly, so as not to curse Frédéric at that instant.

Frédéric sensed Eduardo's ire on the other side of the line but ignored it, continuing callously, "and as to your dealing with the oblique glances of employees, well, that's all just part of the game, isn't it? I regret that you have never experienced that before, but that's the way the corporate world works. And anyway, three months from now, they will have forgotten all about it," he ended blithely.

'That's how the corporate world works!' Eduardo would never forget that phrase. It was suddenly clear to Eduardo that Frédéric had manipulated him into the role of villain in order to maintain an immaculate image of the company for the Brazilian community. He had been nothing more than a scapegoat.

"Fine Frédéric," Eduardo said coolly, "I understand your position perfectly. So, I'll just continue my work here. We'll talk again soon. Good bye," he said, going through the motions.

"Take care, Eduardo. We'll talk soon." And with that, Frédéric ended the conversation, pleased with the results.

Eduardo realized after that that he would not stay at *Beauté*, but at the same time he had to decide what to do with his life. He had just found the love of his life and couldn't be expected to start at a new company that could leave him stuck in *Brazil*. He knew very well that Gabrielle couldn't come for a visit, at least not in the next one or two years.

He continued his daily tasks and waited for Gabrielle to return to *Paris* before bringing up what was going on with him. A few days after she returned from *London*, Gabrielle and Eduardo were talking on the phone when he finally broached the subject: "Brie?" he said.

"Yes, *mon amour*, are you worried about something?" she asked, noting his slight change in tone.

"Truthfully, it is something that I've been meaning to talk with you about for some time now, but since I saw how happy you were in *London*, immersed in the project details, well, I just didn't want to concern you with my problems," he ended somewhat sheepishly.

"But is everything alright with you, my dear?" She asked, even more anxious now. "Please don't make me worry."

"Everything is fine with me, but something happened at my work. Remember that I mentioned the personnel cuts I would have to make when I came back to *Brazil*?"

"Yes, of course. Did everything not go as you hoped?"

"That's just it," and Eduardo went on to explain what had gone on during the past month and how it was affecting him. He explained that he hadn't been able to obstruct the implementation of the lay-off plan, only reduce the total number of dismissals. He told her how he had publicly assumed responsibility at the subsidiary for the lay-off plan in exchange for a transfer to *Paris* in order to be closer to her. And then finally, he revealed how he had been betrayed by Frédéric.

Dismayed, Gabrielle voiced her criticism, "oh *mon amour*, but what a miscreant! What a pig!" She continued passionately, "what xenophobic and protectionist deportment—imagine, to say that he cannot transfer you because of other Frenchmen!"

"True, I know. I didn't want to be the one to say it, but since it's you..." Eduardo went on, "but I'm the one who assumed responsibility for everything. And now it makes no sense to continue at *Beauté*! But what worries me most is that changing jobs now, right when we are engaged, well, I just don't want to be far from you anymore Gabrielle," he moaned, utterly dejected. "And if I find something in *Brazil*, that means we'll be apart for at least six months. And aside from all that, I've made my dissatisfaction with Frédéric's attitude more than clear, so he's going to start boycotting me and cutting my trips to *Paris* too," he ended, clearly frustrated.

"But still, that is the truth *mon amour*!" she confirmed, still indignant. "Ok, we'll think of something: what if you were to come with me to *London* and look for something in your area? *Sincèrament*, if a change is to be made now, then it should be a big one—for both of us," she excitedly voiced the idea as it formed.

"I hadn't thought about that yet, Brie." Eduardo replied pensively, "There is no way I can get a job in *London* legally, not without some company sponsoring me as an expat. And in that case, there would still be the question of my qualifications. I have to find out whether my Brazilian qualifications are even valid in the *UK*."

"I see," she replied slowly, "and if we were married? She asked," suddenly warming to the possibility; rushed on, "that way you would enter as a resident and compete for a position legally, without having to bother with any sponsorship by a company interested in you," she finalized, very pleased with herself.

Eduardo went silent, thinking for some time, "uh," his mouth had gone dry, "*mon amour*," he said thoughtfully, "it's everything that I want in life, to marry you and never leave your side again! But don't you think it's a little early for this?"

"Is this the same Eduardo who asked for my hand in marriage just a little after being together for a month and in the middle of hundreds of strangers," she asked, teasingly. "Wasn't it you who said that you wanted to spend the rest of your life with me?"

"Yes! I did. And I do," he answered, laughing too. "I have no doubt in my mind about that; but I'm not talking about what's going on so that you could make that kind of proposal to me."

"Ok, let's stop with the drama right now," she said unflappably, "you asked me to marry you and now I am deciding when we will get married. Does that suit you better?"

"Yes, dear, you are absolutely right," he quipped meekly. "The two of us must really be *loucos*!" he exclaimed jocosely.

They both laughed raucously.

"Crazy in love you mean," she replied when she had finally stopped chortling, wiping the tears of laughter from the corners of her eyes.

After that day, Gabrielle decided that she would give Pierre one more chance; she wouldn't ask that he stop handling matters with her in behalf of *San-Michel*. She also decided that she would not discuss her private life with him either; including the news about her upcoming wedding.

In London, Still

Chapter Fifteen – Without Fuss

Gabrielle and Eduardo decided that they wouldn't make a fuss about their wedding. They would simply go to the *Mairie* in Paris, taking Tristan and Jordan as witnesses, and only invite Gabrielle's mother since she didn't have her father or grandparents anymore. And that would be that.

That same week that they discussed it, Gabrielle walked to *Rue de Grenelle, No. 116*, the closest *Découvrez Mairie* in the *7th Arrondissement* to her apartment, and requested their marriage license. She also talked to Tristan about the idea she and Eduardo had about the wedding.

"Have you guys gone mad, Gabrielle!" Tristan demanded exalted.

"Why mad, Tristan? If we were engaged less than two months, why not marry in less than six?" Gabrielle calmly justified her question, not without a smile.

"I'm not talking about that! The question is: how can you not have a party?" he demanded.

Gabrielle couldn't resist, and started to chuckle which quickly turned into laughter. "Tristan, what do we need a party for? It's just going to create a media frenzy, and anyway, Eduardo doesn't go for that sort of thing. He is very shy and discreet too. I want to respect his feelings. As for me, I don't care either way," she replied with a careless shrug of her shoulders.

"You don't, really you don't?" Tristan asked more carefully searching for truth in her eyes, not quite convinced.

"I swear I don't," she replied, raising her right hand solemnly.

Despite her swearing to the contrary, deep within and long ago she had dreamt of her wedding day, but that was when she still had her grandparents and her father…she had dreamt of a romantic ceremony on her grandparent's property in the *South of France*.

"Today with only my mother and this madness that is my career, you are my best and only friend. So, what sense would there be in having a party just to invite a bunch of strangers? Not to mention, Eduardo has no parents anymore, and like me, is an only child. So, it's decided! Only a ceremony at the *Mairie* and that's it!" Gabrielle concluded with finality.

"Ok, ok," Tristan conceded, "but could we at least reserve a *salon* and have a lovely cake and toast the bride and bridegroom? I promise that it will be very discreet. Just us; truly," Tristan swore with a straight face.

"Hmmm, that would not be a problem Tristan. We can do that, but if you exaggerate, I swear, you will answer to me after the ceremony," she intoned firmly, but grinning.

Eduardo also agreed that week with Gabrielle that he would try to push for a visit to *Paris* soon, so as not to create any alarm at *Beauté* about the marriage. He didn't want to have to say that he was going to *Paris* to get married, much less with someone so well known in the city.

Frédéric finally scheduled a general meeting of all the financial directors for mid-September, and so Eduardo and Gabrielle scheduled their wedding for the 11th of September, 2009.

Summer's end that year finally arrived, and the forecast was for temperate weather for that day. They wouldn't be able to take time off for a honeymoon, but Gabrielle suggested that they spend that weekend at her grandparent's *villa*. For her, it had a special, a symbolic meaning even; she knew how happy she had been during her childhood and teens, and would like to start her married life with Eduardo precisely in the place where she had always been so happy. There were two sentiments, going back after so many years, and remembering everything that had passed together with her one great love. Eduardo accepted the idea from the very first, more so since he liked to travel.

From the time she had decided to sell the property, she terminated the existing lease with the neighbors who were also considering the possibility of buying it. So, the house was free for her to use, although, in truth, it had rarely, if ever been used by the neighbors who didn't need it, they had only used the land. Only once in a while had they actually used it to house visiting family or friends, and everything had remained as it was since before her grandmother's death, unaltered by her tenant-neighbors.

Eduardo's meetings would only start on the Wednesday after their wedding, so he scheduled his trip for Thursday the week before and would arrive in *Paris* on the day of his nuptials. At the same time, he gave notice at the firm that he would be absent from Friday to Tuesday.

Not having participated in any of the preparations for the wedding, he said that he would take care of the tickets to *Languedoc*. They would stay there for two nights.

Gabrielle and Tristan divided their time between the *London* project, administration of the *Paris* restaurant, and the wedding preparations. Those two months passed very quickly. During that time they managed to put everything in order for the renovation at *Mayfair*. The works would finally start at the beginning of September and the two were installed in their respective new homes a week beforehand.

Tristan had moved to *London* together with Jordan who had easily gotten a job to his liking in his area of expertise. Tristan also promoted and trained one of the supervisors at *Romarin of Paris* to take his place before he left for *London*.

Gabrielle on the other hand, was still going back and forth between *London* and *Paris* on a weekly basis; she still needed to closely accompany the administration of the restaurant and still had to use her own kitchen in *Paris* as a laboratory for the new dishes. Antoine was great help in this process. He was assisting with all of the creations. Antoine even created a dish by himself that Gabrielle, on tasting, immediately approved; she even promised that the dish would receive his own signature. And it would be presented on both the *Paris* and *London* menus. Antoine was over the moon with happiness and deeply appreciative of his bosses' attitude.

As to the preparations for the wedding, Gabrielle had wanted to know absolutely nothing of what Tristan was devising, but she did need him to help her find a dress. And since there would be no party, she decided that it should be something discrete.

The two spent days going in and out of elegant dress shops in the *Place Vedôme* area of *Paris*, but everything seemed so exaggerated to Gabrielle, not at all what she imagined. She finally found it in a shop on *Rue de Marignan*—just a ten-minute walk from *Romarin*—on the other side of *Champs-Élysées*. Gabrielle was simply captivated by the divine dress.

Gabrielle had already known that she didn't really want a traditional bridal gown, and since it was still warm, it had to be something light. Tristan wasn't all that pleased with her choice, not that anything was actually wrong with it; he just wanted her to use something so much more extravagant, 'more bridal and *risqué*' he thought when he saw it, with only the slightest twist of his lips.

What dress would Gabrielle wear? What surprises was Tristan preparing for everyone at the wedding reception? And what about Eduardo, would he prepare something special for such an important day for the couple?

In fact, the wedding of Gabrielle and Eduardo, scheduled for a Parisian summer Friday would be filled with surprises and emotions.

In London, Still

Chapter Sixteen – I Knew I Loved You, Before I Knew You

The big day finally arrived and Gabrielle wasn't going to work at all that day, so that she could wait at home for Eduardo who should arrive around nine that morning.

Gabrielle was in the bath when Eduardo arrived at the apartment calling her name as soon as he was through the door. They had exchanged keys during his last visit to *Paris*, regardless of the ocean that separated their houses. He went to the bathroom, knocked on the door and went in. "*Meu Deus*, how beautiful you are!" exclaimed the madly in love Eduardo, as he watched the woman who would soon become his wife in the shower.

"Won't you join me?" She called out to him from the behind the shower door, her voice enticing and low. He didn't hesitate. Undressing quickly, he opened the glass door and joined his lover. Bathing soon turned into lovemaking; there beneath the warm flow of water.

Eduardo pressed her against the glazed tile wall, hot kisses and hands searching out and exploring every inch of her body: her neck, breasts, and belly, down, down all the way to the tips of her toes and back to the Omega of his beloved's sexuality. Gabrielle had multiple explosive orgasms—she groaned and screamed with pleasure. Eduardo's lips searched out her mouth again and as he kissed her ardently, his weight crushing her against the wall. He made love to her as if there were no tomorrow; all his love and desire exploding inside his beloved. That bath was at the same time both strenuous and incredible.

As they were finally getting out of their bath, Gabrielle made a special request to her future husband. "Eduardo, *mon amour*, after you've finished dressing, I need you to go directly to the wedding venue."

Still dressing, he asked, "sure, but why Brie?"

"It's going to be a simple ceremony but there are some traditions we shouldn't break, isn't that true? So, I would like you not to see me before the ceremony," she replied.

Tying a shoe, he looked up and replied, "oh, I see. Of course, don't worry, I won't be much longer."

"Good," she answered with a smile, "since we're almost late. Tristan will be arriving soon to help me. My mother and Jordan are already there waiting. And Tristan will give me away, his idea, of course," she laughed.

"Fine with me; I can imagine how disappointed he must be not to have been able to prepare a grand party for us," Eduardo replied grinning.

Gabrielle grinned back and quipped, "no kidding! I had to listen to all his weeping and moaning these past few weeks." They chuckled at the image of Tristan wringing his hands over the wasteful simplicity of it all.

"Oh, and your mother; I'll finally get to meet her?" Eduardo asked, finishing the second shoe.

"Yes, finally," Gabrielle agreed sighing. The fact was that Gabrielle had only the most cordial of relations with her mother. They spoke perhaps once a week, always only social amenities and each other's work. *Madame* Vivien was a professor of economy at *PSE – Paris School of Economics*, so Gabrielle's decision to attend *Le Cordon Bleu* was considered well, not quite up to par.

"Who needs a college to learn to...cook, Gabrielle?" Her mother had criticized all those years ago. Her habitual criticism in dealing with Gabrielle's decisions was what initially led Gabrielle to distance herself from her mother. So, with the death of her father that distance became insurmountable and habitual. They both lived in *Paris*, though rarely met.

Gabrielle mentioned Eduardo to her mother only after the two had decided to marry. She touched briefly on how they met, her trip to *Brazil* and how much they were in love.

"But this is insanity Gabrielle!" her mother exclaimed shocked.

"Yes, *Maman*, the same insanity that made me embrace my career rather than one of boring monotony like yours? And from the looks of things, you were quite mistaken, were you not *Maman*?" Gabrielle asked, a slight chill creeping in her voice.

"*Bien*, I didn't mean to..." *Madame* Vivien began to say, recalling the futility of that erroneous chiding of years ago.

"You never do *Maman*. You never *mean* to criticize. But don't concern yourself. He's an executive at *Beauté Cosmetics* in *Brazil*. He has a good life and comes from a good family," she concluded Eduardo's pedigree, in a no-nonsense voice.

"Gabrielle," her mother sighed, though not quite apologetically, "I only want what is best for you." She sighed again, and ended with: "One day you will be a mother and then you will understand."

"Of course, *Maman*," Gabrielle's mind already turning to more pressing matters, she went quickly to the point of the call: "look, you are invited to the ceremony and I hope to see you there."

"Yes, my child," came *Madame* Vivien's voice over the phone, "not to worry, I wouldn't miss your big day for the world. Believe it or not, I am very happy for you," she concluded on a more convivial note.

"Thank you *Maman*. Good bye," Gabrielle replied quickly.

"Until then, my dear…" And with that, the line went dead. The two spoke only of work and amenities over the phone after that exchange, seeing each other again only on the day of the wedding.

Madame Vivien and Jordan were already at the *salon* Tristan had reserved for the wedding when Eduardo and the photographer Tristan had arranged arrived at the same time. The photographer discretely remained in the back of the *salon* and beyond earshot while he waited for the ceremony to begin. No one knew each other personally and Jordan was already somewhat uncomfortable alone in that large salon with Gabrielle's mother who had limited herself to a curt 'good day' when he had shyly introduced himself. Eduardo arrived and managed to break the silence despite his habitual timidity.

"Good afternoon all, you must be Jordan," Eduardo said upon reaching the pair, he extended one hand to Jordan while grasping his shoulder firmly with the other, as Brazilians will do.

"Yes, I am," Jordan replied with a sigh of relief. "And you must be the famous Eduardo!" he smiled brightly and shook Eduardo's hand.

"Yes, that would be me," Eduardo replied grinning, "a pleasure to finally meet you." Eduardo pulled him close and gave him a hug, patting him firmly enough on the back to make a clapping noise. 'More Brazilian custom,' Jordan thought, though pleased, he hesitantly returning the curious gesture.

Madam Vivien maintained her aloof pose while watching the two interact but was quite impressed by Eduardo's handsomeness. 'He is actually jaw-dropping gorgeous' she mused. Nonetheless, she wasn't about to make life easy for him. Noting that he and Jordan were speaking English, she extended her hand toward him, but spoke in rapid-fire French, expecting him not to understand a word. "So, you would be the man who stole my Gabrielle's heart?" she drolly inquired in his general direction, lifting a single eyebrow; simultaneously disdaining and curious, as only a Frenchwoman could.

"And you *Madame*, must of course be *Madame* Vivien," Eduardo replied gallantly in impeccable French, "I see that Gabrielle's beauty comes from family after all," as he briefly touched his lips to the air above the proffered hand he held for only an instant. "Yes, *Madame*, I am Eduardo, and I must say that it was your beautiful daughter who stole my heart. Though I must mention, I am always in doubt as to what I admire most, her intelligence or her beauty. Thank you for bringing into the world the most marvelous woman on the planet," he ended with a slight bow and a smile; his sincerity overwhelmingly apparent.

It was in that precise instance when *Madame* Vivien's barriers came crashing down as she fell a willing victim to Eduardo's easy charm. 'And how well he speaks 'The Language' for a foreigner,' she thought.

Eduardo turned and presented Jordan to his future mother-in-law; with the gelid barriers finally broken, the three never stopped chatting until the arrival of the justice of the peace.

The justice of the peace, a short rotund man sporting an impeccable three-piece suit, his dyed black hair slicked back, entered the *salon*, passed the trio, and took his place on the other side of the table before looking over the top rim of his glasses at all three, he announced solemnly that the bride had arrived and was waiting for the music to make her entry. He gestured for each to take their places before his table. Jordan turned and rushed over to the music playback device he had set up in a back corner of the *salon*, hidden from view by enough empty chairs for at least thirty people, had they been filled. He turned it on before returning quickly to his place next to the bridegroom.

The doors opened and Gabrielle entered on Tristan's arm to the sound of Céline Dion singing Ennio Morricone's "*I Knew I Loved You*" to his earlier "*Deborah's Theme*". Eduardo had loved movies directed by Sergio Leone, and "*Deborah's Theme*" was the instrumental theme song for his 1984 movie, "*Once Upon a Time in America*". Eduardo at one time mentioned to her that he had always watched old westerns on TV with his father when he was little. "One of the best memories that I have with my father," Eduardo had once confided. So she decided to play that song in honor of his father, never realizing that the lyrics were not from the movie.

The song started with the words, "*I knew I loved you, before I knew you, the hands of time would lead me to you…*"

When the music started to play, Eduardo recognized the melody immediately and seeing the love of his life walking down that narrow corridor to that song, he couldn't hold back his tears of joy.

Gabrielle was breathtaking in her two-layered dress of watery blue-green silk shantung. The outer shell was a lace silk organza embroidered with a multitude of delicate, seemingly luminescent pastel flowers that seemed at any moment might float away. The spaghetti-strapped dress showed off her *décolleté* and hugged her graceful curves before spreading

189

softly into a full skirt that beautifully showed off her legs from slightly below the knees. Eduardo was fascinated by her legs.

The color of her dress perfectly reflected that of her eyes although several tones lighter. The embroidery of *appliquéd* three-dimensional petals forming flowers over the lace cascaded lightly down the bodice to the skirt, giving it undeniable levity and charm. It was truly lovely. 'Not a single detail of this dress was anything less than perfect; nor could be considered either too modest or too indecorous—it was just perfect'—Gabrielle sighed, certain that Eduardo would like this dress as soon as he set eyes on it. And he did.

As Gabrielle entered the *salon* she noticed every detail of what Tristan had done for her and it made her very happy. The *décor*, the cake, the bottles of *champagne,* everything was just perfect; not a single exaggeration to be found. It was ultimately her perfect wedding.

"Thank you so very much my dear, dear friend," she whispered while the two gracefully glided down the corridor of the *salon*. When they arrived at the table before the justice of the peace, still tearful with unfettered emotion, Eduardo hugged Tristan and thanked him, enthusiastically clapping him repeatedly on the back until Tristan gasped for air. He turned and received Gabrielle with both hands as he gently placed a tender kiss on her forehead before turning, still holding her hand, to face the justice of the peace together.

The ceremony was brief but lovely. Even *Madam* Vivien was overwhelmed, once dabbing the corner of an eye with a delicate handkerchief. After the solemnity, everyone happily toasted the couple, the bride and groom cut and ceremoniously served the tiny white cake decorated with sugar flowers colored to imitate the flowers on Gabrielle's dress and served on dishes that perfectly matched the color of her dress which Tristan was quick to point out, to the amusement of all.

The little group stayed and chatted on for a while before leaving the *Mairie* for lunch. Gabrielle was so impressed with her mother's behavior and how she seemed so pleased and content to be chatting with everyone, especially Eduardo, she sighed and thought to herself, 'everything is just perfect.'

The little group finally left the Parisian public building and caught two taxies to the restaurant for an uneventful but delicious lunch before the couple would leave them go to the station to have their mini honeymoon on the property that had once been *Madame* Millie's in the *South of France*.

Gabrielle had made a point of asking Tristan not to reserve a table at *Romarin* because she hadn't wanted to make a spectacle of her marriage, she would mention it naturally and little by little to the people at work, including Pierre.

Lunch was a delightful affair, despite her mother's raised eyebrow at the choice of venue, and more so because the place was practically empty at that early hour on a weekday. And so, Gabrielle successfully avoided being seen by anyone of the specialized press or questioned as to why she was having a lunch party at a competitor's *maison*.

While everyone said their good-byes as they rose from their table with much laughter, well-wishing, hugs, and kisses, Eduardo called Tristan aside whispering conspiratorially, "and so—did it work out alright?" he asked.

"Of course," Tristan also lowering his voice, replied with a grin, "I found exactly the model you asked for."

"Great!" Eduardo continued in a loud whisper, "is it outside?"

"*Oui*, right out front," Tristan whispered, theatrically gesturing where with his eyebrows and eyes.

At that Eduardo laughed out loud, "Thank you so much, Tristan. You've been great, *mec*! It's no wonder that Gabrielle thinks the world of you."

Those two conspirators, Eduardo and Tristan, would grow in time to be great friends.

And so, when everyone was standing outside the restaurant, there it was: a classic red 1968 convertible *Alfa Romeo Spider*, all decked out for the bridal trip. Gabrielle couldn't believe her eyes. "What's going on here?" she asked, eyeing the decorated vintage convertible with curiosity and surprise.

"That, my dear, is our carriage. Or did you think I was just going to throw you into a train?" He laughed, "we are going in grand style, my dear. Oh, and we will do it slowly, very slowly, so that we can enjoy the scenery along the way. I've already spoken to Tristan and told him you'll only be back to work on Wednesday," he grinned, delighted with himself.

"*Mon amour*, that is so very romantic! I'm overwhelmed," she cried out, her eyes brimming with unshed tears of happiness.

Eduardo enveloped her in his arms, kissed her, and guided her to the car. The little group clapped and smiled at the sight of them, cheering the couple who, as they were easing from the curb, turned and shouted back, "*au revoir*, see you soon!"

And off the two went on their honeymoon.

Eduardo was resolved that they would avoid the highways and toll roads as much as possible, using secondary roads to better take advantage of the beautiful countryside and castles along the way. With the roof of the convertible lowered, the wind whipped over them and Gabrielle enjoyed every single minute; her face turned toward the late afternoon sun, wearing sunglasses and the pretty straw hat Eduardo had delighted in buying for his beloved while still in Brazil. While her right hand held her new hat firmly to her head, her left rested on Eduardo's leg.

Having tired a little from all the excitement of the day, they decided to stop along the way in the *Lac Vailhan* region. They stopped at a charming hotel in a *villa* near *Clermont-Ferrand*. They went directly to their room and made love. Sometime later, laughing at Eduardo's growling stomach convinced them to leave their room and eat out. Both ravenous, they had a leisurely dinner at a nearby *bistro* and hand-in-hand they went out for an evening walk under twinkling stars only seen far from the big city lights. The weather was balmy and warm so the two strolled without a care into the peaceful country night.

The couple decided to have breakfast on the road that next morning, to better enjoy more sights and experience the novelty of it all. That Saturday was a beautiful day at the tail end of summer.

Eduardo drove them to *Saint-Chély-d'Apcher*, a small town of some four thousand souls, deep within a beautiful valley where they enjoyed a leisurely breakfast and explored the ancient center of the town. From there, they went directly to the property that had once been the warm and loving home of *Madame* Millie.

Gabrielle became overwhelmed with emotion as they arrived at the gates as all those memories suddenly surfaced with a rush.

The neighbor who had rented the place until a little while ago was waiting at the entrance to give them the keys. *Madame* Clementine was a charming middle-aged woman who had inherited her own property from her mother and had been a friend to Gabrielle's grandmother until her death. She and Gabrielle's mother had once been close friends and childhood playmates.

Getting out of the car, still under the impact of the feelings from long ago, Gabrielle walked up to meet *Madame* Clementine at the gates.

"Good afternoon Gabrielle, how are you my child?" was the warm greeting she received.

"Hello *Madame* Clementine, how very good to see you!" Gabrielle hugged her and continued, "I am fine, just feeling a little emotional from the memories of my marvelous childhood in this place, I was overcome by my emotions," she replied, wiping a tear from her cheek as she looked down at the comfortably aging face she had known all her life.

"Oh, my dear, don't distress yourself so," she said gently, "I remember as if it were just yesterday, how much you enjoyed yourself when you were here, and how very close you were to your dear *grand-mère*. She was such an adorable person, *n'est-ce pas?*" *Madame* Clementine replied endearingly.

"Ah, she was everything to me, *Madame* Clementine," Gabrielle replied, affectionately taking both of her hands in her own, as her eyes again filled with tears.

"How good that you are here again to remember such wonderful memories of your time with her, I am certain that they helped mold you into the woman you are today. When I saw you for a moment, I thought I was seeing Vivien. Goodness! How long it's been since I saw or spoke to your mother last. How is she, my dear," Madame Clementine asked kindly.

By then Eduardo had also gotten out of the car and come around it to greet *Madame* Clementine. "Good afternoon," he called out his greeting in French and waved as he closed the convertible's door.

"Good afternoon", the lady replied, releasing one hand from Gabrielle's, waving for him come closer.

Gabrielle answered *Madame* Clementine's question, "my mother is fine, thank you for asking. Please, allow me to introduce my husband, Eduardo;" she continued with a wide grin and raised her voice, "Eduardo, come and meet my friend," as Eduardo walked up to the two women standing at the gate.

Eduardo shook her hand. "*Ravi de vous connaître, Madame, je m'appelle* Eduardo."

"And I am called Clementine, my friend. The pleasure is mine; and I hope you have a good stay in our little town," she replied smiling up at him, squinting against the sun's glare.

"I'm already very happy," Eduardo replied solemnly, "just knowing that this is Gabrielle's favorite place."

"What a gallant young man, he is, Gabrielle!" *Madame* Clementine exclaimed, turning to Gabrielle with a smile of delight.

"He is a gentleman, *Madame*," Gabrielle concurred.

"Excuse me, my children, but I have to get back now. I'll leave you in peace. Here are the keys, and I asked our caretaker to give the house a good cleaning for you. Oh, and I've left some regional products for you to enjoy without having to worry about going to the market," she ended brightly and turned to go.

"Thank you so very much *Madame* Clementine. You really are an angel," Gabrielle replied.

"Oh my dear, it's nothing. Our families are friends for generations; this was the least I could do." *Madame* Clementine began, "Gabrielle," but then paused.

"Yes *Madame*?" Gabrielle looked at her inquiringly.

"I don't wish to interrupt your stay, but before you leave, I would like to talk to you about buying the property. I believe that I have a counterproposal to the amount you are asking," she asked somewhat shyly.

"But of course! You know that you have right of first refusal with me. I wouldn't sell it to just anyone," Gabrielle responded emphatically.

"Of course, my dear, and you are both very welcome here. *Au revoir*," she waved as she walked slowly back toward the lane.

Eduardo returned to the car while Gabrielle opened the gates. He was enchanted with the property and found the house very charming, its simplicity poetic. Entering the house, they found wicker baskets on the table, filled with foods of every kind for them to enjoy: homemade breads, cheeses, milk, wine, fruits and vegetables.

"What a sweetheart your neighbor is," Eduardo declared, moved by her thoughtfulness.

"She really is a darling, so different from my mother," Gabrielle replied.

Eduardo pretended not to have heard the last part of her comment, pained at his own mother's absence. They left their bags on the floor of the living room and she took him by the hand to show him the main bedroom. As they walked in, Eduardo hugged her and said, "have I told you how beautiful you are in that dress? You are perfect."

"No, you haven't, but you may continue with the compliments," she replied laughing.

Eduardo's response was to pull down the straps of Gabrielle's dress while he kissed her from her mouth down to the beginning of her cleavage. When he finally started undressing her, his kisses went lower and lower, from her breasts down her belly to her sex. They made love until dark.

The weekend was perfect. The two took long walks, visited the nearby village and most of all, they enjoyed the house and one another's company. Eduardo made himself the cook for some of their meals and Gabrielle was impressed with his development in the kitchen.

"Hum, have you been taking evening cooking classes these past few months, my love? Your food is very good," she teased.

"Wow, I'm honored to receive such high praise from the great Gabrielle Debois," he grinned and bowed, arms spread wide.

"Silly! I'm being honest. It really is very good," she replied to his clowning.

Unfortunately, their four-day honeymoon finally came to its end when Gabrielle walked to the house of Madame Clementine to return the keys and thank her for her kindness during that long weekend. She had gone to see her a little earlier to have time to talk about the sale of the property while Eduardo wandered for a while in the lane between the two properties, taking in those bucolic sights, sounds, and scents for the last time. As the minutes passed, he sat in the car with its top already down, daydreaming of his future with his bride and simply enjoyed the sun in the quiet countryside. His thoughts only occasionally interrupted by the soft chirping of birds, a sporadic lazy bark of a dog, and the murmur of indistinct human voices drifting from a distant vineyard as he lazily watched high clouds waft slowly by.

"Good morning, my dear. Are you leaving already?"

"Yes *Madame*, unfortunately; I've come to return the keys and thank you for everything—your care, your kindness with us these past few days," Gabrielle replied sincerely. "Thank you so very much."

"Think nothing of it Gabrielle. You are like one of my own."

"I realize that *Madame*," Gabrielle replied, touched. "And now, what would you like to propose about the property," Gabrielle continued, getting down to business.

The two discussed the matter for about half an hour and Gabrielle left with the sale closed. A cycle had just ended in order for another to begin.

The couple left the *villa* around eleven that morning and drove directly to *Paris*, stopping again in *Clermont-Ferrand* for a late lunch. The trip this time was much quicker since Eduardo took the *A75* and then the *A71*; they made it back in just a little less than eight hours.

At one point during the road trip, Gabrielle turned to Eduardo and said, "Thank you so much for our unforgettable honeymoon, my dear. The convertible, the hat, the road trip, your food—it was all so perfect! Now it's time to start a new phase in our lives."

"I'm the one who thanks you, my love!" Eduardo replied, "For everything and for simply existing. I've never been happier than these past few days with you in this place that means so much to you—it is so very you."

"I think our coming here was important before I sell the place, and also because I sold it to someone who I am certain my grandmother would have approved," Gabrielle stated simply.

"Of course, Brie, my love, and now that we are married, I'm going to negotiate my exit package from the company at the end of this week. There's no sense in staying in *Brazil* so far away from you."

"Certainly Eduardo; I agree with you. And as soon as you can, if you could also see about the process for your visa for the *United Kingdom*," she added.

"Yes, my love, I had already thought about that. I'll do that this week too."

Eduardo finished that week in meetings at *Beauté Cosmetics* and at the end of the day on Friday, asked to speak privately with Frédéric. He spoke of his discomfort with the lay-off and proposed a financial agreement to leave the company. Fréderic accepted immediately but asked that Eduardo stay until he found a suitable substitute. Eduardo didn't oppose that request. It was an excellent agreement which would give Eduardo a good amount to start his new life in *London*.

From September of that year, it took almost three months until Eduardo was finally able to leave his job in *Brazil*, obtain his temporary six-month visa as the husband of a French citizen and then rent out the house in *Urca*. He wasn't able to move to *London* before the inauguration of *Romarin of Mayfair*—which took place in early December—but he was able to finally join Gabrielle before Christmas.

As for Gabrielle, she had to return almost immediately to *London*, leaving Eduardo alone in her *Paris* apartment, but before catching the train on Thursday, Gabrielle called Pierre and told him that she had married. That same morning, before the lunch crowd came in, she had already told her entire *Paris* team. They were surprised, but very happy for her. Pierre, on the other hand, was shocked, unable to demonstrate his sentiment over the phone he managed to limit himself to a curt wish of 'much happiness'.

As of October, due to the intensification of her involvement with the renovation of the new restaurant, Gabrielle only managed to go to *Paris* once a month, leaving everything there up to Antoine and Tristan's substitute in *Paris*, Valentin. That was also when she began remotely handling the administrative and financial management of *Romarin of Paris*. And since the statutory and tax matters were already handled by the team at *San-Michel Group* for the restaurant in *Paris*, they took over the same duties and responsibilities for *Romarin of London*.

The renovation work sped by, and on the fifth of December the restaurant was inaugurated with a huge event that was widely and highly commented. Pierre was very impressed with the excellent job she had done and made a point of praising her for it. Gabrielle thanked him rather formally, and then when he tried to turn the subject to her personal life, she limited the conversation in as direct and dry a manner as possible, without being rude.

"I noticed that your husband isn't present on such a special night as this, my dear. I hope that everything is in perfect harmony between the two of you," he commented obliquely at one point.

Gabrielle pretended not to hear Pierre's nasty comment.

"Everything is fine Pierre. I'm so glad that you liked the final results for *Romarin* of *London*. Now if you will excuse me, I must speak with our guests," Gabrielle responded coolly then turned abruptly away.

"Of course Gabrielle, enjoy your big night!" Pierre responded too late for her to see a glint of anger in his eye.

Gabrielle had already turned her back to him and was moving slowly through the crowded *salon* greeting clients and the many journalists from the specialized media who had been invited to the opening. They had come *en masse* and voracious to see what novelties Gabrielle would bring to the new *maison*—she didn't disappoint—the tasting and wines were received with unanimous enthusiasm.

The night had been a great success, but Gabrielle was miserable without Eduardo. From what she had gleamed from Eduardo's explanation, he couldn't enter the *United Kingdom* without a visa in his passport, since that would delay even more his residency process. Nonetheless, she couldn't hide her disappointment. Without Eduardo by her side on that so very important night—for her—it just wasn't perfect.

Eduardo finally arrived in *London* on the fifteenth of December and at last, the two able to start their much-postponed married life together. The couple took advantage of their time together during those final days of the year, even though Gabrielle had very little time for her private life.

When they weren't together during those last days of the old year, Eduardo took the opportunity to research the necessary requisites to practice his profession in *England*, to job hunt, and to do something that he had of late taken enormous pleasure in: cooking for his beloved.

Before the New Year, he had discovered that he would have to choose a professional association among the several existing in *England* and take exams in order to validate his professional capacity for the *United Kingdom*. He lost no time in filing for membership with the association he thought best suited him.

Gabrielle and Eduardo celebrated Christmas and the New Year with Tristan and Jordan as they all were quickly becoming inseparable friends. The four spent the turn of the year 2009 to 2010 in a restaurant that faced the fireworks of the *London Eye*. It was an incredible evening. When the clocks struck midnight, Eduardo pulled Gabrielle into a hot embrace and kissed her deeply.

"Happy New Year, my love!" he cried out. "May this *Réveillon* be the first of many, and may we be very, very happy in this new phase of our lives! I love you!" He shouted over the excited voices and clapping, his mouth only inches from her ear.

"So be it, my love," Gabrielle shouted back over the roar of voices and fireworks. "I love you too! Happy New Year!" She ended, laughing for pure joy.

And so that was how the new lives of Gabrielle and Eduardo began in *London*.

In London, Still

Chapter Seventeen –None Too Easy a Life in London

London's reality had already hit Gabrielle in late 2009 when she made the final move to the city together with Tristan for the pre-operational phase of the new restaurant: accompany the renovation, choose decorative items, kitchen equipment, finalize negotiations with the suppliers, close contracts, and all the rest involved in setting up the new restaurant. For Eduardo, those last days of December were only happiness and exploration of a new town. Although he was focused on what he needed to do before effectively starting his life in the city, he really missed the *Carioca* warm weather of *Rio de Janeiro*.

The old year transitioned into the new, changing everything for Eduardo. Yes, he had his savings grown throughout his life, his settlement with *Beauté*, and a good income from leasing his house, not counting the favorable exchange rate for Brazilian currency and high interest rates in *Brazil* at that time. So, Eduardo's money stayed in *Brazil* earning interest, but he monitored the variations and reactions of the market closely for any news of any possible change.

He brought with him a respectable amount for his upkeep and to help with expenses in his new home for a few months. Even so, Eduardo was a hard worker and three weeks later he was anxious to start a new job, particularly since Gabrielle spent all her time at the restaurant, he ended up staying alone at home a lot. He wasn't idle however; either he was studying for the accounting exams or sending out *résumés* and job applications, or learning new culinary skills by himself.

Since they had started living together, it was rare for Gabrielle to enter the kitchen. Eduardo made a point of cooking for the both of them. And he really enjoyed doing it, even the *mise an place* had a calming effect. Cooking their meals became a personal pleasure for him.

In the first weeks of January, Eduardo started going to interviews, but soon realized that his education and experience in *Brazil*—despite it having been with a European multinational—wasn't worth much in this country. The recruiters simply weren't interested in knowing or even hearing what Eduardo had to say; of how dynamic and advanced things were in *Brazil* with respect to legislation, processes, systems; or his practical experience with important tools for the performance of the job by a professional in his area of expertise after hearing that he was not *British*, or even *European*. Eduardo's lack of experience in the *United Kingdom* was always the reason they gave for 'not fitting the profile'.

During the first few interviews he hadn't been too concerned, primarily because it was the beginning of his search for work. But after three months of hearing the same excuses, even after having taken all the exams and obtaining local certification, it started not only to worry him, but he was becoming extremely irritated about it. It slowly dawned on Eduardo that it wasn't just the qualifications, or even the local experience that were the issue. There was something else the headhunters and recruiters weren't saying, that it manifested in their reactions during the interviews, once they heard Eduardo's reply that he was neither *British* nor *European*. It was unfair and it hurt.

"Calm down, my love, something will show up for you soon," Gabrielle said at one time when he had met her at the *Romarin in Mayfair* after concluding another futile interview. "You've only just arrived and we're still trying to get out of a crisis here. At least we can see that *London* is a world of opportunities."

"Opportunities for Europeans and Brits, Brie," Eduardo replied rather irritatedly. "I'm certain that it has nothing to do with the supposed 'local experience' or anything to do with my being 'over qualified.' And I'm certain I was qualified faster than any of them anyway. It's absurd! We live in a globalized world where rules—especially because of the last crises caused by big corporations' accounting dribbling—are stricter and the majority of countries are adopting them, including *Brazil*," he said emphatically, gesturing toward the west, shaking a hand back and forth, thumb folded against his palm. "So, my knowledge and experience can certainly be very useful to companies here." He gestured down at the floor, same hand; same movement. "That's particularly true because in many aspects, we're much more modern and prepared in *Brazil* than the companies here." Again, Eduardo used his hands, first punching the air, then tapping himself hard on the chest. "Not to mention the fact that I worked for a European company! So I certainly know how to conform to the rules here, I mean of *Europe*," he asserted firmly, spreading both arms out and palms up, making circles in the air, as if to encompass the entire continent.

"I understand, my love, but do try to be calm," Gabrielle said with just a slight turning up of the corners of her mouth at all of his *latino* gesticulating. His hands were like wild birds to her, trying to take flight. "As we discussed before, you have nothing to worry about with household expenses until you get a job." Gabrielle wheedled, trying to coax him into calming down, her own hands resting quietly in her lap.

Eduardo blurt out, "I know Brie, but that's not right for you. I came here not just to be with you, but also to join our efforts, not to divide them. And anyway, I am the husband. I'm the one who should be taking care of you." His frustration raw in his voice and body language—his knuckles whitening as he grasped the arms of his chair with force—his entire body rigid.

"Oh Eduardo, do stop being silly! I didn't know about this chauvinist side of yours. What kind of talk is that? Just because I'm a woman I have to be supported by my husband? What world are you from, huh?" She exclaimed exasperated, repeatedly and rapidly tapping her own forehead to emphasize her point, no longer amused by his wild gesticulations, and forgetting all about being supportive.

Immediately repentant, "I'm sorry Brie," Eduardo said softening his voice, leaning closer to her from where he sat; he tried to take her hand in his, "don't…"

Gabrielle angrily stood and moved away, twisting out of his reach, arms crossed, defiant. And she continued in what quickly escalated into a tirade, "now you look here! I have always been an independent woman! Since I first left my mother's house, I have never called to ask for anything, ever! It's not going to be you who will sweep in now as the breadwinner!" she admonished, her voice continuing to rise.

"What is this?!" Eduardo replied, hurt and angry, altering his own voice as he too rose from his chair, "I come to you to let off steam and you suddenly turn the conversation into a dispute? I am *very* sorry that I may appear a chauvinist!" He moderated his voice as he quickly regained control of his emotions. "But that really wasn't my intent. I know only too well how you don't need me financially, but that doesn't mean that I don't want to protect you. What's the matter with that?" Eduardo ended, raising both hands to shoulder height, gesturing with palms flipped upward as he shrugged once, in a very *latino* age-old supplication for answers.

The two had been talking in Gabrielle's office at the time. Gabrielle became alarmed with Eduardo's reaction and tone of voice; he had never spoken like that to her before. Unaware, he continued, now on the offensive. "You're doing exactly what you did the very first time I tried to invite you out. You can't let a single badly phrased thing pass, that you have to turn it into a reason to spout out about what a strong and independent woman you are! You don't have to keep repeating that—it's one of the things that made me fall in love with you—your strength," his tone softening slightly. "Anyway, enough said, I'm going to leave you to your work and your independence. *Au revoir*," he concluded abruptly and turned to leave.

"But Eduardo, I didn't mean…"

The door slammed shut behind him before she could finish her apology.

From their very first date together, they had never had a fight. Gabrielle, again too late, regretted the position she had taken. She knew full well how anguished Eduardo was about not getting a job, but she let her convictions speak louder anyway. And she did know perfectly well that Eduardo wasn't a chauvinist.

Tristan saw the nervous state Eduardo was in, as he left the restaurant in a huff; so he rushed into Gabrielle's office. "What happened, Gabrielle?" Tristan asked, full of concern, eyes agog. "I just saw Eduardo cut out with an expression on his face…"

"Oh Tristan, we had our first fight," Gabrielle replied deflated, "he was just blowing off steam about his difficulties in finding a job here in *London* and then he went and said something about having to be the breadwinner. So of course, I got worked up." She looked down at her hands, twisting her wedding ring around and around.

Tristan came closer and gave her a hug before he released her, admonishing her with a wagging finger, "You have got to stop with this monomania of yours, raising this 'I am woman, I need no man' banner of yours!" Meanwhile, his hands were doing back-flips. "I'm telling you, there are *a lot* of 'independent' women out there who end up all alone, and only because they can't distinguish men's protective instincts from chauvinism. It's just too much 'mind games' for me!" Tristan insisted emphatically, rolling his eyes dramatically.

"I'm gay, and even so, I have the very same protective instinct. And I think Jordan feels the same way too. The fact that women are becoming more and more independent and have more and more prominent roles in society doesn't diminish men's desire to want to protect their family," he concluded with a final wag back and forth of an index finger gesturing a clear 'no'.

"Oh Tristan, now *you're* going to give me a sermon too?" Gabrielle groaned, "on how I lose control when a man starts to harangue *me* on certain subjects!"

"No Gabrielle, it's not that at all! But, understand it as you will," he said vigorously brushing his hands together as if to wash his hands of the matter. "Anyway, let me say just one thing more, if Eduardo weren't worried about being the breadwinner, or even worried about protecting you, then yes, I *would* have a problem with *him*. I would think he was a malingerer and was trying to freeload on you, a woman of success and financially secure. Now, let me get back to my work." Tristan ended his spiel; whirled around, and launched himself, chin leading, through her doorway without a backward glance.

When Eduardo left the restaurant, he had gone to *Hyde Park* to cool down. After three months of job hunting in *London*, it was clear that not having arrived with a job lined up before quitting at *Beauté* had been a big mistake. It would make it just that much more difficult to find a new job in his area. Coming as an expat, he would certainly have had a number of perks. 'Now it's too late,' he thought, 'since I'm here and already left my job too early to find anything else. But I can't quit now,' he admonished himself.

Deep down, Eduardo felt that the interviewers were simply biased against hiring a Brazilian who they must see as arriving in *London* on the coattails of a European spouse. Not to mention that they seemed inordinately unwilling to honestly analyze a candidate's profile and history; preferring the easier tried and true rule of hiring only local experience and nationality, something never commented in the interviews.

From that moment on, Eduardo resolved to focus on searches in his areas by jobs posted by the companies themselves, not bother using agencies or headhunters. That way, he figured, it should increase his chances to talk with someone with a technical level sufficient to recognize and appreciate his qualifications. At the same time, while nothing was happening in his area, he would try for a job doing anything so that he wouldn't have to bring money from *Brazil* but could still help with the household expenses. Not to mention that he really needed to occupy his time with some kind of activity; doing nothing was just too exhausting.

Excited to put his new action plan to work, he caught a bus home to the apartment in *Chelsea* where he and Gabrielle lived and turned on his computer. He started sending his resume to companies in his area found in search engines and company sites, but not headhunters. He searched for jobs in hospitality, customer service, and sales, both retail and wholesale as well. And there he sat working on this new target until almost eight in the evening, forgetting all about making dinner, until he heard the door opening as Gabrielle came in.

"Good evening Brie," he called from his seat in front of the computer, "sorry, but I still haven't started dinner yet."

"Eduardo, my dear, forgive me for my attitude earlier. We sat down to discuss your problems and I ended up making it all about me," she said as she crossed their living room in his direction.

"Don't worry about that Brie," Eduardo replied lightly as he rose to greet her. "I'll go prepare our dinner while you take a bath."

"But of course, I worry, *mon amour*," Gabrielle insisted, as she grabbed Eduardo around the waist when he tried to reach the kitchen.

"Ok, then, let's do this," Eduardo replied gravely, turning and placing both hands on her shoulders as he looked into her eyes. "You really need to stop letting these convictions of yours which don't always fit into certain context speak louder than our love. For example, if you think I'm being a chauvinist for wanting to give the best to you, even if you don't need me in order to have the best, then yes, I am a chauvinist. Brie! Please understand that I love you and my desire is to protect you and give you everything you deserve, even if you can do that by yourself. Is it so hard for you to understand? Does it hurt you so much for the man who loves you to want also to be the one who takes care of you? That makes me very worried and sad. Am I always going to have to take care of what I say to you? To my best friend?" he asked, feeling dismal.

"I'm sorry, my love. I know you're right, and I will try to control myself. I just wanted you to know that I am not used to this," she replied feeling wretched for having hurt him.

"I understand and respect your positions. More than that, I support them. Regardless, I am not the enemy, do you understand?" Eduardo asked softly.

"Yes, of course," she replied, hugging and kissing him.

"So, go take a relaxing bath and I'll prepare something for us to eat," Eduardo smiled.

"Thank you, *mon amour*," Gabrielle smiled back at him.

During dinner, Eduardo told Gabrielle about his change in strategy. She didn't agree, but decided not to voice her opinion, and when he spoke of looking for jobs in any area, she even suggested that he come and work with her at *Romarin*. Eduardo thanked her and explained that he didn't think it would be a very good idea for her to hire her husband; it would look too much like preferential treatment.

Gabrielle agreed, but then proposed that he might include kitchen experience since he had been doing so well at it. She told him that he could say that he worked as a Kitchen Assistant at *Romarin* of *London*, that she would confirm it.

"Excellent idea, my love," Eduardo replied, "but I'll only work outside of my area while nothing in my own area turns up. I'll continue searching. But at any rate, I'll start earning some money."

Gabrielle smiled, "that's right."

Despite the forged experience as a Kitchen Assistant at *Romarin*, his first interview was for a waiter in a restaurant in South Kensington. Eduardo worked there for a few months and began learning the hard life of an immigrant in the *United Kingdom*, but at least the money was coming in. There he met a lot of people of diverse nationalities and a wide variety of professions in their countries of origin: doctors, lawyers, professors, among the many others who were unable to practice their professions in *London*. The reasons that the recruiters gave to those people were always very similar to those Eduardo himself had heard.

Curiously, Eduardo noted that it was very rare to see any native English working in the hospitality sector and when it did happen, they were, in their vast majority, supervisors or managers. Or they were very young Brits who were only there to earn pocket money to pay for their expenses while they studied.

Around the end of June of that year an opening for a kitchen position opened at the restaurant where he worked. Eduardo asked to be allowed to take the test despite his bosses' resistance, his service being very much appreciated where he was. He got the Kitchen Assistant position.

The restaurant's *chef* soon recognized Eduardo's talents in the kitchen and offered him a chance to become one of his *sous chefs*. Eduardo accepted then and there since his salary would increase by at least sixty percent.

Although Eduardo grew more and more enchanted with the kitchen, he never gave up his desire to get back to his own profession for which he had studied and prepared all his life. And so, he was always sending out resumes and every once in a while, he was called for an interview.

Although almost three years had passed before Eduardo was called with an offer to finally work in his own area of expertise at *Tottenham Equity*, he had never lost contact with accounting, always helping Gabrielle review all the numbers of the company and deliveries that her *London* accountant sent to *San-Michel* holding company. And it was because he—through

Gabrielle's initiative that year—included in his resume that he worked as a consultant to *Romarin*, that *Tottenham Equity*'s HR called him to interview at the company's headquarters for a position.

Eduardo had finally come back to his own profession, even though indirectly; yet leaving the restaurant left in him with an inexplicable and curiously hollow sensation, as if something were missing. At that moment, he couldn't admit even to himself how much he had enjoyed that work.

In London, Still

Chapter Eighteen – Welcome to *Romarin* of London

The first person Eduardo saw on his first day at *Tottenham Equity* was Martin Porter waving him over and indicating a place for him to sit. It was still early, and the two were in the HR reception to go through the hiring process, hand in their documents, be shown around and then conducted to the area where they would work.

"Good morning, Martin right?" Eduardo greeted him as he seated himself facing Martin in the indicated chair.

"Yes. Sorry, I've forgotten your name," Martin replied.

"Eduardo Jardim. Were we the only ones called for the positions?" Eduardo asked.

"I believe so, yes. A friend who had told me about this opening said that there were only two positions open, and one was for someone with experience in *Latin America*. I guess that's you," Martin grinned.

"Yes," Eduardo replied, "I'll be the specialist taking care of assets in that region."

"Where in the *UK* are you from?" Martin asked.

"Umm, actually I'm not, I'm Brazilian," Eduardo said smiling.

"Gee, your English is very good. Where are you from originally?" Martin asked, now curious.

"I'm from *Rio de Janeiro*."

"Great!" Martin exclaimed, as he started to give a low appreciative whistle before he remembered where he was, "I hear that it's a very pretty city."

"It's a marvelous city," Eduardo replied.

Martin continued his cheerful inquisition, "and you learned English in *Brazil*?"

"Yes, I studied at a very good language school in my hometown. I also worked at a multinational for many years and there spoke either English or French almost the entire time" Eduardo offered by way of explanation.

"Damn! I only speak English, and that's probably because it's my native language," Martin responded with a droll laugh.

Eduardo caught his self-depreciative English humor.

Martin and Eduardo got along well and would go on to become great friends. Whenever they could, they would go out together for a beer before going home; and since they had the same technical position, each would cover the other in his absence.

Eduardo hadn't had very positive experiences with the English up until then. He found them rather arrogant, with forced and excessive manners. Martin, however, was different, and so he slowly began to change his opinion.

"So, do you have more experience in assets or accounting?" Eduardo asked.

"Neither actually," Martin replied honestly. "I've just gotten my ACA certification and what I've done in accounting is mostly entries and some reconciliations—mostly operational".

"Of course, that makes sense." But what Eduardo really wanted to say was that these companies in this country were real bastards for ignoring the experienced professionals simply because of nationality. 'Perhaps we Brazilians should be more like that, instead of sucking up to foreigners that come to our country,' he thought.

"What about you, a lot of experience, Eduardo?" But before Eduardo could reply, one of the HR manager's assistants came in and called for them to accompany her to hand in their documents.

That first day passed quickly and the two were introduced to all of the company procedures together. They did the entire employee induction process together: introduction to all the company policies, meeting their colleagues, and in the end, they were handed over to their respective managers to begin their work.

At the end of that first day, as Martin was saying good bye to Eduardo, he was invited to a celebration. "Today my wife and I and a couple of friends are going to celebrate my new job. Wouldn't you like to come with us? After all, it's your first day at a new job too," Eduardo proposed.

"I wouldn't be imposing?" Martin asked suddenly shy.

"No, of course not," Eduardo replied magnanimously, patting him on the shoulder.

Martin grinned, "ok, then let's go." And off they went together to their celebratory dinner.

Tristan and Jordan had become very close to Eduardo since he had arrived in *London*. Tristan and Gabrielle, already close friends, grew even closer. And even Jordan got to know Gabrielle much better. In *Paris*, Gabrielle's and Tristan's social interactions were mostly limited to their work place and their encounters at times when Jordan couldn't join in because of their very different work schedules. So, during those next three or four years, from the time they moved to the English metropolis, the four would become inseparable friends.

Everyone had agreed on *Romarin*, where they would toast the conquests and eat great food, while Gabrielle and Tristan seized the opportunity to review their respective teams in real time from the client's point of view, something they did on a fairly regular basis for quality control. Exiting at *Hyde Park Corner Station*, Martin and Eduardo walked along Mount Street toward the restaurant. As it dawned on Martin where they were going, he felt a combination of excitement and anxiety; he knew the bill could well overrun his entire months' entertainment budget.

"Is this commemoration going to be at *Romarin* by any chance?" he asked.

"Yes," Eduardo smiled, "do you know it?"

"Of course, it's only one of the hottest restaurants in *London*. How did you guys manage a reservation there and on such short notice? And better yet, where are we going to get the money to pay the bill?" He raised his eyebrows inquiringly as he looked over at Eduardo while the two continued walking.

Eduardo laughed. "Not to worry, my friend. You are my guest tonight."

"Oh my God, really?" Martin exclaimed excitedly. "First day of work at a cool job and it ends with celebrating at a restaurant of this caliber—and for free? Fantastic!" He shouted, pumping a fist in the air.

Eduardo laughed again and continued walking. He thought to himself, 'good thing I invited Martin' He decided then and there that he liked him—honestly—he was authentic, unpretentious, and enthusiastic about everything.

Martin was a young guy, around twenty-five at the time, perhaps six years or so younger than Eduardo. Everything for him was incredible and exciting. He thrived on new experiences and was game for just about anything. He was diligent, though not terribly intelligent; and he was always cheerful—at least as far as his British sense of humor would allow anyway.

Martin Porter was good looking, more or less the same height as Eduardo, had very light skin that took on a light tan in summer, with blonde hair and grey-blue eyes that changed with the weather. He had an athletic build—being a somewhat avid body-builder—he working out daily after work. Nonetheless, he smoked a lot, and never refused a good beer, or a good meal, for that matter.

The two arrived at the restaurant and once inside, Eduardo was immediately greeted by the hostess. "Good evening, Mr. Jardim. How are you this evening?" she asked brightly pronouncing his name perfectly.

"Good evening Anna. Aren't Mondays your day off?" Eduardo inquired somewhat surprised to see her at her post.

"Yes sir, but Fran asked me to stand in for her today," Anna responded still smiling.

"I see," Eduardo nodded, "but please, don't call me sir. And please, call me Eduardo; I've already asked you before," Eduardo said politely, finding these formalities unnecessary, "and it makes me seem really old," he ribbed gently.

"Alright...Eduardo," she replied, her smile slipping just a slightly as she tried it out.

"Ah, and this is my friend from work, Martin," Eduardo turned and indicated his new friend. "He'll be joining us tonight. Do you think we can find a seat for him?" Eduardo continued in a joking tone.

"Of course, sir; I mean Eduardo," Anna's eyes had widened in surprise at his query, "of course that won't be a problem."

"Is everyone already here?" Eduardo asked as he glanced around the restaurant.

"No Eduardo, you're the first. Please follow me," Anna turned and led them to their table. "Please, be seated. I'll call your waiter so you can order your drinks," she continued.

"Thank you, Anna," Eduardo replied.

"Thank you, Anna," Martin chimed in with a smile. She had barely turned away when Martin, unable to contain his curiosity asked, "are you some kind of secret millionaire Eduardo?"

Eduardo let out a bark of a laugh on hearing that. "Why do you ask, Martin?"

"Ah, come on! First you invite me to a celebration only for me to discover that it is in one of *the* best and most disputed restaurants in *London*, if not all of *Europe*. Then, before I can get over that shock, we arrive at the *Romarin of London* and you tell me I'm your guest. So, I don't have to cough up a single nugget. And now, you're received like some kind of celebrity by the hostess?"

Eduardo grinned, "calm yourself Martin. You'll soon understand everything. And by the way, have I told you that I am an excellent cook?" Eduardo's grin grew even wider, "I really like to cook, and I owe that passion to my beautiful wife..." Eduardo was about to continue as he caught sight of Gabrielle, Tristan, and Jordan moving in their direction. "And speaking of her..." Eduardo stood to greet the three. He hugged and kissed Tristan and Jordan on both cheeks, and finally, he hugged Gabrielle affectionately, kissing her passionately on the mouth, while Martin stood by, his jaw dropping as he recognized her.

"Good evening, my love. How was your first day at work," Gabrielle asked him softly as the kiss ended, looking into Eduardo's eyes with a private smile.

"My first day went very well. I've even made a friend," Eduardo responded, now speaking in English, "everyone, this is Martin. Martin, may I present to you my wife Gabrielle, and my dear friends Tristan and Jordan." He gestured toward each in turn, delighted at Martin's expression.

"Oh, my God!" Martin exclaimed mesmerized, "Man, are you telling me that you are married to *the* beautiful and celebrated Gabrielle Debois? How could you not have prepared me emotionally for this?" he exclaimed theatrically, hand over heart, eyes wide.

Everyone laughed and shook his hand one by one. He lingered slightly over Gabrielle's, perhaps trying to decide whether or not he should try to kiss it before she pulled it gently from his grasp.

"Didn't I tell you that you would come to understand everything?" Eduardo laughed as he pulled out a chair to seat Gabrielle between himself and Martin, while Jordan and Tristan seated themselves in the two remaining chairs.

"My apologies everyone," Martin said, sounding slightly disconcerted, "but I had no idea that Eduardo was married to *the* Gabrielle Debois. Forgive me Gabrielle." He said as he turned in his seat to look directly at her, "but I think you are one of *the* most beautiful women in the world," he said flustered. Embarrassing himself again, he leaned one forearm on the table and steadied himself with his other hand on the back of his chair.

"Please, Martin. Do stop; you exaggerate, surely," Gabrielle said smiling as she covered his hand with hers for only an instant.

Eduardo leaned forward to peer at Martin from the other side of Gabrielle, "hey Martin, are you hitting on my wife?" he deadpanned, raising a single eyebrow.

Martin's cheeks and neck grew ruddy, "who m-m-me? No, wha…what do you mean Eduardo?" He croaked, getting more nervous by the second.

"Oh, don't pay any attention to Eduardo, Martin. He's just teasing, trying make you nervous," Tristan pronounced with the wave of a hand while making a face at Eduardo to break the ice.

"Believe you me, he's succeeding," Martin said, somewhat relieved. At that everyone laughed again; even Martin smiled this time.

"All right," Gabrielle interrupted their antics, back to the business at hand, "shall we order champagne to toast your new jobs?"

"Excellent idea Brie," Eduardo still chuckling replied as he put an arm around her shoulders.

Gabrielle asked their waiter for a bottle of *Veuve Cliquot Vintage.* They all lifted their glasses to Eduardo and Martin for their new jobs several times throughout the evening. The champagne and high spirits of the group made for an extremely enjoyable night for everyone.

Martin got to know a little about each one and how they had ended up in *London* through much laughter, more toasting, and constant interruptions from one another, each of the four adding to everyone else's narrative, none bothering to let the teller finish before butting in. But what most impressed Martin was Eduardo and Gabrielle's love story, and how Eduardo had had the courage to leave everything behind in the name of love.

The five finally left the restaurant at around eleven that night, and on the way out, Eduardo pulled Martin aside, and without lowering his voice asked him to be discrete about his marriage to Gabrielle. He told him how proud he was to have married a woman with such an incredible personality, but that he didn't want to be judged on that alone.

"Not a problem Eduardo. You can count on me; I won't tell a soul," Martin swore. "Anyway, not even I can believe that I shared a meal with *the* Gabrielle Debois—who else would? Man, I have got to tell you: she is even prettier in person than in the newspaper and magazine photos. And she's incredible!" he confided in a loud whisper.

"I know." Eduardo continued his voice slightly burred with emotion and champagne, "she's everything to me. I wouldn't be who I am without her in my life."

"I can imagine, and you're not bad looking yourself. Not that you're my type though." Martin and Eduardo roared with laughter, slapping each other on the back. The others turned and stared, shaking their heads at the two of them.

"I'll see you tomorrow Martin. I hope you enjoyed the evening."

"Did I ever? I don't even think I'll sleep tonight!" Martin said straight-faced, before bursting into laughter again. Eduardo hugged Martin, slapping him on the back, who immediately returned the gesture. And so, the great friendship between the two began and grew steadily from there on.

Martin said goodbye to the others, turned and walked off into the night—tie thrown over one shoulder, his blazer hanging on his finger over the other—toward *Oxford Street* to the subway station. After Martin left, Jordan and Tristan said their goodbyes too, and caught a cab. Gabrielle and Martin hailed the next cab and got in. As soon as Eduardo closed the door, Gabrielle turned and said, "I didn't understand why you asked that of Martin."

"I'm sorry my love, it's just because I don't want the people to look at me as if I'm just the husband of a celebrity," he replied.

"Unfortunately, the fame is unavoidable," Gabrielle, pragmatic as ever, pronounced after a few moment's consideration. "But even so, if you prefer to remain in the shadows...I just think that you should relax a little with respect to it," she concluded with a shrug of her shoulders.

"Perhaps you're right, *mon amour*. I just don't want people to think that I'm with you for any reason other than because of the love I feel for you. I worry that they won't understand that for me, you are so very much more than someone famous," he answered honestly.

"And who cares what other people think Eduardo," she challenged him. "What's important is what *I* think. What *we* think about each other," she cried as she caught his hand and squeezed it between hers, as if her gesture would convince him of the truth in her words.

"You're probably right, Brie," Eduardo conceded slowly, "I'll try to change that. Could you have a little patience with me?" he asked as he enveloped both her hands gently between his own.

"Of course, *mon amour*," she said, and taking advantage of the moment, she went on to propose: "anyway, there is going to be a grand event of the *San-Michel Group* in *Paris*, and I would like it very much if you would go with me. I know you don't like to involve yourself too much in *Romarin's* events, but this time I must insist that you accompany me. May I count on you?" she asked solemnly.

"Of course, Brie," Eduardo replied, unwilling to disappoint her, "I promise I'll go."

"Wonderful!" she replied smiling, delighted at having convinced him to participate a little more in her world.

The two arrived home and before going to bed, took a long hot bath together.

In London, Still

Chapter Nineteen – The Family's Going to Grow

Eduardo accompanied Gabrielle whenever he could on her trips to *Paris*. Nonetheless, Eduardo had only met Pierre on one of these trips, some time after he had married Gabrielle. He had noticed how Pierre looked at his wife from the very first time, and didn't like it. But since he knew Gabrielle and her principals, he never thought to ask her if the guy had more of a personal interest in her; he trusted her implicitly.

It was only a little over a year after they had married, that the couple casually discussed the beginnings of *Romarin* over a glass of wine during a late dinner, when Gabrielle mentioned Pierre's advances at the beginning of the partnership. She also made a point of clarifying to Eduardo that when things started getting physical, Gabrielle made it very clear to Pierre that there would never be anything between them, particularly since they were partners. What she never told Eduardo, however, was about that day Pierre had effectively attacked her in his office. Although a turning point in their relationship; for her it was already water under the bridge; unfortunately, not for Pierre.

Eduardo was aware that he would encounter Pierre at the *San-Michel Group* event but thought nothing more of it; their infrequent encounters would probably always be a few degrees above frigid. Eduardo didn't care, and Gabrielle didn't seem to mind.

The event was to be on Saturday evening, so the two caught the train to *Paris* at *Saint Pancras Station* on Friday so they could enjoy the Parisian evening. The next day they strolled through the familiar city streets, hand in hand always, returning to their hotel late in the afternoon to get ready for the event—a commemoration of the twenty-five years of the *San-Michel Group*, and as *Romarin* was part of the conglomeration, Pierre had thought it would be an excellent excuse to see Gabrielle.

In Eduardo's suit bag Gabrielle had brought a lovely *bustier raffiné* black taffeta dress with a *jupe évasée* long in the back and shorter in the front, showing off her legs wonderfully—to Eduardo's delight—while he was in a black suit of fine English wool and a gray *Gucci* bee tie; they looked good together.

The couple arrived at the Group's event in a taxi and was greeted by a smiling Pierre as they entered the *salon*. Every time he saw the two together, he gritted his teeth and felt a burning in the pit of his stomach, but he never let anything transpire, or so he thought. This obsessive passion he had for Gabrielle was almost impossible to endure and would be even less so should anyone has noticed.

"Gabrielle, *ma chérie*, you are more beautiful each day that passes," Pierre murmured as he hugged her, glancing over her shoulder through narrowed eyes at Eduardo who watched him closed-faced.

"Stop that, Pierre," Gabrielle said quietly but firmly into his ear, equally discrete. When Pierre still hadn't released her after a few moments, she turned aside so that he had no choice but to release her. She was careful not to grimace as she caught the look in Eduardo's eye.

"Eduardo, so how is your life as a cook in *London*?" Pierre turned with an undeniably disdainful smile for Eduardo as he shook his hand. "Are you adapting well to your new condition?" he asked rather smugly.

"And what condition might that be Pierre? All professions and paid activities are honorable," Eduardo barely acknowledging the dig and smirk with a closed-lip smile; he squeezed the older man's hand in his just a little too tightly and a little too long as he leaned in, releasing his hand only when Pierre gasped and took a single step back.

"My apologies, *mon cher*. I did not intend any offense," Pierre replied pulling his hand back, his smile slipping slightly as he discretely rubbed his hand with the other behind his back.

"Oh, but you haven't offended me...*mon cher*," Eduardo gave him a wolfish grin, "but not to worry, I am no longer working as a cook. I am back in the financial sector again."

"Ah, but that is wonderful news, *n'est-ce pas?*" Pierre responded already disinterested, his hand still aching from the crushing handshake. He turned back toward Gabrielle and was about to speak when she interrupted him, "excuse me Pierre, but we must circulate. And after all, you too must see to all your other guests." Eduardo took her arm and they both walked toward some people she wanted to introduce Eduardo to. As they were moving slowly through the crowd, Eduardo murmured in her ear that he didn't want to stay very long at the party, she laughed relieved, and immediately agreed. "How about going to *Le Queen* to dance," Gabrielle suggested with a twinkle in her eye.

"Great idea," Eduardo agreed with his brightest smile since the evening had begun, "when do you want to go?"

"How about right now?" she grinned, "we can eat something and go directly from there."

"Perfect, Brie. The sooner we leave the better. I don't like the way that partner of yours is always checking you out," he said quietly as he scanned the people around them.

"Don't worry about Pierre, *mon amour"*, she said, her mouth not far from his ear. "He would be the last man on the face of the earth for me to get involved with," she said a little louder. As soon as the words were out of her mouth Eduardo saw Pierre passing just behind her, but he couldn't be sure whether or not he had heard her.

"*Shhhhh*, do you think he heard you, Brie?" Eduardo asked, not realizing that he had.

"Honestly! That is of absolutely no importance," Gabrielle said firmly, rolling her eyes and shrugging one elegant bare shoulder as she glanced at Pierre's receding back. "*Mon amour*, I'm going to the *toilettes* and then we can leave, ok?"

"Fine Brie, I'll be right here waiting for you," Eduardo replied as he let go of her hand.

Gabrielle weaved her way through the crowd that had formed dozens of small groups of grey and black attired somber business people, all celebrating quietly staid with only an occasional laugh or raised voice to be heard above the tinkling of toasting drinking glasses as she moved toward the tiny restroom.

Though small, the *Ladies Room* was beautifully appointed. Silk *gris moiré* covered walls, matching sink and dressing table of *Calacatta* marble with its delicate grey veins running through a soft white background, and what looked to be a set of 19th Century silver leaf *Louis Philippe* mirrors hanging in the opposing alcoves, multiplying images to infinity. The toilet was opposite the entry, enclosed discretely behind the watered silk-covered walls and an identically upholstered door, distinguished only by its button tufting, replicated only in the single backless seat placed in the dressing table alcove.

She used the toilet, washed and dried her hands, then looked down, opening her evening bag to take out her *maquillage*. Gabrielle took out her lipstick twisting it open and looked up into the mirror over the sink when stunned; she caught sight of Pierre standing behind her in the recessed alcove of the dressing table. Dismayed, she turned and demanded, "what are you doing in here Pierre? Are you insane?"

"No Gabrielle, I just wanted to have a moment in private with you, away from that guard dog of a husband of yours. He never leaves you alone for a second! So, I followed you in here," he ended with a slight shrug and a smirk, his voice deceptively mild.

"But this is absolutely unacceptable and completely beyond the pale Pierre—even for you!" Gabrielle's voice growing more shrill and louder as she grew more and more indignant, "Please *do not* try to do what you attempted the last time we were alone!" she ended forcefully, her eyes dark and flashing with anger. Her lipstick, forgotten on the marble sink vanity rolled into the sink unnoticed, leaving a garish smear behind as it rolled to the drain and stopped.

"You have no need to worry about that," Pierre said in the same soft voice with a dismissive wave of a hand. "So, not even if I were the last man on the planet, would you have me? Don't you think that is just a little too cruel to say about me, even for you Gabrielle?" his voice taking on a disagreeable whine.

"Pierre, *c'est précisément* how I feel. Now please leave, my husband is waiting for me outside and if I delay, he will come looking for me," she said emphatically.

"Of course, *ma chérie*, but we shall continue this conversation another day," Pierre oozed cordiality, unconcerned with her none too discrete threat or even her anger, which he short-sightedly found irresistibly charming.

"I don't know about that, Pierre," she replied calmer now that he had moved slightly to the side to let her pass. "Thank you for

232

the invitation," she said formally and only a curt nod without offering her hand, much less her cheek, she left the *toilettes* hastily to find Eduardo without a backward glance.

Once more she said nothing to Eduardo about what had happened in that awkward encounter. "There you are. Let's go, *mon amour*. I'm ready," she said rather breathlessly when she finally found him in the same place where he had said he would be.

"*Nossa!* You took a long time, Brie. What happened?" he replied, taking her hand in his and moving toward the exit.

"It was nothing, my love. I just met Linda in the *toilettes* and we chatted a little. That's all," she replied nonchalantly and smiled at him.

The two left the event, had a leisurely dinner at a nearby restaurant and moved on much later to the *Le Queen Nightclub* right next to the *Champs-Élysées*. When they arrived, the line was enormous, but it didn't even take five minutes before one of the bouncers recognized Gabrielle.

"*Mademoiselle* Debois," he enquired politely in recognition.

"*Monsieur*, please! I'm a married woman now," she said in a serious voice while grinning widely at the uniformed man who towered over her and was twice Eduardo's width, at least. She had known him since her schoolgirl days when she and her friends would try to sneak past him unnoticed. He would occasionally let them in for a while, but would always keep a close eye on them, promptly kicking them out if they tried to order drinks or were being accosted.

"Oh, I'm so sorry *Madame* Debois," the bouncer corrected himself, his white teeth and bald head gleaming under the streetlights, "you don't need to wait in this line. Please, follow me." He spoke rather mildly for such an imposing figure. Gabrielle and Eduardo left the back of the line and went through the front doors of the nightclub. They danced and had fun all night, returning to the hotel when the dawn was almost breaking over *Paris*. They slept until late into Sunday and brunched around two in the afternoon. They had a leisurely meal, rested a little more, got dressed, and then travelling the reverse route by train back to *London*.

Their workweek began the next day in *London,* with the two of them back at their routines. Eduardo enjoyed his new job very much and after a while, he began travelling to *Brazil* and other countries in the region to visit the company's local operations.

The years passed with everything in perfect harmony between the couple. Both Eduardo and Gabrielle were very happy. Whenever they could, they would travel within *Europe* during extended weekends or holidays, but when they could both take longer vacations at the same time; they would journey to countries on other continents.

They visited *China, India, Madeira Island, Australia, New Zeland, Mauritius Island, the Philippines* and *Thailand* among other countries and islands especially where they could enjoy the warm weather. And they even returned to *Rio* a few times. These trips were always filled with fascinating sights, intriguing if not exciting foods and flavors, and they nearly always took time and delighted in going to as many beaches as possible, each one so different from the ones before. They snorkeled often, and learned scuba diving in *Cebu,* then tried out parasailing in *Boracay,* while in the *Philippines*. They surfed at nearly every Australian beach from *New South Wales* to *Queensland* one year. Then the very next year they went white water rafting in *New Zealand,* and although Gabrielle put her foot down when it came to shark cage diving, she did enjoy the sea kayaking. They thrilled at kitesurfing on *Mauritius Island.*

They even sailed the *Koh Samui* coastline in *Thailand* on a private charter where Eduardo delighted everyone one day by barbequing Brazilian-style the catch of the day.

When they were in *London*, they were always together with Martin, Tristan and Jordan. The five were great friends and one of their favorite pastimes was trying out any restaurant, bar, pub, deli or café that caught their fancy in and around *London*. Once in a while Martin would bring along a girl, but they never lasted more than a month. He loved the romance of the chase, but once the novelty started to wear off, he was soon glancing around for a new conquest.

"You have to try and settle down Martin," Gabrielle said one time when he was between girlfriends and had showed up alone. "You really should try to date someone a little more seriously."

"Ah, I don't know, Gabrielle," he said with a slow mischievous grin. "There are just so many, I just can't choose!" He replied lazily sipping his beer, not even pretending to take her suggestion seriously.

"You are such a Casanova," Gabrielle exclaimed with a huff, "you're going to end up all alone!" They all laughed at Martin's antics when he stuck out his tongue at Gabrielle then quickly straightened, as a pretty blonde passed behind Gabrielle's chair and glanced his way with just the slightest of smiles. Even Gabrielle laughed and shook her head in mock despair when he stood and followed the blond to her table to get her number.

Nearly seven years passed before Gabrielle came home with understandably exciting news for Eduardo. She was just a little apprehensive, not quite sure what his reaction might be. "Eduardo, I have something to tell you," she said one night, placing her hands over his then patting the bed, indicating for him to sit on the bed beside her.

"What is it Brie, what's going on?" Eduardo asked anxiously, immediately thinking of their friends. "Did something happen to Tristan or Jordan?" He hadn't seen either since dinner on the previous Saturday at the then newly inaugurated *Core* by Clare Smyth.

She was the first female chef in the *UK* to run a restaurant with three *Michelin* stars—*Restaurant Gordon Ramsey*—and she had just opened her first solo restaurant. Gabrielle held her in the highest regard, an example for all female chefs, so the five had gone to experience the *Core*. "No, no, it has nothing to do with the company or our friends. It's us." She was so mysterious; Eduardo grew distressed as tiny beads of sweat formed on his forehead. "What's all this suspense," he finally cried out, giving her a slight shake with one hand as if to get her talking.

She took a deep breath. "Ok, I'll go straight to the point. You are going…"

He couldn't contain himself anymore and interrupted her, "What? What?" He was agonizing now, horrible images passing through his head.

"You are going to be a daddy, *mon amour*," she said so softly he almost missed it in his angst.

Eduardo froze. He was in shock. The color drained from his face and he remained immobile, staring at her, mouth hanging open.

Slowly, his mouth started to move, but no words came out, until finally, "wha…what? Who? How? When?" He babbled on, making no sense whatsoever to Gabrielle. Then, taking several deep breaths, he seemed to collect his thoughts; managing to stand, he embraced Gabrielle, wrapping his arms around her and pulling her up from the bed. "I can't believe it!" He laughed and cried at the same time, spinning her around, her feet only inches off the floor. "*Mon amour*, this is the best news that you could have *ever* given me!"

"Goodness, for a moment there I thought you didn't want it," she laughed happily relieved.

"Are you crazy Brie?" He shouted, tears of happiness running down his cheeks, "me—a father; and with the most beautiful woman in the world?" He couldn't contain his joy. In truth, he was actually even more excited about the pregnancy than Gabrielle herself.

"When did you find out, *mon amour*?" he asked, still not calm enough to sit or wipe the silly grin off his face.

"I received confirmation today. My period was late and so I decided to take that pharmacy test, but I didn't want to say anything to you until I got confirmation from a laboratory," she replied calmly.

"*Ai, meu Deus*! What a happy, happy day this is!" Eduardo kept repeating as he laughed and cried and paced and spun about again and again.

"I'm also happy, my love," Gabrielle said as she sat calmly, hands folded in her lap with a *Madonna* smile on her lips as she watched him from the bed. And ever the practical one, she continued, "and now we should think about getting a larger apartment."

"Of course, of course," Eduardo replied, finally stopping, sitting beside her. "We can buy one. I have the money from my savings and with the money from the sale of the house in *Urca* when the real estate market in *Brazil* was a seller's market.

Well, those savings grew significantly. I just have to see what the best way to transfer the money here will be."

"Hmmm, buy one," Gabrielle said almost to herself, "I had almost already forgotten about that. Soon after I moved to *London*, I had told myself that this apartment would only be temporary; so that we could live near the restaurant. But so many things happened that I ended up forgetting all about it. I have some savings too, and also part of the money from the sale of *grand-mère* Millie's property that I had separated for precisely this purpose."

"So, it's decided then," Eduardo concluded, "we'll buy something with two bedrooms wherever you want."

Eduardo and Gabrielle were thrilled with the changes. Not just the move to a new apartment, but the changes in their life, as a growing family. It was the beginning of a new phase for the couple. They visited all the available apartments near *Romarin* that they thought they might like. At the same time, Gabrielle had started visiting shops for baby articles to see what she would want to buy for their baby boy—or girl.

By the time they visited the apartment on *Davies Street* Gabrielle was already three months pregnant. "This is the one, *mon amour*!" Gabrielle declared passionately. "This is the home where I want us to raise our daughter," she said as they finished seeing the apartment and had returned to the living room.

They had found out the baby's sex in Gabrielle's last ultrasound. Eduardo was thrilled when he discovered that it would be a girl. And when Gabrielle, still lying on the examining table said that she wanted to name her Julia, he cried; unable to contain his tears of joy in front of the obstetrician who kindly turned her eyes to the knobs and dials of her machine, giving them a moment.

"Isn't it too big Brie?" Eduardo asked.

"A big living room will be good for Julia to run around and play," Gabrielle responded. Her smile illuminated her entire face. She had never been more beautiful Eduardo thought than at that moment.

"All right then, my love. This is the one," Eduardo concurred, imagining their little girl playing as he looked around that huge empty space.

They sent a proposal to the owner the next day and unsurprisingly, it was accepted almost instantaneously. Their down payment was forty percent of the property value and the rest would be financed in fifteen years—a rarity even for that neighborhood.

"But we're going to try to amortize the last payments first in order to decrease the duration of our loan," Eduardo suggested when they signed the agreement.

"Of course, *mon amour*, Gabrielle agreed, but let's not concern ourselves about that just now. After all, we will soon have our baby girl, and must prepare everything for her arrival."

The apartment was impeccable and required very little by way of renovations, only a few touches here and there, except for the kitchen, which was quickly configured to Gabrielle's very specific specs. And of course, the baby's room was painted, wallpapered, furniture delivered; everything perfect, awaiting only the arrival of the new baby, and perhaps just a few more toys and dresses.

The couple moved in almost immediately and decided that any other renovations or changes could be done while they were living in the apartment. That way they could be released from the expense of the rent for the *Chelsea* flat.

On the day of the move Gabrielle and Eduardo toasted the event with an excellent wine and a dinner made especially by Gabrielle in her new professional kitchen. It had been a long time since Eduardo had allowed her into their home kitchen to cook for them.

"To us and our Julia, my love," Eduardo proposed as he raised his glass.

"To our new life," Gabrielle exclaimed, tired but happy; as she raised her glass to her beloved husband, "I love you Eduardo."

"I love you more, Brie," Eduardo replied with a tender smile before he drank.

The only other new thing they had bought for the apartment and which had arrived on the day of the move was the new mattress. It was hard put to the test that night.

In London, Still

Chapter Twenty – One Day, Two Incidents

The mini renovation of the *Mayfair* apartment was very quick. Gabrielle and Eduardo enjoyed buying every single item to furnish Julia's bedroom and her complete layette including outfits and accessories. They went to several stores to personally choose each tiny detail related to their daughter, always together.

Ever since the press had caught word, there was a frenzy of candid photos or notes about Gabrielle's pregnancy in the news. Even Eduardo gave an interview about their expectations of his daughter Julia's arrival. He was rather reluctant, but since he had promised his wife some years ago that he would try to be more present in her public life, he ended up giving in, and talked to the reporter. The interview took place during the fifth month of Gabrielle's pregnancy. She was particularly pleased with the article, a declaration of Eduardo's love.

Gabrielle had already entered the seventh month of her pregnancy when she decided to take a final auditing trip to the restaurant in *Paris* before the baby was born. She left on a Thursday morning and would be back late Saturday afternoon.

Gabrielle woke up early, got dressed in the dark and didn't even have breakfast so that she wouldn't miss the first *Eurostar to Gare du Nord, Paris*. Before she left, she woke Eduardo up with a kiss. "Good morning, *mon amour*," she said softly into his ear, followed by a light kiss on the lips.

"Good morning, Brie. Are you going already?" Eduardo asked, stretching and grabbing Brie before she could stand up, pulling her close for a more lingering kiss.

"Yes" she laughed, trying to pull away. "Let me go, I have to run, otherwise I'll miss my train. Sorry to have to rush off like this."

"Not a problem *mon amour,"* he replied. Sitting up, he hugged his wife, "have a good trip."

"Thank you. I'll see you on Saturday night. I love you," she said softly.

"I love you too," Eduardo replied resting his head against her huge belly for a moment, whispering "I love you too Julia. Don't be jealous." He gave Gabrielle another squeeze before releasing her. Gabrielle jumped up, smiling she turned and gave Eduardo a final kiss. And with that, she was out the door and on her way in the near dark of *London's* early morning hours.

The train ride went calmly, and Gabrielle went directly to *Romarin* of *Paris* with her overnight bag rolling along behind her on the sidewalk as she got out of the taxi where she was greeted by Antoine. She had decided to check into her hotel at the end of the day, so as not to lose any time, hoping she might even catch an earlier train back and enjoy a late afternoon with Eduardo showing off the exquisite little dresses she had secretly ordered and was picking up tomorrow morning at the specialty baby shop down the road. She smiled at the thought of his expression of delight when he saw the extravagant little French dresses for their English baby.

"Good morning Gabrielle," Antoine greeted her with his gentle smile and bright eyes as he gave her a kiss on each cheek. He took her little bag in one hand and locked his other arm through hers, guiding her into *Romarin.*

"Good morning, Antoine," she smiled, basking in the special care and attention she was receiving from everyone. Gabrielle entered the restaurant, greeting everyone there with her customary bright "good morning," and proceeded to go over the organization of the salon and the kitchen before finally settling into to her old office, now shared by Antoine and Valentin. She had asked the two to accompany her there and they all took their seats before she began the first meeting of the day.

"Well my friends, as you can see for yourselves, I'm already at that stage of my pregnancy when I soon won't be able to travel anymore," she began, smiling and spreading her hands over her very pregnant tummy, "but I was determined to come this week to take a final look at the *maison* and everyone's work before Julia arrives. And I am very pleased with the work that you've both been doing. Everything is impeccable, and that gives me peace of mind for my absence from *Paris,* which will be at least four months as of this week."

"Thank you so much Gabrielle for your feedback," Valentin replied. "Your recognition of our hard work makes us even more motivated to continue our best efforts. Your generous praise encourages us all," he concluded with a smile on his normally somber face.

"And I make Valentin's words my own Gabrielle," Antoine chimed in, "we're all very happy to be part of your team. Not to mention that, aside from being a great chef, you are also one of the few celebrities in our business that doesn't need a TV program to keep the media spotlight on you," he enthused, his open face reflecting his boyish admiration for his boss.

"Oh, don't be so silly, Antoine," Gabrielle laughed, just a little embarrassed. "I care nothing for all the spotlights. But I do thank you both for your recognition of my own efforts," she said by way of thanks. "Anyway, I've been thinking that it's time to start testing some new dishes and offer some new experiences to our clients. Unfortunately, I won't have a lot of time to dedicate myself to this right now; at least until after the birth of baby Julia. So, since you are my oldest pupil Antoine, I would like very much if you were to present me with a few of your creations in *London*. What do you think?"

Antoine's eyes widened, his mouth making an "O" of surprise. "Are you serious?" He whispered in disbelief, his eyes swimming with emotion.

"Very! Any dishes approved will carry your signature," Gabrielle responded seriously.

"Gosh Gabrielle, I don't know what to say!" Antoine replied in earnest.

"Then say nothing at all; just do your best to maintain the excellent quality that we have served our clients. And when we launch the new dishes, let's make a grand event and I am going to want you by my side" Gabrielle replied.

"Wow! This is a dream come true," Antoine murmured, already lost in thought.

"All hands on deck then!" Gabrielle finalized, slapping the table with both hands, knowing that she was doing the right thing, very pleased with herself and her pupil.

Valentin patted Antoine on the shoulder as he brought his arm around him and gave him a hug, congratulating him on his continued good fortune as the two left Gabrielle in the office to herself. There she remained until one in the afternoon, by which time the restaurant was already packed for lunch. She returned to the kitchen to review station coordination and accompany the flow of dishes. Satisfied, Gabrielle went out to the *salon* to greet clients and compliment the employees, especially those who had shown improvement since her last visit. The clients were delighted to see Gabrielle's glowing beauty at this stage of her pregnancy. And there she remained, circulating in the *salon* until the restaurant was almost empty.

Finally returning to the kitchen, Gabrielle ate with the entire crew, returning immediately to her old office to work some more. In no time, the restaurant was almost empty except for her. Both the kitchen crew and the *salon* team had gone out for their break after lunch.

Antoine was the last to leave, dropping by her office on his way out. "Everyone has already left for the afternoon break. Do you mind being here by yourself?" Antoine anticipated, considerate of her state.

"Of course not, Antoine," Gabrielle replied with a laugh, "I'm pregnant, not sick. Go on you, I'll be fine. In a little while you'll all be back."

"Ok, but I can stay if you need me for anything," Antoine offered.

"Antoine, please; go and take your break," she insisted.

"Ok, I'll see you later. I'll be back by six," he promised turning to close the door.

"Fine, *a bientôt*," she replied automatically, her attention already settling again on the computer screen in front of her.

Antoine closed the office door softly, leaving Gabrielle alone in the restaurant, but as he was leaving he saw Pierre arriving.

"Good afternoon *M.* Pierre", Antoine called out as he held the door of the restaurant open for him.

"Good afternoon Antoine," Pierre responded as he came around his car, "I'm fine. Are you closing for the afternoon break?"

"Yes, we'll be back at six," he responded politely as Pierre strut toward him.

"And Gabrielle, has she gone back to her hotel?" Pierre inquired, pausing in the doorway where Antoine still held the door open for him.

"Not yet, *Monsieur*. She said that she would stay and work a little longer."

"Excellent," Pierre replied and continued his forward trajectory, entering the restaurant. "Then I've come to the right place. You don't mind that I come in to have a brief word with her?" He asked with half a smile, no response expected.

Antoine was in fact, a little concerned about letting Pierre come in. He had heard the gossip about his being in love with Gabrielle, but he couldn't think fast enough of even a single excuse to stop the owner of the restaurant from going in.

"Of course not, sir," he responded after a moment's hesitation, "let me accompany you to the office," he continued politely, moving to let the door close behind him.

"That won't be necessary, *cher Monsieur le Cook*. I know the way," Pierre replied sardonically with a dismissive wave of his hand, making it abundantly clear that Antoine was dismissed.

"As you wish, *M.* Pierre, good bye then," Antoine said, noting a yeasty smell of whiskey as Pierre passed by. Nonetheless, he let him go alone, reluctantly closing the door behind himself. He walked pensively toward *Champs-Élysées*. Arriving in front of the stairwell of the *George V Metrô* entrance, Antoine stopped before descending. He stood there for quite a while at the top of the stairs—a staid obstacle to the flux people moving around him, some grumbling—until finally, he decided that it would have been better had he stayed close by, just in case Pierre wanted to try something on, and with Gabrielle in such a delicate state, he thought. So, he turned around and went back the way he had come, moving faster this time, back toward *Romarin,* and Gabrielle. The hair on the back of his neck standing on end seemed to forebode something not quite right.

Pierre walked slowly through the *salon*, touching an occasional chair back on either side, as if to steady himself, or perhaps just to confirm ownership. He sauntered in, heels tapping out an erratic tattoo as he moved toward the back of the kitchen to Gabrielle's office. Knocking only once, he twisted the knob open before he even heard an answer.

"Come in Antoine," Gabrielle called out. "Did you forget some…" she glanced up from the monitor, seeing that it was Pierre standing in the doorway. "Pierre?! What are you doing here? How did you get in," she asked surprised, leaning back in her chair.

"And a good afternoon to you too Gabrielle," Pierre satirized, "how nice to see that you are happy to see me."

"I do apologize, Pierre. I hadn't been expecting to see you here. After all, hadn't we scheduled our meeting for tomorrow morning?" Gabrielle replied smoothly, ignoring his affront.

"Ah yes, that is true *ma chérie*, but I was passing by and stopped to see if you were still here," he replied with a smirk, his *esses* sounding slightly sibilant. The liquid courage he had imbibed at lunch was giving him courage but might have been just a bit too much after all, he thought. But then, he wouldn't have risked stopping by to see her otherwise, 'this was the only way', his bleary mind concluded.

That's when Gabrielle realized the drunken state Pierre was in, sowing seeds of concern about his true intentions. She wished that she hadn't let Antoine go and leave her alone with him.

"Is there a problem, Pierre?" She asked.

"Nooooo, no problem at all Gabrielle," he slurred slightly, leaning against the doorjamb and slipping slightly before stopping himself by grabbing at, and missing the doorknob. The door banged loudly against the wall.

Gabrielle fearing he might hurt himself in the state he was in, stood and demanded, "please, sit down Pierre. You're drunk, for the love of God! Why would you want to show up here in this state?" She navigated around the desk, her belly making for a rather tight squeeze. She took him by an arm and tried to help him to sit in one of the chairs facing the desk.

"I'm very sorry, *Mlle*. Gabrielle, I wasn't aware of any rule saying that the owner can't show up after a few drinks," he replied belligerently, yanking his arm from her grip, sliding into the chair, perfectly demonstrating *Newton's Third Law of Motion.*

"Pierre, you don't look well to me. Let me make you a cup of coffee," she offered.

"Coffee," he blustered. "I don't want your damn coffee. I want you. You!" he shouted suddenly jumping up from the chair as Gabrielle tried to leave the office to go to the kitchen. He grabbed her arm and yanked her back around and toward him.

"What is this Pierre; what do you think you're doing? Please, let go of my arm," she said trying desperately to remain calm, and at the same time, get away from him.

He not only refused to let go, he grabbed her other arm and forced himself on her, trapping her against the wall with his entire body, pressing himself painfully against her breasts and belly. He tried to kiss her as she jerked her head away, avoiding his lips and sour breath; but she couldn't get him to release her arms. His grip on her was too tight.

"You are even more beautiful pregnant," he mumbled huskily into her ear. "This child should be mine! You should be mine," he shouted, shaking her with each word as he stepped slightly away to look her in the eyes; his voice cracking with fury.

"Stop it Pierre! You are out of your mind!" Gabrielle cried as she continued to struggle to get away from his grip; away from him.

"Yes," he cried anguished, "I'm out of my mind, and it's all your fault! You did this to me," he whined, spittle flying, as she desperately turned her face, fighting to avoid him and break loose. "Until when did you think I could support this situation? You—married to some other man, not me," he blubbered. Shaking her violently with each word, "you—should—be—mine! Mine! Do—you—understand?" he screeched, his face turning a deep crimson, the vein in his temple throbbing violently.

That last bout of fury seemed to exhaust him and for an instant he lessened his grip. Gabrielle sensing this, managed to push violently against his shoulders and step away from the wall, backed now against the table while Pierre stood between her and the door.

"I tried to be reasonable about all this, but I just can't do it anymore, I'm sick of it! And seeing you with that idiot at MY company's party just made me furious," he rant hoarsely, almost to himself.

"You really are a stupid chauvinist, aren't you Pierre? This is all because the great Pierre San-Michel can't have the woman he wants?" She hissed, furiously.

"Slut! Ungrateful bitch!" he screamed, in an unthinking instant, he lashed out with his hand. He hit Gabrielle with such force that she spun around losing her balance; as she fell, her head hit the edge of the table and she lay crumpled, immobile, curled between the desk and the broken overturned chair.

Hearing screaming as he opened the restaurant door, Antoine flew past the *salon* and into the office in time to watch helplessly horrified, Gabrielle falling belly-first onto the overturned chair, and then hit the floor. Two stains of pooling blood widened on the floor, one spreading through her hair, the other from between her legs.

"What have you done Pierre?" Antoine cried, dropping to his knees beside Gabrielle, lifting her head to his lap, trying to stem the flow of blood with his hands. Already the bright red imprint of Pierre's hand on her chalky cheek condemned him.

"Wha...what? Me...I didn't mean..." Pierre mumbled. Befuddled, he stood staring at Gabrielle's fallen body; unwilling to connect that dreadful sight with what he had done, he turned and fled. "I'm sorry. I'm sorry. Please, I didn't mean to..." he whimpered as he raced through the restaurant, knocking over chairs before stumbling out the door.

"Pierre, wait! We need to take her to the hospital!" Antoine yelled to Pierre's receding back, though never taking his eyes from Gabrielle's face. All he heard was the scrapes of scrambling feet, the front door slamming shut and then, silence. Antoine reached over grabbing the telephone that had fallen from the table, dialed 15 for SAMU, then 112 for the police. He told them what had happened and that Pierre had run away; probably driving off drunk in his car. He described the black Bentley Continental GT, what he remembered of the license plate, and the drunken fugitive.

Putting the phone down, he pulled off his sweater, tucking it tenderly under Gabrielle's head, then jumped up and ran into the kitchen where he grabbed half a dozen clean towels from the rack and raced back to try and staunch the flow of blood from Gabrielle's head. He had followed the emergency operator's instructions and checked for a pulse at her throat, which he reported seemed weak, but that she remained unconscious and unmoving. He waited alone for the ambulance to arrive, repeating over and over: "please, please hold on Gabrielle. The ambulance is coming soon," that became his mantra all the while he sat there, her blood slowly soaking into the towels.

Antoine was in such a state of shock that he never even remembered to call Eduardo or anyone else; he just waited, holding her, repeating his mantra, until help finally arrived.

While Antoine remained with Gabrielle, Pierre fled the restaurant and got into his car driving down the *Champs-Élysée* at high speed, drivers and pedestrians fled from his path, fearful for their lives. Less than two minutes had passed since his wild flight began; police sirens screamed their warnings as several police vehicles, lights flashing, followed the suspect in high speed pursuit, trying to cut him off. Reaching the *Place de la Concorde*, Pierre abruptly spun the steering wheel, desperate to turn onto the *Pont de la Concorde*. Losing his grip, hands flailing, he unwittingly hit the gas pedal with both feet trying to brake. His car—spinning out of control, engine whining—crashed head first through the protection rail, took flight in a shallow arc off the bridge, plummeting into the River *Seine*. Pierre died instantaneously; crushed as he hit the water. His car slowly drifted then finally sank into the dark smooth waters of the *Seine* as the officers who had given chase stopped to watch, blocked the bridge, called in the death, and requested recovery of the body and vehicle in a matter of seconds, then finally, turned their sirens off.

Though it seemed an eternity to Antoine, the ambulance arrived in little more than five minutes at *Romarin*. He watched their movements mutely, reminded of his own precise movements when he was *Poissonier*; long before he was *Sous Chef* or, thanks to Gabrielle, *Chef*—methodical—neat—swift.

His mind wandered to better times, trying to protect him from the horror, as he rode beside Gabrielle in the ambulance racing toward the hospital.

"I said: are you family?" the first responder seated beside him in the ambulance repeated again, a little louder.

Suddenly, coming out of his daze, Antoine realized that he hadn't called Eduardo. "Ah *mon Dieu*, I must call her husband. I'm sorry, I'm not. I work at the restaurant. I'm going to call her husband now," Antoine replied, pulling his cell phone from his pocket, smearing it with her blood that was still drying on his hands and clothes. Tears finally welled in his eyes as the first responder handed him some paper towels to clean it off with, and told him grimly, "ok, but please, tell him to get to the hospital as fast as possible. Her pulse is very weak. She's still losing blood from her womb, and I can't hear the baby's heartbeat."

Flipping through his contacts, Antoine realized that he didn't even have Eduardo's number, so he called Tristan instead.

Tristan had been surprisingly stalwart as he repeated Antoine's message to Eduardo. He spoke in slow, clear French, repeating himself in English, just to be sure. Though his entire body trembled as he put on his coat after hanging up, his voice was firm, resolute even, as he left instructions with his Number Two at *Romarin of London*.

Eduardo was in a state of shock by the time he finished talking to Tristan. As though moving under water, he stood up from his desk, turned and walked toward Martin's, his face completely drained of blood. "Gabrielle has had an accident Martin," he said, his voice lifeless.

"What? What are you talking about Eduardo?" Startled, Martin jumped up, afraid of hearing a confirmation, he steadied his friend.

"Please, could you go with me to the station? I need to catch the train to *Paris*, now," Eduardo replied, ignoring his question. "Gabrielle is being taken to hospital."

The two ran out of the office and flagged down the first cab that came into sight to take them to the train station. "*Saint Pancras Station*, as fast as you can, please; this is an emergency," Martin directed the driver as Eduardo leaped into the back seat and he followed close behind. The car sped off before he had quite closed the door behind him.

Eduardo told him what had happened on the way. Twenty-five minutes later, the taxi was dropping them as close to the main entrance of the busy station as possible.

"Do you want me to go with you, Eduardo," Martin asked tentatively, not wanting to intrude but not wanting to abandon his friend either.

"I don't want you to go out of your way Martin," Eduardo responded, falling back on childhood drilling in proper manners by *Dona* Julia, still in a state of shock. "Tristan is coming to meet me here at the station."

"Think nothing of it, Eduardo. I'll call the office and explain the situation. Tomorrow I can catch the first train back," he replied, brushing off Eduardo's feeble protest as he followed him in.

Eduardo put his arm around Martin's shoulders as they entered the station, "thank you, my friend. Then I gladly accept your offer."

Eduardo and his companions only managed to catch the train scheduled for six that evening. The three had a quick meal at the station while they waited for their train; the trip was mostly in silence. Arriving in *Paris* around nine that evening, they jumped off the train, ran to the taxi stand, and were off to the hospital before most of the other passengers had even left the train. Eduardo tried calling Antoine again from the taxi, having tried unsuccessfully from the train several times.

"Hello Antoine, this is Eduardo. We're already leaving *Gare du Nord* and on our way to the hospital. How are Gabrielle and Julia?" Eduardo asked when the connection finally went through. "Please, give me some good news," he pleaded.

"I'm sorry Eduardo, but since I'm not family, they won't tell me anything. I can't get any update on their status since the ambulance ride," Antoine replied woefully.

"What about her mother, *Madam* Vivien?" Eduardo asked.

"Oh, I did manage to contact her just a while ago. She's on her way here too," Antoine answered quickly, heartened to finally be able to deliver some positive news.

"Great! We should be arriving at the hospital in a few minutes, see you then," Eduardo responded.

"Ok, I'll be waiting for all of you inside the front entrance," Antoine replied before ending the connection.

The trio arrived in front of the hospital just slightly before nine-thirty and as they were getting out of the taxi, Eduardo saw his mother-in-law getting out of the car in front of them. "*Madam*

Vivien," Eduardo called out as he moved quickly in her direction, leaving the others to follow. The men greeted her somberly as the group moved together toward the reception where Antoine stood waiting.

News reporters loitered in front of the hospital. The news of Pierre San-Michel's wild car chase ending in death and Gabrielle's admission through *Emergency* had spread like wildfire from the police band. The group pushed through photographers with their blinding flashes, and reporters shouting out questions, without stopping or replying; finally reaching the hospital doors with the aid of hospital security. They hurried to meet the attending doctor who stood when he saw them. He had been talking with Antoine who held a large paper bag looking odd wearing the scrubs he had been lent.

"*Monsieur* Eduardo Jardim," the doctor asked.

"Yes," Eduardo replied, extending his hand and shaking that of the doctor.

"Pleased to meet you, I'm Dr. Gilles."

"And this is *Madame* Vivien, Gabrielle's mother," Eduardo replied, turning to introduce his mother-in-law.

"Please, *Docteur*, could you tell us how my daughter is," *Madame* Vivien asked, her hand that gripped the doctor's was cold, trembling in her evident distress.

"Of course, *Madame*. Please, let's sit down."

In London, Still

Chapter Twenty-One – In London Still, But Why?

"Eduardo! Eduardo! Wake up! Please, wake up!" That voice, coming from so far away, it was almost nine in the morning, the beginning of the cold and rainy Spring 2019, and Eduardo thought he had heard someone calling to him. Not wanting to wake from his dream of happier times, he ignored it.

"Eduardo, *mon chérie*, get up. You have to go to work." He heard that voice calling softly again.

"Brie, is that you?" Eduardo croaked, struggling to wake up. He wanted to open his sleep crusted eyes, but felt the Universe spinning too rapidly to risk taking a peek.

"No Eduardo, it's me, Tristan," his old friend responded, a little louder this time.

"Wha…what?" He finally woke up, "Tristan, is that you? What are you doing here?" Eduardo asked, unsure of where 'here' actually was, as he glanced around confused.

"Eduardo, what are YOU doing here in front of your tenant's door?" Tristan asked, wrinkling his nose, not sure he really wanted to know. "Martin called me early looking for you because you hadn't gone to work. I called you, but since you didn't answer…" he glanced around, looking for Eduardo's cell phone, "I went around to your place. Obviously, I didn't find you THERE," Tristan's hand waggled, palm up to the right, other hand on his hip. "But it occurred to me to call the concierge HERE," Tristan's other hand waggled, this time, to the left. "And then HE told me that you had come in around six this morning, but he hadn't seen you leave." Both hands flipped around, palms upward, emphasized by a raised eyebrow, "so," he drawled, pursing his lips, "what's going on?" he asked expectantly, resisting tapping a foot.

Unexpectedly, Eduardo burst out in tears—heartbroken—they dripped down his face, wetting his shirt. This was the first time he just totally lost it since the incident. "Why, Tristan? Why did everything have to end like that?" Eduardo sniffed, wiped his tears with the backs of his hands, and scrubbed his head frantically with both hands, as if trying to erase an unwelcome image in his head.

"I don't know my friend. I just don't know," Tristan lamented, looking down at his old friend in so much pain.

Tristan sat down beside Eduardo, sighed and laid his head on his shoulder.

"That bastard Pierre," Eduardo said through gritted teeth. "I'm glad he's dead, otherwise I would have killed him!" he snarled.

"Calm yourself Eduardo. Don't be thinking like that. It was a fatality." Tristan replied soothingly, lifting his head to look at his friend as he spoke.

"How can I not Tristan!" Eduardo moaned, "because of that bastard my family was destroyed! I didn't even get the chance to see my daughter born, or say good bye to my wife," Eduardo sobbed inconsolably, "my Brie, my beautiful Brie, my baby girl, my darling baby Julia."

"I know Eduardo," Tristan commiserated his face drawn, dark eyes dulled by sorrow, "I still miss her too, I can't even imagine your pain. But I also miss us. I miss our outings and our dinners—everyone together."

"Forgive me for avoiding you guys these past two years, Tristan," Eduardo said, clearing his throat. "You and Jordan are my closest friends, but for a long time I couldn't look at you two without remembering the good times we had together, without remembering her. I promise, I'll try to change that," Eduardo said, trying hard to smile, not quite succeeding.

"It's alright, my friend. Let's schedule a dinner at our place then," Tristan offered. "You can invite Martin too," he smiled encouragingly.

"Oh Tristan, I just can't get that terrible night in the hospital in Paris out of my head. That doctor telling us that Gabrielle was in a coma without any hope of recovery. And worse, he said they didn't even get the chance to try and save my baby, my Julia," he moaned. "It's all so very hard to get over. I've never told anyone, but I feel like I'm only alive on the outside; like I died with them, understand?"

"Eduardo, you have got to try to go on. I'm certain that Gabrielle wouldn't like seeing you like this," Tristan said, nudging Eduardo's shoulder with his own.

"It's hard Tristan, very hard, but I swear, I am trying. Since then, I've tried to be strong…act normally, but there comes a time when you just can't go on anymore. Funny thing is, until yesterday; I was doing ok. I was coming back from celebrating a promotion with Martin when I started feeling sick in an Uber. I got out and went walking home through *Hyde Park*. Honestly, I can't even remember how I got here. Now tell me, how could I celebrate a milestone like that without remembering her? She was my 'everything'!" Eduardo's voice trailed off as the sharpness of her absence stabbed him again and again.

"I can only imagine your pain, my friend," Tristan said as he rose easily from where he sat on the floor, "ok," he said firmly, "but now we are going to get up and I will take you home. Can you walk?" he asked as he helped pull Eduardo to his feet.

"That way you can get rid of all that alcohol in your system. And we had better get going soon, before the neighbors see you in the state you're in," Tristan concluded, smoothing his hair back with one hand; always conscious of his own appearance.

With Tristan's help, Eduardo got to his feet then hugged his friend, slapping him on the back until Tristan began to cough weakly. "Thanks for taking care of me my friend, even though I abandoned you guys," Eduardo said gruffly.

"Oh Eduardo, don't bother about that. We're friends, and that's that! No time or distance can ever change that."

The two walked out of the building arm in arm and talking softly, making their way slowly toward the apartment where Eduardo actually lived.

"Can I ask you something, Eduardo?" Tristan asked mildly, as they waited at a cross-stop.

"Of course, anything," Eduardo replied, squinting up at the heatless sunlight filtering through the naked trees. The breeze was icy regardless of the season. Eduardo shivered.

"What are you still doing here in London? What I mean to say is: Gabrielle is gone. She left you a good inheritance, money from her life insurance. And the San-Michel Group paid better than top dollar to buy back her share in *Romarin* of *London*. And you paid off your mortgage on the apartment with part of what you received. And you must be charging a good amount for the rent too; it is in *Mayfair* after all. And even so, you insist on living in this grey city where it always rains, it's stressful, people are always ill humored, or pretending to be refined and sophisticated—when obviously—they can't even speak French!" Tristan twisted his lips, harrumphing in disdain. "And you work at a job that you don't need, and which I doubt very much if you even get any joy from!" Tristan proclaimed with a flourish, flouncing forward into the crosswalk, practically dragging Eduardo along with him.

Eduardo gave a sharp bark of a laugh at Tristan's diatribe and his even more than usual national superbity. But once they stepped back up onto the sidewalk on the other side of the street, he replied somberly, "curious you should ask that. I was just thinking the same thing yesterday: still in *London*, without even a motive to be here."

Tristan stopped and looked his friend in the eye, "so, why then?"

"I don't know," Eduardo replied simply, as they began walking again. "I think it's because I was the happiest man in the world here or maybe because here I can still hold on to some kind of a connection with Gabrielle. I don't know! Sometimes I'm just afraid to move on and be unfaithful to her memory—to the memory of our happiness—does that make any sense to you?" Eduardo sighed deeply, glanced at Tristan and continued walking, apparently closely examining the crevasses in the sidewalk to cover his embarrassment at such frankness.

"It makes a whole lot of sense, but don't you also think that all this self-martyrdom is keeping you from being happy again?" Tristan sighed deeply, inhaled and then, more emphatically this time, "after all Eduardo, you aren't even forty yet. You have every right in the world to start over again. You have your whole life ahead of you, my friend."

"Do you think I could ever have another love as great as the one I still have with Brie," Eduardo responded wistfully. He wasn't even asking a real question, or expecting much of an answer, for that matter. Eduardo was just unsure whether he really wanted to leave his dream world, however painful it might be, for a reality that could become a nightmare.

"Of course not," Tristan replied startled. Then, as if speaking to someone simple-minded, he continued slowly, "who would want to make such comparisons, Eduardo? I'm talking about a new love story. Something entirely novel, without comparisons to your past, otherwise you will never be happy again." Looking slightly exasperated, he concluded, "honestly! I think it is about time that you started moving on."

"Do you? Do you really think so, Tristan?" Eduardo asked seriously.

The two finally arrived in front of the building where Eduardo actually lived and they both stopped on the sidewalk in front. "You're home! Delivered safe and sound," Tristan grinned, self-satisfied. "Now please, call Martin so that he can relax. Oh, and by the way, congratulations on that promotion. After everything you've been through in this damp and dreary place where an immigrant like you isn't always seen for his value instead of just his nationality, this promotion is more than well deserved."

"Thank you, Tristan," Eduardo smiled wryly.

"Nevertheless, I really do think you deserve to be happy and to begin again. And who knows, drop everything you have here and begin somewhere else, since *London* is only holding you to a past that can never return. You've reached the top, *formidable*! You proved that you could reach the top by merit, *incroyable*!" Tristan clapped lazily; deliberately extravagant. "But what is all that worth if you still feel empty? You may have done this all your life, but it was never your passion! You know that deep within," he said tapping Eduardo in the chest hard with a long index finger.

Eduardo looked quizzically at his friend, "and what might that passion be, Tristan" he enquired, rubbing his chest where Tristan had poked him. "So, you tell me."

Tristan raised a sardonic eyebrow knowingly, "you know very well what made you happy in this town aside from your marriage to Gabrielle."

"What?" A tiny crease of concentration appeared on Eduardo's forehead.

Explaining the obvious to the fool, Tristan blurt out: "The time when you worked in a restaurant kitchen, of course! How could you be so dumb and blind Eduardo?" Exasperated, Tristan threw his hands up in the air.

Eduardo stood there staring at him in silence.

Disappointed, Tristan said with a final shrug, "well, I have to go. I open *Romarin* today," The two hugged each other and Tristan left. Not another word was exchanged, both feeling oddly let down.

While Eduardo waited for the elevator, his head now cleared by their walk in the fresh air, he thought, "is it possible that Tristan might be right? Is that what I need, a change like that, after all my effort and sacrifice to get where I am today in my profession?" He gave up on both—the elevator and his thoughts—as he bound up the five flights of stairs to the home he had loved.

In London, Still

Chapter Twenty-Two – You Have to Move On

It was almost midday before Eduardo finally left his house for work on his second day in his new position at *Tottenham Equity*. And since he still hadn't had anything to eat that morning, he stopped by *Pret À Manger*, got a double espresso and a *croissant* with almond butter then jogged the rest of the way to the subway. He was certainly in need of that caffeine and sugar boost.

Eduardo caught the subway train at the *Mable Arch Station*; then the connecting train at *Oxford Street*, as usual. By the time he arrived at the *London Bridge Station*, it was almost one in the afternoon. Martin caught sight of him crossing through the reception of *The Shard*, as he was on his way out to lunch.

"Eduardo!" Martin shouted, waving at him—arm high above his head—ignoring the irritated glances of those around him.

Wearing earphones, Eduardo neither heard nor saw Martin as he made his way to the elevators, jumping when his friend who had gone back after him grabbed him by the arm from behind.

"Oh, it's you," startled, Eduardo glanced quickly behind him to see who that hand belonged to. "What happened, Martin?"

"You're the one who must say what happened, Eduardo. Where did you end up after you left yesterday? I thought you were going home," Martin said punching him lightly in the upper arm.

"Yesterday? Oh, you mean today, don't you," Eduardo responded wryly.

Martin persisted, "Whatever! What happened, man?"

"Well, I started to feel queasy in the *Uber* car, so I asked him to stop about a kilometer from my house, at *Hyde Park*," Eduardo began, "it so happens that where I got dropped off is also very close to my old apartment…"

"Don't tell me you went there, man!" Martin interjected, eyes widening with incredulity.

"Yes, but unknowingly. I mean, I don't remember anything; I just realized where I was when Tristan arrived and woke me up…in front of my old apartment door," Eduardo replied, feeling rather foolish.

Shaking his head in disbelief, Martin slapped his forehead with one hand, "man, that is insane! But are you all right?"

"All right? No, not really Martin, but I do need to get there. I need to try to get on with my life. Tristan said a whole lot of things. And he was right about a lot, you know? These past few years have been very difficult for me, and once again I find myself grabbing onto my work just to hide from life. After everything that I lived and learned with Gabrielle, I simply can't let my losses define me again. I can't close off my heart," Eduardo confessed to his friend as office workers by the dozens walked around them, getting on with their own lives, oblivious to Eduardo and his life-changing realizations.

"Yeah, I've got to hand it to Tristan on that point," Martin conceded, slightly envious of Tristan's success where his own attempts had failed.

"But it's not easy, you know," Eduardo replied in earnest.

"Yeah, but you are at least trying, man," Martin affirmed, shrugging off his own momentary sense of inadequacy and grinned at his friend encouragingly.

Eduardo hesitated just for an instant: "no, the truth is, I haven't been trying."

"But you must, Eduardo! You have to get out more, see people, just soldier on! Understand?" Martin growing more enthusiastic at the prospect of getting his old friend back; reassured him eagerly.

"Of course; so, I told Tristan that I would set up something with him and Jordan. Would you like to come too?" Eduardo asked, the most animated he had been yet at this chance encounter.

"Awesome! Those guys are great...even though they are French," Martin joked. "Where will we go, somewhere new?" he asked, ebullient.

"I hadn't really thought about it yet," Eduardo stalled, immediately trying to backpedal.

"I heard there's this *bistro*, very charming and all, and with delicious food on *Bute Street* in *South Kensington*. Nothing expensive or too chic—no stars," he grinned. "We could go there. What do you think?" Martin asked, happy to contribute.

"Perfect," Eduardo replied. "But I really have to go. I'm already kind of late for someone who's just become an executive director," he ended, turning to get in line.

"Ok, go on then," Martin replied, giving Eduardo's shoulder a light tap with his fist by way of leave-taking. "We'll talk after lunch." Martin left the building and Eduardo swiped his ID card over the glass access panel of one of the electronic turnstiles, passed through, used the first available elevator to his floor, and went directly to his office.

On the way to his office, Eduardo was stopped by Anton's secretary who informed him that he was expected. Eduardo turned a shade lighter thinking it had something to do with his tardiness.

"Good afternoon Anton, you asked to see me," Eduardo said as he was ushered in.

"Eduardo? Yes, of course. How have your first two days of your new position been?" Anton inquired, glancing up over his glasses from behind his laptop sitting atop of a wide glistening expanse of glass and brushed steel bound together, serving as his desk.

"Yesterday was very useful. As soon as I got installed in my new office, I had a conference with the entire team—here and abroad—presenting myself as the new director and had each one introduce themselves, their individual scopes of work, and their results for the last six months. I also took the opportunity to ask that they send me their monthly reports for their last six months work by end of day yesterday, so that I could analyze them in more detail. By next week I'll be prepared to talk to each and every one individually. Moving forward, I'll be making any modifications that might be necessary—I would like to see them all working more collaboratively than they have been, many have no idea what their colleagues in LATAM are doing. And there are younger members of the team who would benefit from closer mentoring from some of the regional senior members. Meanwhile, those senior members will get some international experience in monitoring, so it's a win-win."

"Very good; that is very good," Anton intoned nodding.

Eduardo continued, "except that today I was slight indisposed and couldn't come in this morning, but I was able to talk to Martin earlier and informed him that I would be in this afternoon. I apologize for any inconvenience, Anton. It is certainly not my style to be absent from work."

"Come, come, Eduardo, don't concern yourself with that. I didn't call you in to talk about anything of the sort," he said with a wave of his hand, brushing the matter aside.

"Thank you, Anton; how may I help you then," Eduardo inquired relieved, leaning slightly forward in his seat, hands open and spread wide.

"Since you assumed asset management direction of LATAM, nothing more logical than for you to tour the region to present yourself locally and get to know everyone in person. That way you can take the opportunity to get to know all of the operations you will be managing as assets, aside from meeting your local teams, your peers and counterparts, of course."

"Excellent idea," Eduardo enthused, "and when would you like me to schedule this trip?"

"I think as soon as possible would be best, my dear fellow. Get the secretary of your sector to coordinate and block in the visits schedule. Have her arrange everything with our travel personnel—they'll take good care of you. As soon as you've close the program, ask them to send it all to me so that I can authorize the expenses," Anton instructed, taking off his glasses pinched the bridge of his nose lightly between a thumb and forefinger.

"Perfect! I'll get on to that now." Eduardo continued, "is there anything else you would like to discuss with me?"

"Did you request your new corporate credit card with HR yesterday? It'll take a while to arrive, but you can use the one you have now for this trip," Anton continued as he cleaning his glasses.

"Yes, thank you for asking. Will that be all?" Eduardo replied, rising.

"Yes, you have a good afternoon now, Eduardo," Anton said, putting his glasses back on and turning back to the screen of his laptop.

"Good afternoon, Anton," Eduardo replied. He turned and left his boss's office and went directly to his own to set up his travel plan, after all, it would include several countries aside from Brazil. Next, he sent an email to the sector secretary asking her to confirm the country schedules with the offices he would be visiting and if no changes were necessary, then to ask for quotes for the flights and hotels. Later that afternoon, she confirmed his trip schedule and attached a list of available flights and hotels for him make his choices. He quickly marked his preferences and asked her to confirm everything and send the chosen flights and hotels costs for Anton's approval with a copy for himself. Finished with that, he began reading the reports he had received from his new team, getting on with his new activities.

Coming back from lunch, Martin went directly to Eduardo's office. "Hi, I brought you something to eat. Some lovely soup and crackers," he said, his grin wicked.

"Hi Martin, thanks, but I'm not feeling up to eating at the moment," Eduardo replied, ignoring the jibe. "I've got a beast of a hangover from our night out."

"Not to worry my friend, anyway, I'll leave it here on your desk, and when you're feeling better, you can have it," he replied. Only mildly repentant for enjoying his friend's misery just a little, he took out a little bottle of aspirin from his pocket, shaking it near his ear, offered it to Eduardo, who accepted gratefully. Gabrielle and Eduardo had always been on him for his 'excesses', so a little payback couldn't hurt. "Oh, and Kristin told me you're going on a trip," he segued.

"Kristin, yeah?—what a little gossip she's turning out to be! I was just going to tell you," Eduardo said chuckling.

"Don't blame her," Martin said hastily, "and please don't tell anyone, but we went out a few times when I was still an Analyst. After that, we became friends and now she tells me all kinds of things," he grinned unashamedly.

"That's good to know, Martin," Eduardo now turned the tables, teasing, "good thing we're friends" he ended, raising a single eyebrow.

"Don't be so suspicious, man," Martin admonished, wagging a finger at him. "But tell me, so you're going to visit the operations in *Latin America*! That's great. I love these little jaunts, too bad mine are all here in *Europe*. Hey, can I go with?" Martin begged, pretending to pout and plead, palms pressed together.

"No." Eduardo deadpanned then abruptly about-faced, continuing enthusiastically, "I'm really excited and it's coincided with your advice. I think I am going to take advantage and explore new places like I used to, when I was single. That way, I can disconnect a little too," Eduardo replied smiling at the prospect.

"Way to go, Eduardo! It's going to be great; even if I don't go," Martin replied, glad to see his friend spirits improving. "Too bad we're going to have to postpone our outing with Tristan and Jordan."

"No way," Eduardo rebutted, "we can still go this week, how's that? We could have an early dinner."

"Fantastic!"

"How about this Thursday, I think that's Tristan's night off," Eduardo proposed.

"Fine by me," Martin agreed and stood up from where he had been sitting on a corner of Eduardo's desk, walked over to the window that faced the *Thames* and looked out.

"Then I'll call Tristan, see about their availability and confirm with you later. I'll try to set it up for sevenish, that way we can leave directly for *South Kensington* from here, ok?" Eduardo said; talking to Martin's back.

Martin turned reluctantly from the view he didn't have from his own office, "I'm fine with that Eduardo. Just confirm that that's ok with them too. Now let me get back to my own office."

"Great! See you later than," Eduardo replied as Martin walked out, leaving him to himself with his view and his plan to implement, feeling more alive than he had in quite a while. So that he wouldn't forget to talk to Tristan about Thursday, He called him as soon as Martin closed the door behind him. "Hi Tristan, how are you? This is Eduardo," he said into his mobile.

"Eduardo my friend, still alive," Tristan laughed on the other side of the line. "I thought you might be curing your hangover at home."

"Not a chance! I couldn't kill an entire day, not after just being promoted," Eduardo replied laughing.

"True," Tristan mused. "So, what goes?"

"It's like this: we talked earlier about setting something up to do, and Martin suggested a *bistro* in *South Kensington* on Thursday. So, are you in?"

"*Uh*, I don't know about that, Eduardo," Tristan responded slowly after a few seconds of consideration. "I work on

273

Thursday, and the *Romarin* is booked full. Couldn't we do this another day? I don't work Mondays," Tristan asked slightly deflated.

"The thing is, I'm going to be away from *London* for about a month, beginning next week. I'm going personally to see the company's operations in *Latin America* and introduce myself to the teams there," Eduardo explained.

"That's fantastic! The timing couldn't be better. You could use a change of scenery, my friend," Tristan exclaimed delighted for his friend.

"Yeah, I know," Eduardo replied pleased. "So, you're sure you won't be able to get away to have an early dinner before I take off? Otherwise, I'll only see you guys a month or so from now," he concluded.

"Yes, I understand. Can I check and get back to you later? Anyway, I still have to talk to Jordan," Tristan concluded.

"No problem. At any rate, I'll ask Martin to make the reservation. I'm sure everything will come out well in the end," Eduardo replied, determined to remain positive.

"I hope so. We'll speak again later. Bye," Tristan ended before disconnecting.

"See you later, Tristan." Eduardo disconnected and went back to analyzing the reports he had asked his team for that were piling up in his email inbox.

It was after five-thirty in the afternoon when Martin sauntered into Eduardo's office again; not stopping until he reached the place he decided would be his favorite—centered in front of the window overlooking the *Thames*—and with his back to Eduardo said, "aren't you ready to leave yet?" He watched the boats moving slowly up and down the river attentively, each one making a sparkling trail of ripples the afternoon sun hit in their wakes—mesmerized—he almost forgot what he was doing there.

"Martin! No man, I have too much to take in before my trip and I don't want to arrive at the sites not knowing everything I can about them," Eduardo replied, stretching, he looked up and smiled knowingly at his friend's back.

"Oh, got it! I was going to ask you to have a pint with me over at the *Borough Market*." Martin still hadn't turned to talk to his friend, fascinated by the movement on the river, not a little envious of this great view.

"Thank you, my friend, but I have to focus on these reports. Not to mention that I still have a brutal hangover," Eduardo passed on the invitation, careful not to move his head too fast, in order to avoid that bitter taste at the back of his throat.

Martin laughed then turned and gave the unsympathetic grin of someone younger and more accustomed to late nights and week-day drinking, "right old man; see you tomorrow then. Good night." Crossing the office swiftly, he was out the door almost before he heard Eduardo call out, "Good night Martin, See you tomorrow!"

Eduardo examined a few more pages before he sighed, stretched and got up, went to the break room and got a cup of black coffee. He came back using curiously gliding movements, balancing his head carefully. No one was there to notice. He took a sip and grimaced at the weak blandness of the English coffee, set his cup carefully on his desk—missing the Brazilian *cafezinho*—then promptly forgot all about it as it turned icy, developing an oily patina on the surface, untouched. He continued his work for three or so more hours. By the time he left the building it was past eight. He caught the subway and went home.

As he walked up the stairs of *Marble Arch Station*, he saw that he had a missed call from Tristan. Arriving finally at street level he pressed redial, holding his mobile to his ear as he walked homeward. "Hi Tristan, you called?"

"Yes, can you talk now?" Tristan's voice sounded clearly.

"Yes, of course. I was in the subway and didn't see your call. I just left work a while ago. I needed to make up for my absence this morning. So, is everything set for Thursday?" Eduardo said in a single breath.

"Yes, all good. I almost couldn't get a substitute, but he's finally confirmed. I'll leave around seven and meet you at the *bistro*. Jordan will be going directly too." Tristan replied, pleased that everything was working out as he had hoped.

"Perfect!" Eduardo intoned. "Martin and I will go directly from the office too. He's reserved a table in his name for seven. Whoever gets there first can hold the table. From what he told me, the *bistro* is small and tables are at a premium," he concluded slightly out of breath.

"*Formidable*, no problem; I'll tell Jordan too, in case he gets there before any of us," Tristan agreed.

"Great. Then we are agreed. Until Thursday Tristan, I'm very happy about our dinner," Eduardo ended truly pleased.

"I'm also very happy, Eduardo. See you Thursday, *tchau*" Tristan replied.

Eduardo pressed END, put his phone back in the inside pocket of his suit coat and continued to walk, a little faster now that he was getting closer to home. Once inside his apartment, he put a

Spotify playlist on his *IPhone* to play through the *Bose* speakers strategically placed for maximum effect, tossed his backpack on the sofa, and walked past the counter into the kitchen to make himself something to eat. Eduardo loved cooking, but his greatest pleasure had been having his food appreciated by Gabrielle. Since losing his wife, he cooked less frequently; but having skipped lunch, he decided to make something for himself that night.

Opening the refrigerator, he took out a deboned and divided duck breast neatly resting in its marinade to make *Magret de Canard à l'Orange* with potatoes. Using coarsely ground sea salt and rosemary, he scored then seared the duck over high heat, separating some of the reduced duck fat to make the orange sauce. Eduardo popped the seared duck and potatoes with the rest of the fat into the oven to finish.

As he cooked, Eduardo opened a bottle of *Pinot Noir 2011* from *New Zealand*. As he stood leisurely sipping his wine and keeping an eye on the oven, he listened to *Sarah Blasko, Joni Mitchell, Nina Simone, Dave Matthews Band, Of Monsters and Men, Cesária Évora, Zaz,* and *Tori Amos,* among other musicians he enjoyed. It had been a while since he had listened to good music, savoring a good bottle of wine while he cooked. The clock seemed to slow down, giving him time to focus more on the good things in his life.

While the duck and potatoes were roasting, he set the table and placed his *Notebook* next to his dish so that he could continue reading a little more while he ate. Oranges squeezed, and water boiling, with the peel at ready; he took just a little more rendered fat from the duck in the oven. Methodically, he whisked together the juice, the infusion, the rendered fat, the vinegar and the honey, swirling it over the flame as he whisked the concoction until reduced, ready to drizzle over the lovely rare brown duck breast. Flame off, he took the sauce off the stove and set it aside.

Shortly afterwards, when the scored duck was beautifully rare, but not underdone and potatoes ready, he removed them from the oven and began to plate the dish. Neatly slicing half of the duck breast, laying each slice slightly overlapping the previous, he placed the potatoes to one side of the duck, orange slices to the other, with a sprinkle of fresh rosemary. Finishing with the warm brown sauce drizzled over the meat, the pink tinged centers barely peeking out. He finished off the rest of the wine in his glass, refilled it. Balancing his glass in one hand and plate in the other he took them to the table. Eduardo set them down and savored his fabulous dinner for one. At that moment he felt good about himself.

He ate and drank while he continued to read the reports on his *Notebook*. When he finished, he cleared the table, cleaned the kitchen and put everything away. The leftovers he packed for lunch the next day. Carrying his *Notebook* and backpack to his room, it was already nearly eleven.

Eduardo brushed his teeth, changed into his pajamas, got into bed and adjusted his pillow. He was asleep almost before his head made a dent in it.

The next day he worked as usual and after lunch, an email popped into his inbox containing his trip approval. He would be on his way to *Mexico* on Sunday, the first leg of his trip. He was pleased to be going to *Mexico*, a place he wanted very much to get to know. His itinerary included *Bogotá, Santiago do Chile, Buenos Aires* and then *São Paulo*—it was going to be a grueling trip—five countries. At the end of the day he went with Martin to *Borough Market* for a pint and then dinner at the memorable *Padella*. The wait was almost two hours, but well worth it; the pasta there was out of this world. As they were leaving,

Eduardo remembered to confirm with Martin the dinner scheduled with Tristan and Jordan for the next day.

Leaving the restaurant a little after ten in the evening, Eduardo begged off Martin's suggestion of a nightcap and went directly home where he fell asleep almost immediately. 'This has been a good week,' was his last thought as he closed his eyes and drifted off to sleep.

Chapter Twenty-Three – The Bistro in South Kensington

That Thursday Eduardo woke up excited about the dinner that evening with his friends. It had been a long time since they had gotten together around a table to eat, drink and shoot the breeze.

Since he woke up early, he decided to have a nice breakfast, so he dressed, pattered out barefooted to the kitchen and made a scrambled egg with *crème fraîche* and bacon, some toast and espresso with milk. When he finished eating, he washed the dishes, brushed his teeth, put on his shoes and walked toward the subway station. It was a beautiful sunny day, a real spring day. Eduardo used the same route as always. Arriving at *Tottenham Equity* around nine, he got a cup of coffee from the break room and went down the hall to his office.

It was an average day at work, rather uneventful actually. He worked nonstop all morning, including a few meetings with operations under his direction in *Latin America*. He had his leftover duck for lunch in the break room and at the end of the day walked together with Martin toward the *bistro* in *South Kensington*. The two crossed the *London Bridge* on foot and down the subway stairs in order to avoid the evening rush hour traffic. Squeezing into the train at *Monument Station,* which was bulging at the seams with commuters, they alighted at *South Kensington Station.*

"Man, it's been a long time since I've seen the guys," Martin said enthusiastically, walking shoulder to shoulder with Eduardo toward their exit, "I can't wait to see them, this is going to be great!"

"They'll be happy to see you too," Eduardo replied, "I just hope that our table is free when we get there."

"Well, our reservation is for seven, and I think we'll get there a little before that." Martin estimated. "So, we'll probably have a place to sit when we arrive. What time did Tristan and Jordan say they would arrive?"

"Around the same time as us, but I told them to give your name on the reservation in case one of them arrives before we do," Eduardo elaborated.

"Excellent!" Martin replied. Both remained silent, engrossed in their own thoughts until they reached the *Old Brompton Road* exit and walked toward the bistro on *Bute Street.* It was already dark and the streetlights illuminated their way in the penumbra.

The place appeared unexceptional but cozy—typical French décor, paintings with bucolic scenes, a tiny vase of wildflowers on each tables—a family atmosphere, as if their clients were very familiar with the staff. It felt like one of those mom and pop places, the kind where the owners do everything themselves and only have a few helpers. It wasn't that big either, only five tables inside in front of a bar where you could also see various delicacies in the showcase counter, and you could see the food being prepared too, through a doorway just beyond the counter. Outside there were three small tables, all occupied. All of this explained the   reservations being in such high demand. The bistro didn't have much formality at its entry either. When Eduardo and Martin walked through the door, they were greeted by a teenager who looked like she might be seventeen at most, in jeans, a black polo shirt, and high-top red trainers, her hair tied back with a black ribbon.

"Good evening gentlemen, how are you?" She greeted them politely with a British accent. This struck Eduardo as curious, since it was clear that this was a French bistro and she certainly didn't appear to be one of the local employees.

"Good evening, we're fine, thank you for asking. We have a reservation in the name of Martin Porter," Martin offered, not waiting to be asked.

The girl took out a piece of paper containing a hand written list from her shirt pocket to confirm their reservation. "For four, is that right?" She asked, looking up, inquiringly.

This time it was Eduardo who replied, "yes—a party of four—the others are on their way".

"That won't be a problem," she clarified, breaking into a smile, showing a dimple in her right cheek, "but since you are a little early, your table isn't available yet. Would you mind waiting a little?"

"Of course not," Eduardo smiled back, "might we have a drink outside while we wait?"

"Of course Sir, what would you like to drink?" The girl asked politely. There was something familiar about him, but she couldn't quite place where she had seen him before.

"A glass of *viognier*, if you have it," Eduardo replied, turning to Martin he asked, "what about you?"

"I'll have a beer, if it all the same to you," Martin grinned, then asked the girl, "Do you have an *IPA*?"

"Certainly Sir," showing her dimple again, "I only have to verify that we have a *viognier*."

The girl went around the counter while Eduardo held the door as he and Martin stepped outside. The two were chatting when a forty-something woman came out with a tray bearing a sniffer, a bottle of beer, and a glass of white wine.

Blonde, perhaps a meter sixty, tops, light brown eyes, nice curves that were apparent even in her faded blue jeans and white linen blouse. Even in such informal attire and with light or no makeup, which somehow seemed appropriate for a little family-run restaurant; she had a natural grace and was easy on the eyes.

Sophie Baron was one of the proprietors of this tiny restaurant and it was easy to see that the girl who had greeted them was her daughter, Camille Brown, a younger, leaner version of herself with light brown hair and golden eyes.

"Good evening gentlemen," Sophie greeted them with a dimple identical to that of their original greeter.

The two stopped their talking when she spoke; and greeted her. Eduardo —almost with his back to the door—turned his head quickly to greet her, not really noticing her. Martin on the other hand, had already forgotten what they had been talking about as he openly admired this very attractive woman in front of him.

"The ale is for…" Sophie asked.

"That would be me. Thank you very much Miss," Martin replied raising an index finger, his eyes twinkling with anticipation as she poured his *Greene King India Pale Ale.*

"Then the *viognier* would by yours…" she deftly handed the glass of wine to Eduardo, who finally turned and thanked her, "a nice choice of white wine, by the way," she added, looking him full in the face.

As Eduardo took his glass, he glanced at her. Sophie recognized him immediately. *"Ah Mon Dieu!"* Sophie exclaimed softly in French.

Confused, Eduardo automatically responded in French, "I'm sorry, is there something wrong," not realizing what had happened.

"You don't remember me, do you?" Sophie's lips twisted in mirth, but she tried hard not to laugh.

"I'm sorry Miss, but I don't recall ever being introduced," Eduardo replied, now in English, becoming slightly irritated at her sudden cavalier manner, taking a step back.

"Forgive me, I didn't mean to disconcert you, but a few days ago, I knocked you down with my bicycle at *Hyde Park*. It was early morning and you were stepping into the cycling lane and when I realized it; well, it was already too late. I ended up knocking you down. My daughter was with me, Camille. She greeted you just a little while ago. Anyway, she had stopped just a little beyond us when I stopped to help you up," her words tumbled out, not stopping for a breath. "By the way, how is your arm and your new job?" She finally inhaled then smiled charmingly at Eduardo.

Watching in amazement, Martin burst out laughing, spilling a little of his beer, unable to contain himself as her tale unfolded. "Man; that was the morning you went home in an *Uber* after our commemoration!" He poked Eduardo in the ribs. "How could you forget something like that, eh? And what's worse, not remember such a beautiful woman," he demanded of Eduardo, still chuckling while he admired Sophie. Turning back to the storyteller, "With all due respect, Miss..."

"Sophie Baron, I'm the owner of the restaurant," she replied holding the tray and empty bottle, not quite sure what to think.

Eduardo's face had gone beet red to the roots of his hair with mortification. Crossing paths with Sophie before had been embarrassing enough, but not remembering her just made matters that much worse. "I do apologize for not remembering you *Madame* Sophie. I remember getting out of the *Uber* before arriving home...I wasn't feeling well in the car. And I vaguely remember falling and someone helping me up, but I was very drunk..." his voice trailed off, clearly disconcerted. He didn't quite know what to do with himself.

"Man that is insane!" Martin burst out. "What a small world! Eight million inhabitants in *London,* and you two tripped over one another twice, and in such a short space of time?" Martin grinned widely, looking first at one then the other, then back again, shaking his head in disbelief. That was just too unbelievable and funny at the same time.

Eduardo cleared his throat, "so," he continued—ignoring Martin's razzing—looking directly at Sophie, "as I was saying, because of my state, I don't remember very well what happened that morning. As a matter of fact, when I woke, I remember feeling some pain in my arm, but I had no idea in truth, of its cause. But it's fine now. Thank you for asking Sophie...I may call you that?"

"That is my name, isn't it? So, of course you may," she responded with typical French sarcasm. "Regardless, I apologize again for the incident, Mister..."

With that, Eduardo replied, "I do apologize for not introducing ourselves. Eduardo Jardim, my pleasure," he extended his hand and shook hers. "And this very funny guy beside me is Martin Porter," he indicated as he released her hand.

Martin stepped forward to grasp her hand, "a pleasure Sophie," he said. "Apologies for that, but it was all just too ludicrous;

and his expression…" he began chuckling again nearly spilling his drink again; he quickly extended his arm as far as it would go so as not to get the drink on him again. After a few moments he finally managed to stop chuckling long enough to sip his drink.

While Sophie chatted with them, a man watched the three from behind the counter inside the restaurant. His eyes skittered from one to the other, back and forth. He looked very unhappy about the extended conversation she was having with two good-looking men and out of earshot.

"Not a problem, but you're right, it is very curious that I ran you over with my bicycle," Sophie responded to Martin, but looked directly at Eduardo, "only a few days ago and now you are here dining at my bistro. By the way, who indicated us to you?"

"Oh, that was a friend at work," Martin replied. "She gave a rave review of your place." He grinned up at her as she smiled her appreciation.

Just then Camille came out of the restaurant, stopping beside her mother, "your table is ready now," she said, looking at both men.

Sophie put an arm around her daughter and gave her a squeeze before releasing her and handed her the tray, "You're very welcome here boys. Now I have to get back to work," she said; returning inside taking the empty bottle with her, leaving Camille to escort their clients to their table.

Eduardo and Martin were about to follow too when Tristan and Jordan, still a little ways down the block spotted them. "Eduardo!" Tristan shouted waving as he and his boyfriend quickened their step, rushing hand in hand, to catch up with two.

"Tristan! Jordan! Perfect timing," Eduardo said, "our table has just become available," as his friends reached the bistro.

"Hello you two!" Martin whooped, greeting the newcomers first with hugs, then pats on the back once they reached the waiting party. Everyone greeted each other then quickly followed Camille to their table.

"What will you two have?" Eduardo inquired of the newcomers before Camille could open her mouth to ask.

"We'll accompany you *avec le vin,*" Jordan replied with a wink and the curve of a smile at Tristan.

"*Mademoiselle* Camille, could you bring us a bottle of this fine wine that I'm drinking? And two more glasses for my friends, please," Eduardo asked.

"Of course," Camille replied giving Eduardo an enquiring look when he used her name which she found odd.

Camille walked over to her mother who was behind the counter and asked for the bottle of wine and two glasses. "Thank you, *ma chérie*; I'll take care of it," her mother replied with a smile.

"Thank you *Maman*. But how does he know my name—do I know him?" she asked in that quiet but direct way of hers, so typical of Sophie's daughter.

Sophie laughed and explained that she had had the sensation that she had seen him before too, but hadn't recognized him from the park until she saw him up close.

"Bizarre," Camille replied. "I thought I had seen him before, but not from the park. I was too far away when you knocked him down for that. I think I've seen him somewhere else," she said thoughtfully looking at the back of his head.

287

"How strange; well, I…" Sophie was interrupted by the man who had observed them from behind the counter when she had been outside talking with Eduardo and Martin. He came up beside her, interrupting her just as she was commenting, "What is it that's strange, Sophie," he asked cocking his head slightly to the side, narrowing his eyes suspiciously as he looked back and forth between Sophie and the men at the table. Sophie, Camille and Michael, despite his being English, always spoke in French among themselves.

"Nothing Michael, nothing," she replied exasperated, turning away from him as she reached for the wine and glasses. She walked over to Eduardo's table without a backward glance.

The evening passed marvelously well for Eduardo and his friends. It was as if no time at all had passed since they had all last met. The flow of conversation was relaxed and happy, interspersed with bottles of wine and some excellent food. Yet three of the companions carefully avoided bringing Gabrielle's memory to their table; particularly because of Eduardo's relapse just days ago.

Since her death, almost two years ago, the group that had once been inseparable had only come together for her funeral and perhaps one or two times more after that. Eduardo however, had not grown away from Martin; probably because they had to see each other every day at work rather than any actual effort on Eduardo's part to do so though.

Apparently Eduardo was finally trying to overcome his loss and resume his life among the living. They all thought his spirit was lighter that evening. Could it have been the frank talk Tristan had had with him when he found him in front of the door of his old apartment in that lamentable state? All three felt more than a twinge of guilt for not having tried harder and earlier to help

Eduardo out of his funk, but maybe nature just needed to take her course.

While the evening progressed tranquilly for the four friends, the same could not be said for Sophie who had made a point of giving considerable attention to that happy table of four. And that didn't please Michael at all, Camille's father, and her ex-husband.

Although they were no longer together, Michael believed it his right to meddle in Sophie's life. While she, on the other hand, being the independent woman that she was, simply ignored him utterly.

At one point during the evening, he made a point of growling at her, "don't you think you're giving too much attention those men at table three?" He glowered at them from behind the counter.

"I'm sorry Michael, is something bothering you?" Sophie asked blithely. "I happen to have liked the group and I am giving them special attention. What's the problem with that," she replied pointedly smiling at them from where she stood.

He deliberately turned his back to the group and continued in a low voice, "What's bothering me is that I don't think it's appropriate for the mother of a teenage girl to be carrying on like that in front of her daughter!" he snapped.

"My daughter is almost a woman! And honestly, there is nothing wrong with being pleasant. You should try it," she looked over at him and smiled sweetly.

"But I am your husband and I demand that you respect me!" Michael hissed loudly, the vein in his temple throbbing visibly as he lost his temper.

Sophie grabbed him by the upper arm and pulled him toward the back of the restaurant, asking Camille that she take over the counter as she passed her. "Lower your voice, please!" She whispered emphatically. "And don't you dare make one of your scenes here in the restaurant. That's already given us more than enough negative publicity," Sophie's voice hardened along with her stance, "what's more, you are NOT my husband anymore. You haven't been for a very long time. And if we still work together," she continued, gritting her teeth in anger and frustration, "it's because I can't buy out your part in the restaurant yet to see myself totally free of you. And you certainly can't afford my part either. As a matter of fact Michael, you know very well that without my skills in the kitchen this restaurant wouldn't even exist, and not even the good reviews we have on the internet would save you then. So why don't you go look for a job somewhere else and let me grow our business in peace? I would make it a point to continue your monthly withdrawal in exchange for not having you cross my path again!"

Michael raised a threatening hand to hit Sophie.

"What are you going to do, big man?" Sophie demanded lifting her chin, eyes smoldering, "you going hit me like you did when we were married? I'm not afraid of you anymore! That foolish and frightened little woman that you exploited and beat died a very long time ago! You killed her!" Sophie pushed him away forcefully with both hands and returned to the *salon* as if nothing had happened. Michael lowered his hand as quickly as he had raised it, holding it to his chest as if had a mind of its own; he turned abruptly away from the *salon* as she walked away.

"What's happened *Maman*?" Camille asked softly, looking worried as her mother came to her side.

"Just another of your father's ridiculous jealous tantrums *ma chérie*, but everything is resolved now," Sophie said quietly. She went off to oversee affairs in the tiny kitchen and later returned to go around the tables to see if anyone needed anything, stopping last at Eduardo's table where she lingered, her back deliberately to the back of the restaurant, either hand placed nonchalantly on the backs of Eduardo's and Tristan's chairs.

Michael returned to the *salon* and spoke quickly and quietly into his daughter's ear then walked out of the restaurant through the front door, slamming it behind him, startling the clients.

Sophie rushed to her daughter's side and looked questioningly at her. "It was nothing *Maman*. Papa said he didn't feel well and that he was leaving," Camille replied calmly, mature beyond her years.

"Fine with me; his absence doesn't make the least difference here," Sophie's voice irritated, unrelenting.

"Please, *Maman*, don't be so hard on him."

Immediately repentant, Sophie softening her tone; "I'm sorry, *ma chérie*. I didn't mean to speak badly of your father in front of you." Sophie knew that she would never reveal to Camille what had really gone on while she was married to Michael. The girl idolized her father.

The night was ending and the restaurant was almost empty; only Eduardo's table remained. Sophie went over and asked them if they would like something more to eat, informing them that because of the house license, in fifteen minutes she wouldn't be able to serve any more alcohol.

Eduardo, Martin, Tristan, and Jordan gave her marvelous feedback on their dishes, highlighting the charm and simplicity of the place in such an expensive neighborhood as *South Kensington.*

"Our contract is an old one, so we have been able to maintain the *maison* here," Sophie explained. "The owner of the building has been very generous with us and with our bistro which attracts a lot of people to this street. He appreciates us because he has several other properties nearby which are always occupied."

"Brilliant!" Martin exclaimed. Intelligent and good-looking he thought.

"Could we possibly order a last bottle of *viognier*," Eduardo asked.

"But of course!" Sophie exclaimed. "But I must warn you, we will be closing in an hour, ok?"

"No problem," Tristan said lightly, "we won't need that much time to finish off another bottle. By the way, Martin was telling me what happened between you and Eduardo at *Hyde Park.* Wouldn't you like to join us and tell this story in more detail," he proposed with a wink and an inviting smile.

The others at the table laughed, except for Eduardo. "Stop it, Tristan," Eduardo said blushing with embarrassment. "We are not going to bother Sophie; otherwise she won't be able to close her *maison.*"

"Not in the least," Sophie replied delighted. "I'll ask Camille to take care of everything. I'll just get another bottle and a glass and will be with you momentarily," she smiled her dimple making another appearance.

Sophie spoke quietly and quickly to Camille who went to the kitchen to advise the others that there were no more orders for the evening.

Sophie sat down with the four and served everyone wine, including herself and then, she retold the story. They also regaled her with tales about themselves for the rest of the evening which she greatly enjoyed. The night only grew a little tense when Eduardo was explaining that he had been married but was now a widower, he had barely touched on the matter before he was swiftly interrupted by Martin who told her the story of how the two met.

Sophie brought out yet another bottle of wine—on the house this time—and told them a little of her marriage, her daughter, the opening of the bistro and her separation. She tried to focus on the success of her food and her restaurant, not dwelling on the rest. She didn't care for dramas, despite having had many with her ex-husband.

At the end of the evening, her employees had finished cleaning up and had all gone home. Only the four, Camille, and Sophie remained. "Boys, we have to go now, Camille has classes tomorrow," she said standing reluctantly.

The four had already paid the bill earlier, so they said their good-byes to her among kisses on cheeks, brief hugs, and promises to return. Eduardo, however, was more aloof, limiting himself to shaking her hand. "Thank you for a lovely evening Sophie; it's been a while since I've enjoyed myself so much," Eduardo said rather formally as he shook her hand.

"It was a pleasure to have you all here, Eduardo," she replied. "It's been a long time since I've had such pleasant moments for myself. I am always so absorbed in my work and my daughter, it's hard to break such a cycle," she shrugged. "I too end up not allowing myself to socialize. I isolate myself too much from the world," Sophie confessed softly so that only Eduardo heard.

"I understand perfectly what you are saying," Eduardo responded, also quietly. "Of course, we all have our own personal dramas and must always learn to deal with them."

"True," Sophie mused; then turned to include everyone, "good bye boys, do come back whenever you like. Good night to all!"

It was late and the subway had already stopped running, so they hailed two taxis, one for Eduardo who went off toward *Hyde Park* while the remaining three all climbed into the second taxi, since they lived in neighboring boroughs.

It had been an exceptional night for the four, and for Sophie too, who had made new friends. And they had made a new friend too—it seemed almost like the old times were back again.

Camille was the last to leave the restaurant, locking the front door carefully behind her. "Are you ready to go home *ma chérie?*" Sophie asked with a soft smile, pocketing the set of keys Camille handed her. "Yes, *Maman.*" Before Sophie could say anything more, Camille added, "do you remember I mentioned earlier that I thought I had seen Eduardo before, but that it wasn't at the incident in the park?"

"Yes," Sophie replied looking inquiringly at her daughter, squinting under the streetlights, "and from where do you know him? As a matter of fact," she went on, "he is quite an interesting man. Apparently he has something of a somber past with his wife. He didn't go into details, but I noticed that there was *something.*"

"I wouldn't just say somber, *Maman*. Do you remember that tragedy with that famous French chef about two years ago?"

"Gabrielle Debois—yes, of course I remember. She was an incredible woman, a reference to French *cuisine*," Sophie recalled.

"Well, Eduardo was her husband who tragically lost his wife and unborn daughter," Camille announced matter-of-factly.

Chapter Twenty-four – For Better Or For Worse, In Sickness And In Health

Sophie was only seventeen when she met Michael. He was the same age as she when he asked his parents to send him on a summer exchange program to *France* to learn the language. He stayed in the city of *Orleans* for almost three months. When it came to choosing where to stay, he preferred a family residence over the dormitories at the Universities associated with the course, although they were almost empty during summer. Michael opted for *Orleans* because of its proximity to *Paris*, and because it was cheaper than the French capital.

At seventeen, Michael was extraverted and liked very much to learn new cultures. Since French was his second language choice in school, he decided to expand his knowledge. At that age he was already almost 1.80m, skinny, but with developed legs from his love of long distance running, his hair was golden—more so from the summer sun—his nose was definitely Roman, blue eyes, narrow jaw finished off with a squared chin. He was barely recognizable as the man Eduardo and his friends glimpsed briefly at the bistro.

Arriving at the house where he would be hosted, he met *Madam* Amélie and *Monsieur* Olivier Baron. "Good afternoon, Michael," *Madam* Amélie said as she opened the door and greeted him in French. "Welcome to our home. My name is Amélie Baron. And there, sitting on the sofa is my husband, Olivier," she pointed with her free hand and smiled.

"*Bonjour Madam* Baron. It's a pleasure to meet you both," Michael replied, attempting his salutation in his schoolboy French, but instead ended with, "do you speak English too?" and a grin.

"Of course," Madam Amélie replied, "but we will try to speak a combination of both languages, and in time, we will progress to speaking only French, yes? Is that acceptable for you?" She looked at him inquiringly, though not expecting any objection.

"Yes, ma'am," Michael replied relieved.

Still smiling, "please, no need for formalities with us," she continued. "You must call us Amélie and Olivier, we insist," she proclaimed.

"Of course *Madam*; sorry, I mean Amélie," his teeth flashed giving her a winning smile.

"Good afternoon, young man," *Monsieur* Olivier called out, not rising from his comfortable seat on the sofa.

"Good afternoon, sir," Michael replied after he had come closer, extending his hand. "It's a pleasure to meet you, my name is Michael Brown," the teenager said solemnly.

"A pleasure Michael, but please, you may call me Olivier," giving him a nod and pointing at his own chest.

"Michael," Amélie interrupted, "we have one more member of the family to present to you, but she is probably enjoying summer in some other part of town." After briefly watching him standing in front of her husband—neither speaking—she said, "your room is upstairs. Let me help you with your luggage." She took hold of his backpack and left him to follow.

Michael was shown his room where he remained for some time settling in. After a few hours he could hear Amélie's voice calling him for dinner. Sophie was already seated at the table by the time Michael arrived in the dining room to share the evening meal. She had her back to the stairs and couldn't believe her eyes when she turned around and saw him traipsing down the flight of stairs. 'How handsome and such a beautiful smile,' she thought. She promptly changed her mind about English teeth, the previous boarders had all had such awful teeth.

"Michael," Amélie called out as soon as she saw him, "come meet our daughter, Sophie."

Sophie rose from where she had sat twisted around in her seat watching him as he entered the dining room, "Good evening Michael," she said, shaking his hand and looking him straight in the eye, "welcome to *Orleans* and to our home."

"Uh, *merci Mademoiselle*," Michael stuttered, a little intimidated by this self-confident girl.

In fact, Sophie had always been both determined and self-assured from a very young age. She wasn't the prettiest among her school friends, but she certainly won everyone over with her charisma, good humor, and aplomb. Plus, she had just been freed from the braces on her teeth, which she thought auspicious as she greeted Michael.

"Please call me Sophie, Michael. And if you need any help with your French classes or even getting to know the city, I am at your disposal," she said firmly and sincerely as she smiled up at him, finally releasing his hand.

"*Merci*, Sophie," Michael smiled back, walking around the table to sit opposite her without taking his eyes off her.

Amélie noted the exchange and saw the two glancing at each other from across the table throughout the meal, but she was sure that Michael was a good boy, so she was pleased that there seemed to be this instant connection between the two. They never separated that summer. When Michael finished his morning classes, the two would meet and go off together exploring.

Michael ended up getting to know the entire region as well as *Paris* through Sophie. And after a time, unsurprisingly, they ended up becoming emotionally involved with one another.

Sophie and Michael had their first sexual experience together, and from then on, swore undying love to each other. But when summer finally ended and the time for Michael to go home had arrived, that first heady rush of uncontrollable teenage love had also ended. Michael went back to *Richmond* on the outskirts of *London*, resuming his normal life and Upper Sixth.

On the day Michael left, Sophie went with him to the train station in *Paris* where he would soon catch his connection to *London*, "You promise we'll stay together even at a distance?" Michael asked, looking deeply into her eyes before passing through the turnstile leading to his platform.

"Of course, we'll be together forever!" She stated matter-of-factly. "You can come here whenever you want, and I will ask my parents so that I can go visit you too. Of course, if your parents allow it."

"Of course they will!" He replied with the same teenage certainty. "When I get home I'll tell them all about my summer, about us and how you helped me to learn French so much faster. Just don't be surprised the first time you meet them. They're rather stodgy and deep down probably believe themselves to be near aristocrats, living the good life in *Richmond* and all." They both laughed at that and then kissed madly before he rushed off to catch his train, leaving her to watch until his train finally left the station.

In fact, they both kept their word and their love for one another. They spoke constantly by telephone and whenever possible, travelled to each other's home. Yet they both preferred when Michael would come to *Orleans*; particularly because they had the blessing and support of Sophie's parents.

Sophie finished high school the next year and decided to study for a degree in administration with specialization in tourism. She wanted to move to *Paris* and work in a sector that had always been strong in the region. Although she was quite bright, she already knew that she didn't want to be a boring old executive, unhappy behind the desk of some corporation. What she liked were people. Michael finished that same year too, but after a year had passed, still didn't know what he wanted to study at university. He had thought about French literature, but that was sternly rejected by his father who declared that he would only finance studies that would provide security in the future. Unable to think of anything else, and tired of nowhere jobs, still not ready for school again, Michael finally decided that he was going to enlist. The war in *Afghanistan* had begun—and he wanted to go!

He would be one of Britain's soldiers going as part of the *Nato-led International Security Assistance Force in Afghanistan (Nato-ISAF)*. At the same time he told Sophie that he wanted to go to *Afghanistan*, Michael asked her to marry him, insisting that he couldn't possibly leave for his first mission unless they were married.

"You don't think this is all too precipitated Michael? We're not even twenty, I haven't finished my degree yet, and you still haven't decided what you want to do with yourself," Sophie responded, always the practical one. They were both together in *Richmond* at the time, seated in his parent's pergola, overlooking their elegant garden. Michael's parents were hopeful that Sophie could convince him to give up on the idea of going to war where they had failed.

"No, my love; I have everything planned out," he replied, holding her hand in his. "I'll be gone only a few years, and when I come back I'll have enough money to start our lives wherever you want: *London* or *Paris*," Michael swore.

In the end, Michael enlisted at nineteen and they married at twenty, just a few months before he would be shipped out. Sophie stayed in *Orleans* with her parents, which was where Michael insisted on staying whenever he could when he was in *Europe*. Sophie's parents agreed to help them, supporting them both in their home, under the condition that Michael wouldn't spend any more than four years away from his wife.

In their second year of marriage, Sophie got pregnant. She gave birth to Camille–not long after their third anniversary—who was very much welcomed by everyone. Even the paternal grandparents travelled to *France* to meet their only granddaughter; and it was Camille's arrival that softened the hearts of Michael's parents. They insisted that Sophie come live with them while she finished her last year of university. Michael was reluctant, as were Sophie's own parents, but Sophie convinced them all that what Michael needed was to reconnect with his own parents and that this would be best for the new baby too.

So when Michael came back from the *Middle East* to accompany the birth of his daughter, he brought along with him the promise that the next would be his last year away from *Europe* and that his next homecoming would be to stay with his wife and daughter permanently. Michael fell in love with Camille the first time he caught sight of her—he couldn't hold back the tears of joy. Sophie could still see him as the loving boy that she had fallen for so long ago.

Michael finally went back to *Afghanistan* for what he hoped would be his fourth and final tour, but something happened that would change his life forever. On his last mission, his convoy suffered a violent attack; nearly his entire section was killed or captured. Michael escaped with a concussion and only a few scrapes and bruises having been thrown from his vehicle when a terrorists' mine exploded under the truck in front of his. The blast was so violent that it flipped his truck onto its side crushing several within as it slid down the embankment. Michael was thrown clear but unconscious. The terrorists attacked the convoy, took several hostages and killed the rest, leaving him for dead at the bottom of the embankment.

Michael was located by a search party three days later; alone, dehydrated, and almost lifeless, but he survived. Sophie was only informed a week later, after Michael had been brought in via *medevac* to *Kabul's Daoud Khan Military Hospital.* She was desperate for news, unable to reach her husband for almost twenty days. When they were finally able to talk, Michael calmed her fears telling her that he would be home as soon as he was in conditions to catch a flight back.

Not long after, his four years were up; Michael got his discharge. Miraculously, he had suffered no lasting physical consequences from his last mission. The same was not true of the psychological damage—he began having horrific nightmares, reliving the event over and over—his entire personality began to change. He was never the same again. When he finally came home, this time to his parent's house, Michael had lost that sparkle of happiness in his eyes. The war had destroyed him. The only person who could still bring out any vestige of the old Michael was Camille.

During those early years, Sophie would frequently insist that he get psychological help to cope with his issues, but he resisted, equally convinced that everything was fine.

The years passed and things only got worse. Michael closed himself off from everyone as more and more his fears and traumas took over his life. Sophie however, never stopped trying to help him, putting her love for him above everything. By then Sophie was working in the restaurant sector in *Richmond* where she could be closer to her daughter.

Sophie's dedication to her husband and daughter was recognized and profoundly appreciated by her in-laws Albert and Margaret Brown; they grew closer and closer to her as the years passed. It was Margaret who, seeing her son sinking deeper and deeper into his traumas, unable to find his way through them and unable to establish himself in any kind of work, suggested that the couple open a bistro with her and her husband's financial help.

Sophie hesitated. She was sadly aware that what was helping to keep her marriage together and her own sanity, was the fact that she could spend at least ten hours away from that whole situation. She loved him, but she also realized that she was reaching her limit.

Camille had just turned five when Sophie and Michael opened the bistro in *South Kensington*. Things had even started well with Michel taking care of supplies, the physical infrastructure, and finances, while Sophie administrated the business, coordinated the kitchen crew, and attended to the clients–areas that she dominated with her knowledge, articulation, and charisma.

Regardless of their initial success, in less than six months from its inauguration—watching Sophie's innate ease with the diners and the help—Michael began to develop a blind and incontrollable jealousy. Their moments of intimacy had long become few and far between, so in Michael's head, he was absolutely certain that she must be having affairs with clients and the help. It reached a point where he attacked the then bistro's chef, positive that he was being cuckolded. The leap from crises of jealousy to physical aggressions against Sophie was sadly inevitable.

By the time the restaurant completed two years, Sophie couldn't shoulder the situation anymore, even though she had yet to react. In the beginning, she tried to brush it off with the excuse that he had suffered such grave traumas during the war; later, it was because Camille had never witnessed any scene of violence. Up until then, the aggressions still hadn't gone beyond shouting and shoving.

The first time Michael physically attacked Sophie was on a night that the two had returned to his parent's home from the restaurant—where they still lived and shared the same bedroom—when Michael's jealousy led to violence because Sophie had hugged one of their habitual clients. It hadn't mattered that the guy's wife was there at the time or that Sophie had hugged her first.

They were in their bedroom when it started: "you think I didn't see you hitting on that guy?" Closing the door, Michael suddenly berated her.

"What are you talking about now, Michael?" Sophie asked tiredly, seated at her dressing table, her back to him as she brushed her hair. "You know I like to treat people well. Just as I like to be treated too. Anyway, he was with his wife. Have you become deranged—did you not see her?"

"Too well too, wouldn't you say? You think I'm blind? And you have the gall to pull that kind of stunt in front of me?" Spittle flew as Michael raged, working himself into fit of fury. Fists clenched at his sides, his entire body rigid.

Sophie continued calmly brushing her hair. "You really must be going mad. I've tried and tried to tell you that you need to get help Michael. You're destroying our marriage." Tired of his tantrums, she turned to walk past him, intending to go down the hall toward the bathroom. Michael had turned into an old man, his body bloated, humorless, angry and vindictive; no vestige remained of that fun, handsome boy—inside and out—whom she had known what now seemed a lifetime ago and fallen in love with, she thought as she looked at this pathetic lump. She didn't even recognize him anymore.

She had just opened the door when he grabbed her by the arm forcefully, "Don't turn your back on me when I'm talking to you," he demanded.

"What do you think you're doing Michael?" She tried to pull her arm loose, "I'm getting tired of your threats and aggressions," Sophie continued speaking calmly so as not to irritate him more or wake Camille.

"And I'm tired of having a slag for a wife!"

Sophie yanked her arm to get away from Michael, but he raised his hand and hit her with such force that she flew back, falling to the floor as she cried out in pain and shock, covering her face with her arms crossed over her head, terrified of what might come next.

"Papa, what are you doing?" Camille sobbed standing in the hall. Her eyes round as saucers, she ran to her mother covering her with her own seven-year-old body sobbing hysterically. She had seen the entire scene of her beloved father striking *Maman* as she stood in their doorway awakened by their fighting.

Michael couldn't stand the shame of the one he loved most in the world seeing the monster within him exposed. He threw himself on the bed and wept uncontrollably, curled in the fetal position as he hid his face in his pillow.

Sophie jumped to her feet, picking Camille up, carried her toward her room, trying to calm her daughter, her voice tremulous, "it is nothing, my child. *Papa* is just nervous, that's all." Tears continued to slide silently down her cheeks, one side of her face, bright pink where he had struck her, as she put the child back in her bed and lay down beside her, holding her tightly until they both fell asleep, exhausted.

That was the first and last time Michael ever physically attacked Sophie in such a violent manner. Nothing would ever be the same again.

The next day he tried to apologize, begging her forgiveness, promising to get help. But it was too late. Sophie told him that she would leave their home taking Camille with her and asked Margaret only for a few days to stay in the house, dividing the room with her daughter, until she could find a place to live.

Although Margaret and her husband knew what was happening under their roof, they had always kept a distance, not wanting to get involved, giving the young couple room, they always insisted to one another. So, the night before neither one of them left their room, ignoring the shouting as usual. But that next day, when Sophie asked for their help and told them she was separating from her husband, they supported her decision immediately. Remorseful that they hadn't interfered the night before once they saw the hand-shaped bruise on her face, they insisted on offering their full assistance, even to pay the deposit and rent of an apartment for her and their beloved granddaughter.

And so, Sophie finally abandoned her marriage when her daughter was only seven years old, yet she was careful never to let her daughter lose the admiration and love she had for her father. In their separation, the two agreed to hold one half each of the restaurant and maintain their same functions. Sophie however, put her foot down and only agreed to work with Michael if he sought psychiatric or psychological help. Michael, in order to stay close to his daughter—she would go every day to the restaurant after class—agreed immediately, though he never took his treatment very seriously.

As the years passed, Michael's comportment did improve, but every once in a while, he would fly into a fit of jealousy over his ex-wife. He honestly believed that he still loved her very much. Sophie on the other hand, always put him in his place, that of ex-husband, nothing more to her than the father of her daughter.

Sophie and Camille moved into a small apartment near the restaurant. In the divorce agreement it was determined that the expenses would come out of the bistro's income before any financial results of the business.

Until she completed fifteen years of age, Sophie and Michael agreed that Camille would stay no later than six-thirty at the restaurant with them, and that they would agree which of the two would take her home each day. When it was Sophie's day to close the restaurant, Michael stayed with Camille until her mother arrived home. Camille was usually asleep by that time, and Sophie would call ahead so that Michael could be gone before she arrived. In order for all these arrangements to work to Camille's best interests, Michael needed a copy of the apartment key—Sophie wasn't too pleased about that in the beginning, but as time passed, so did any concerns she had.

By the time Camille finally turned fifteen, she had grown to be a very pretty girl with blue eyes like her father's, thin and tall, with golden-brown hair cut in a long bob barely touching her shoulders. She always went directly to her parent's restaurant after classes, would have a snack in the kitchen, then studied from four in the afternoon until around six-thirty, using one of the tables in the salon until the movement in the bistro would begin to pick up. She would then happily rush to put her books away to help take orders, serve, and bus dishes for their clients. She had grown to be good-tempered and responsible, her parent's pride.

From then on, Camille no longer needed one of her parents standing such close watch over her. The fact that Michael never returned his copy of the apartment door key however went unnoticed by Camille or her mother.

In London, Still

Chapter Twenty-Five – Back To The Origin

Eduardo finally took off for *Latin America*, bringing with him great memories of a week that had just ended.

His flight left Heathrow at two in the afternoon, arriving in *Ciudad Del Mexico* at around seven in the evening due to the number of time zones he passed through to get there. Since it had been a long flight, Eduardo decided to have dinner at his hotel and sleep early to be rested for the upcoming days of work that would be long and hard. He would be in *Mexico* until Friday for work but decided to program his flight to *Santiago do Chile* on Sunday so that he could enjoy at least one full day in the city.

Eduardo's five days in *Mexico* were overflowing with meetings on balance sheet analyses, fiscal discovery and audits, and project costs of the entire region and he still managed to fit in at least four visits to wind or solar farms. One had been a combo of wind towers and solar panels. Eduardo didn't know this world of renewable energy and was impressed by what he saw.

He ended the week satisfied with what he had seen and had taken note of several points for improvement of costs and tax credit benefits. What disappointed him though was the mediocre technical level of the professionals at the company in general, as well as the generalized deficiency in English fluency, even written. The usefulness of the visit, as far as communications was concerned, only wasn't worse because he spoke Spanish fluently. These issues would need to be addressed, and quickly.

Despite the challenges of his first visit to *Tottenham Equity's* operations in that country, they were more than compensated by the excellent local food. He learned on that trip that the best Mexican food could only be found in *Mexico*.

On Friday, Eduardo managed to finish up his work a little early. Thanking his team for an incredible week and for the experience, he said his good-byes to everyone at the main office and left. After leaving the office, he went directly to the downtown area and enjoyed visiting a few touristic spots in the historic center—the *Plaza de la Constituición*, the Palace of Fine Arts, and *La Casa Azul*, a cobalt blue-walled museum dedicated to Frida Kahol's life, one of his and Gabrielle's all-time favorite artists. There he remained for over two hours and was moved by the visit.

He took the opportunity to dine before returning to the hotel and ate at *Villa Maria* in *Polanco*, a *barrio nobre* of the city. He loved the food. Arriving, he asked for a bottle of *Zinfandel*, a California red he enjoyed on infrequent trips to the *United States*. To start he had *tacos de pescado al pastor* and for his main dish *Manchamanteles de Sor Juana*. An absolute delight! The servings were large, so he decided to skip dessert and had a *carajillo* to finish his meal. Arriving back at his hotel, it was nearly eleven that evening; he fell asleep almost immediately.

The next day he visited the pyramids of *Teotihuacan,* some fifty kilometers outside of the city limits. It was truly an exceptional day.

Sunday Eduardo caught his flight at noon for *Santiago do Chile.* He would only stay two days there since he already knew the region, and it not being one that he particularly cared for, he decided to focus only on his work and leave as soon as possible. By Tuesday evening, he was in *Buenos Aires* where he took advantage of his early arrival, taking a stroll around town before dining at one of the innumerous restaurants that specialized in barbequed meats that the city had to offer.

In *Argentina* he visited not only farms in operation, but also the new 300MW project under construction far to the south which he found enlightening, never having visited a construction site before—it was truly a whole new world—where the single-minded goal was all about meeting deadlines.

To cut down on his travel time between the *Buenos Aires* office and the widely spread wind farms, Eduardo decided that flying would be more expedient. Using commercial flights to take him as close as possible to the wind farms; then from the small domestic airports he and the team designated to accompany him would use huge rented SUVs to complete the trips, they were comfortable and up to par for the often rugged road conditions.

In *Argentina* as he had in *Chile*, Eduardo made a series of notations and shared with his teams a few points they could implement immediately. He promised all the members of his teams in all three countries full reports about his visit and made clear that he was not conducting an audit, rather a visit to get to know everyone personally and establish a relationship of collaboration moving forward.

Eduardo left the last Hispanic city of his tour on Friday night and caught a direct flight to *Rio de Janeiro*. Although the main offices of *Tottenham Equity* in *Brazil* were in *São Paulo*, Eduardo had asked for and received authorization from Anton to make a stop in his home town before returning to work on Tuesday of the upcoming week.

En route from *Tom Jobim Airport* to his hotel in *Ipanema*, Eduardo was overcome with emotion at the sight of the *Cristo Redentor* as he travelled the *Linha Vermelha*. During the taxi ride through the *Centro, Glória, Aterro do Flamengo, Botafogo* and *Copacabana* before finally reaching *Ipanema*. Even at night, Eduardo could see the situation of abandon of his marvelous city. It was a depressing sight.

During the entire ride to his hotel, his taxi driver droned on and on about the tragedies that afflicted the city. 'My God, what have they done to my *Rio*? What have they done to my *Brazil*?' flashed through Eduardo's mind along with a profound sense of sadness.

Eduardo used that final week in his home town to return to *Urca*, see the house where he had been born, admiring it from the other side of the street, and look up a few old friends. He went to the beach in *Ipanema* alone and although it was autumn, it was *Rio* weather—the temperature was hitting 28 degrees *Celsius*—slightly better than *London's* hottest summer days— so he sat on the beach in the hot sand—idly sifting it through fingers and toes—enjoying that beautiful panorama and wondered if this might not be the time to be come back.

Among the few friends he met up with on this trip was Flavio de Lucca, still the CEO of *Beauté, Brazil*. The two arranged to have lunch on Monday at *Marius*, on the beach in *Leme*. Eduardo was hankering for a good *rodízio de carnes* and catching up on all the latest news.

The two chatted for hours about what had happened to Rio de Janeiro and in *Beauté* over the past ten years. Flavio told Eduardo that thanks to the crisis that had been deteriorating the country since 2014 and Frédéric's pernicious influence, operations in the country had almost closed but, with the possibility of leaving some two thousand workers jobless, the labor union demanded government intervention, and simply put, the government threatened to impose import taxes so high on their brand products that it would surely cause the demise of the brand in *Brazil* should the French choose to close *Beauté* in *Brazil*.

"Those French sons–of–bitches got the message and backed off from that decision," Flavio said with an air of one having his soul washed clean. "Between us, and may it never leave this table," he said kissing two fingers, "but I made certain that the union boss heard about the company's intent before the shit hit the fan," he ended with a bark of laughter.

"You did the right thing Flávio," Eduardo replied. "Those people are a band of reprobates. They think we're some sub-human race and still a colony. I learned that lesson very well since I moved to London. Until today, as a Brazilian I still have to prove myself time and again as a professional, otherwise I become the 'incompetent immigrant' that doesn't understand anything," Eduardo ended with an air of disappointment, "and then it's just sour grapes if we even imply that they're being racists or hypocrites."

"I can only imagine, my friend. I think it's really courageous of you to make such a radical change in your life," Flávio replied, carefully avoiding mentioning Gabrielle's death.

"So, what about Frédéric—is he still putting his finger on the scale to benefit European operations?" Eduardo queried, bringing the discussion back to *Beauté*.

"After that confusion that almost closed Brazilian operations, Frédéric was 'invited' to retire by the board. Today he is only a consultant to *Beauté*, limited to Europe; but I did hear that the bastard is filthy rich from certain dealings he had with company directors in Africa," Flávio gossiped half-enviously.

"Wow!" Eduardo looked surprised, "I never would have thought that of him. He never even hinted at anything of that type anywhere near me."

"He was a rogue Eduardo, and most likely was aware that you were too honorable to go for any of that! Maybe that's even why he didn't go too far out of his way to help you or keep you in the company," Flávio speculated.

"Anyway, that's all behind me now," Eduardo brushed that entire line of thought away, savoring another bite of his fantastic *picanha*.

The two talked on for another hour or so as they gorged—on thin slivers of tender rare meats, flavored only with rock salt—cooked high over a Brazilian-style barbeque pit—which the waiters circulating between tables on huge sword-like spits balanced on tiny concave trays and served delicately with huge knives—until finally, the two were unable to take another bite. They went their separate ways after they shook hands and pounded each other on the back at the entrance of the restaurant with promises to 'do it again' next time Eduardo was in town. Eduardo caught a taxi back to his hotel, picked up his bag with reception having already checked out, and took another taxi to the *Santos Dumond Airport*, admired its latest facelift, and caught the next shuttle to São Paulo; it being the off season, they only took off every thirty minutes.

Leaving *Congonhas Airport* in *São Paulo* less than an hour later, his turn finally arrived in the line for taxis and he made his way to his hotel near *Avenida Faria Lima* where *Tottenham Equity's* offices were located in Brazil. He remained four days in *São Paulo* and then visited a few wind farms in the Northeast of *Brazil*. Particularly memorable was *San Miguel do Gostoso,* in *Rio Grande do Norte,* a 125km drive from the state capital, *Natal*. Since it was a short drive and the roads were in good conditions, Eduardo decided to rent an SUV and drive himself to the wind farm where the Operations & Maintenance Manager was already waiting to show him his first working wind farm in *Brazil*.

Eduardo was dazzled with the drive to *San Miguel*, a road following along the beachfront. He contemplated the green seas of the region and the beautiful pristine sand dunes marked only by the wind. At one point along the way Eduardo decided to make a quick stop on the roadside and walked down to the beach. Where the rough grass ended and the sand began, he removed his shoes and socks, rolling his pants up a bit he continued on to where the gentle waves lapped the beach wetting his hands and feet in the transparent sea. 'How warm the water!' he thought surprised, his mind flashing back with longing to earlier adventures in his ten-year relationship with his beloved.

Eduardo had left *Natal* at dawn and was able to finish up his visit to the *Rio Grande do Norte* wind farms before noon. By sunset he was stepping out of the *Vitória da Conquista* airport, the only commercial airport of the region. He would stay overnight in a hotel and leave early by helicopter to the wind farm site in *Caetité, Bahia.* This was the company's largest wind farm in production and couldn't possibly be overlooked, despite being located over 750km from the state capital, *Salvador*, and accessible by only two rather difficult roads, all of which made another helicopter ride his best and fastest option.

One final short flight, and Eduardo would conclude his trip to *Brazil* with visits to the wind farms in *Traíri, Ceará.* His flight arrived in *Fortaleza*, the state capital by late afternoon, so he stayed the night in a hotel on the beautiful seafront aptly named '*Beira Mar'*, *Fortaleza's* prime beachfront where kilometer after kilometer was filled with fine hotels and magnificent luxury apartment buildings where he took advantage of the balmy evening to enjoy a long walk on the six kilometer boardwalk and drink coconut water straight from the nut, freshly opened and pierced by its sidewalk vendor. *Delicioso!*

Despite the beautiful seaside roads that traced the gently curving eastern seafront of the state, leaving *Fortaleza*, Eduardo again preferred the commodity and noisy speed of a chartered helicopter. The view from above was mesmerizing as they flew

316

along the lovely seacoast. It was breathtaking. Limpid waters, and practically deserted beaches along the route–emptying more and more of people—as they flew further and further from the capital. 'Brie would have loved this trip,' he mused watching the white crested waves hitting beach after sandy beach. He stopped at all three sites in *Traíri* County, laid out one beside to the other. There was an elevator in one turbine. Excited at the novelty, he geared up with the mandatory PPEs, went 160m up the tight tower and into the hot, stifling, and shockingly confining space of the turbine—his admiration expanded for the guys who erected and maintained these monoliths to energy. Disappointed that he wasn't allowed to look out through the hatch on the top without several days of safety training, he returned directly to the airport in *Fortaleza*, catching the direct flight to *Lisbon*.

That week Eduardo saw a new face of *Brazil* for him. He thought on the immense diversity of his country with its twenty-six states, and the *Distrito Federal*, often called "Fantasy Island" by the more cynically-minded of his countrymen because of the politicians' distance from reality. Always having worked for foreign multinationals while still living in *Rio de Janeiro*, his trips were always overseas. Even for his vacations he opted for foreign airs, far from this *South American* behemoth.

Eduardo's trip ended back in *London* with a sense of personal satisfaction for a job well done. While he flew from the *Lisbon International* to *Heathrow* his mind often wandered back to thoughts of returning to *Brazil* to get to know his own country better.

Chapter Twenty-Six – Back to Sophie's

Since the evening Eduardo and his friends had come to her restaurant a few weeks ago, Sophie had been unable to get her daughter's last words of that evening out of her head, "Eduardo was the husband of Gabrielle Debois," trailed through her thoughts like some mournful dirge.

'He must have suffered terribly these past two years,' she found herself musing time and again, 'I can't imagine what must be going on in his heart and mind all this time. It must be so difficult to overcome such successive tragedies she empathized. What emptiness and pain he must feel, even now,' were her *idées fixe*, as she tried to imagine the unimaginable.

Although everything was going as usual for Sophie since that night, the truth of the matter was that Sophie could hardly wait for the next visit from that delightful group of men: Eduardo, Martin, Tristan and Jordan. Since that night, she had thought a great deal on how good it would be to have such dear friends that could be by one's side as often as possible.

Unfortunately, the course of her own history had separated her from her own good friends. And the prince that Michael once was had become a monster in her eyes; one who had stolen her youth. At least she still had two great loves in her life worth fighting for: her beloved daughter Camille and her bistro, both into which she deposited all her dedication and energy. But it had been forever since her last vacation or even a carefree moment to herself. Sometimes, she dreamed of a single 24-hour period just for herself, without having to think or worry about absolutely anything. Twenty-four hours of the pure pleasure of having absolutely nothing on her mind.

Eduardo arrived in *London* on Saturday and was still in the baggage area of *Heathrow* when he began calling his friends to try and set something up for that evening. It was still early in the morning and Tristan was home. "Eduardo, *mon cher ami*, how is everything in *Brazil*?" Tristan blurted out enthusiastically as he answered Eduardo's incoming call.

"I'm already back in *London*—just flew into *Heathrow*—but I really want to see you guys," Eduardo responded happy to hear his friend's voice. "As for my beloved *Brazil*, my friend, things aren't going very well there, I'm afraid. There's a new government, but I don't know whether they can resolve the basic problems that the country has. Anyway, I want to talk about happier things, and I would like very much to have dinner with you two and Martin tonight. Are you guys in?"

"Oh, unfortunately, I can't get away tonight," Tristan lamented, "the restaurant on Saturdays is non-stop full. We've got reservations booked all the way through to midnight! We even had to reject some last-minute VIPs for you to have an idea," Tristan replied already imagining the evening frazzle. "But I can ask if Jordan wants to go with you guys," he concluded, glad that his dear friend was seeming more like his old self, not wanting to see a relapse from neglect.

"I'm in, for sure," Eduardo replied. "It's a shame that you won't be with us; but we can send you photos," he ended with a laugh.

"Funny, you are so very funny, no?" Tristan chuckled, not rising in the least to Eduardo's bait. "Hold one moment please, let me ask him." Tristan put his phone on mute. While waiting, Eduardo fiddled with the zippers on his suitcase. Two minutes later, Tristan was back on line, "Jordan is up for it," he said rather breathlessly, "where are you planning on going?"

"Well, I really liked that bistro we went to last time. I'll message him later with the place and time," Eduardo replied.

"Perfect!" Tristan replied as he flagged down a taxi in the middle of the street. "We'll talk later, I have to run," he gasped, opening the taxi's door, "*Romarin,* please...good bye my friend." And with that the line went dead.

Eduardo looked at his phone and said, "later," to no one in particular then punched in Martin's number. No answer. 'He must be sleeping it off,' he thought.

Eduardo went home, taking the *Piccadilly Line,* and while he waited on the subway station platform, he sent a message by *WhatsApp* to Jordan confirming their encounter for seven that evening in front of *Sophie's Bistro.* Jordan's response came back immediately with a grinning *emoji.* Next he sent the following message to Martin: "Good morning sleepyhead. Back in London. Tried to call earlier. You must be hung over, sleeping it off. Jordan and I are going to that bistro you indicated. Dinner and Talk at seven. If you're up for it, meet us there, ok? *Hugs (emoji)*"

Finally arriving home, Eduardo took a shower and went directly to bed to rest for the evening. He woke late afternoon, around four, ate a light snack that wouldn't ruin his appetite for dinner and got ready to meet Jordan and Martin.

It was only when he was already in the bus and on his way that Martin's message pinged on his *WhatsApp*: "Hey man, good to hear you're back. *London* isn't the same without you. Sorry but will have to decline your invite, my friend. Met a fantastic girl on one of those new *Apps* and I am going to meet her for the first time in the flesh. Let's do something next week? Don't cry, you'll see me on Monday, ok? *Hugs (emoji) I'm outta here! (GIF)"*

Eduardo's fingers flew over his mobile's keyboard as he typed in his response, "No problem, Martin, no tears in my beer. Enjoy your evening. See you Monday. *xoxo*." Simultaneously, he sent the message and rose from his seat, exiting the subway at *South Kensington,* he walked slowly toward the street of the bistro. As he turned the corner and saw the restaurant, he stopped in his tracks, astonished at the sight of the crowd lined up at their door, undoubtedly waiting for their tables. Arriving at the front door of the restaurant he pushed it open and went through to find out how the waiting list was faring. It was none other than Camille at the reception. He recognized her and smiled, "Good evening. Camille, isn't it?"

"Good evening Eduardo!" She recognized him immediately— and how could she not? Her mother had been going on about him for ages. "I do hope you have a reservation with us for tonight, it is absolute insanity here today. And this is just the end of spring!" She replied with a bright smile and a dimple.

"Wow—yes, I can see that!" He grinned rather foolishly. "Unfortunately, I came hoping to get a table for me and my friend. I just arrived today from a long trip and didn't even remember to call in a reservation."

"Oh, unfortunately I'm going to have to let you down," Camille replied rather disappointed herself.

At that moment Sophie drew up alongside her daughter after coming through the kitchen door. "Eduardo? What a delightful surprise! How nice to see you back at *Sophie's,*" she dimpled her face aglow with pleasure at the sight of him.

"Thank you, Sophie," Eduardo leaned over to kiss her on both cheeks. "We very much enjoyed your food and the special attention when we were here last. That's why we decided to come again today. But only Jordan is coming to meet me this time," Eduardo laughed.

"And the other two, Martin and Tristan," Sophie asked over the chatter around them, then interrupted herself, "I'm sorry Eduardo, but its just crazy here today, shall we go outside to talk a little?" She proposed.

"Of course, no problem," Eduardo replied, holding the door for her as he followed her out.

Glancing up after the door closed behind him, Eduardo saw Jordan as he turned the corner and waved to him. "Hey Jordan, I'm over here!" He shouted to his friend and then went back to explaining the situation to Sophie, "Martin had a date and Tristan couldn't leave *Romarin* to be with us. The *maison* was full too."

"Ah, but what a shame," she said disappointed that she wouldn't see the two of them tonight, "at any rate, we wouldn't be able to receive anyone else without a reservation today, as you can see for yourself," she replied glancing at the line before looking back up at him.

At precisely that moment Jordan reached them. "Sophie, how delightful to see you again," Jordan exclaimed, kissing her cheeks and embracing her delicately. "Wow!" He said looking around delighted, "this is crazy, right? How wonderful! I hope our reservation doesn't take too long" he concluded as he shook hands and hugged Eduardo, patting him on the back.

Eduardo released him and gave him a rather foolish lopsided grin as he explained that he hadn't thought to call in a reservation before confirming his choice of restaurant.

"Are you crazy Eduardo? Have you forgotten how the restaurants get at this time of year, especially the better ones,"

Jordan mildly berated his friend, shaking his head back and forth in mock disgust as Sophie immediately jumped in to defend Eduardo, "oh Jordan, poor Eduardo isn't to blame. He was just telling Camille how he had arrived today and hadn't even thought to make a reservation," she said patting Eduardo on the arm to console him.

"I know Sophie," Jordan replied with a sly smile, "it's just that Eduardo always does all the right things, never a step out of place; so we all try to make a point of sticking it to him when he screws up royally, like now," he poked Eduardo in the ribs with his elbow laughing at Eduardo's downfallen expression. Then the two men burst out laughing.

"You are just so cute, *n'est-ce pas*," Eduardo chuckled, pinching Jordan's cheek in jest and shaking it back and forth as he grinned foolishly at him, not in the least upset by his teasing.

"Gee guys, I'm so sorry; but I'm going to have to owe you one for today. *Je suis vraiment désolé*," Sophie said looking back and forth between the two, actually the most disappointed of the three.

"Please don't worry about it," Eduardo replied gallantly.

"Hold on, just a moment while I check with Camille to see if there have been any cancellations between seven-thirty and eight-thirty. At any rate, would you like something to drink while you wait? Yes?" She looked at them both enquiringly.

"Of course!" Eduardo interjected before she had even finished speaking.

Sophie smiled and went back into the restaurant to speak with Camille. She was also unknowingly being watched by Michael from behind the bar, where he had kept his eyes on her since she and Eduardo had exchanged their first words of the evening.

"I don't know Eduardo, but I think Sophie has her eye on you," Jordan said poking him in the ribs, mischievously provoking Eduardo.

"Oh, *arrête* Jordan! No way," Eduardo's cheeks turned dark red nudging his friend back with an elbow in the ribs. "And with all the responsibilities she carries, not to mention her ex hanging around her neck, I can't believe she has time to think about relationships right now. Anyway, from the little she told us the last time, that was the impression I got," Eduardo concluded lamely.

"You straight guys are really dumb, aren't you?" Jordan poked him in the chest this time as he broke into laughter.

"You think? I don't know about that," Eduardo retorted harrumphing his notion.

"You *wanna* bet she's going to get a table for us," Jordan wagered, sticking his chin out defiantly, still grinning.

"Oh, I doubt it; she's just being polite," Eduardo replied.

"Stop playing the fool, Eduardo. It's obvious she's interested in you. Now if *you* aren't, that's another thing altogether," Jordan replied letting his voice trail off nonchalantly as he glanced at his friend from the corner of his eye.

"No. No, I didn't say that man," Eduardo fumbled, "I just don't know whether I'm prepared to involve myself with anyone just now and I don't want to give any false hope to anyone either, especially someone as interesting as she is," he continued more firmly.

"Oh, so you *are* interested…" Jordan looked squarely at Eduardo, raising his eyebrows in tandem with the corners of his mouth.

"I don't know anything about that Jordan," Eduardo responded solemnly.

Exasperated, "look, neither you nor she is obligated to do anything; but that doesn't mean that you can't get to know each other. Right?" Jordan pressed his point.

"Right!" Eduardo concluded, ending the subject.

As the two were talking, Sophie was also discussing the possibility of getting them a table with her daughter. "*Ma fille*, have you started calling for the reservations of the next hour to see if there are any cancellations?" Sophie asked more hopeful than not.

"Yes *Maman*, but all are confirmed and some are even outside waiting," Camille responded calmly eying her mother. "*Madam* Sophie, I see that you have second intentions with Eduardo, ok?"

"Ah, *mon Dieu*, is it so obvious?" Sophie replied flustered.

"Don't worry, he hasn't noticed yet, but I think his friend may have," Camille glanced out the window toward the two men deep in conversation.

"Are you sure Camille?" Sophie glanced surreptitiously in their direction.

"You can bet on it!" was the firm affirmation her daughter proclaimed.

Sophie sighed, "at any rate, we don't have a table, so we can't very well hold them here, can we?"

Camille glanced back at her mother, "true, we can't really hold *them* here, but we can find a way to get *you* a night off, right?" She proposed with a perfectly innocent expression on her face.

"What are you saying, you silly girl? How could I possibly leave the restaurant with all these patrons here? And what about your father—he would go berserk," Sophie insisted, shocked more by the proposal than who was doing the suggesting.

"Oh, we can always find a way," Camille replied flipping one hand carelessly at shoulder height. "As for my father, don't worry, I can get him off your trail so that you can 'escape'," Camille replied greatly enjoying the novelty of the whole thing.

Sophie went back to the sidewalk to give the men the sad news of the impossibility of getting a table at all that night.

"Don't worry Sophie," Eduardo replied trying to cheer her up, "we'll all come back next week, for sure."

"Oh, but I am so sad that we won't have the pleasure of having you here with us today. I was already so happy that I would be able to stop by your table a little in between attending to one patron and another," she replied coyly.

"And what if I were to try and get a table at *Romarin*," Jordan suggested, as if the idea suddenly dawned on him, "would you agree to come with us Sophie? Take a night off?"

"Ah, I don't know if I can leave my *maison* alone," Sophie responded her face brightening for an instant before it fell and she was back in reality.

"No, I won't accept your refusal!" Jordan insisted.

"I would love for you join us Sophie," Eduardo ratifying the invitation, both men looking hopefully at her.

"But are you sure I wouldn't be intruding?" Sophie asked looking from the face of one man to the other and back.

"What do you mean, 'intrude'?" Jordan asked quizzically his eyebrows arched high, "how could you possibly intrude on a dinner between friends, particularly when one is gay and the other straight? You're more than welcome, my dear," he concluded his head cocked to the side and a slightly crooked smile dancing on his lips.

They all laughed together this time.

"Let me try to talk to Tristan," Jordan finally said, stepping away to call his husband.

While Jordan was on the phone, Sophie again asked Eduardo if he was sure that she wouldn't be intruding on their night out. "Not in the least, Sophie. You're already practically a member of the gang!" Eduardo insisted.

"Oh, you flatter me!" Sophie replied tickled as she blushed. "Well, then let me see with Camille how they can get by in my absence."

A few minutes had passed as Eduardo idly watched the crowd before Sophie and Jordan reformed the little trio.

"Done!" Jordan said wrinkling his nose delighted with his success, "we've got a table for 8:30. It's almost 8:00 so Sophie, my angel, we must run," he said tapping his watch in emphasis.

"Ah *mon Dieu*! I'm going to *Romarin*! I can't believe it," Sophie almost squealed with excitement grinning from ear to ear her dimple deepened. She rushed back into the bistro, said something to Camille and disappeared. Camille came out and served them the white wine they had ordered. "Hello again, *mecs,*" Camille said as she handed Eduardo one glass and Jordan the other, "the wine is on the house. My mother has gone home to get ready and asked that you meet her in fifteen minutes in front of the *Museum of Natural History*. She also said that she would get an *Uber* for everyone. Have a great evening!" She grinned, her dimple a replica of her mother's.

The two men looked at one another, eyes round with surprised pleasure, thanked her and sipped their wine, continuing their conversation as she left. After about fifteen minutes they handed their empty glasses over to one of the waiters circulating outside and walked off to the meeting place.

As soon as Camille had returned from giving them their wine and message, she was stopped by her father who held onto her arm and whispered into her ear, "where is your mother?" his tone pithy.

"She asked me to take care of things here while she went home to take some medication, she isn't feeling well," Camille's soft contralto soothing and her lovely blue eyes looking guilelessly into her father's.

"Well, I hope she doesn't take her time, we can't work with one person down," he replied gruffly softening his tone as he looked into his beloved daughter's eyes.

"Don't worry papa, everything is under control," she replied turning back to her work. Camille had already called for reinforcements—one of her friends from school who always picked up hours at the bistro during school holidays. As soon as her friend arrived she quickly updated her then ran home to help her mother.

"Oh, you look beautiful, *maman!*" Camille cried out as soon as she caught sight of her mother through her bedroom door. She was filled with pride and excitement. She couldn't remember when she had last seen her like this, simply stunning!

"Oh, stop that, *ma petite fille*! What nonsense, I'm just going out to have dinner with some friends," Sophie replied pleased with the compliment and excited about her night out.

"Uh huh, right," Camille answered, smiling with her usual perceptiveness far beyond her years.

"Now help me with this make-up because I don't even remember how to do this," Sophie replied giggling girlishly.

"You'll have a wonderful evening," Camille said as she picked through her mother's make-up choosing colors for a care-free evening. After Camille finished helping her mother, she ran all the way back to the restaurant while Sophie got into the *Uber* she had ordered. She smiled to herself, 'a night just for myself, and I can barely wait,' she thought gazing out the window of the moving car that would take her to pick up Eduardo and Jordan in front of the museum and then off to *Romarin*.

Chapter Twenty-Seven – A Silver Lining in Every Cloud

Sophie sat in the front seat of the *Uber* so that she would be able to see Eduardo and Jordan as she arrived at the *Museum of Natural History*. The two were standing in front of the west garden of the museum when Sophie spotted them and asked the driver to stop to pick them up.

"Let's go boys," she called waving from inside the car where they could barely see her. The two got in and all three were driven to *Mayfair*. It took no more than seven minutes for the driver to drop them at their destiny.

The two men stepped out of the *Uber* and Jordan rushed to help Sophie out. "Wow! You are beautiful! Is that really you Sophie?" Jordan half serious, half playfully cried out as she stepped out under the light of the streetlamps.

True, she looked nothing like that simple woman who wore no makeup and used department store blouses and jeans to work. Sophie had taken advantage of the warm night and wore a black sleeveless dress that showed off her curves—ending just below her knees—emphasizing a well-cared for curvaceous body. Completing the look were high heels and a little black lace bolero carried over her arm, just in case the weather changed. Being *London*, it could and would without notice.

Sophie had taken special care with her make-up which transformed her into a beautiful woman looking at least ten years her junior. Not that her skin wasn't smooth and clear, but the make-up brought out her qualities and gave her a skin an extra luster. The greenish flecks in her light brown eyes stood out thanks to Camille's artfully application of eye shadow and liner. Not having had enough time to style her hair, she simply twisted it into a loose *chignon* at the nape of her neck that exposed her lovely neckline. All this was with the expert help of a teenage daughter who at most was only ever seen sporting a light pink lipstick on special occasions.

"Oh stop teasing Jordan," Sophie retorted, blood rushing up her delicate neck to suffuse her cheeks, only making her even more lovely under the glow of the streetlights.

"Not at all Sophie; he is absolutely right. You look wonderful," Eduardo pitched in, reinforcing his friend's compliment.

"How did you manage such a quick transformation, Cinderella," Jordan quipped, still holding one of her hands while the three walked up to *Romarin's* doorway.

Sophie dimpled at his generous praises, "Camille came to my rescue just as I was trying to put on my make-up." She added simply, "I'm not used to using it anymore."

"Well, you should be," Jordan insisted, patting her hand. "You are naturally very pretty, but I think that you should try to explore a touch of good make-up in your day-to-day look. Something light, of course," he went on, "nothing too overdone" he counseled seriously.

Sophie knew that that wouldn't be possible, precisely because she didn't want to provoke Michael's extreme reactions. She preferred to avoid the siphoning off of her energies that those fights resulted in.

As the three entered the *Romarin*, Tristan was there to greet them. He had made certain that he keeps a close eye on the door, to be sure to welcome them. Through the windows to the street it was easy to see who was arriving at the packed restaurant. Jordan kissed his husband discretely. Then it was Eduardo who hugged Tristan, kissing his old friend's cheeks.

Finally, Tristan looked over Eduardo's shoulder, "ho, ho, and who have we here? Wasn't Sophie going to come with you guys?" Tristan teased, making his way toward Sophie, arms wide open to embrace her.

"Oh stop your silly nonsense Tristan! You three are disconcerting me," Sophie pretended to complain. "I couldn't come my first time to *Romarim* dressed in just any old thing, could I? Especially in the company of such handsome men," she insisted with a bright smile.

"Oh, so you think we're handsome, do you?" Tristan continued in the same mien—his back carefully to the salon—he smoothed out one of his perfectly trimmed sideburns with the tip of a finger, turning his head towards his shoulder, in a picture-perfect pose he vapidly batted his eyelashes. They all laughed.

"Of course you are," Sophie blushed as her eyes flitted over the three, finally stopping on Eduardo.

"Well, let's go in then. Welcome to *Romarin*," Tristan said with a slight bow. He turned and led them to a table of four and said that he would be back as soon as he could. Not less than ten minutes from when they first took their seats, barely having taken a first sip of their drinks and still examining the *menu* Jordan jumped up, apologized and made for the restrooms. After some delay he came back and announced that he had to leave. "Forgive me my friends, but I am not feeling well. I've already spoken with Tristan. Unfortunately, I am unable to stay with you," Jordan apologized bowing his head; making an effort to swallow, he put a hand to his throat as if in pain.

It was all a ploy devised by Tristan and Jordan to leave the two alone that evening. Eduardo and Sophie immediately offered to take him to the closest Emergency Room, insisting that it made no sense to stay and dine without him. Jordan insisted that Tristan would be with them intermittently throughout the evening, and said: "It's just too distressing to accept that your dinner would be ruined because of my silly indisposition. After all, it isn't every day that Sophie has a chance to escape work on a Saturday night to be among friends—her newest friends." He was quite convincing.

Sophie had been moved, but being an intelligent woman, she realized exactly what was going on—and she was loving it— they really were accepting her into their inner circle!

Jordan finally left the restaurant alone and soon after, Tristan offered them a smaller table in a more secluded part of the *salon*. Eduardo still had no notion of what had transpired.

Eduardo and Sophie had a very nice evening; they dined unhurriedly going into greater details about their marriages and their lives. For the first time, Eduardo was feeling comfortable talking about Gabrielle's death with someone. Perhaps it was because he was just getting to know Sophie. He told her everything, including what had transpired at the hospital, things he had never said aloud to anyone.

"When that doctor told us there at the hospital, that Gabrielle was in a coma and that they hadn't been able to save our daughter, I froze," Eduardo said quietly at one point that evening. "I don't know where I gathered the strength from so that I wouldn't collapse right then and there. My hope was always that Gabrielle would recover. While I was there at the hospital by her side, having to support the agony of seeing my wife in that state and at the same time take care of the burial of our daughter…I cried and begged God the entire time to at least save my Gabrielle."

Eduardo's eyes filled with tears, but he continued with his catharsis, "I would sit beside her and talk nonstop, willing her to hear me, to come back to me; but she never moved, not once. Two weeks after the incident I was at the hospital, sitting beside her, holding her hand. I must have dozed off from exhaustion and dreamed that she spoke to me. She told me never to give up on my happiness. And in that dream she told me that she was well, and that she loved me, and felt the love I had for her, but despite all our love and all our history, she wanted me to let her go. She told me to open my heart to new possibilities and then smiled her beautiful smile. I woke abruptly to the racket her monitor was making, the lines flat. I panicked! I ran down that hospital hallway screaming for help, but she was already gone. I'd never felt so abjectly alone. In less than a month I had buried my daughter and then my wife. And the reporters! My God, they wouldn't stop their incessant clamor! They hounded me for months. I even changed my telephone numbers more than once. But as the weeks and months passed, so did they; chasing after fresher stories of someone else's agony for *voyeurs* pretending it was news."

He took a sip of wine and only after he managed to control himself again did he look up at her. Sophie sat across from him and covered his hand with hers, the compassion evident in her eyes: "what a terrible, terrible thing Eduardo. I am so very sorry that you had to go through all that."

"I often think," he went on, almost to himself, "that I would have preferred that she had lived, regardless of what it might have been like. Anything would be better than to have lost her forever, even if she had sustained some permanent injury…" his voice trailing off, loosing himself in his memories, drifting.

"Eduardo," Sophie softly spoke his name. He came out of his reverie; looked directly at her—unfocused, momentarily puzzled—she wasn't Gabrielle. Continuing as if she hadn't noticed his confusion, recognizing if for what it was, "since you have been so open with me, I would like to be very frank with you too." In a voice that inexplicably soothed him, she laid out the flip side of that coin: "Thousands looked to Gabrielle as a real hero who won her way in that the male-dominated market in the very exclusive world of *haute cuisine*. I don't believe that she would have been able to be happy if she had woken from the coma to be less than she had always been: a strong, talented and independent woman. Who knows, perhaps living in a vegetative state, or bedridden forever, or voiceless? Wouldn't it be just a little selfish on your part to want her, regardless? Of course, *your* love for her was greater than any enduring injury, but would it have been fair to her? And more, with time this immense pain of yours will eventually transform into a sweet aching for a perfect love that you were so very privileged to have. Nothing and no one can ever take that memory from you."

"It's possible. Only time can tell if you're right," Eduardo reflected still not convinced, but willing to consider her viewpoint.

"I believe that your dream of her—minutes before her death—is of crucial importance. And you really should follow the counsel Gabrielle gave you; whether it was her or your subconscious," Sophie concluded.

"Maybe you're right, Sophie," Eduardo said with a sigh, finally acknowledging the inevitable.

"Look," Sophie said, bring home her point. "It may seem terrible of me, but sometimes I wonder what my life would have been like if Michael hadn't come back from that last mission in *Afghanistan*. Because honestly, my Michael died during that attack, or at most, by the time they found him at the bottom of that embankment. The fact is, I will never know, because he won't speak of it with anyone, not even me. But what I want to say is that if he had never come home, perhaps I would have held onto my marvelous image of him to this day untainted, and would have eventually moved on with my life with just my daughter. Would I have suffered the pain of loss? *C'est une vérité absolue!* And I did suffer, terribly too." She bowed her head, mourning her own loss for an instant, then looked him in the eye, "but time cures all, *n'est-ce pas*? I sent one man off to war but received a monster in return," Sophie shook her head in dismay. "And it took a very, very long time until I could find the courage to leave that situation. And what's worse, I still haven't freed myself completely. We must be very careful of what we wish, *mon chérie*. When Michael was reported missing, what I wished for most, was that he come home alive—regardless the conditions."

"*Nossa*! I don't know if I can share such a pragmatic way of thinking Sophie. But I also haven't gone through what you did with your ex-husband. Speaking of whom, couldn't you get financing to buy him out?"

"The problem is that he will not sell his part, or buy mine; maybe he just can't, I just don't know," Sophie replied vexed, "what I do know, is that what he wants is to stay in my life for as long as he can. For you to have an idea," Sophie continued. "After we separated, I've lived only for the restaurant and for my dear Camille. I never again had a relationship with anyone. Simply because I was afraid of what he might do to me or to a boyfriend," Sophie confided with a slight fatalistic shrug.

"But that makes no sense. You can't accept to live your life in a prison like that," Eduardo exclaimed indignant at the unfairness.

"And you would tell me?" Sophie flashed him a grin of gaol humor. "Anyway, Camille finishes school in a few months, and in autumn she will start at a university. With her out of the house and the restaurant, I can begin thinking of some way to start my life again somewhere. If he insists and still refuses to buy me out, I'll abandon everything and Michael can do what he wants with *Sophie's*. The only *idée fixe* I have now is that I know I can be happy. And I will be too, someday!" She slapped the table lightly in emphasis.

"And your daughter supports these ideas of yours," Eduardo asked.

"She loves her father, but she also knows of what he is capable, so she supports me, so much so that she has already told me that I should never have waited so long. Only I wouldn't feel good about going away without my daughter at least being on her way to having a career," Sophie explained with a sigh.

"That's really good, Sophie," Eduardo assessed. "From the little I've seen, you seem to be very good friends."

Sophie smiled, "Camille is my best friend...but what about you? What are your projects for the future?"

By this time, they had already consumed their appetizers and main dishes, all between generous servings of wine, and were well into their second bottle. After this intimate meal and conversation, both were relaxed and at ease with each other. Eduardo had even managed to disregard the fact that he was eating in the restaurant that had once been owned and commanded by Gabrielle, though he hadn't entirely been able to avoid that cold sensation in the pit of his stomach when he had first walked through *Romarin's* doorway. Yet here he was, enjoying a meal and making a new friend.

"Well, I've just been promoted to a position in top management at the firm where I work, but after that drunken bout that you yourself witnessed, I had grief relapse resulting in a very serious conversation with Tristan. He advised me to revise my priorities—put the things I really love first." Eduardo continued sharing, "for the last two weeks I've been visiting a few countries in *Latin America*, including *Brazil*, and there I realized how little I know my own country, my culture..." He hesitated and appeared to lose steam, stopping mid-sentence.

"And with this you mean to say..." Sophie prompted him, gently dabbing her lips with her napkin then setting it neatly beside her plate.

Looking up at her from the glass of wine that he had just finished off, he went on, his voice dropped conspiratorially: "I want to tell you something that very few people know about me: I love to cook. And this I owe to Gabrielle." Gaining more confidence, now that his secret was out, Eduardo continued more normally, "But for the past few years, I have been so obsessed with wanting to prove to myself and to people here in *Great Britain*—that I could reestablish myself as a professional in my own area—I forgot all about my passions. When I first moved to *London*, I gave up a great career in *Brazil* and only found work as a waiter for a while. I did all that for love and have nothing to regret," he said, smiling wanly at those memories.

"Now, every beginning is hard, and believe you me, there are lots of idiots in management positions and as *chefs* in the restaurant business. I had to deal with a good many of them over the years. But a time came when I finally got the opportunity to work in the kitchen of a restaurant, and I was never happier in my life! I found myself there. Not just because I could feel closer to my wife, but because for me, it was pure pleasure putting into practice everything I had ever learned from her. The hardest was always dealing with the egos of idiots who thought they were better than everyone else, especially the managers and *chefs*. Nonetheless, I can't deny that I earned a certain respect as a cook, and so when I went to work in the kitchen of that restaurant, I found that I did very well as a *chef*. But then, the opportunity to go back to my own area of expertise came up, and I must confess, I didn't even hesitate! Am I unhappy doing what I do? No, I don't think so. But then again, I'm not happy. Does that make any sense? I'm not sure you can follow what I mean," he ended looking expectantly at Sophie.

"I understand perfectly. And don't even get me started on the idiots that I have to deal with in this business! My good luck was that I started in it at the top—since I had the opportunity to open my own business—I started at the apex of the pyramid. But don't worry; I'm not one of those idiots you mentioned," Sophie chuckled and continued, "now let me ask you a question: what is it you're waiting for to transform your life? I don't imagine that it could be money that holds you back."

"No. No—far from it," Eduardo said after a moment's pause. "What I'm lacking is courage. You know when you settle for something, even if it's not necessarily good for you, but it seems comfortable enough? Well, that's where I am at the moment."

"Hmmm, comfort—it's been a long time since I've had that sensation," Sophie mused for a moment, gathering her thoughts, then continued, "be courageous Eduardo! There is nothing holding you back, not what you're doing now, not even *London*—food for thought!" She ventured firmly.

Their conversation turned to lighter topics, they ordered dessert, and then finally, asked for the bill. Their waiter came back almost immediately, informing them that 'it had been taken care of'.

"What do you mean?" Eduardo asked with a slight frown, "I insist on paying, please."

"I'm sorry *M.* Eduardo, but I have no way to charge anything to you now sir. The bill has been closed already," their waiter offered by way of explanation.

Eduardo was about to insist again when Sophie placed her hand gently over his, effectively interrupting him. "Now Eduardo, stop being silly; when someone extends us a courtesy, we must always accept with gratitude. When we leave we can thank Tristan." She patted his hand.

"Of course Sophie, you're absolutely right. I was just being proud."

"Precisely, shall we leave now," she asked smiling.

"Of course, let me call an *Uber* for you," Eduardo replied, taking his mobile out of his inner jacket pocket.

"Absolutely not," Sophie replied with a smile, "after this wonderful evening what I really want is to walk home and think about life and everything we've talked about. It won't take me more than twenty minutes."

Eduardo put his mobile back in his pocket, "ah, then I must insist that I accompany you," he said with a smile.

Having agreed, the two rose from their seats, thanked their waiter for whom Eduardo left a very generous tip, then moved toward the exit. They found Tristan near the reception and thanked him profusely for the marvelous evening as he accompanied them out. Eduardo helped Sophie put on her little bolero then they walked into the night, heading toward *Hyde Park*. Tristan watched them go, turning, he stepped back into *Romarin* with a small smile of satisfaction.

Sophie and Eduardo continued to chat as they walked arm-in-arm at a comfortable pace. Sophie spoke of her *bistro* which was quite successful she admitted, pleased with herself. She was proud to have saved enough for a down payment on Michael's part, but he simply refused to sell she explained, frustrated. Eduardo counseled her to find a good lawyer, explain the situation, and see if a way out for her couldn't be found.

"What irritates me most," she said, "is that he knows that if I leave the business, the restaurant will lose its primary force. After all, it's not just the dishes that are my creations; I am the connection to our patrons and suppliers too."

"Don't delude yourself Sophie, no one is irreplaceable," Eduardo interjected.

"That may well be, but I need a way out of this hell that my life has become!" Sophie replied exasperated.

"And you have every right to be free," Eduardo agreed, "but like me, you need to find your courage to do it too."

"I know that. Well, in the worst-case scenario, I'll transfer my share to Camille, just cut my losses and get on with my life. I know she wants to make a life for herself here in London and I am certain that her father would never do anything to harm her," Sophie affirmed.

"That might just be your way out," Eduardo had stopped and turned to look at her as he uttered those prophetic words. They continued on in a comfortable silence until they reached her block, each one mulling over the ideas they had exchanged.

"Well, we've arrived," Sophie said stopping as they reached her building. She invited him up for a nightcap.

"Thank you, Sophie, but I still have a few reports to finish. I'm presenting them on Monday morning to my boss, so I had better go home now and get a good night's sleep."

"Ok, that sounds rather dull, but no problem. I'll forgive you this time, but you'll have to make it up to me with an invitation for a proper date," she teased.

"Agreed," Eduardo replied elated at the prospect. "Now I just need your telephone number," he said bringing out his mobile.

"True," Sophie laughed and grabbed his arm to steady herself, a little tipsy from all the wine they had consumed, not to mention the high heels that she was now so unused to, "take note…"

The two said their goodbyes, hugged one another and exchanged two kisses, one on each cheek before she went happily through the door of her building and Eduardo turned and walked—still smiling—to stand directly under a streetlamp and stopped. On the opposite side of the street a man watched from behind a tree from where he had been observing them silently. Eduardo didn't notice him as he watched Sophie disappear behind the front door of her building. He didn't see him as he took out his mobile and called for an *Uber* to take him home. And he didn't see him come out of hiding as Eduardo passed by in the car that had arrived minutes later to take him home.

The man watched Eduardo's car drive away, turning the corner before he went silently through the same door Sophie had passed through just minutes earlier. Eduardo was at his own doorstep not ten minutes later.

Sophie was alone at home, taking off her make-up in the bathroom when she saw reflected in the mirror a shadow flicker past the partially open bathroom door. "Camille, is that you *ma petite*? I thought you were going out with your friends after the *bistro* closed," she called out to the silent unlit hallway. Not hearing an answer, Sophie shrugged and thought no further on the matter. She was mistaken, it was probably just the make-up remover that must have momentarily dulled her sight, she presumed.

Concluding the removal of the last vestiges of powders, pencil and lipstick, she brushed her teeth, turned off the light and walked back to her room in the dark when she suddenly felt someone grab her arm. "You are just a little whore, aren't you," came a guttural rasp in her ear along with hot breath making the hair on her neck rise in fear.

She froze for a fraction of an instant then, recognition: "Michael, how did you get in here? Go away! Now!" She hissed angrily, hitting the light switch and turning to face him.

"How could you just drop everything at the restaurant to sneak out on a date with some other man!" his voice was hoarse, his outrage growing out of control. He blinked at the sudden bright light.

"*What-are-you-talking-about*?" She enunciated each word emphatically. "Are you spying on me? Yes, I went out to dine with friends. I have that right. I work day and night at *Sophie's* and I have every right to have fun with whomever and whenever I wish! As a matter of fact, Michael," her breathing calmer, she modulated her voice, "you should do the same. Why don't you find someone to go out with and leave us alone once in a while? And let go!" she cried, suddenly jerking her arm free from his grasp, moving swiftly to the other side of her bedroom.

The bed between them now: "ah, so Sophie has some friends now, does she?" He sneered in falsetto, taunting her. "You still owe me satisfaction! You can't just make up your own hours without consulting me first," he insisted pointing his thumb at his chest. "You had the *obligation* to tell me where you were going," he complained, suddenly feeling sorry for himself.

343

"We unfortunately may still be partners in business, but you don't *own* me! I *owe* you nothing of the sort, least of all *sa-tis-fac-tion*! Now, *leave-my-house-Michael*! Now! Otherwise, I am calling the police!" She retorted angrily reaching for the phone on her bed stand.

"You know very well that I still love you and can't stand the idea of you being with another man," Michael sniveled. Then, in a flash, Michael projected himself across the room, launching his corpulent body onto Sophie; he landed on top of her as both fell across her bed.

"Michael, get off!" she struggled to get out from under him, crying, "stop, please! You're hurting me!"

Michael swiftly pinned her arms above her head, and with one hand yanked her skirt up and pulled down his pants. Tears of anger and pain ran down Sophie's face but she didn't stop struggling for one instant against what she knew was about to happen. Relaxing slightly his grasp on one of her arms as he tried to force himself on her, one of her hands broke free. Instinctively, she grabbed the lamp from her bed stand and slammed it down on his head with all her strength. The blow made a sickening sound. Air exploded from her lungs as Michael's dead weight fell on her as he suddenly fell limp. His body rolled and fell to the floor with a thud as she gave a might push, her entire body heaving with exertion, her breath rasping so loudly it was deafening to her.

"Damn you! You bastard!" She shrieked as he opened his eyes and looked up dazed at her standing above him on her bed, her arms waived wildly with her fury: "I have tolerated you for a lifetime in the name of our daughter, but now I want you definitively out of my life!" She roared. He had passed all limits. "Get out, get out now. Go!" she shouted, jumping down off the other side of her bed, as far away from him as possible,

344

pointing stiff-armed at the door, her other hand clenched tightly by her side.

Michael rolled over and got to his knees, fumbling to pull up his pants and close his zipper while simultaneously trying to hold his throbbing head. "I'm sorry Sophie, please! I didn't mean to," he groaned, looking at the hand he had held to his head, showing her, "look, I'm bleeding," he whimpered pathetically, trying to staunch the blood trickling down his face and onto his shirt, succeeding only in smearing it into a grisly mask.

"Get out of my house Michael, now!" She repeated less loudly, but still outraged. "I don't want to talk to you. I don't want to see you ever again! Just go, you monster!" She hissed.

Michael stumbled to his feet, running out the front door. It slammed behind him. Sophie's knees buckled—adrenaline spent—she sat on the floor, arms wrapped around her legs, knees to her chest, she leaned her head against her bed as she wept convulsively. After some time had passed, she got up, changed into her nightgown and lay down on her bed crying softly into her pillow until sleep finally overtook her.

Chapter Twenty-Eight – The Japanese Garden

Sunday morning came finally. Sophie got up early, took a bath, dressed, and went discretely to her daughter's door to check that she had arrived, and then left the house without breakfast. She needed to think.

Sophie walked along the streets of her neighborhood without any particular destiny, eventually stopping at a café where she ordered a *cappuccino* to go and walked on until she arrived at *Holland Park*, cup still in hand. For her, the Japanese garden was a place of much peace and tranquility—just what she needed. She sat for seemed hours on a bench with a clear view of the waterfall, watching people pass by, admiring the plants, the occasional squirrel chattering away overhead. An occasional tear would slip down her cheek unnoticed. She went over her entire life in her mind like a movie, pausing occasionally to replay a bit. 'At what point should I have said *enough,* and then gotten on with my life, far away from all of this, all that I capitulated to?' She wanted to go back in time and reclaim something; she didn't quite know what—that confident Sophie, her indomitable spirit, her youth perhaps?

Around ten that morning her mobile vibrated. It was Eduardo sending her a message on *WhatsApp*: "*Good morning Sophie, I hope you slept well. I really enjoyed our unexpected dinner last night. It was a very pleasant evening. Enjoy your Sunday. By the way, this is Eduardo. And this is my number (emoji □).*"

Reading this, Sophie couldn't hold back anymore, bursting into tears. She couldn't even cope with answering the message. Among that mixture of feelings, resentments, and regrets going through her head, came the singular notion that she actually was interested in Eduardo. But she couldn't possibly bring him into this mess. Not before untangling her relationship with Michael definitively at any rate. After a while longer had passed, she managed to recompose herself. With her mind made up, she stood; on leaving the park, she caught a taxi directly to *Sophie's*.

Walking through *Sophie's* front door, she couldn't believe that Michael was there as if nothing had happened. Striding up to him, she took him by the upper arm and said firmly, her eyes blazing, "Let's go into the back. Now!"

"Hold on, calm down Sophie," Michael tried to stall, "can't we talk some other time? There are people already arriving for lunch," he reasoned, glancing around at patrons already sitting or being seated.

"No. Now!" She retorted abruptly, not letting go of his arm. Then turning to her daughter said, "Camille, please take care of everything out here, I need to talk to your father."

"Leave it to me, *Maman*," Camille replied startled with her mother's tone, "is everything ok?"

"No, *ma fille*, nothing is 'ok'. We will talk later, you and I. Ok? *C'est possible?*

"*Bien sûr Maman*," Camille concurred as Michael, led by Sophie, left the salon and went to talk in privacy inside the Waste Storage Chamber behind the kitchen where two gleaming compactors took care of all of the restaurant's waste, with standing room to spare for two.

"I'm going to give you two options," Sophie said turning on the light then facing Michael. She released his arm once the WS Chamber door closed behind them, effectively sealing them off from prying ears and eyes. "Either you sell me your damn part in the business or I'm passing my part to our daughter and leaving for good. This time there is *no* negotiation," she declared the terms of her ultimatum firmly.

"Ah Sophie, you don't have to threaten me like that," Michael replied meekly. "You know how much I need this."

"All right then," she replied, still giving no quarter. "If you want the restaurant so much, keep it. But you will never, ever show your face to me again. What you did was unforgivable! I've tried and tried to tolerate your absurd jealousy during all these years and only didn't move on with my life because of our business and our daughter. But now, I want to get as far away from you as possible. I'm sick of you! I want to forget that you exist!" She vented.

"Don't talk like that to me Sophie or I'll..." he began working his lips in and out, trying to think of what to say and intimidate her all at once; puffing out his chest like a toad.

"Or you'll what? You will what Michael?" In a voice hardened by her fury, she glared at him, chin out, fighting mad. Sophie went on issuing her terms of rendition, "I will give you two months for me to get everything resolved regarding my leaving the business and organizing the kitchen. After that, the problem will be yours. At least there's one thing that I can still believe in; you wouldn't want to ruin everything and end up jeopardizing our daughter. She will be your new joint owner of *Sophie's*. So please, don't let her down too."

Michael opened his mouth and started to say, "But there's no way that I can..." She interrupted him again, her rudeness deliberate, pointing a finger at him, stabbing the air, "And if you insist on trying to hold onto me, I'll go to the police and incriminate you for attempted rape," she hissed. "Then our daughter will finally see what kind of man her father *really* is."

His jaw dropped flabbergasted. Sophie went on, lowering her finger and her voice, as she took a step back, out of his personal space, but still firm, "but you don't have to worry. From now on, I'll do everything in my power, so I don't have to look at you again. Ah! And during these next two months, while I am here organizing everything to hand over the restaurant to you and Camille, I want you far away from the operation."

This time Michael's voice took on that distinctive and all too familiar whine, both churlish and belligerent, "but I can't possibly stay away. I have my own duties, and, and..." She interrupted him one last time, "So, do your duties in the daytime and I'll come in only after five in the afternoon. And do me a favor," she glared at him under hooded eyes, her abhorrence for him undeniable, even to him, "see that you're out of here at least an hour before I arrive. Take good advantage of your day's work today, because I am giving myself the day off. Good bye Michael!" She said with a finality even he couldn't doubt. She turned her back on him, and with head held high, opened the door and marched back through the kitchen into the salon and up to the reception and her daughter. She ignored the sudden scramble and furtive glances of the kitchen help who had most likely tried to hear everything she had said with their ears glued to the door.

"*Ma fille*," she said in a low voice to her daughter, "let's go home. We need to talk."

Camille immediately called to one of the waiters to man the reception, taking out a piece of paper from her shirt pocket, she handed him the list of reservations for lunch and dinner—not sure how long this might take—then followed her mother out the front door. Neither said a word as they walked briskly back to the apartment.

Arriving home, Sophie sat on the sofa and patted the place beside her for Camille to do the same. She calmly explained to her daughter that any social coexistence with her father had become impossible. Without going into detail, she told her that Michael had invaded the apartment the night before and tried to force himself on her, but carefully mentioned nothing of the attempted rape. She simply said that she had kicked him out. Camille covered her mother's hand with her own, saddened and shocked. The fact was, Sophie continued, it had become simply intolerable to have anything further to do with him and that she had gone to the restaurant today to try to resolve the situation by convincing him sell her his part, but again, he refused.

She went on to inform Camille that given the circumstances, she would be transferring her rights to the restaurant to Camille within two months, and from then on the business would belong to her and her father.

Mature beyond her years, Camille supported her mother's decision, but she couldn't hide the sorrow in her eyes. "And what will you do *Maman*?" She asked, as practically minded as her mother.

"I haven't decided yet, *ma chérie fille*," Sophie replied with a deep sigh. "I've managed to save a bit during all these years, but I had hoped to use it for your education."

"Don't worry about that *Maman*. I can get a loan," Camille replied sensibly. "And now with your share in the restaurant I can use my earnings to pay for my expenses. I just hope *Papa* doesn't ruin everything."

"Camille, even if he does run the restaurant into the ground, we will still have each other. But I need you to understand that I have to be far away from him now. I can't go on *not* living my own life," Sophie explained.

"I do understand *Maman*. Look, don't worry; everything's going to be fine. If you took this drastic decision you had good reason," Camille replied placatingly.

"Thank you my dear, I knew that I could count on your support," Sophie concluded. The two hugged each other tightly for a long time. Sophie buried her head in her daughter's neck and breathed deeply the sweet scent of her beloved child for whom she had sacrificed everything.

Camille walked quickly back to the restaurant, her mind racing. Soon after, Sophie also left the apartment for the second time that day, again walking without any particular destiny, when after a few blocks she suddenly and decisively took out her mobile, finally tapping out an answer to Eduardo's message: *"Bonjour Eduardo, thank you for your message. I also loved our evening together, made all the more special because it was so unexpected. Believe me, in some ways, thanks to last night, a lot is going to change in my life. Don't worry it has nothing to do with you. Enjoy your Sunday and your reports (emoji □)"*.

Eduardo messaged her back immediately: *"What happened? Are you at the bistro now? Could you come have coffee with me? We could meet half way."*

Sophie smiled and her eyes lit up at his response. She called him as soon as she finished reading his message.

"Sophie? Is everything alright with you," Eduardo asked slightly apprehensive.

"No, but it will be," she replied, with a deep sigh.

"*Nossa*, now you've worried me even more. Wouldn't you like to go out for coffee and talk?" he insisted concerned.

"Of course I would! Today I've given myself a day off. I'm free as a bird," she grinned widely, even though he couldn't see her.

"Oh—ok—great! We could meet at that little café that's on the lake at *Hyde Park*, that way we can both walk," he asked suggested. "What time do you want to go?"

"I'm free, I can go right now!" Sophie replied cheered by the prospect.

Relieved and elated, Eduardo agreed immediately and the two met at *The Serpentine Bar & Kitchen*. They were soon seated outside on the deck overlooking *Serpentine Lake*. They lingered for hours over coffee and later, sandwiches discussing the events that followed after he had left her the previous night up until now.

Shaking his head, "I can't even imagine the horror of what you went through last night Sophie!" Eduardo repeated more than once. "But don't you think you're being just a little precipitated in your decision? I mean giving up what's yours? And you really should seriously consider reporting this attempted rape to the police. I can go with you if you like," he offered.

"No Eduardo," Sophie replied emphatically, "it's better not to involve the police in this. Camille would be devastated. And to tell you the truth, I think this was the push I needed." She covered his hand on the table with her own and continued earnestly, "Eduardo, I have to remake my life for *me*. I love this place, but I need a life, and as long as I'm near Michael, that will never be possible. I want to meet someone, make love, travel," she continued dreamily. "All my life I've taken care of my daughter—that task is finally completed. *Donc, assez!* It's my turn now! And what's more: I leave, but I take all my know-how with me," she grinned mischievously, "I can work anywhere in the world I want! My will to work certainly isn't lacking!" She laughed, thrilled at the possibilities.

"I understand," Eduardo agreed. "Well, you're right, but what do you think you'll do?"

"I don't know yet, but one thing is certain, I've had enough of *London*. I have the next two months to think about what to do with my life, and until then, I'll have to resolve all of the restaurant's issues so I can definitively cut my connection with *Sophie's*," she replied earnestly.

"Well, I certainly admire your courage Sophie," Eduardo said, looking directly into her eyes, his expression openly reflecting the sincerity of his words.

"You should have the courage to do what you want to do with your life too Eduardo. If it's only accumulating money and giving satisfaction to others about what a great executive you are, then you're on the right path." She noted his suddenly deflated manner. "I'm sorry Eduardo," Sophie apologized, "I realize we've only known each other for a little while, but I really like you, truthfully. And I would like to see you happy too."

"Don't worry about it," he replied, still rather crestfallen. "I prefer that you be honest with me." Eduardo liked the idea of Sophie liking him, but he didn't want to return the sentiment yet, ancient lessons learned encroaching on his decision-making.

"But seriously!" She caressed his hand that rested on the table then shook it playfully, "what *are* you still doing in *London*?"

"I've been asking myself that same question every day for the last few weeks. And to tell you the truth, *London* isn't even one of my favorite cities," he smiled sheepishly at his acknowledgement. "I never even wanted to visit it before I came to live here, can you believe it? I really came because of love. I don't regret it, not for an instant," he went on more seriously. "On the other hand, after you get used to the place and can actually sustain a decent life in this city, you do get used to it, and you do enjoy it. We can't deny that it is a culturally rich and remarkably pulsating city," he replied with a grin of one accustomed to taking full advantage of such things.

"I agree," she said smiling back. "But it is also a very grey city, and cold for the greater part of the year," she ended with an irrepressible shiver despite the warm day.

He chuckled, "that's true. And it can be very cruel to those unable to take full advantage of it. I remember my mates at work when I was working in restaurants, always complaining that the salaries they earned were very far removed from the life style the city has to offer. Many abdicated their privacy— sharing rooms with strangers—so that they would have a little left over for some kind of leisure, or refuge, or escape from their daily drudgery. I can't complain because although I did submit to jobs outside of my profession, I never had to give up on any creature comforts. I don't say this to diminish any minimum wage activities, rather to illustrate what little spending power these wages provide. I arrived in *London* living comfortably in one of the most elegant neighborhoods of the city, but not everyone can marry a successful professional recognized worldwide in their profession," he concluded unapologetically.

"That really does make it easier," she nodded in agreement. "I also cannot complain of *London*. I was very happy here for a time. I never had to make any great sacrifices either, but I know very well what migrants and immigrants who come here go through. I myself give jobs to some. It's not a paradise here, but it is certainly *infinitely* better than the situation of these people in their own native cities and countries. Otherwise," she concluded with a fatalistic shrug, "they wouldn't choose to come here at all, *n'est-ce pas*."

"That's for sure," Eduardo nodded in agreement. "For me, what seems sadder is that someone can 'live in' *London* and still not 'live' *London*. And isn't that the whole reason why so many venture here in the first place, for the theaters, restaurants and fantastic parties? It's just not within the means of the majority's pockets–those who make this giant wheel keep spinning."

The two had finished off their respective coffees and sandwiches some time ago. Sophie looked across to the other side of the lake, mesmerized by all the people that walked, pedaled, or just sat enjoying the sun and asked, "would you like to take a walk in the park?"

"Of course," Eduardo replied, already standing. He pulled out her chair for her and they wandered along the lakeside then through various walkways in the park for some time. As they ambled leisurely, side by side, admiring the formal gardens, they continued to talk on a myriad of subjects interspersed with comfortable intervals of silence. During one of these intervals, Eduardo wondered again to himself what was he doing in *London*? What was it he needed to find the courage to make a really big change in his life? He also wondered what he was waiting for to take Sophie in his arms and kiss her; certain that he was as interested in her as she was in him.

He wasn't in love with her or anything like that he thought; but he was taken by her strength, her personality, her good looks, and her determination to reinvent herself. Eduardo noticed wryly that he had a thing for strong independent women.

During those same momentary silences, Sophie also considered taking the lead and kissing him right then and there. But the fact was, she didn't even know how these things were supposed to be done anymore. She had forgotten all those rituals of conquest between two people. Not that she hadn't been courted after the divorce, or even flirted with while she was still married to Michael, but she had tended to sidestep advances of any kind to avoid problems for her and the *bistro* with Michael, her *bête noire*. Not to mention the fact that she had had so many problems in her life up until this precise moment, even after the divorce, that a love life had seemed something sadly beyond her reach.

As they were finally leaving the park and saying their good-byes, the two moved to kiss each other's cheeks as was their custom. But turning their heads for this polite farewell, they both moved in the same direction, and their lips inadvertently met. Sophie waited a fraction of a second for Eduardo to take the initiative of finally kissing her, but since that advance didn't come—perhaps for fear of her rejection —she did, kissing him squarely on his full-lipped Latin mouth. With a slight tremble, Sophie feared that he might turn away, but Eduardo responded warmly. And there they stood embraced, kissing timelessly, under a shady canopy of trees on a lazy summer afternoon in beautiful *Hyde Park*.

Pulling away, "oh, I'm sorry Eduardo," said the somewhat flustered and blushing Sophie, "I didn't mean to…"

"Don't say another word," Eduardo murmured, his lips searching out hers, this time with desire.

In London, Still

Chapter Twenty-Nine – Friends with Benefits

For the next two months Eduardo e Sophie saw each other as often as possible, having decided to let things flow and develop naturally between them, without any pressure. And so, they maintained an atmosphere of friendship in their relationship, their feelings growing for one another unperceived as the weeks sped by.

Meanwhile, Sophie focused on resolving her problems with Michael, while adroitly avoiding her ex-husband as much as possible. On his part, he did actually manage to respect her demand for different work hours, so they didn't meet. Deep down, his hope was that she would forgive him and as usual— things would just fall back to the way they always had been— she'd retract her decision eventually. But Sophie remained unswerving.

The two finally met at the office of his family's lawyer, barely a month into Sophie's ultimatum to finalize her exit from the business and Camille's entrance. The three met on a Friday afternoon, in a sterile wood-paneled meeting room of the law offices—oddly devoid of decoration or distraction—within walking distance of *St. Paul's Cathedral* in *The City*. Sophie and Camille heard the quarter hour bells peal as they arrived together.

"Sophie please, you don't have to do this, I know how much you love the *bistro*," Michael, appealed to her from across the table, "and I promise that I'll change. I won't interfere in your personal life, I swear! We can even keep the same work schedule we have now. And you can have the weekends off if you want," he implored before the lawyer came in. Camille looked out the window concentrating on the street below, her back to her parents, embarrassed to hear her father's supplications, not wanting to see him beg.

Michael seemed sincere in his pleadings. Truth be told, since the 'incident' he had finally sought out psychiatric help again, and this time, he was taking his treatment seriously, medication and all, and it was helping a lot. Sophie never said a word to Michael. Whether he was better or not was irrelevant to her now.

"*Maman*," Camille said, turning away from the window, looking down at her mother as the silence became deafening, "I want you to know that I'm not opposed to your holding on to your part in the restaurant, if you want to change your mind," hoping her mother might be persuaded.

Sophie looked up at her daughter from where she sat, "*Ma chérie*, my decision is made," she replied not unkindly, but in a tone that brooked no argument. "The only thing I really want is to leave *London* for a while, then decide where to make my own life," she reached out grasping her daughter's hand lightly in hers for a few moments before letting it go; she never so much as glanced Michael's way.

Their lawyer came in minutes later, shuffling several color-coded folders. He went over the details, his voice as dry as the papers themselves, he handed Sophie several documents to sign. After verifying the signatures, he took out his *Mont Blanc* fountain pen and signed at the bottom of a few, initialing others. Pushing his spectacles up on his forehead where mysteriously, they remained anchored, he looked at Sophie. "It's done. We'll get these filed and have a copy sent to you," he said somberly. Standing he extended his hand. With that, she shook his hand once—firmly—got up and walked out without another word or backward glance.

Camille stayed behind with her father but couldn't help but feel pride in her mother's attitude to liberate her self from that abusive vortex she had lived in for so many years. Yet, she couldn't help but fear that *Maman* might have been too impulsive and eventually come to repent her actions. Regardless, Camille thought coolly, she was ready and willing to give everything back to her mother, if ever that was her wish.

Eduardo had invited Sophie to dinner at his house for the first time on that same night to celebrate her new life. They had yet to spend a night together, though neither was particularly concerned. They were taking their time. These first weeks had been filled with encounters in *cafes*, parks, museums, and restaurants where they would talk and enjoy each other's company, occasionally holding hands and kissing.

Tristan, Jordan, and Martin were already aware of what was developing and had even gone out with them after they had become, 'officially together' as Tristan called it. The five had enjoyed a very pleasant brunch in *Richmond*. That day, these three had been unable to dissemble their happiness at seeing Eduardo with his new lighter countenance, all thanks to Sophie.

"I for one am very happy for Eduardo and Sophie. His bereavement seems to finally be coming to a close," Martin commented to the other two standing on the sidewalk watching, as the new couple walked away arm-in-arm after brunch that Sunday.

Tristan was the middleman of the trio on the sidewalk watching the couple. "But don't you think he's moving too fast," Tristan asked the other two still concerned. Eduardo's doorway confession of only a few short months ago was always waylaying his thoughts, causing him to worry about his old friend.

"Oh, Tristan!" Jordan exclaimed, taking hold of his husband's hand. "There is no *right* time for people to feel that they can be happy together. Eduardo and Gabrielle lost almost a year before they met again and that, only by good fortune. They lost all that time for happiness, missing their chance to be together longer before the tragedy struck," he contended.

"*Weeeeell*, putting it that way…" Tristan made a *moue*, sighing dramatically through pursed lips.

Martin jabbed him sharply in the ribs with an elbow, effectively deflating his high drama with a single poke, making Tristan gasp, as he continued, uncommonly serious, "man, I think their relationship is going to be something more mature. And it can only evolve…not that Eduardo and Gabrielle didn't have something incredible, to the contrary," he added quickly. "Especially since no one gets the same kind of love twice around—each one is unique. That's what I mean!"

"And that from the mouth of a confirmed bachelor—specialized in love—to a *gay* couple," Jordan ironized; leaning forward to eye Martin from Tristan's other side. The three howled with laughter—impervious to snobbish glances their way, pedestrian noses askew—as they slapped each other on the back, simultaneously ecstatic and relieved by their friend's newfound happiness.

The afternoon Sophie walked out of the law office, she had decided to pamper herself and be especially pretty for the upcoming date that night at Eduardo's apartment. She would go to a spa not far from her apartment and have her hair, nails and make-up done. But before that, she splurged, buying a beautiful dress, something really special for that night's date. As she was leaving the *boutique,* she also decided to buy a French wine she was certain he would appreciate at a shop she knew was on her way home from the spa. She chose an excellent 2014 *Mont Rocher Vieilles Vignes, Viognier, Pays d'Oc*.

Their dinner was set for seven that night, but Sophie arrived a few minutes early. Inhaling deeply, she got out of the *Uber* that had brought her, walking up to the entrance of Eduardo's apartment building. She entered the number of his apartment pressing the back-lit numbers of the black glass plate beside the door. "Hello, it's me, Sophie".

"Come up, please" Eduardo replied pressing a button on his interphone. The door lock released immediately with a loud clacking sound, she pulled the door open and walked through. It wheezed closed behind her.

On the way up, she checked her make-up in the elevator mirror—satisfied—she smiled at what she saw. Sophie rang the bell and Eduardo ran to answer the door. His jaw dropped. He simply couldn't believe his own eyes seeing her standing there, bottle in hand.

When choosing her dress at the *boutique* earlier, Sophie had been a bundle of nerves; wanting the perfect dress to wear to Eduardo's dinner. She really wanted to cause a good impression. After looking at single dress in the shop, she finally opted for a two-piece silk outfit. The skirt was layered black silk tulle gathered tightly at the waist and ending just above her knees showing off her shapely calves. The upper part was a pearl white with asymmetric sleeves—one arm more exposed than the other. But the really special detail—which she absolutely loved—was the *décolleté* in a deep "V" cut asymmetrically with the wider side on the left and in perfect balance with those sleeves. It was elegant and sensual, not in the least overdone.

She used make-up that was more natural this time too: a nude lipstick with a gloss, and a light touch to her cheeks to give her a healthy blush. Exaggerating slightly on the eyeliner and eye shadow, going for a more *femme fatal* look, decidedly emphasized her light brown eyes. With her hair cut fashionably in a long bob, she opted for gel to fix it totally to the side opposite from her *décolleté,* sensuously exposing her neck and ears adorned with a pair of dangling crystal earrings. The finishing touch, no less important, was her scent—*J'adore*— refreshing and light, perfect for summer. Looking in the mirror when she was done, it took a moment to realize that that attractive woman was the new Sophie.

"Wow! I mean...wow!" Eduardo's jaw still dropped in amazement. "You look absolutely stunning!" He said without guile.

"Oh stop exaggerating, Eduardo," Sophie replied blushing.

"I *am* being serious," Eduardo insisted, taking her into his arms and kissing her warmly. "Come in, please. Welcome to my home," he said as he continued to admire her while ushering her in.

Eduardo received the wine Sophie had brought enchanted that she had remembered his favorite type of white.

"What a beautiful apartment Eduardo. I love your *decor*. And what have we here?" She asked looking curiously at the bottle of wine on ice and the appetizers Eduardo had already laid out on the coffee table: a camembert cheese filled and baked with a *confiture de Mirtille* surrounded by toast points served on a small footed opaline glass platter; an antique silver tray filled with a variety of *pâte feuilletée canapés;* and served in a small, highly polished Brazilian hardwood dish—Eduardo had told her was called a *gamela*—were tiny *coxinhas*, a favorite Brazilian *croquette* in the form of miniature drumsticks. This *croquette* is filled with a creamy chicken salad, first covered in a *choux* and finally breaded and deep fried he had explained, just a small introduction to Brazilian cuisine.

Eduardo offered her the dish. Sophie didn't hesitate to try this novelty. On the first bite her eyes lit up, "oh but it *is* delicious Eduardo," she complimented.

"Thank you," Eduardo grinned, "would you like a glass of champagne to accompany that," he enquired, already taking the bottle from its sleek silver champagne bucket.

"Of course I would," she replied, settling comfortably on his sofa while carefully arranging her skirts.

It wasn't his custom, but making it an occasion, Eduardo let the champagne cork fly with a loud pop. He sat down beside her and poured the wine into the two champagne tulips next to the bucket resting on a large antique ornate silver tray that sat to one side of the *hor d'oeuvres* and proposed a toast: "to you and your new life," Eduardo discoursed, glass raised, "may it be filled only with good things and happy days from now on. Cheers!"

"Cheers!" Sophie replied turning her cheek for Eduardo to kiss. "Thank you, Eduardo. Thanks to you these past weeks have been so much more enjoyable for me."

"I'm happy to be at your side. Our time together has been marvelous. Count on me if you ever need anything. Really, anything," Eduardo replied, his sincerity endearing.

Sophie's eyes shone with unexpected tears of gratitude realizing that she really could count on him. Eduardo was truly a very decent man, yet she also knew that she should only count on herself, after all every fairytale must end sometime.

The two chatted comfortably during dinner about what they had done while apart. Sophie spoke of all the things she had done to prepare for her leaving the *bistro*. Eduardo listened more than he spoke.

Dinner was simple yet marvelous. Eduardo had roasted a Brazilian cut of meat in the oven accompanied with potatoes and a green salad. For dessert, he had prepared thick rounds of sliced pineapple grilled to tenderness, then dusted with cinnamon and flambéed—another touch of *Brazil*. Sophie clapped at the fiery presentation.

When they had finished, Eduardo put on one of his playlists using his surround sound connected to his home internet and the two sat on the floor of the living room. Before sitting, Eduardo got a bottle of cognac, serving it as a *digestif* for both of them.

At one point between kisses and embraces, both had grown very excited, and as they were at the point of exploding, suddenly pulling back from his embrace, Sophie announced: "It's getting late. I had better be going."

"No, wait," Eduardo exclaimed surprised and slightly breathless, "wouldn't you like to stay here tonight?"

"You want me to sleep *here*?" Sophie asked suddenly shy.

Eduardo was almost bursting. "Do I want it? That's everything I want!"

The two went back to kissing and made love for the first time there on the floor of the living room, then on the sofa, in the bedroom, and when they woke the next morning, in the shower. It seemed as if the world was ending.

Returning from the bath, Sophie cuddled against Eduardo's chest and said, "Eduardo, I have something I must tell you."

"Of course, anything," he responded, gently moving a wisp of wet hair from her eyes.

"You do know that I don't want to live in *London* anymore, don't you?"

"But is it something you've already decided?"

"Well…yes! I don't intend to change my mind. There is nothing more for me here and, I don't know if I could deal with remaining in *London* knowing that I left a lifetime project behind that fell apart, and for so many reasons that don't even matter anymore."

"I see," Eduardo said slowly, pensively. "I just thought that now that we're together, things might change a bit. Even though we agreed to take things slowly—no pressure—I thought that with time, things might evolve," Eduardo pondered the situation while trying not to demonstrate what he really felt in that regard. And yet, he couldn't help but feel disappointed.

"Well yes, if we had enough time and I didn't have a psychopath for an ex-husband who might come back and stalk me at any moment; everything could be rethought. But I don't want that for me, or for you. I like you very much, but I don't think you deserve that kind of stress. Neither do I, for that matter. Not any more anyway," she insisted vehemently. "But we can continue to see each other whenever we want, in *Paris* or anywhere else in *Europe,* wherever it's convenient for both of us," Sophie proposed hopefully, unaware of his discomfort.

"Of course, of course," Eduardo agreed guardedly. "So, you're going to *Paris*," he asked with a nonchalance he felt safe behind.

"Yesterday I spoke to my mother before coming here and she invited me to stay for a while with her and my father in

Orleans. She said I could stay with them as long as I needed, until I decide where to go or what to do with my life," Sophie replied.

"And when are you planning on going," Eduardo queried, that queasy feeling in the pit of his stomach starting to spread.

"A month from now," she replied happily. "I've already bought the train tickets to *Paris* and after that, on to *Orleans*. But look," she went on more seriously, "I'm not asking for anything or trying to pressure you into anything. Truthfully, if you agree, I would like very much to spend my last month in *London* with you and our friends. Now that I've met you all, I wouldn't want to lose you from sight. After this period, if you agree, then yes, we could continue seeing each other. At least once a month, and then see what happens from there," she suggested looking optimistically up at him.

"I would like that very much. But I can't tell you how sad I am to know that a month from now we'll be spending less time together instead of more," Eduardo told her truthfully.

"But you'll be ok with this, won't you? We can continue together even knowing that I'll just be here for a short while?" A wrinkle of concern began spreading from the bridge of Sophie's nose across her forehead, fine at first then deepening as she began to realize there might be a glitch in her otherwise perfect plan.

"Of course," Eduardo replied. "And if the distance should become a problem for me, I would tell you before that. Anyway," he shrugged, as if to rid himself of a problem, "we can always see each other in *Paris* or *Orleans* or anywhere else in *Western Europe, n'est ce pas?*"

"Yes, certainly Eduardo," she exclaimed delighted. "Aside from my daughter and the friends I've made in these last few months, you are the only good memory I take with me from *London*," Sophie insisted. "I don't intend to come back here. Perhaps just for the graduation and eventual wedding of my daughter," she ended smiling at the possibility, that wrinkle in her forehead dissolving.

Eduardo was saddened but realized at the same time that he couldn't demand anything more from Sophie; first, because they were just getting to know each other and second, because he understood Sophie's reasons perfectly. Regardless, he was determined to make the most of this month together, and who knows, she might still change her mind. Mollified, he got up to prepare their breakfast: scrambled eggs and French toast—they both laughed over that name—and coffee, of course. Just before she left, Sophie gave Eduardo one last loving kiss.

In London, Still

Chapter 30 – The Last Encounter Among Friends

The weeks before Sophie was to leave passed unhurriedly as she and Eduardo continued seeing each other. After that first dinner at his apartment, the two slept together as often as possible.

As Sophie's travel date came closer, it became torture for Eduardo knowing that in a few days he wouldn't be able to see Sophie all the time. He already liked her a lot. But there was something different, something that not only made him want to be with her all the time, kiss her, hug her and make love to her, but something more, something that brought him an assurance, a certainty too. And all that was going to end and yet, he was clueless about how to fix it.

For Sophie, things weren't too different either. It pained her to have to leave, but she also knew the risks that continuing in *London* with Eduardo could bring. She was fully aware that sooner or later Michael would become a problem. And she didn't want that for herself, or for Eduardo. Leaving was the only solution, to go wherever; anywhere but here. For now, what she had was her parents' home as a safe haven. And she knew that soon she would start up her own project—a new beginning. 'It would be wonderful with Eduardo, but I can't design my life around someone who has their feet deeply rooted in *London*,' she believed.

That Friday night she would travel, and the guys had scheduled a going-away dinner for the night before. Summer had finally shown up on *London's* doorstep, the days were hot and the nights marvelously cool, so far. They would all be there: Tristan, Jordan, Martin, Camille, and of course, Eduardo.

Last to arrive at *Romarin* were Camille and Sophie, it was nearing seven-thirty and the sun was still well above the horizon. The other four had arrived earlier, already seated at their table, but still on their first round of drinks. Eduardo and Martin had come directly from work together, enjoying their sunlit walk from the Underground station. Jordan had rushed in just moments earlier having come by *Uber* from the *atelier* where he was finishing next season's men's apparel for approval—he didn't want to miss a second of what he was sure was going to be a great evening. Tristan was already working at the *maison,* stopping after Jordan arrived. He had given himself the rest of the evening off—to enjoy the farewell party of his new friend—he deserved it. While they waited for Sophie and her daughter, the four drank their beers and chatted.

"Man, what's the situation going to be like between you two," the ever-curious and none-too-discrete Martin asked Eduardo point-blank, draping a comradely arm over his friend's shoulders and giving him a shake.

"Look Martin, for now, we'll continue to meet in *Paris* or some other city on the *Continent,* a quick trip for us both. If this situation is going to become a problem or not, there's no way we can anticipate that," Eduardo replied after taking a sip of his beer with a slight grimace. 'Would he never get used to the temperature it was served here,' he wondered.

Jordan leaned forward, rolling his half full glass between his artist's hands, "but seriously, Eduardo, what are you going to do about this?" Inquisitively, he asked, "I mean, what do you really feel for her?"

Eduardo didn't hesitate, answering as honestly as he knew how, "I really do like her very much Jordan, but I just can't pressure her to stay," he replied, trying to justify his inaction.

Leaning back in his seat, almost tipping it back before he caught a warning glance from Tristan, Jordan straightened and settled more comfortably in his seat. "And whose talking about her staying," he asked. "What's keeping you here, Eduardo? And don't tell me it's that director's salary! Because even I doubt that you like very much what you do, and I still don't even know what that is!"

That brought laughs from everyone—Eduardo included—but he wavered, "Well, I certainly don't dislike it," he intoned diplomatically.

Martin pulled away, and turning, looking at Eduardo. A blank, rather puzzled expression on his face. He didn't understand what Jordan was going on about, much less Eduardo's odd response. 'What was there not to like? He had it all, including the view!' Martin thought.

Jordan leaned forward, pressing Eduardo again, "so, you mean to say that you don't love what you do either. What's more, you don't even need that money Eduardo. It's just something that you wanted to prove to yourself; ok, so you've proven yourself. Now what are you waiting for to go out and find your happiness?" Jordan insisted, his hands at rest, glass empty.

"What *are* you guys going on about?" Martin cut in, his eyes widening as Jordan finished, his beer forgotten. "Surely, you're not suggesting that Eduardo should just drop everything because of some woman, are you?" He looked truly shocked.

Tristan pressed his knee against Jordan's and answered Martin, "not exactly because of a woman Martin," he responded, "in all seriousness, we think that Eduardo should leave here and go after his true happiness—whether it's alone or with Sophie, or someone else—do what he loves, and he knows very well what that is. Only he's been living in this state of denial for years, since he started working at *Tottenham Equity* actually."

"Ok, enough you guys, please!" Eduardo interrupted them all, "Sophie and Camille are here," he said rising from his seat as they crossed the salon trailing behind the new hostess.

The other men rose as one and greeted the new arrivals with kisses, hugs, and teasing about tardiness. Eduardo was the last to greet Sophie as she gave him a hug and a light kiss on the mouth. The two seated side-by-side spent the entire dinner holding hands, only unlocking them when they needed both of their hands to eat, or when one or the other went to the restrooms.

Dinner was excellent. The six talked throughout the meal, maintaining a festive mood the entire time. They capitalized laughs remembering the first time they met Sophie, retelling of how Eduardo had literally tripped over her, but hadn't the slightest recollection of that obstacle. "And it will probably still be told when we're all old and grey," Eduardo pretended to grouse. The hours of fraternizing, true friendship, and love were many.

Eduardo and Sophie exchanged glances and secret smiles throughout the evening. Having endured so many devastating experiences in their lives, neither still quite realized how involved they were with one another.

Long after dinner had ended, the men's goodbyes to Sophie and Camille were complemented by many loving hugs and kisses. It seemed as if those friendships had evolved for years instead of only those few short months. "Are you coming home with me?" Eduardo asked Sophie quietly at one point as they stood on the sidewalk in front of *Romarin* while the others animatedly debated the number of cars needed to take them all to their respective homes amid much joking and laughter.

"No, my dear, I have a lot to get ready by tomorrow. Anyway, I couldn't possibly let Camille go home alone," Sophie replied justifying her absence that night.

"Don't miss out for my sake, *Maman*," Camille interjected rather loudly trying to be heard above the men's banter. "After all, it will be your last night together in *London*," she lowered her voice as silence abruptly fell—all eyes on them.

"Camille! Don't talk to your mother like that!" Sophie chided her but blushed, contradicting her rebuff.

"Oh *Maman*, I can go home by myself!" Camille grumbled, her 'grown-up' mask slipping slightly.

"No, *ma fille*," Sophie insisted more mildly, but with that glance that only a mother can use in public to successfully silence her willful child.

Standing slightly to Sophie's other side, Eduardo hadn't noticed, but at that rebuke, the three men watching the back-and-forth like a tennis tournament suddenly stepped back a pace in tandem. Dissembling, they huddled, discussed yesterday's football scores in hushed voices.

Heedless of the movement, Sophie turning back to Eduardo continued: "Eduardo, really, there is too much that needs still to be organized, but I do hope to see you at the station, *n'est ce pas?* Besides, we'll meet in *Paris* next weekend, *d'accord?*"

"Yes, of course Sophie," Eduardo agreed quickly. "I understand perfectly. You have to go." His lips smiled, but his eyes looked pained. Of course he didn't understand! How could he? He was hardly able to bear up under the circumstances, but he held himself together with determination. There really didn't seem much else that he *could* do.

Oblivious, Sophie reminded him, "oh, and don't forget: my train leaves *Saint Pancras* at ten in the evening. So I would like it very much if you could arrive an hour earlier so that we can have some time together."

"Of course!" Eduardo replied kissing her lightly on the lips and then holding open the door of the first *Uber* to arrive for Sophie and Camille to get in.

"Good bye, my friends!" Sophie called, waving through the open window of the car. "I hope to see you all in *Paris*, or *Orleans*, or wherever in the world I may end up!"

The four remaining on the sidewalk waved to Sophie until the car turned the corner, disappearing from sight.

"Are you all right man?" Martin asked breaking the sudden silence. "You look awful!" He said peering at Eduardo under the yellow streetlights.

"I'm fine my friend," Edward replied wearily. "I'm just tired," he said. "I'll see you my dear friends," he said to Jordan and Tristan; "and I'll see you tomorrow, Martin."

The three said good bye to Eduardo, got into their shared *Uber* that had just pulled up, then drove off toward southeast *London*. Eduardo turned and walked home arriving some twenty minutes later. He got ready for bed, but didn't lie down; he just couldn't. He spent that entire night awake, thinking hard.

The next day Sophie was so overwhelmed, it slipped her mind to even message Eduardo. There was simply too much to do, things to donate, others to throw away. "How do we manage to collect so many things in a lifetime, is that not true my dear,"

Sophie asked Camille as her daughter helped her with the baggage.

"Really *Maman*, it's unbelievable!" Camille glanced around despairingly at the growing piles of clothing separated only by destiny.

"From now on, I only want the minimum necessary. Because I certainly don't want to be dragging around so many heavy suitcases," Sophie said decidedly, separating a few more items from her 'travel' pile and putting them into the 'donate' pile. By late afternoon, she and Camille had finally achieved order, so Sophie went to take a well-deserved soak. While she luxuriated in that little bathtub for the last time, she examined her entire life as if it were a film with a private showing in her head, and in the end, she decided that she *was* happy with the decision to relinquish the *bistro* and leave town. The only thing she couldn't quite manage to stop thinking about was what her life might be if she and Eduardo could stay together forever. She admitted however, that that was a sacrifice she simply couldn't make—not in *London*—not so close to that ex-husband of hers who would never leave her alone, no matter how hard he tried.

The time finally came for her to go to the station. Camille offered to go with her, to help with the bags. "No *ma chérie*, don't worry. I ordered a large car. We will say good bye right here," Sophie said.

Camille's eyes suddenly filled with tears.

"No, now don't cry," Sophie said, tenderly patting her daughter's cheek as she put her other arm around her. "This is not good-bye *ma chérie fille*, we'll only be a few hours away from one another."

"But for how long *Maman*," Camille sobbed, "I can't believe this is happening. Everything is moving too fast! I know I supported you in all your decisions, but now seeing you actually go, it's just too hard," she lamented sniffling, her head on her mother's shoulder.

"Child, in very little time you'll be starting a new life too. And we'll always be together as often as possible, wherever I may be," Sophie comforted her, smoothing her hair, running it through her fingers as she had since Camille was a child and had come running to her crying over something or other.

Camille sniffled then brushed away her tears with the backs of both hands, "ok. I love you *Mme* Sophie," she replied bravely, her eyes still glistening.

"And I love you more. You are my life. The best of me," Sophie whispered back, repeating their lifelong litany of love. She kissed each of Camille's cheeks, then her forehead, and then finally, reluctantly, released her.

Sophie and Camille wrestled the suitcases down to the minivan already waiting for Sophie in front of their building. On the opposite side of the street, Michael stood fidgeting, half hidden in the dappled shadows behind a tree. Sophie recognized those unmistakable furtive stirrings from the corner of her eye, pretending not to. When she got into the car she smiled sadly, wishing that he really could remake his own life. She just couldn't quite manage to hate him forever, but she could let him go.

She turned in her seat and watched Camille walk back into the building as the car drove off to toward the train station. It pulled up around eight-thirty in front of the *St. Pancras* entrance. Looking up, she could see the warm hues of the summer sky contrasting with the dark outlines of the beautiful *Gothic Revival* building. Plenty of time to spare, she thought. Before nine, she was seated in the *café* in front of the *Eurostar*

Departures Entrance, her suitcases carefully out of the way beside her.

Fifteen minutes had passed, and then thirty. And still, no Eduardo. Another fifteen and finally, she stood and rolled her bags like two cumbersome double sidecars, joining the queue that had formed. She stood turning to search first one way then the other, her eyes surveying the crowded hall, as the line shuffled forward. With just five minutes to final boarding, she saw him come through the crowd, running toward her.

"Sophie," he shouted, waving at her seconds before she passed her ticket's bar code over the turnstile's card reader. "Wait, please!" He gasped, skidding to a stop beside her.

"Eduardo, I have to go through, otherwise I'll miss my train," she said slightly exasperated, though tremendously relieved. Even so, she moved slightly to the side to allow the passengers behind her pass before anyone could grumble.

"No, wait, please! After you hear what I have to say, I'll buy you a new ticket and you can leave on the next train," he blurted out, slightly out of breath from his run. Eduardo commandeered both her suitcases out of the way.

"Eduardo, what's going on," she asked following him and her suitcases.

"Please, listen to me," he implored when she turned as if to reenter the line.

Sophie hesitated for a moment but couldn't resist. With a sigh, "all right, let's sit down over there," she pointed to the café where she had waited for him earlier.

"Look," he said when they were finally seated. "I couldn't sleep last night thinking that we wouldn't be together anymore, or that we would see each other less and less as time goes by until finally, we wouldn't see each other again after you decide to move someplace else. The idea of losing you nearly drove me mad!"

"I don't understand what you are trying to say Eduardo," Sophie whispered. But she did.

"Listen to me please. Just listen," he insisted.

"Of course, go on," her voice quavering. She listened.

"I know that I'm a 'feet on the ground kind of guy,' maybe even too much so. And I have a hard time opting for the things in life that are good for me. The fact is, I've lost a lot of the people I love, and that makes me afraid, very afraid. Afraid to make the wrong choices; afraid to give up on what's safe, when safety isn't even a real issue. But it's all nothing more than ego, and vanity. And fear; fear that things might go wrong between us too." Eduardo gasped, his face flushing but he continued, "I know that this fear makes me freeze up, and I always end up letting it take over. But more than anything, I fear losing you."

Sophie opened her mouth to speak, but Eduardo wasn't to be stopped. He kissed her open lips and continued, "listen, just listen, please!" His words tumbled out, "The truth is, I've been very unhappy for the last few years and that began to change after I met you. I don't know whether it's love or not, or a passion, or even if it's something that's still growing inside me—and who knows—will change into one or both. I only know this: *I-do-not-want-to-be-far-from-you!*" he insisted, hoping that she would understand, even when he could not.

"Tell me then Eduardo, how shall we resolve this?" She asked frankly, reining in her emotions. "I am leaving for *France*. Couldn't we talk more about this when we *rendez-vous* in *Paris* next week?"

"No!" Eduardo insisted emphatically. His knuckles whitening as he gripped the arms of his chair, "I *need* to talk to you now." Immediately softening his tone at her startled look, he went on, "but you're free to choose what you will Sophie."

"But what is there to decide here, now, Eduardo?" she argued.

"Well, today I called the owner of my apartment and cancelled my lease. As soon as I arrived at the firm, I handed in my resignation without notice. So, I lost my rent deposit and will have to pay *Tottenham* a month's salary as a penalty for breaking my contract. When I left the office, I called Tristan and asked him to arrange for a storage unit to hold my things until I decide what to do with them," he replied matter-of-factly.

"What! Are you mad?" She cried shocked.

"No," he insisted, as he took one of her hands and cradled it in both of his, "I'm doing what I should have done some time ago; I'm going to live my life. Discover myself and do something that I love."

"What are you talking about? For the love of God," she cried, half rising from her seat, her mouth an 'o' of amazement.

Eduardo clasped her arm, gently pulling her back into her seat as if she might suddenly float away. "I'm talking about leaving *London*, restarting, but before that: living, experimenting and enjoying life, making use and sense of all that money I have. I know I should have made this decision before, but I don't think it would have made any sense without the right person…you!" he exclaimed, grinning lopsidedly.

"But Eduardo, I…" her mouth repeatedly opened and closed wordlessly.

"Sophie," he chuckled delighted that for once, he had left her speechless. "Sophie, I'm not asking you to marry me, or swearing eternal love, but I do have two tickets to *Rio de Janeiro* and I'm going now. From there, I'll buy a car and travel around my country and the rest of *South America*, introducing myself to cultures, flavors, scenery and everything else that comes my way. No date to finish. Only a starting date: *tomorrow!*" Eduardo continued exhilarated, "I'm going one way or the other, but everything will have another flavor, another meaning by your side," he ended watching her, hopeful.

"Eduardo, are you ..." she began, but he held up a hand indicating for her not to speak; she felt as if her stomach was doing non-stop flip-flops, she was so dumbfounded.

"Sophie," he leaned forward, taking both her hands in his, he said softly in a calm voice, "would you like to come with me on this journey so together we can see what happens? If we survive this adventure side-by-side, you might even—who knows— want to open a new restaurant with me, somewhere on this planet?" He shrugged his shoulders, grinned, and looked inquiringly at her, hoping. "And more, after everything, or in the middle of this journey, perhaps you might like to marry me. I mean, if that's what you and I might want," he proposed.

"E-du-ar-do!"

"At this moment, I only want to hear one of two answers from you Sophie," Eduardo cut in again, "yes or no," he said excitedly. "You can come with me now to *Heathrow,* or I can buy you a new passage to *Paris.*" He held his breath.

Sophie was still speechless. Giving up trying to answer, she grabbed him and kissed him with a passion that belied any doubt of her enthusiasm. "Of course, I'm going to *Heathrow* with you," she murmured. Finally finding her voice, "and yes, I accept your proposal to go adventuring together!" she said between kisses and laughter, "and we *will* try all those new flavors together".

No one knows whether Eduardo and Sophie survive this grand adventure together, or if they'll be happy just adventuring, or even if there is an 'ever after' to their happiness. Perhaps time *will* tell—I certainly don't know, at least not yet.

THE END

Printed in Great Britain
by Amazon

67037738R00217